MORE ACCLAIM FOR NICCI FRENCH'S
PREVIOUS NOVEL KILLING ME SOFTLY

"A compulsive read . . . peak psychological suspense."
—*People*

"First rate . . . Genuine chills run down the spine. . . . French can show John Grisham and Patricia Cornwell a thing about good writing."

—*Orlando Sentinel*

"Undeniably fascinating. . . . You can't stop reading this book once you've picked it up. . . . French whips up a perfect confection."

—*Washington Post Book World*

"Elegantly chilling." —*Philadelphia Enquirer*

"A sleek, utterly gripping tale."

—*Mademoiselle*

"French pulls off [sexual obsession] as well as anyone in recent memory."

—*Chicago Tribune*

"Stunning. . . . every decade or so a psychological thriller appears that graphically recounts an intelligent woman's willing sexual subjugation; this gripping novel joins that group." —*Publishers Weekly*

"An elegant, chilling take on love, murder, and obsession."
—*Kirkus Reviews* (starred review)

Also by Nicci French

The Memory Game

The Safe House

Killing Me Softly

BENEATH THE SKIN

NICCI FRENCH

WARNER BOOKS

A Time Warner Company

WARNER BOOKS EDITION

Copyright © 2000 by Nicci French
All rights reserved. No part of this book may be reproduced in any form or by any electronic or mechanical means, including information storage and retrieval systems, without permission in writing from the publisher, except by a reviewer who may quote brief passages in a review.

Cover design by Diane Luger
Cover photo by Franco Accornero

Warner Books, Inc.
1271 Avenue of the Americas
New York, NY 10020

Visit our Web site at
www.twbookmark.com

For information on Time Warner Trade Publishing's online program, visit www.ipublish.com

 A Time Warner Company

Printed in the United States of America

Originally published in hardcover by The Mysterious Press
First Paperback Printing: June 2001

10 9 8 7 6 5 4 3 2 1

BENEATH THE SKIN

In the summer, their bodies catch heat. Heat seeps in through the pores on their bare flesh; hot light enters their darkness; I imagine it rippling round inside them, stirring them up. Dark shining liquid under the skin. They take off their clothes, all the thick, closed layers that they wear in winter, and let the sun touch them: on the arms, on the back of the neck. It pours down between their breasts, and they tip back their heads to catch it on their faces. They close their eyes, open their mouths; painted mouths or naked ones. Heat throbs on the pavement where they walk, with bare legs opening, light skirts fluttering to the rhythm of their stride. Women. In the summer I watch them, I smell them, and I remember them.

They look at their reflections in shop windows, sucking in their stomachs, standing straighter, and I look at them. I watch them watching themselves. I see them when they think they are invisible.

The ginger one in an orange sundress. One of the straps is twisted on her shoulder. She has freckles on her nose; a large freckle on her collarbone. No bra. When she walks, she swings her pale, downy arms, and her nipples show through the tightened cotton of her dress. Shallow breasts. Sharp pelvic bones. She wears flat sandals. Her second toe is longer than the big one. Muddy green eyes, like the bottom of a river. Pale eyelashes; blinking too much. Thin mouth; a trace of lipstick left at the corners. She hunches under the heat; lifts up one arm to wipe the beads of moisture from her forehead, and there is a graze of ginger stubble in the scoop of her armpit, maybe a few days old. Legs prickly too; they would feel like damp sandpaper. Her skin is going blotchy; her hair is sticking to her brow. She hates the heat, this one; is defeated by it.

The one with big breasts, a squashy tummy, and masses of dark hair, you'd think that she'd suffer more—all that weight, that flesh. But she lets the sun in; she doesn't fight it. I see her, opening out her big soft body. Circles of sweat under her arms, on her green T-shirt; sweat running down her neck, past the thick, straight braids of her hair. Sweat glistening in the dark hairs on her arms, her strong legs in their high shoes. Her underarm hair is thick; I know the rest of her body when I see it. She has dark hairs on her upper lip, a mouth that is red, wet, like a ripe plum. She eats a roll that is wrapped in brown, waxy paper with grease spots on it, sinking white teeth into the pulp. A tomato pip is caught on her upper lip, grease oozes down her chin and she doesn't wipe it away. Her skirt catches in the crease between her buttocks; rides up a bit.

The heat can make women disgusting. Some of them get all dried up, like insects in the desert. Dry lines on their face, stitching their upper lips, crisscrossing under their eyes. The sun has sucked away all their moisture. Especially the older women, who try to hide their crepey arms under long sleeves, their faces under hats. Other women get rank, rotten; their skin can barely contain their disintegration. When they come near, I can smell them: Under the deodorant and soap and the perfume they've dabbed on their wrists and behind their ears, I can smell the odor of ripeness and decay.

But some of them open like flowers in the sunlight; clean and fresh and smooth-skinned; hair like silk, pulled back or falling round their faces. I sit on a bench in the park and look at them as they walk past, singly or in groups, pressing their hot feet into the bleached grass. The light glistens on them. The black one in a yellow dress and the sun bouncing off the shining planes of her skin; rich, greasy hair. I hear her laugh as she passes, a gravelly sound that seems to come from a secret place deep inside her strong body. I look at what lies in the shadows; the crease in the armpit, the hol-

low behind the knee, the dark place between their breasts. The hidden bits of them. They think no one is looking.

Sometimes I can see what they are wearing underneath. The woman with a sleeveless white shirt and the bra strap that keeps slipping onto her shoulder. It is gray-colored, stained by wear. She put on a clean shirt but didn't bother about her bra. She thought no one would notice. I notice these things. The slip under the hem. The chipped nail varnish. The spot they try to cover with makeup. The button that doesn't match. The smudge of dirt, the grimy rim of the collar. The ring that's got too tight with years, so the finger swells around it.

They walk past me. I see them through a window, when they think they're alone. The one that is sleeping, in the afternoon, in her kitchen, in the house down the quiet street I sometimes visit. Her head hangs at an awkward angle— in a minute she will jerk awake, wonder where she is—and her mouth is slack and open. There is a thin line of spittle on her cheek, like a snail's trail.

Getting in a car, the dress hitched up, a flash of underwear. Dimpled thighs.

The love bite under the carefully arranged scarf.

Pregnant, and I can see the tummy button through the thin material of the dress.

With a baby, and there are milk stains on the blouse, a tiny patch of vomit where the baby's head lolls on her shoulder.

The smile that shows the swollen, receding gums; the chipped front tooth; the porcelain cap.

The track of brown down the parting in the blond hair, where the dye is growing out.

The thick, yellowing toenails that betray her age.

The first sign of varicose veins on the white leg, like a purple worm under the skin.

In the park, they are lying on the grass while the sun beats down on them. They sit outside pubs, froth from the head of beer on their lips. Sometimes I stand among them in the underground; the press of hot flesh in the stale air. Sometimes I sit beside them, my thigh just touching theirs. Sometimes I open a door for them, and follow them into the cool interior of a library, a gallery, a shop, watching the way they walk, the way they turn their heads or push their hair behind their ears. The way they smile and look away. Sometimes they do not look away.

For a few weeks more, it is summer in the city.

PART ONE
Zoe

ONE

I wouldn't have become famous if it hadn't been for the watermelon. And I wouldn't have been in possession of the watermelon if it hadn't been for the heat. So I'd better start with the heat.

It was hot. But that may give you the wrong impression. It may make you think of the Mediterranean and deserted beaches and long drinks with colorful paper parasols dangling out of them. Nothing like that. The heat was like a big old fat smelly mangy greasy farty dying dog that had settled down on London at the beginning of June and hadn't moved for three horrible weeks. It had got sweatier and slimier and the sky had changed day by day from blue to a sort of industrial mixture of yellow and gray. Holloway Road now felt like a giant exhaust pipe, the car fumes held down at street level by a weight of even more harmful pollutants somewhere above. We pedestrians would cough at each other like beagles released from a tobacco laboratory. At the beginning of June it had felt good to put on a summer dress and feel it light against my skin. But my dresses were grimy and stained by the end of each day and I had to wash my hair in the sink every morning.

Normally the choice of books that I read to my class is
dictated according to fascist totalitarian principles imposed
by the government, but this morning I'd rebelled just for
once and read them a Brer Rabbit story I'd found in a cardboard box of battered childhood books when I'd cleared
out my dad's flat. I'd lingered over old school reports, letters written before I'd been born, tacky china ornaments
that brought with them a flood of sentimental memories. I
kept all the books because I thought one day I might have
children myself, and then I could read them the books that
Mum had read to me before she died and left it to Dad to
tuck me into bed each night, and reading aloud became
just another of those things that were lost, and so in my
memory became something precious and wonderful. Whenever I read aloud to kids, there's a bit of me that feels as
if I've turned into a soft, blurred version of my mother;
that I'm reading to the child I once was.

I wish I could say that the class was held enthralled by
this classic old-fashioned piece of storytelling. Maybe there
was just a bit less wailing, nose-picking, staring at the ceiling, or nudging than usual. But what mainly emerged as I
asked them about the story afterward was that nobody knew
what a watermelon was. I drew one on the blackboard for
them with red and green chalk. A watermelon is so like a
cartoon anyway that even I can draw them. A complete
blank.

So I said that if they were good—and for the last hour
of the afternoon they were alarmingly well behaved—I'd
bring in a watermelon for them the next day. On the way
home I got off the bus a stop later than usual, after it had
turned up Seven Sisters Road. I walked back down the road
past the greengrocers and stalls. In the very first one I
bought a pound of golden nap cherries and ate them greed-
ily. They were tart, juicy, clean; they made me think of

being in the countryside where I grew up, of sitting under the green shade as the sun goes down. It was just after five o'clock, so the traffic was already starting to grind to a halt. The fumes were hot against my face, but I was feeling almost cheerful. I was fighting my way through crowds of people as usual, but many of them seemed in good spirits. They were wearing bright colors. My urban claustrophobia meter was down from its usual eleven to a more manageable six or seven or so.

I bought a watermelon the size of a basketball and the weight of a bowling ball. The man needed four carrier bags one inside the other, and there was virtually no practical way of carrying it. Very gingerly I swung the bag over my shoulder, almost spinning myself into the traffic as I did so, and carried the melon like a man with a sack of coal on his back. It was only about three hundred yards to the flat. I'd probably make it.

As I crossed Seven Sisters Road and turned into Holloway Road, people stared at me. God knows what they thought I was up to, a skimpily dressed young blonde hunched over and carrying what must have looked like her own weight in iron ore in a shopping bag.

Then it happened. What did it feel like at the time? It was a moment, an impulse, a blow, and then it was in the past. I only really reconstructed what had taken place through the action replays in my mind, by telling people about it, by what people told *me* about it. A bus was coming toward me on the inside lane of the road. It had almost reached me when a person jumped off the platform at the back. The bus was going as close to full speed as anything ever gets on Holloway Road during rush hour. Normal people don't jump off buses like that, even Londoners, so at first I thought he may have been recklessly crossing the road behind the bus. It was the speed at which he hit the pavement, almost losing his balance, that showed he must have come off the bus.

Then I saw there were two of them, apparently joined together by straps. The one behind was a woman, older than him. But not really old. She really did lose her footing, horribly, when she hit the ground, and rolled over. I saw her feet crazily high in the air and she crashed against a bin. I saw her head hit the pavement; heard it. The man wrenched himself free. He was holding a bag. Her bag. He held it in two hands, chest high. Somebody shouted. He ran away at full speed. He had a strange, tight smile on his face and his eyes were glassy. He was running straight for me, so I had to step out of the way. But I didn't just step out of the way. I let the watermelon slip off my shoulder. I leaned back and swung it. I had to lean back or else it would have fallen vertically, taking me down with it. If it had continued on its circular progress around me I would quickly have lost control of it, but its progress was very suddenly halted as it hit the man full in the stomach.

They talk about the sweet spot. When I used to play rounders at primary school and I swung at the ball, mostly it would hit the edge of the bat and dribble off pathetically to the side. But every so often, the ball would hit the right place and with almost no effort, it would just fly. Cricket bats have sweet spots too, except that it's called the "Meat." And tennis rackets have sweet spots. So do baseball bats. And this bag-snatcher caught my watermelon right in its sweet spot, right at the perfect point of its arc. There was the most amazing thud as it struck him in the stomach. There was a whoosh of ejecting air and he just went down as drastically as if there were no body inside his clothes and they were attempting to fold themselves up on the pavement. He didn't go down like a falling tree. He went like a tall building being demolished by explosives around the base. One minute it's there and then there's just dust and rubble.

I hadn't made any plan of what to do next if the man was going to get up and come at me. My watermelon was only good for one shot. But he wasn't able to get up. He clawed at the pavement a bit, and then we were all surrounded by a crowd. I couldn't see him any longer, and I remembered the woman. Some people got in my way, tried to talk to me, but I pushed my way past them. I was lightheaded, exhilarated. I felt like laughing or talking wildly. But there was nothing funny about the woman. She was slumped and twisted on the pavement, her face down. There was quite a lot of blood on the stone, very dark and thick. I thought she must be dead but there were odd twitches from her leg. She was smartly dressed, a business suit with quite a short gray skirt. Suddenly I thought of her having breakfast this morning and going to work, and then heading home thinking of what she was going to do this evening, making mundane and comforting plans for herself, and then this suddenly happening and her life being changed. Why hadn't she just let go of the stupid bag? Maybe it had been caught round her arm.

People were standing around her looking uncomfortable. We all wanted somebody official—a doctor or a policeman or anybody in a uniform—to step forward and take charge and make this a regular event that was being dealt with through proper channels. But there was nobody.

"Is there a doctor?" an old woman next to me said.

Oh fuck. I'd done a two-day first-aid course in the second term of my teacher-training. I stepped forward and knelt down next to her. I could sense an air of reassurance around me. I knew about administering medicines to toddlers, but I couldn't think of anything relevant here except for one of the key maxims: "When in doubt, do nothing."

She was unconscious. There was lots of blood around the face and mouth. Another phrase came into my mind: "the recovery position." As gently as I could, I turned her face toward me. There were gasps and expressions of disgust from behind me.

"Has anybody called an ambulance?" I said.

"I done it on my mobile," a voice said.

I took a deep breath and pushed my fingers into the woman's mouth. She had red hair and very pale skin. She was younger than I'd thought at first, and probably rather beautiful. I wondered what color her eyes were, behind the closed lids. Perhaps she had green eyes: red hair and green eyes. I scooped thick blood out of her mouth. I looked at my red hand and saw a tooth or a bit of a tooth. A groan came from somewhere inside her. There was a cough. A good sign probably. Very loud and close by I heard a siren. I looked up. I was pushed aside by a man in uniform. Fine by me.

With my left hand I found a tissue in my pocket and carefully wiped the blood and other stuff off my fingers. My melon. I didn't have my melon. I wandered back in search of it. The man was sitting up now, with two police officers, a man and a woman, looking down at him. I saw my blue plastic bag.

"Mine," I said, picking it up. "I dropped it."

"She did it," a voice said. "She stopped him."

"Fucking KO'd him," someone else said, and close by a woman laughed.

The man stared up at me. Maybe I expected him to look vengeful but he just seemed blankly puzzled.

"That right?" asked the female officer, looking a bit suspicious.

"Yeah," I said warily. "But I'd better be getting on."

The male police officer stepped forward.

"We'll need some details, my darling."

"What do you want to know?"

He took out a notebook.

"We'll start with your name and address."

That was another funny thing. I turned out to be more shocked than I realized. I could remember my name, though even that was a bit of an effort. But I just couldn't think of my address even though I own the bloody place and I've been living there for eighteen months. I had to get my appointment book out of my pocket and read the address out to them, with my hand trembling so much I could hardly make out the words. They must have thought I was mad.

TWO

I had reached "E" in the register; E for Damian Everatt, a skinny little boy with huge spectacles taped together at one hinge, waxy ears, an anxious gappy mouth, and scabby knees from where the other boys pushed him over in the playground.

"Yes, miss," he whispered, as Pauline Douglas pushed her head round the already open classroom door.

"Can I have a quick word, Zoe?" she said. I stood up, smoothing my dress anxiously, and joined her. There was a welcome through-breeze in the corridor, though I noticed that a bead of sweat was trickling down Pauline's carefully powdered face, and her normally crisp graying hair was damp at her temples. "I've had a call from a journalist on the *Gazette.*"

"What's that?"

"A local paper. They want to talk to you about your heroics."

"What? Oh, that. It's . . ."

"There was mention of a melon."

"Ah yes, well you see . . ."

"They want to send a photographer, too. Quiet!" This last to the circle of children fidgeting on the floor behind us.

"I'm sorry they bothered you. Just tell them to go away."

"Not at all," Pauline said firmly. "I've arranged for them to come round at ten forty-five, during break time."

"Are you sure?" I looked at her dubiously.

"It might be good publicity." She looked over my shoulder. "Is that it?"

I looked round at the huge green-striped fruit, innocent on the shelf behind us.

"That's the one."

"You must be stronger than you look. All right, I'll see you later."

I sat down again, picked up the register.

"Where were we? Yes. Kadijah."

"Yes, miss."

The journalist was middle-aged and short and fat, with hairs growing out of his nostrils and sprouting up behind his shirt collar. Never quite got the name, which was embarrassing as he was so aware of mine. Bob something, I think. His face was a dark shade of red, and wide circles of sweat stained his armpits. When he wrote, little shreds of shorthand in a tatty notebook, his plump fist kept slipping down the pen. The photographer who accompanied him looked about seventeen; cropped dark hair, an earring in one ear, jeans so tight I kept thinking that when he squatted on the floor with his camera they would split. All the time Bob was asking me questions, the photographer wandered round the classroom, staring at me from different angles through the camera lens. I'd tidied my hair and put on a bit of makeup before they arrived. Louise had insisted on it, pushing me into the staff cloakroom and coming after me with a brush in her hand. Now I wished I'd made a bit more effort. I sat there in my old cream dress with its crooked hem. They made me uncomfortable.

"What thoughts went through your head before you decided to hit him?"

"I just did it. Without thinking."

"So you didn't feel scared?"

"No. I didn't really have time."

He was scribbling away in his notebook. I had a feeling that I should be making cleverer, more amusing comments about what had happened.

"Where do you come from? Haratounian's a strange name for a blond girl like you."

"A village near Sheffield."

"So you're new to London." He didn't wait for me to reply. "And you teach nursery children, do you?"

"Reception, it's called. . . ."

"How old are you?"

"Twenty-three."

"Mmm." He looked at me musingly, like someone assessing an unpromising item of stock at an agricultural auction. "How much do you weigh?"

"What? About seven and a half stone, I think."

"Seven stone," he said, chuckling. "Fantastic. And he was a big chap, wasn't he?" He sucked his pen. "Do you think society would be a better place if everybody got involved the way you did?"

"Well, I don't really know." I fumbled for some sort of coherent statement. "I mean, what if the melon had missed? Or if it had hit the wrong person?"

Zoe Haratounian, spokeswoman on behalf of inarticulate youth. He frowned and didn't even make a pretense of writing down what I'd said.

"How does it feel to be a heroine?"

Up to then it had been amusing in a way, but now I felt a little irritated. But of course I couldn't put it into words that made any sense.

"It just happened," I said. "I don't want to set myself up as anything. Do you know if the woman who was mugged is okay?"

"Fine, just a couple of cracked ribs and she'll need some new teeth."

"I think we'll take her with the melon." It was the boy-photographer.

Bob nodded.

"Yes, that's the story."

He pulled the fruit off the shelf and staggered across with it.

"Blimey," he said, lowering it onto my lap. "No wonder you took him out. Now look at me, chin up a bit. Give us a smile, darling. You won, didn't you? Lovely."

I smiled until the smile puckered on my face. Through the doorway I saw Louise staring in, grinning wildly. A giggle grew in my chest.

Next he wanted the melon and me with the children. I did my impersonation of a prim Victorian schoolmarm but it turned out that Pauline had already agreed. The photographer suggested cutting it up. It was a deep, luscious pink, paler at the rind, with polished black pips and a smell of fibrous coolness. I cut it into thirty-two wedges; one for each child and one for me. They stood round me on the sweltering concrete playground, holding their melon and smiling for the camera. All together now. One, two, three, cheese.

The local paper came out on Friday and I was on the front page. The photograph of me was huge; I was surrounded by children and slices of melon. MISS HEROINE AND THE MELON. Not very snappy. Daryl had a finger up his nose and Rose's skirt was tucked into her knickers, but otherwise it was all right. Pauline seemed pleased. She pinned the piece on the notice board by the foyer, where the children gradually defaced it, and then she told me that a national paper had rung, interested in following up the story. She had provisionally set up an interview and another photo opportunity for the lunch break. I could miss the staff meeting. If that was all right with me, of course. She had asked the school secretary to buy another melon.

I thought that would be the end of it. I was bewildered by the way a story can gather its own momentum. I could hardly recognize the woman on an inside page of the *Daily Mail* next day, weighed down by a vast watermelon, topped by a large headline. She didn't look like me, with her cautious smile and her fair hair tucked neatly behind her ears; and she certainly didn't sound like me. Wasn't there enough real news in the world? On the page after there was a very small story at the bottom of the page in which a bus had fallen off a bridge in Kashmir and killed a horribly large number of people. Maybe if a blond British twenty-three-year-old schoolteacher had been on board they might have given it more space.

"Crap," said Fred when I said as much to him later that day, eating soggy chips doused in vinegar after a film in which men with bubbling biceps hit each other on the jaw with a cracking noise like a gun going off. "Don't do yourself down. You did what heroes do. You had a split second to decide and you did the right thing." He cupped my chin in his slim, callused hand. I had the impression that he was seeing not me, but the woman in the picture with the sticky little smile. He kissed me. "Some people do it by throwing themselves on top of a grenade; you did it with a watermelon. That's the only difference. Let's go back to your place, shall we? It's still early."

"I've got a stack of marking and forms that are about a yard high."

"Just for a bit."

He chucked the last of the chips in an overflowing bin, sidestepped the dog turds on the pavement, and wrapped his long arm round my shoulder. Through all the exhaust fumes and the fried reek from kebab houses and chip shops, he smelled of cigarettes and mown grass. His forearms, where he had rolled up his shirt, were tanned and scratched. His pale hair flopped down over his eyes. He was cool in the industrial warmth of the evening. I couldn't resist.

Fred was my new boyfriend, or new *something*. So maybe we were at the perfect time. We were past the difficult, embarrassing first bit where you're like a comedian going out before a difficult audience and desperately needing laughter and applause. Except in this case very much not needing laughter at all of any kind. But we hadn't remotely got to the stage where you walk around the flat and don't happen to notice that the other person hasn't got anything on.

He had been working most of the year as a gardener and it had given him a wiry strength. You could see the muscles ripple under his skin. He was tanned on his forearms and neck and face, but his chest and stomach were pale, milky.

We hadn't got to the stage either of just taking off our clothes and folding them up on separate chairs in some clinical, institutional sort of way. When we got into my flat—and it always seemed to be *my* flat—there was still an urgency about getting at each other. It made everything else seem less important. Sometimes, in class on an afternoon when the children were fidgety and I was tired and listless in the heat, I would think about Fred and the evening ahead and the day would lift itself.

We lit cigarettes afterward, lying in my little bedroom and listening to music and car horns in the street below. Someone shouted loudly: "Cunt, you cunt, I'll get you for this." We listened to the sound of feet pounding down the pavement, a woman screaming. I'd got used to it, more or less. It didn't keep me awake at night, like it used to.

Fred turned on the bedside lamp and all the dreary, dingy nastiness of the flat was illuminated. How could I ever have bought it? How would I ever manage to sell it? Even if I made it look nicer—got rid of the flimsy orange curtains the last owner had left behind, put down a carpet over the grubby varnished boards, wallpapered over the beige woodchip, painted the blistering window frames, put mirrors and prints on the walls—no amount of clever interior design could disguise how cramped and dark it all was. Some developer had carved up an already small space to make this hole. The window in the so-called living room was actually cut in half by the partition wall, through which I sometimes heard a neighbor I'd never met shouting obscenities at some poor woman. In a spasm of grief and loneliness and the need for a place I could call home, I'd used up all the money my father had left me when he died. It had never felt like home, though, and now, when property prices were soaring, I was stuck with it. In this kind of weather, I could clean the windows every day and still they'd be smeared with greasy dirt by the evening.

"I'll make us some tea."

"I've got no milk."

"Beer in the fridge?" Fred asked hopefully.

"No."

"What have you got?"

"Cereal, I think."

"What's the use of cereal without milk."

It was a statement of fact rather than a question I was supposed to answer. He was pulling on trousers in a businesslike kind of way that I recognized. He was about to give me a peck on the cheek and leave. Purpose of visit over.

"It's all right as a snack," I said vaguely. "Like crisps."

I was thinking about the woman who had been mugged; the way her body flew through the air like a broken doll hurled out of the window.

"Tomorrow," he said.

"Yeah."

"With the guys."

"But of course."

I sat up in bed and contemplated the marking I had to do.

"Sleep well. Here, there's some post you've not opened."

The first was a bill, which I looked at, then put on the pile on the table with the other bills. The other was a letter written in large, looping script.

Dear Ms. Haratounian, from your name I gather you are not English, though you look it from the photographs I have seen. I am not a racist, of course, and I count among my friends many people like yourself, but . . .

I put the letter on the table and rubbed my temples. Fuck. A mad person. All I needed.

THREE

❧

I was woken by the doorbell. I thought at first it must be some sort of joke or a wino who had mistaken the street door for the entrance to a hostel. I opened the curtains slightly in the front room and pushed my face against the glass, trying to see who it was, but the angle was wrong. I looked at my watch. Just after seven. I couldn't think of anyone who could possibly be calling at this time. I wasn't wearing anything so I pulled on a bright yellow plastic raincoat before going downstairs.

I opened the door just a fraction. The street door of the building opens directly onto Holloway Road, and I didn't want to stop the traffic with my appearance just after I've woken up. It was the postman and my heart sank. When the postman wants to hand his mail to you personally, this is not generally good news. He usually wants you to sign for something in order to prove that you have received a horrible bill printed in red threatening to cut off your phone.

But he looked happy enough. Behind him I could see the beginnings of a day that was still cool but was going to be very hot indeed. I'd never seen this particular postman before, so I don't know if it was a new thing, but he was wearing rather fetching blue serge shorts and a crisp light blue short-sleeved shirt. They were obviously official summer issue, but they looked jaunty. He wasn't exactly young, but there was a *Baywatch*-postman air to him. So I stood on the doorstep looking at him with interest, and he looked back at me with some curiosity as well. I realized that my raincoat was on the skimpy side and not joined very well in the middle. I pulled it tightly together, which probably made things worse. This was starting to feel like a scene from one of those sleazy British comic sex films from the early seventies that you sometimes see on TV on Friday nights after you've got back from the pub. Porn for sad bastards.

"Flat C?" he asked.

"Yes."

"There's mail for you," he said. "It wouldn't go through the box."

And there was. Lots and lots of different envelopes arranged in piles held together with elastic. Was this a joke? It took some complicated maneuvering to receive these bundles with one arm while holding my coat closed with the other.

"Happy birthday, is it?" he said with a wink.

"No," I said, and pushed the door shut with a naked foot.

I took them upstairs and spilled them onto the table in the main room. I picked a dainty lilac envelope to open but I already knew what they were. One of the things about having a great-grandfather or great-great-grandfather who walked out of Armenia about a hundred years ago with nothing but a recipe for yogurt is that you're very easy to look up in the phone book. Why couldn't he have changed his name like other immigrants? I read the letter.

> *Dear Zoe Haratounian,*
>   *I read of your heroic exploit in this morning's news-*
> *paper. First may I be allowed to congratulate you on*
> *your courage that you showed in tackling that person.*
> *If I may trespass a little longer on your patience . . .*

I looked ahead and then over the page and then the page
after that. There were five of them, and Janet Eagleton
(Mrs.) had written on both sides of the paper in green ink.
I'd save that one for later. I opened an envelope that looked
more normal.

> *Dear Zoe,*
>   *Congratulations. You did brilliantly, and if more*
> *people behaved the way you did, London would be a*
> *better place to live. I also thought you looked lovely*
> *in the photograph in the paper and that's really why*
> *I'm writing. My name is James Gunter and I'm twenty-*
> *five and I think I'm quite presentable looking, but I've*
> *always had trouble meeting the right girl, Miss*
> *"Right," if you will. . . .*

I folded up the letter and placed it on top of Mrs. Eagleton's. Another letter was more like a package. I opened it
up. There was a bundle of paper half folded, half rolled
up. I saw diagrams, arrows, subjects arranged in columns.
But sure enough, on the first page it began as a letter addressed to me.

> *Dear Ms. Haroutunian,*
>   *(That's an interesting name. Might you be a Zoroas-*
> *trian? You can let me know at my box number (below).*
> *I will return to this subject (Zoroaster) below).*

*You have defenses against forces of darkness. But
as you know there are other forces that are not so
easily resisted. Do you know what a kunderbuffer is?
If you do you can skip the following and begin at a
section I will mark for your convenience with an as-
terisk. I append one for demonstration purposes (*).
The section I will mark for your convenience I will
mark with two (2) asterisks in order to avoid unnecessary confusion.*

I put the letter on top of James Gunter's. I went into the
bathroom and washed my hands. That wasn't enough. I
needed a shower. That was always a bugger in my flat. I
liked showers with frosted doors that you could stand up
in. I once went out with someone whose only redeeming
quality, in retrospect, was that he had a power shower with
six different nozzles apart from the normal one above. But
the shower in my flat involved squatting in the bath and
fiddling with decaying valves and twisting the cable. Still,
I lay back for several minutes with a washcloth over my
face, showering it. It was like lying under a warm wet blanket.

I got out and got dressed in my work clothes. I made a
mug of coffee and lit a cigarette. I felt a bit better. What
really would have made me feel better is if the pile of letters had gone, but it was still stolidly present on the table.
All those people knew where I lived. Well, not quite all.
Another brisk inspection of the letters showed that several
of them had been redirected from the newspapers where
they had been originally sent. Some of them were probably nice. And at least, I thought to myself, they were writing instead of phoning up or calling round.

At that moment the phone rang, which made me jump.

It wasn't a fan. It was Guy, the real estate agent who was allegedly trying to sell my flat.

"I've got a couple of people who want a look around the property."

"Fine," I said. "You've got the key. What about that couple who saw it on Monday? What did they think?" I had no hopes of them, really. He had looked grim. She had talked in a friendly way, but not about the flat.

"They weren't sure about the location," Guy said breezily. "A bit on the small side as well. And they felt it needed too much work on it. Not keen, basically."

"The people today shouldn't come too late. I'm having some friends around for a drink."

"Birthday, is it?"

I took a deep breath.

"Do you really want to know, Guy?"

"Well . . ."

"I'm having an anniversary party because it's six months since this flat went on the market."

"It's not, is it?"

"Yes, it is."

"It doesn't seem like six months."

He took some convincing. After the call I looked around the room rather desperately. Strangers were going to be coming in and looking at this room. When I moved to London my aunt had given me a book on Household Hints and Handy Tips. It had advice on how to tidy if you've only got fifteen minutes. But what if you've only got one minute? I made my bed, straightened the rug by the door, rinsed my coffee mug and put it neatly upside down by the sink. I found a cardboard box in a cupboard and I tipped all the letters into it and stowed it under my bed. A minute and a half and I was late at the school. Again. Sweatily late and the day was only starting to get hot.

* * *

"So, my love, what can we do to make this more salable?"

Louise was standing at the window with a bottle of beer, brandishing a cigarette at Holloway Road.

"It's very simple," I said. "Get rid of the road. Get rid of the pub next door and the kebab house next to that. Decorate. It's horrible, isn't it; everything about it. I hated it from the moment I owned it and even if it means losing money I've got to get out. I want to rent a small cozy flat with a garden or something. We're meant to be in the middle of a housing boom. There must be somebody mad out there." I took a drag of my cigarette. "Granted, lots of mad people have already looked at this flat. I need the right kind of mad person."

Louise laughed. She had come early to help me get things ready and to have a proper talk and basically because she's a good person.

"But I didn't come all the way here to talk about property. I want to know about this new man. Is he coming tonight?"

"They're all coming."

"What do you mean all? Have you got more than one?" I giggled.

"No. He goes round with this gang of boys. I think they've all known each other since primary school or something ridiculous. They're like those six-packs of beer. You know, not to be sold separately."

Louise frowned.

"This isn't some sort of strange five-in-a-bed sex thing, is it? If so, I want to hear about it in detail."

"No, they leave us alone some of the time."

"How did you meet?"

I lit another cigarette.

"I met them all together. A few weeks ago I went to a

party at a gallery over in Shoreditch. It was one of those typical disasters. The person I knew turned out not to be there. So I wandered from room to room holding a drink and pretending to be on my way to somewhere important. You know what I mean?"

"You're talking to the world champion," said Louise.

"Anyway I went upstairs and there was a group of good-looking young men round a pinball machine, banging at it, shouting, laughing, having a better time than anyone else there. One of them—not Fred, as it happens—looked round and asked me if I wanted to play. So I did. We had a great time and the next evening I met them again in town."

Louise looked thoughtful.

"So you faced the difficult choice of which one of them actually to go out with on a one-to-one basis?"

"It wasn't exactly like that," I said. "The day after *that* Fred rang me at home and asked me out. I asked him if he had the permission of his gang, and he was a bit sheepish about that." I leaned out the window a bit. "And here they are now."

Louise peered out. They were some way down the road and hadn't noticed us.

"They look like nice boys," she said primly.

"That's Fred in the middle carrying the large bag, the one with very light brown hair, almost blond."

"So you grabbed the nicest-looking one."

"The one in the very long coat, that's Duncan."

"How can he wear it in this heat?"

"Apparently it makes him look like a gunman in some spaghetti western. He never takes it off. The other two are brothers. The Burnside brothers. The one in the glasses and the cap is Graham. The one with the long hair is Morris. Hi!" This last was yelled down at them.

They looked up, startled for a moment.

"We'd love to come up," Duncan shouted. "Unfortunately we've got to go to a party."

"Shut up," I said. "Here, catch."

I dropped my bunch of keys and, with what I have to say was remarkable style, Graham took off his cap and caught the keys in it. They disappeared from view as they let themselves in.

"Quick," said Louise. "We've got thirty seconds. Which one of them should I marry? Who's got the best prospects? You can leave out Fred for the moment."

I thought for two seconds.

"Graham's working as a photographer's assistant."

"Got it."

"Duncan and Morris work together. They do all sorts of different stuff to do with computers. I don't understand it at all, but then I don't think I'm meant to. Duncan's the life and soul of any party; Morris is rather shy when you actually get him on his own."

"They're the ones who're brothers, right?"

"No, that's Morris and Graham. Duncan has red hair. He looks completely different."

"All right. So for the moment the computer people seem the better bet. Morris the shy brother and Duncan the talkative redhead."

And then they were in the room, filling it. When I'd talked to them about this event they had been asking brashly what sort of women would be there and they had been noisy down on the street, but in my flat they went a bit quiet and polite as they were introduced to Louise. That was something I liked about them, in a way.

Fred came over and gave me a lingering kiss, which I couldn't help thinking was a public demonstration to everyone in the room. Was he showing affection or marking out territory? Then he produced something that looked like a brightly colored drape.

"I thought this would be helpful. It's to hang over the damp patch," he said.

"Thanks, Fred." I looked at it dubiously. It was a bit bright; its colors clashed. "But I think that surveyors are allowed to move bits of cloth out of the way to see what's behind them."

"Let's get you to the surveyor stage first. Hang it up then."

"Oh. Okay."

"Zoe says you're geniuses with computers," Louise was saying to Duncan.

Morris, who was standing with us, blushed slightly, which was sweet.

"She'd think so," Duncan said, pulling the ring top off a can of beer. "But she's got low standards. That's just because we showed her how to use her own computer." He took a sip. "Admittedly that was an impressive achievement. It was like teaching a squirrel how to find nuts."

"But squirrels are brilliant at finding nuts," Morris objected.

"That's right," Duncan said.

"But they're good already," Morris persisted.

"That's right. Zoe is now as good with her computer as a squirrel is at finding nuts."

"But you should have said it was like teaching a squirrel how to juggle."

Duncan looked puzzled.

"But you can't teach squirrels how to juggle."

I topped up Louise's drink.

"They can go on like this for hours," I said. "It's a bonding thing. Something to do with having been on the playground together."

I went off to get some crisps from the kitchen and Louise came with me. We could see the boys in the room.

"He's lovely-looking," she said, nodding over at Fred. "What's he smoking? He looks very relaxed. Exotic."

"He's got a hippie side to him. Relaxed is good, though."

"Is it serious?"

I took a sip from her glass.

"I'll have to get back to you about that," I said.

A few other people arrived. There was John, a nice teacher from our school, who had asked me out just a few days too late. And a couple of women I had met through Louise. It had turned into a real miniature celebration. After a couple of drinks I was starting to feel benevolent toward them, this new circle of people. All they had in common was me. A year ago I was lonely and lost and I hadn't met a single one of them, and now they were all coming to my so-called home on a Friday evening. Suddenly there was a chinking sound. Fred was rapping on a glass bottle with a fork.

"Silence, silence," he said when there already was silence. "Unaccustomed as I am, et cetera. I'd just like to stand up and be counted and say that I *like* this flat and I'd like us all to raise our glasses and hope that we'll all be able to meet here again in six months' time and have another good evening." There was a general raising of glasses and bottles. A flash went off in my face as Graham took a photograph. He was always doing that—you'd be chatting away to him and he'd suddenly lift up his camera and aim it at you, like a third eye. It could be quite disconcerting, as if all the time he was talking or listening to you, he was really in search of a good shot. "Also," continued Fred, "it's also our anniversary." There were starts of surprise all round, not least from me. "Yes," he said, "it's nine days since Zoe and me first . . . erm . . ." There was a pause. "Er . . . met." There were some suppressed laughs behind me from Duncan and Graham, but not from anybody else. I felt for a moment as if I were trapped at a rugby club dinner.

"Fred," I said, but he held up a hand to stop me.

"Hang on," he said. "It would be sad if such an evening were not marked in a solemn way but . . . what's this?" He said this last in a pathetically false tone of amazement as he bent down and rummaged behind my armchair. He pulled out a large parcel wrapped in brown paper. "Either this is another offering from one of Zoe's anonymous fans or else it must be a present."

"Idiots," I said, but in a nice way. It looked like a picture. I ripped off the paper and then saw what it was. "You bastards," I said, laughing. It was an entire framed page of the *Sun* featuring the headline ME AND MY MELON and in smaller writing: HAVE-A-GO BLONDE ZAPS MUGGER.

"Speech," said Louise through cupped hands. "Speech."

"Well," I began, before I was interrupted by the ring of the doorbell. "Wait," I said. "One minute."

I opened the door to find a man dressed in a brown corduroy suit and rubber boots.

"I've come to see the flat," he said. "Is that all right?"

"Yes, yes," I said eagerly. "Come on up."

As I led him up the stairs, the talking of the guests became audible.

"You seem to be having a party," he said.

"Yes," I said. "It's my birthday."

FOUR

~

The letters gradually fizzled out. The first flood turned into a trickle, then stopped altogether. For a little bit it had seemed funny. One time I took a bunch of them with me when I was meeting Fred and the guys. We sat at a table outside a bar in Soho, drank very cold beer and passed them among us, occasionally reading choice phrases aloud. Then while Morris and Duncan were conducting one of their impenetrable conversations, which involved them challenging each other to name the Seven Dwarfs or the Magnificent Seven or the Seven Deadly Sins, I talked more seriously about it with Graham and Fred.

"It's the thought of these people sitting all over Britain and writing eight-page letters to someone they don't know and looking up my name in the phone book and buying a stamp. Haven't they got better things to do with their lives?"

"No, they haven't," said Fred. He put his hand on my knee. "You're a goddess. You and your melon. We all loved you before. Now you're a male fantasy. This powerful beautiful woman. We all want someone like that to walk up and down our bodies wearing high heels." Then he leaned over and whispered in my ear, his breath warm. "And you're all mine."

"Stop it," I said. "It's not funny."

"Now you know what it's like to be a celebrity," said Graham. "Enjoy it while you can."

"Oh, for God's sake, is nobody going to give me any sympathy? Morris, what have you got to say on my behalf?"

"Yeah," said Fred. "Tell us, Morris. What advice would you give to a beautiful woman about coping with the pressures of fame?"

And he leaned over and slapped Morris several times very gent-ly on the cheek. Sometimes I was baffled by the boys, as if they were conducting rituals from a strange exotic culture I didn't understand. One of them would say or do something to another and I couldn't tell whether it was a joke or an insult or a joking insult. I didn't know whether the victim would laugh or flare up. For example, Fred never seemed to say anything nice to Morris, yet he sometimes talked of him as his best friend. There was a sudden silence and I felt a twist in my stomach. Morris blinked in the face of our attention and ran his fingers through his hair. I used to think he did it to show how impressively long and thick it was.

"Who can name ten films with letters in them?" he said.

"Morris!" I said furiously.

"*Letter from an Unknown Woman*," said Graham.

"*Letters from Three Women*," said Duncan.

"*The Letter*," said Fred.

"This is too easy," said Morris. "Ten films with letters in them that don't have 'letter' in the title."

"Like what?"

"Well . . . like *Casablanca*, for example."

"There aren't letters in *Casablanca*."

"There are."

"There aren't."

The serious conversation was over.

After that I stopped even reading them. Some I could recognize just by the writing on the envelope, so I didn't even bother to open them. Others I glanced at cursorily and chucked into the cardboard box with the rest. They weren't even funny anymore. A few were sad, a few obscene, and most were simply tedious.

If I wanted a reminder of the derangement around me I only needed to look out of the window, the frame of which was rotting, incidentally. Young men in beat-up cars, leaning on their horns, faces red with rage. Solitary old women with their baskets on wheels, stumbling through the crowds, muttering to themselves. The winos who sat in the doorway of the boarded-up shop a few doors down from me, smelling of piss and whiskey, with their unbuttoned trousers and their skewed leers.

Madness was coming through the door as well, in the shape of prospective buyers of the flat. There was one man, about fifty perhaps, very small with cauliflower ears and a dragging limp, who insisted on kneeling on the floor and knocking against the skirting boards, like a doctor checking a patient for a chest infection. I stood ineffectually beside him, wincing at the music pounding into the flat from the pub. Or the young woman, probably about my age, with dozens of silver studs around the rims of her ears in a bumpy ridge, who brought her three huge smelly dogs into the flat while she looked round. The thought of what the flat would be like after a week with them in residence made my stomach heave. There was hardly room for a person. One of them ate my vitamin tablets off the table and another lay by the front door, making horrible smells.

Most of the visitors stayed only a few minutes, just long enough not to seem rude, before beating a retreat. A few didn't mind being rude. Couples sometimes talked loudly to each other about what they thought.

Perhaps on superficial, casual acquaintance, Guy was more like a normal member of the human race. But due to his failure to sell my flat, we were becoming long-term associates. He was always smartly dressed in a variety of suits and colorful ties, some of which had cartoon characters on them. However hot the weather became, he didn't sweat. Or rather he sweated very discreetly. There would be just one single drop running down the side of his face. He smelled of shaving lotion and mouthwash. I would have assumed my flat had become a symbol of failure that he would have avoided. It wasn't as if it needed an expert guide. But he kept accompanying viewers, even at awkward times, in the evening or on weekends.

So maybe it should have been less of a surprise when, after a thin, anxious-looking woman had scuttled out, he looked me deep in the eyes and said:

"We must get together for a drink one evening, Zoe."

I should have come up with some monumentally savage put-down reflecting the deep hatred I had for him and his fake tan and his infuriating euphemisms, but I couldn't think of anything, so instead I blurted out:

"I think we should lower the price."

The man who had come to look round on the evening of my not-moving party returned with a tape measure, a notepad, and a camera. It was early evening and Fred was away on some strange regional TV assignment in the Yorkshire Dales, spending thirty-six hours transforming a large and overgrown garden for a program to be shown in about a year's time. He'd rung me from a pub, his voice thickened by alcohol and lust, and told me how he was imag-

ining the things he would do to me when he returned. Not
what I needed to hear: I was struggling with the literacy
hour report on the computer. I was trying to produce a pie
chart. It had seemed so easy when Duncan, or was it Morris, had done it. The sentence "A type 19 error has occurred" kept flashing on my screen. So I smoked and cursed
while the man who might or might not buy my flat poked
around. He measured floor space, pulled open cupboards,
lifted up the tatty rug, lifted Fred's ghastly wall hanging
and inspected the damp patch that seemed to be spreading
in spite of the hot, dry weather, turned on the tap in the
bathroom and stood for a minute or so watching the
wretched splatter of water. When he went into the bedroom
and I heard the sound of drawers being opened, I followed
him.

"What are you doing?"

"Checking things out," he replied, quite unconcerned,
gazing into my jumble of knickers and bras and laddered
tights.

I slammed the drawer shut and went into the kitchen. I
was hungry but when I opened the fridge all I found there
was one bag of ancient spring onions, one white roll with
mold growing on it, an empty brown bag with a cherry pit
in it, and a can of Coke. In the freezer compartment was
a bag of prawns, probably well past their sell-by date, and
a small bag of peas. So I drank the Coke, standing by the
fridge, then returned to the computer and wrote: "We aim
to produce not just competent readers, but interested readers. A carefully considered Whole School Curriculum Plan
ensures that all pupils reinforce . . ." Oh fuck. This wasn't
what I became a teacher for. Soon I'd be writing words
like "satisfactory attainment levels" and "inputting."

I put three multivitamin tablets in my mouth and
crunched them crossly. Then I picked up the homework—

if that's not too grand a word for it—that I had set the class to and brought home that evening. I had asked them all to draw one of their favorite stories. Some of the pictures were pretty incomprehensible. Benjamin's zigzag pattern in green and black was "The Big Bad Wolf." Abstract art, I supposed. Jordane had drawn a round pea-green circle, nothing else, for "The Princess and the Pea." Lots of them had done pictures of Disney films: Bambi and Snow White and things like that. I went through them and wrote encouraging remarks on them and then put them all in a folder under the table.

"I'm going now."

The man stood in the doorway, camera round his neck. He was tapping his pen against his teeth and gazing at me. I saw that the bald spot in the center of his head was a cruel pink, and his hairy wrists were sunburned as well. Good.

"Oh, right."

Not a word about coming back. Bastard.

I left a few minutes after him, to go and see a film with Louise and a few of her friends I had never met before. It was lovely sitting in the dark with a group of women, eating popcorn and giggling. It was so safe.

I came back quite late. It was dark, starless. I pushed open the door and there was a letter on my doormat; someone must have pushed it through the letterbox. Neat italic writing, black ink. It didn't look like another nutter. Standing in the doorway, I opened the letter.

Dear Zoe, When does someone like you, young and pretty and healthy, become frightened of dying, I wonder. You smoke (there's a nicotine stain on your finger by the way). Sometimes you take drugs. You eat bad food. You stay up late and the next morning you don't get hangovers. Probably you think that you will live forever, that you will be young for a long while yet.

Zoe, with your white teeth and your one small dimple when you smile, you will not be young for much longer. You have been warned.

Are you scared, Zoe? I am watching you. I am not going to go away.

I stood on the edge of the pavement while crowds of people flowed past me, jostled against me, and I stared at the letter. I lifted up my left hand and there was a yellow stain on the middle finger. I crumpled the letter into a tight ball and threw it into a bin with all the other rubbish, all the crap of other people's lives.

Today, she is wearing a pale blue dress with straps. It comes down to her knees, and there is chalk dust near the hem that she has not noticed yet. She is not wearing a bra. She has shaved under her arms; her legs look smooth, soft. There is pale nail varnish on her toes, but it is beginning to chip on her left big toe. Her sandals are flat, navy blue, old, scuffed. She is tanned; the hairs on her arms are golden. Sometimes I can glimpse her milky underarms; the whiter skin behind her knees; if she stoops down I can see that the honey color on her shoulders and throat fades between the beginnings of her breasts. Her hair is piled on top of her head. It has bleached in the sun, so it is much darker underneath than on top. She is wearing small silver earrings, in the shape of little flowers. Every so often, she twists them round between her finger and thumb. The lobes of her ears are quite long. The vertical groove above her upper lip is quite pronounced. When she is hot, like today, sweat gathers in it. Every so often she wipes it with a tissue. Her teeth are white, but I have seen several fillings at the back of her mouth. They glint when she laughs or yawns. She is not wearing any makeup. I can see the pale tips of her eyelashes; the slight dryness of her bare lips. There is a sprinkling of freckles on the bridge of her nose that was not there last time I looked. The yellow stain on her middle finger has gone. Good. She wears no rings on her fingers. On her wrist is a large-faced watch, with Mickey Mouse in the center. She uses a ribbon for the strap.

When she laughs, she makes a pealing sound, like a doorbell. If I told her that I loved her, she would laugh at me like that. She would think I was not serious. That is what women do. They turn what is serious and big into a small thing, a joke. Love is not a joke. It is a matter of life and death. One day, soon, she will understand that. She will know that the way she smiles, or opens her eyes wide when she is listening; the way her breasts flatten when she lifts her arms above her head—these things matter. She smiles too easily. She laughs too easily. She flirts. She wears skimpy clothes. I can see her legs through her dress. I can make out the shape of her nipples. She is careless of herself.

She talks very quickly, in a light husky voice. She says "Yeah," not yes. She has gray eyes. She is not frightened yet.

FIVE

Everybody knows that schools, almost everywhere except perhaps in busy places like Japan, finish at about four or three-thirty, although the little things that I teach clock out even earlier, at quarter past three. Even people who know nothing else about children know that. They see boys and girls being led along high streets, holding the hand of their mother or trailing behind carers, carrying schoolbags, lunch boxes. I'd already learned that the rush-hour traffic in London was about half composed of vast people-carriers ferrying glum-looking kids in uniform the huge distances between their nice houses and the schools that were considered worthy of them. Because, of course, as I'd also newly discovered, one of the main status symbols of any parent in London is the distance they have to transport their children. The school next door is for poor people, like the ones I teach.

The big joke when people discover I'm a teacher is about how they envy me the short hours and the long holidays. Fair enough, of course, since this was one of the less worthy motives that brought me into this job. My school career had not been a major success, so I didn't have the qualifications for studying something really important like looking after sick pussycats, which was what I had wanted to do when I was much younger. I had only done well enough to teach small children. That suited me. I liked children, their transparency, their eagerness, and their sense of possibility. And I liked the idea of standing around a sandbox all day and wiping the noses of toddlers and helping mix paints.

Instead I found myself in a job that was more like being an accountant in the middle of a zoo. And the hours were longer than being an accountant. The official school inspection was coming at us like a train. After the kids had been collected and taken back to their apartment blocks, we had meetings, form-filling, planning. We stayed on until seven, eight, nine o'clock, and Pauline would have been better off installing a camp bed and a Primus stove in her office, since she never seemed to leave.

I got away earlier that evening because I had an appointment to meet a man at the flat. Naturally the bus didn't arrive for ages, so when I ran panting along the pavement only five minutes late at twenty-five to eight, he was standing there in the doorway reading a newspaper. Bad start. I had already given him too much time to look at the area. Fortunately, he seemed engrossed in what he was reading. Maybe he hadn't noticed the pub, or at least hadn't taken in its full implications. He was wearing a suit that was a slightly odd shape with lapels that were askew, so it was probably very expensive. He must have been in his later twenties, maybe thirty. His hair was cut very short, and he looked cool in the blistering heat.

"I'm really sorry," I panted. "Bus."

"That's all right," he said. "I'm Nick Shale. You're Miss Haratounian." We shook hands in a sort of continental style. He smiled.

"What's so funny?"

"I pictured you as a grim old landlady," he said.

"Oh," I said, trying to smile politely.

I opened the street door. There was the usual rubbish on the doormat, leaflets for takeaway pizzas, window cleaners, taxi cabs, and one hand-delivered letter. I recognized the writing immediately. It was the creep who had sent me the letter before—when was it?—five days ago. He'd been back to my door. How boring and irritating. How very nasty. I looked at it for a moment, then over at the man, Nick, who had a puzzled expression.

"What did you say?" I said.

"Your bag," he said. "Can I take it for you?"

I handed it to him without speaking.

I had my guided tour of the flat down to a skillful three minutes, brilliantly taking in all the points of interest while deftly avoiding areas that were not necessarily to the advantage of the property. Occasionally Nick asked questions that I had now become used to.

"Why are you moving?"

Did he think he could trap an old hand like me so easily?

"I want to move closer to my work," I said, falsely.

He looked out the window.

"Is the traffic a problem?" he asked.

"I've never thought about it," I said. That was laying it on a bit thick. At least he didn't laugh. I placed the envelope on the table. Unopened. "It's handy for the shops."

He put his hands in his pockets and stood in the middle of my living room as if he were rehearsing being the owner. He looked like the squire of a very small estate indeed.

"You're not from London," he said.

"Why do you say that?"

"You don't sound like it," he said. "I'm trying to place you. With your name you should be Armenian. But you don't sound Armenian. Not that I know what Armenians sound like. Maybe they all sound like you."

I felt oddly sensitive when people looking around the flat turned personal as if we were all going to be good friends, but I couldn't help smiling.

"I grew up in a village near Sheffield."

"Different from London."

"Yeah."

There was a pause for mutual thought.

"I'd like to think about this," Nick said with an earnest expression. "Would it be all right if I came back and had another look sometime?"

I was dubious about whether it was specifically the flat he was interested in, but it didn't bother me too much. Even a crumb of enthusiasm was something.

"Fine," I said.

"Can I ring you or do I need to go through the estate agent?"

"Whatever," I said. "I'm at work quite a lot."

"What do you do?"

"I'm a teacher in a primary school."

"That's great," he said. "All those holidays."

I forced a smile.

"Your number," he said. "Can you give it to me?"

I told him and he typed it into what looked like a chunky pocket calculator.

"Good to meet you, erm . . . ?"

"Zoe."

"Zoe."

I heard him trip down the stairs two at a time and I was left alone with my letter. I pretended to myself to be casual about it for a bit. I made myself an instant coffee and lit a cigarette. Then I opened it and spread it out on the table before me:

Dear Zoe,

I may be wrong, but I think you aren't as scared as I mean you to be. As you know, I'm looking at you. Maybe I'm looking at you as you read this.

It was stupid but I glanced up and around, as if I might catch someone next to me.

As I said before, what I'm really interested in is looking at you from the inside, the bits of you that you'll never see but I will.

Maybe it's that you feel secure in your horrible little flat that you can't sell. You're not secure. For example: your back window. It's easy to climb up on the shed in the yard behind and then through it. You should put a proper lock on it. The one you've got at the moment is too easy. That's why I left it open. Go and look.

P.S. You look happy when you're asleep. Being dead is only like being asleep forever.

I put the paper back on the table. I walked across the room and out onto the landing. Sure enough the window that looked down on the garden I wasn't allowed to go into was raised a couple of feet. I shivered. I almost felt that there was a chill in the flat, like in a cellar, though I knew it was a clammy hot evening. I went back into the living room and sat by the phone. I wanted to be sick. But was it an emergency? Was it anything?

I compromised. I looked up the nearest police station in the phone book and phoned it. I had a slightly complicated conversation with a woman at the desk, who seemed to be looking for excuses to put the phone down. I said there had been a break-in and she asked what had been stolen and what damage had been done. I said no damage and I wasn't sure what had been stolen.

"Is this a police matter?" the voice asked wearily.

"I've been threatened," I said. "Threatened with violence."

The discussion went on for quite a few minutes more, and after a conversation with a third party, inadequately masked by a hand over the receiver, she said that somebody would call round "in due course," whatever that meant. I went from window to window, locking them when I could, fastening bolts. As if somebody was going to climb into a first-floor window in full view of Holloway Road. I didn't switch on the TV or play music. I wanted to be able to hear anything. I just smoked cigarette after cigarette and sipped a beer.

It was over an hour later that the doorbell rang. I walked down to the street door but didn't open it.

"Who's there?"

There was a muffled sound from behind the door.

"What?"

Another muffled sound. Awkwardly I pulled back the stiff-sprung opening of the letterbox and looked out. I saw dark blue cloth. I opened the door. There were two police officers. Their car was parked behind them.

"Do you want to come in?"

They didn't reply but looked at each other and stepped forward. I led them up the stairs. Both of them took off their caps as they entered the house. I wondered if it was an ancient form of respect toward women. To make things worse, I get nervous around the police. I tried to remember if there was anything illegal in the flat, in the fridge or on the mantelpiece. I didn't think so but my mind wasn't working very efficiently, so I couldn't be sure. I pointed to the letter on the table. Maybe I shouldn't touch it. It might be evidence. One of the officers stepped forward and leaned over the table, reading it. It took him quite a long time. I saw he had a long Roman nose, with a lump where it met his head.

"You've had another letter from this person?" he asked finally.

"Yes, I got one a few days ago. On Wednesday, I think."

"Where is it?"

I'd been waiting for this.

"I threw it away," I said, a bit guiltily, and then quickly started speaking before he could get cross with me. "I'm sorry. I know it was a stupid thing to do. I just got upset by it."

But the officer didn't get cross. He didn't seem worried at all. Or even especially interested.

"Did you check the window?"

"Yes. It was open."

"Can you show us?"

I led them out of the room. They followed in rather a heavy sort of way, as if they were being asked to do too much for something so trivial.

"The pub garden's down there," the other officer murmured, peering through the window. Roman Nose nodded. "He could've seen the window from down there."

They turned and walked back to the living room.

"Can you think of anybody who might have sent this? Old boyfriend, someone at work, that sort of thing?"

I took a deep breath and told them about the melon and the mail it had provoked. They both laughed.

"That was you?" said Roman Nose rather cheerily. He turned to the other officer. "Danny was first at the scene at that one." He turned back to me. "Nice one. We've got your picture up in the station. Quite a heroine you are to us." He chuckled. "Watermelon, eh? Better than a truncheon any day." There was crackling in his radio. He pressed a button and a voice said something that was unintelligible to me. "That's all right. We'll be along in a minute. See you there." He looked back at me. "That's it, then."

"What?"

"You get your face in the paper, this sort of thing happens."

"But he's broken in, he's threatened me."

"You're not from London, are you? What was your name again?"

"Haratounian. Zoe Haratounian."

"Funny old name. Italian, is it?"

"No."

"It's just that there's a lot of strange people about."

"But hasn't he committed a crime?"

Roman Nose shrugged.

"Has anything been taken?" he asked.

"I don't know. I don't think so."

"Are there any signs of forced entry?"

"Not that I could see."

He looked across at his companion and gave a little nod toward the door that clearly meant Let's get out of here as soon as we can shut this little woman up.

"If anything serious happens"—he put a gentle but unpleasant stress on the word "serious"—"then give us a ring."

They turned to go.

"Aren't you going to take the letter with you?"

"You keep it, love. Put it in a drawer. Somewhere safe."

"Aren't you going to take a statement? Don't I need to fill out some form?"

"If you have any more trouble, we'll do all that, my dear. All right? Now you get some sleep. We've got work to do."

And they went to work. I looked out of the window as their car pulled out into all the other lights and hubbub of the hot city.

Six

There was loud music and laughter outside on Holloway Road, as if there was a slightly sinister late-night street party going on. Somebody was clapping wildly. A car horn blared. The hot air held all the smells of the night together: spice, frying onions, exhaust fumes, patchouli, garlic, cinnamon, and the unexpected drift of roses. Occasionally a feeble twitch of wind fluttered the half-open curtains through the wide-open window, but otherwise the heat was thick and deep and saturated. It was the middle of the night but there were no stars, no moon, only the street lamps that cast a dirty orange glow round the room. And noise. People. Cars. I felt for a moment I'd like to be out in the middle of a forest or desert or on the open sea.

I didn't close my eyes. I looked at Fred and he looked back, slightly smiling, sure of himself, while the sweat from his forehead dripped on my face, my neck, and our hands slipped on each other's drenched bodies. He was still strange to me: his high forehead, full mouth; his long, slim, smooth, rather soft body. Even after an evening of dancing and then sex he smelled clean, yeasty. Lemon soap and earth, grass and beer. I pulled the damp sheet off us and he stretched out on the narrow bed and put his arms under his head and grinned at me.

"That was nice," I whispered.

"Thanks," he said.

"You're not meant to say that," I said. "You're meant to say something like, Yes, it was nice."

He shook his head.

"Have you ever had sex that's as good as that?"

I couldn't help giggling. "Are you serious? You want me to say, Oh, Fred, I never realized it could be like this."

"Shut up. Shut the fuck up."

I looked at him. He wasn't smiling. I'd hurt his feelings. He looked humiliated and angry. Men.

I sat up, legs crossed, shook two cigarettes out of the pack lying on the floor, lit them both, and handed one to him.

"I've never had sex with a gardener before."

He took a drag and blew a perfect smoke ring into the air, where it hung for a second before dissolving.

"I'm not a gardener. I garden. I help out."

"Like: I'm not a teacher, I teach?"

He blew another smoke ring and watched it.

"You're a teacher. I'll be out of this job as soon as I can."

"Oh." I felt a surge of resentment. "Thanks a lot. Well, have you had sex with a teacher?"

He raised his eyebrows at me. His face broke into a leer.

"Never with a *famous* teacher."

I didn't want to think about that. All evening I'd been drinking and giggling and dancing and getting stoned and trying not to think. I'd had enough of stupid jokes about watermelons, and of newspaper articles calling me petite, blond Zoe, and weird letters on the doormat. Of people whom I'd never met thinking about me, having fantasies about me. Maybe there was someone standing outside the flat at this moment, looking up at my open window, waiting for Fred to go. I felt completely sober now.

I dropped my cigarette into the glass by the bed and heard it sizzle.

"Those last letters . . ."

"Ignore them," Fred said briskly. He closed his eyes. "What are you doing this weekend?"

"They scared me. They were . . . oh, I don't know, purposeful."

"Mmm." He stroked my hair lightly. "We were thinking of a picnic on Saturday. Out of town. Want to come?"

"Do you do everything as a group?"

He leaned down and kissed me on my breasts. "I can manage some things on my own. And what's the problem?"

"Nothing." There was a silence. "Would you stay the night, Fred? I mean the whole night. If you'd like to, that is."

It was as if I'd told him there was a bomb under the pillow. His eyes snapped open and he sat up.

"Sorry," he said. "I've got to be at some old lady's house near Wimbledon first thing tomorrow." He stepped into his boxer shorts, his cotton trousers. God, what a speedy dresser he was. Shirt on, buttons done up, socks, shoes from under the bed, patting his pockets to make sure his change was in there. Jacket from the back of the chair.

"Your watch," I said dryly.

"Thanks. Shit, look at the time. I'll ring you tomorrow, make plans."

"Sure."

"Don't worry about things." He ran his hands over my

face, kissed me on the neck. "Beautiful woman. Good night."

"Bye."

After he'd left I got up and closed the living room window, in spite of the dense heat. The room felt more claustrophobic than ever. I looked out at Holloway Road. It would be light in a few hours. I checked the landing window, which I'd already checked several times that evening, got my watch from the bathroom: 1:45. If only it were morning already. I was tired, but not sleepy, and time creeps when you're scared. My sweat prickled on my skin, suddenly chilly, and I picked up the sheet from the floor and wiped down my body with it, before wrapping myself up in its thin folds and lighting another cigarette. I wished I had tea in the flat. Maybe there was some whiskey somewhere. I went into the kitchen and pulled a chair up to the high cupboard. There were a load of empty bottles, which one day I was going to take to the bottle bank, and no whiskey. But there was some peppermint liqueur that a parent had given me at Christmas and I'd never touched. I poured a slug of it into a mug that had lost its handle; it was green and viscous and cloyingly sweet, and rolled in a burning ball down my throat.

"Ugh," I said out loud, and noticed suddenly how quiet it had become; just the occasional minor earthquake of a passing lorry, the slap of someone's feet passing under the window. It was 2:15.

I shuffled to the bathroom in my sheet; cleaned my teeth and splashed water on my hot face. Then I lay down in bed and tried not to think about it. I couldn't help it. I turned over the two last letters in my mind. The first, of course, I'd thrown away. But I remembered most of it. The second I had put on my desk. The police obviously weren't convinced it was by the same person; I knew it was. They weren't treating it seriously; they didn't know how it felt to be a woman lying alone in a shabby flat on Holloway Road, fearing there was someone out there, watching.

Despite myself, I got out the letter and read it again, lying in bed. I knew this man had looked at me; I mean, really looked at me. He'd seen things that even I hadn't bothered to notice about myself: like the stained finger. He was learning me, the way we never learn even lovers. Maybe he was memorizing me, like for an exam. He'd been in here, I knew he had, whatever the police said, and looked at my things, touched them. Maybe he'd gone through letters, photographs, clothes. He might have taken things away. He'd seen me asleep. He wanted to see inside me, he said. Not be, see. I felt nauseous, but maybe that was just the peppermint liqueur, which still lined the inside of my mouth like glue, and the drink I'd had earlier, and the sweaty sex, and the tiredness, and—oh fuck it.

I closed my eyes and put one arm over them so I was in complete darkness. London crouched outside my window, full of eyes. I heard a drop of rain, then another. My mind wouldn't stop; I couldn't make it slow down. I went over and over the letter in my mind.

"As I said before": That was the funny thing. What was it? He would like to see inside me. As he had said before. But he hadn't said it before, had he? I tried to reconstruct the first letter, the one I'd thrown away, in my mind. I could remember only fragments. But I would have remembered. What could that mean?

A thought stirred, something I wished I could ignore. I sat up, dry-mouthed, swung my legs out of bed, and went into the living room, where I dragged the cardboard box out from under the sofa. There were dozens of letters in there, some not even opened. This could take ages. I went back into the bedroom, pulled on my tatty old tracksuit; then I poured myself another horrible mug of the liqueur, lit a cigarette, and began.

I just needed to glance at each letter to make sure, although actually I could tell by the handwriting on the envelopes that they weren't from him. My dear Zoe . . . Miss Haratounian . . . Go back to where you came from, bitch. . . . Have you found Jesus? . . . You smile, but your eyes look sad. . . . Good for you . . . If you would care to donate to our charity . . . I feel we have met somewhere. . . . If you're into S&M . . . I'm writing this from prison. . . . I would like to offer you a word of hard-earned wisdom. . . .

And there it was. Suddenly I could hear my heart beating hard, too fast. My throat felt too narrow to breathe. The handwriting, black italic. I picked up the envelope, which hadn't been opened. There was a stamp on this one; my address, post code in full. I took a violent swig from the mug, then slid a finger under the flap and tore open the envelope. The letter was short but to the point.

Dear Zoe, I want to see inside you, and then I want to kill you. There is nothing you can do to stop me. Not yet, though. I will write to you again.

I stared at the words until they blurred. My breath was coming in little ragged gasps. Raindrops burst against the windows, slow, heavy summer rain. I jumped to my feet and bumped the sofa over the floor, until it was rammed against the front door. I picked up the phone and dialed Fred's number with shaky, inept fingers. It rang and rang.

"Yes." His voice was thick with sleep.

"Fred, Fred, it's Zoe."

"Zoe? What time is it, for fuck's sake?"

"What? I don't know. Fred, I got another letter."

"Jesus, Zoe, it's three thirty."

"He says he's going to kill me."

"Look . . ."

"Can you come round? I'm scared. I don't know who else to ask."

"Zoe, listen." I could hear him strike a match. "It's all right." His voice was gentle but insistent, as if he were talking to a small child who was worried about the dark. "You're quite safe." There was a pause. "Look, if you're really scared, then call the police."

"Please, Fred. Please."

"I was asleep, Zoe." His voice was cold now. "I suggest you try to sleep yourself."

I gave up then.

"All right."

"I'll call you."

"All right."

I called the police. I got a man I'd never talked to before who took down all my details with painstaking slowness. I spelled my last name out twice, H for horse and A for apple. Every time I heard a sound, I stiffened and my heart raced. But of course no one could get in. Everything was locked and bolted.

"Hold on a minute, miss."

I waited, smoked another cigarette. My mouth felt like the inside of an ashtray.

In the end he told me to come into the police station in the morning. I suppose I had wanted policemen to rush around and protect me and sort everything out, but this was all I was going to get. If anything, I was reassured by the tone of dullness and routine in his voice. Things like this happened all the time.

* * *

At some point, I fell asleep. When I woke it was nearly seven o'clock. I looked out the window. It had rained heavily in the night, and the downfall had cleaned the road; the leaves on the few plane trees looked less bleached and shriveled, and the sky was actually blue. I'd forgotten about blue.

SEVEN

I got to see more important policemen this time, so that was something. If the officers in uniform who had called round at the flat looked like members of the school rugby team, then the detective who talked to me in the police station looked more a geography teacher. Perhaps a little more smartly dressed than any geography teacher I had had, in a navy blue suit and a sober tie. He was large, heavyset. I mean almost fat. His brown hair was cut short and precise. He introduced himself as Detective Sergeant Aldham.

I wasn't led to an interview room or anything formal like that. He met me at the reception area and then punched some numbers to open a door to let me through into the real police bit behind. He made a mistake the first time and had to punch in the numbers again, more slowly, with some cursing under his breath. He led me to his desk and sat me down by the side of it, which made me feel even more like an awkward pupil going to see her teacher after school. Or before school, in this case. I had had to phone Pauline to say I'd be in late and she wasn't pleased about that. It was not a good time, she said to me.

Aldham read the two letters very slowly with a frown

of concentration. I spent five minutes fidgeting and staring around the room at people arriving, talking on the phone. A couple of officers were laughing about something I couldn't hear at the far end of the open-plan office. Aldham looked up.

"Would you like a cup of tea?"

"No thanks."

"I'm getting one for myself."

"All right, then."

"Biscuit?"

"No thanks."

"I'm having one."

"It's a bit early in the morning."

It was quite a long time before he hustled awkwardly back, the plastic cups almost too hot to hold. He dipped a digestive biscuit into his tea and carefully bit the wet crescent of biscuit.

"So what do you think?"

"What do *I* think? Well, but I—that's your job, isn't it?"

"I don't know. What did the other letter say?"

"It was horrible so I threw it away. It had some weird stuff about what I ate. And there was something about being afraid of dying. It sounded as if it was someone who had been spying on me."

"Or somebody who knows you?"

"Knows me?"

"It might be a joke. Don't you think you might have some friend who's doing this for a laugh?"

I hardly knew what to say.

"Someone's threatening to kill me. I don't see any joke."

Aldham shifted uneasily in his chair.

"People have a funny sense of humor," he said. There was a silence. I was thinking desperately: Could I just be wrong about this? Maybe it was nothing to make a fuss about. "Hang on a moment," he said at last. "Let me have a word with someone."

He took a folder out of his desk and inserted the two letters. He took that and his tea and walked heavily across the room and out of my sight. I looked at my watch. How long was this going to take? Was it worth getting my own files out of my bag and doing some work on the corner of Aldham's desk? I wasn't quite in the mood. When Aldham finally returned, he was with another man in a suit. He was a smaller, slighter man, graying, who looked as if he was a bit farther up the food chain. He introduced himself as Detective Inspector Carthy.

"I've looked at your letters, Miss . . . er . . ." he mumbled something that was apparently an attempt at my name. "I've looked at the letters and DS Aldham has filled me in on the details of the case. These are certainly nasty pieces of work." He looked around and pulled a chair over from an unattended desk. "The question is, What's actually going on here?"

"What's going on is that somebody is threatening me and they've broken into my flat." Carthy grimaced. "And I'm being harassed. That's a crime now, isn't it?"

"In certain circumstances. We have every sympathy for your concern," he said. "But it's difficult to know how to proceed exactly."

"Don't you think this person sounds dangerous?"

"Maybe. Maybe not. Look, miss, I understand you've had other mail of this kind."

I gave yet another recapitulation of my moment of fame, and the two detectives exchanged a brief smile.

"The melon thing?" Carthy said. "That was great. We've got the newspaper photo on a notice board somewhere. Everyone thinks you're a heroine here. Maybe you could go and say hello to some of them before you go. But about the letters: I reckon that in all probability this is just the sort of thing that happens when you become a celebrity. There are sad people out there. This is their way of meeting people."

I finally lost patience.

"I'm sorry, I just don't think you're taking this seriously enough. This person hasn't just written letters. He's been in my flat."

"He *may* have been." Carthy gave a long-suffering sigh. "Very well. Let's think about a couple of things." There was a moment's pause. "Your flat. Is it easy of access?"

I shrugged.

"It's just a normal conversion. There's a common entranceway from Holloway Road. There's a pub patio thing next to the backyard behind."

Carthy wrote something on a large pad of paper that was balanced on his knee. I couldn't see whether he was taking notes or just doodling.

"Do many people visit your flat?"

"How do you mean?"

"One a week? Two a week? On average."

"I can't answer it in that way. I've got friends. A bunch of them came round for a drink last week. I've got a new boyfriend. He's been around quite a few times." More scribbles on the pad. "Oh, and the flat's been on the market for six months."

Carthy raised an eyebrow.

"Which means that people have been visiting the flat?" he said.

"Obviously."

"How many?"

"A lot. Over the entire six months there must have been sixty, seventy, maybe more."

"Have any people come more than once?"

"A few. I *want* them to come more than once."

"Have any of them seemed strange in some way?"

I couldn't help laughing grimly.

"About three-quarters of them. I mean, they're complete strangers rummaging through my cupboards, opening drawers. That's what it's like trying to sell your home."

Carthy didn't smile back.

"There are various motives for harassment of this kind. The most common is of a private nature." He was sounding embarrassed. "Do you mind if I ask you some personal questions?"

"Not if they're relevant."

"You said you have a new boyfriend. How new?"

"Two or three weeks. Very new."

"Does that mean that a previous relationship ended?"

"Not exactly."

"What do you mean?"

"I mean no. I wasn't in a relationship."

"But have you had a recent personal, that is, er, sexual liaison?"

"Well, fairly recent." I was blushing hopelessly.

"Did it break up painfully?"

"It wasn't like that," I said. Now it was *my* turn to go red. "I've seen a few people at different times."

"A few?" He and Aldham exchanged a significant look.

"Look, that sounds wrong." I was flustered. I knew what they were both thinking, and there was nothing I could say that wouldn't make it worse. What made it so ludicrous is that compared to almost anyone I know, I'm a nun: an awkward, embarrassed, inarticulate nun, too. "I've gone out with, seen, whatever you call it, two men in the last year or so." They both went on looking at me as if they were not at all convinced by this low number. "The last of them was months ago."

"Did it end badly?"

I thought of sitting opposite Stuart in a café near Camden Lock. I gave a sad laugh.

"It just fizzled out, really. Anyway, the last I heard he was hitchhiking across Australia. You can cross him off the list of suspects."

Carthy gave a loud click of his ballpoint pen and stood up.

"DS Aldham will help you fill out a case form and take a brief statement."

"What are you going to do?"

"I've told you."

"I mean, to catch him?"

"If anything else happens, give Aldham a ring and we'll take it from there. Oh, and take sensible precautions in your private life for a while."

"I told you, I've got a boyfriend."

He nodded curtly and turned away, muttering something I couldn't hear under his breath.

EIGHT

I was late arriving at school. Even later than I'd said. When I walked out of the police station, I felt so tired I thought my legs would give way beneath me. My skin felt dusty, gritty, under my cotton dress. My scalp itched. My mouth was ashy. My shoulders were full of vicious little knots, bubbles of stress. When I walked out into the glare of the sunlight, my eyes, which already felt sunken back into their sockets, throbbed painfully. I screwed them up against the dazzle and fumbled in my bag for my dark glasses. Damn. I'd forgotten them. And my vitamin tablets. And I had only one more cigarette left. For a moment, I thought of going back to the flat and having a bath, cleaning my teeth, pulling myself together, before going to school. Or even just going to one of the nearby parks and sitting on the yellowing patches of grass by the side of a pond, watching the ducks, closing my eyes.

Instead I bought two packs of cigarettes, a cheap pair of sunglasses from a roadside stall, and then guiltily slunk into a greasy-spoon café. I ordered two cups of black coffee and a poached egg on toast. I ate slowly, watching people pass outside the smeary window. A Rasta in a yellow cap. A teenage couple, arm in arm, who stopped to kiss every couple of steps. A group of Japanese tourists with cameras and wearing jerseys. Surely they must be lost. A man carrying a baby in a sling; I could just see its tufty head. A woman screaming at the minute, red-faced child at her side. An Indian woman draped in a scarlet sari, picking her way in delicate sandals through dog shit and litter. A flock of schoolchildren carrying swimming bags, herded across the blaring, fume-filled road by a harassed young woman who reminded me of me. A cyclist in fluorescent yellow shorts, head down, swerving in and out of the traffic on thin wheels. A woman with a wide-brimmed hat, a bosom like a shelf, and a tiny poodle, who looked as if she had stepped into the wrong story.

I had stepped into the wrong story. He could be looking at me at this moment. Maybe I could see him, if I knew where to look. What had I done, that this should happen to me? I lit a cigarette, drank my cooling, bitter coffee. I was so late now a few more minutes wouldn't make any difference.

Before catching my bus up Kingsland Road, I passed a phone box and I had the stupidest impulse to phone my mother. My mother who hadn't been alive for twelve years. I just wanted her to tell me everything was going to be okay.

Pauline was politely chilly with me when I arrived. She told me a man named Fred had called. He had asked me to phone him on his mobile during the day. She didn't seem happy to be collecting messages from a boyfriend for an absent member of staff. The primary assistant who was sitting in for me had the children in plastic pinafores, mixing up paints with thick brushes. So I told them they all had to draw a portrait of themselves to put up on the wall before parents' evening. Raj painted himself with a pale pink face and brown hair, and legs sticking straight out of his chin. Eric, who never smiles, gave himself a red mouth that stretched from ear to ear. Stacey spilled water all over Tara's efforts and Tara hit her in the neck. Damian started crying, tears dripping onto the paper. I took him into the home corner and asked him what was wrong, and he told me that everyone picked on him, called him sissy, pushed him over on the playground, locked him in the toilet. I looked at him: a pale and snuffly creature with clothes that hung off his skinny frame and dirty ears.

Fred wanted me to come and watch him play five-a-side football that evening. They played every Wednesday, he said—a regular lads' feature. He was cheerful and laid-back, as if nothing had happened last night. He told me he was deadheading roses in suburbia, but he kept thinking about my body.

Pauline told me I had to have my literacy-hour material ready by the end of the week and did I think that was possible. Oh yes, I replied, unconvincingly, head throbbing. I usually buy a roll with cheese and tomato at the sandwich bar on the way to school, but today I'd forgotten, so while the other teachers ate healthy sandwiches and fruit, I had boiled potatoes and baked beans from the obese dinner lady, followed by steamed pudding and custard. Comfort food: It made me feel better.

I made the children write the letter *f* over and over again, following the dotted lines on their work sheets. *F* for fox and frog and fun. "And fuck," said four-year-old Barny, an August baby and youngest in the class, to the hoots of his admiring friends.

At circle time, we discussed bullying. I didn't look at Damian when I talked about everyone trying to care for each other, and all the children gazed at me with their cruel and innocent eyes. He sat quite near me, picking bits of fluff out of the rug, eyes swimming behind his thick glasses.

"Better?" I asked him as they left for the day.

"Mmm," he mumbled, head hanging. I saw that his neck was grubby; nails dirty. I felt suddenly irritated and angry with him, and wanted to shake him out of his hopelessness. Maybe that's how I was being, I thought: Maybe I was letting myself be bullied.

It's amazing how much noise ten men can make. Not just shouting at each other, but grunting, screaming, howling, yelling, hitting the ground with a thwack, hurtling into each other, kicking each other's shins so I thought I could hear the bones crack. I was amazed not to see blood gushing, bodies on stretchers, fisticuffs. But at the end of the hour they were all sweaty, smelly, fine; clapping each other round the shoulders. I felt a bit stupid, standing on the sidelines and watching them like part of the fan club. There were four other women there, as well, who obviously knew each other, were part of some kind of group who went out every Wednesday to watch their men getting pulped. Clio, Annie, and Laura, and someone whose name I never quite got and didn't like to ask again. They asked me how I'd met Fred, and wasn't he a charmer, and were friendly in a restrained kind of way that made me think there was a different girl most weeks and they didn't want to commit themselves. I guess I was meant to have cheered Fred on, as he rushed past me in a hot blur, eyes glazed, yelling something, but I couldn't quite bring myself to do it.

Afterward, he came over and draped an arm round my shoulder and gave me a kiss.

"You're sweaty."

I didn't mind that much, but on the other hand I didn't

intrinsically take huge pleasure in it in some primitive hormonal way.

"Mmmm." He nuzzled me. "And you're all cool and lovely."

After work, I'd been to Louise's flat to have a bath, and she'd lent me a pair of gray cotton trousers and a sleeveless knitted top to put on. I hadn't wanted to go back to my place. "Coming for a drink?"

"Sure." The last thing my body needed was a drink, but I wanted company. As long as I was with other people, in a public place, I felt safe. Just the thought of it getting dark again, and me in my flat, on my own, made me breathless.

"I'll see you after the shower."

One drink turned into several, in a dark pub whose landlord obviously knew them all well.

"And she's been getting all these mad letters," continued Fred, as if it were all a big joke. His hand moved round to my side, feeling its way down my ribs. I shifted nervously, lit another cigarette, tipped the last of the lager down my throat. "Including ones that threaten to kill her. Haven't you, Zoe?"

"Yes," I mumbled. I didn't want to talk about it.

"What did the police say?" asked Fred.

"Not much," I said. I made an attempt at lightness: "Don't worry, Fred. I'm sure you'll be suspect number one."

"It can't be me," he said cheerfully.

"Why not?"

"Well . . . er."

"You've never seen me sleep," I said and immediately wished I hadn't, but Fred just looked puzzled. It was a relief when Morris started telling me how they used to come here on quiz night.

"It's cruel, really," he said. "It's just too easy. It feels like helping ourselves to their money. We're lucky they don't just take us out back and break our thumbs."

"The Hustler," said Graham.

"What?" I said.

"Is my idiot brother boring you?"

"Don't be mean," I said.

"No, no," said Morris. "It's another reference. That's what Herman Mankiewicz said about Joseph Mankiewicz." Now he grinned over at his brother. "But Joseph was the more successful one in the end."

"I'm sorry," I said. "I don't know who these people are."

Unfortunately, they then started to tell me. To me the interplay of these old friends and brothers was a bewildering mixture of ancient jokes, obscure references, private catchphrases, and I generally thought the best thing was to keep my head down and wait for something I could follow. After a while the frenzied, competitive cross talk subsided and I found myself talking to Morris once more.

"Are you together with any of . . ." I said in a subdued voice and giving a discreet nod in the direction of the various young women around the table.

Morris looked evasive.

"Well, Laura and me are sort of, in a way . . ."

"In a way what?" said Laura across the table. She was a large woman with straight brown hair pulled back in a bun.

"I was telling Zoe that you've got ears like a bat."

I assumed that Laura would get furious with Morris. *I* would have. But I was starting to see that the three women hovered on the edge of the group, mostly talking among themselves and only being brought into the general conversation when necessary, which didn't seem to be very often. The boys, fresh-faced, bright-eyed after the football, looked more like little boys than ever. Why had I been embraced by their little group? As an audience? Morris leaned over very close to me and I almost thought for a moment he was going to nuzzle my ear. Instead he whispered into it.

"It's over," he said.

"What is?"

"Me and Laura. It's just that she doesn't know it yet."

I looked across at her as she sat there, unaware of the sentence hanging over her head.

"Why?" I asked.

He just shrugged, and I felt I couldn't bear to talk about it anymore.

"How's work going?" I said, for want of anything better.

Morris lit a cigarette before answering.

"We're all waiting," he said.

"What do you mean?"

He took a deep drag and then an even deeper gulp of his beer.

"Look at us," he said. "Graham is a photographer's assistant who wants to be a real live photographer. Duncan and me go around showing stupid secretaries how to do things with their software that they should have read in the manual. We're waiting for one or two of our ideas to, well, come to fruition. The way things are now, you need one halfway plausible idea and you're worth more than British Airways."

"And Fred?"

Morris looked reflective.

"Fred is digging and sawing while trying to decide who he is."

"But in the meantime there's that tan and those forearms," said Graham, who'd been eavesdropping.

"Mmmm," I said.

We sat there for a long time and drank too much, especially the boys. Later Morris moved across to be close to Laura, at her request, which sounded more like a command, and Duncan sat next to me. First he talked about his work with Morris, how they were out on the road every day, working mainly separately in different companies, teaching idiots with too much money and no time how to operate their own computers. Then he told me about Fred, how long they'd known each other, their long friendship.

"There's just one thing I can't forgive Fred for," he said.

"What's that?"

"You," he said. "It wasn't a fair fight."

I made myself laugh. He stared at me.

"We think you're the best."

"The best what?"

"Just the best."

"We?"

"The guys." He gestured around the table. "Fred always chucks his women in the end," he said.

"Oh well, we'll cross that bridge when we come to it, shall we?"

"Can I have you afterward?" he said.

"What?" I said.

"No, I want her," Graham said from across the table.

"What about me?" said Morris.

"I was first," said Duncan.

There was a little bit of me that recognized that this was one of their jokes, and maybe at some other time I might have laughed and made a flirtatious attempt to play along, but this wasn't one of those times.

Fred pushed himself against me. Pushed his hand against my trousers, Louise's trousers. All of a sudden I felt nauseous. The thick, noisy atmosphere of the pub was curdling around me.

"Time to go," I said.

He gave me a lift back to my flat in his van, dropping Morris and Laura on the way. He must have been way over the limit.

"Do you mind when they talk to me like that?"

"They're just jealous," he said.

I told him how the police had asked about my personal life.

"They made me think it was my fault," I said. "They asked about my sex life."

"A long story?" There was a gleam in his eyes.

"A very short story."

"That many?" He whistled.

"Don't be stupid."

"So they think it's one of your ex-lovers?"

"Maybe."

"Did any of them seem like nutcases?"

"No." I hesitated. "Except, when you start thinking like that, of course, everyone seems odd, a bit sinister. Nobody's just normal, are they?"

"Not even me?"

"You?" I looked across at him as he drove, thin hands on the steering wheel. "Not even you."

He seemed pleased. I saw him smile.

He pushed me back in my seat and kissed me so hard I tasted blood on my lip, and pressed a hand against my breast, but he didn't ask to come in. And I'd learned my lesson from last night. I didn't ask him. I waved him off, in a reasonably convincing charade of cheerfulness, and instead of going into the flat I walked down the still crowded road to the nearest pay phone. I called up Louise: Maybe

I could go there for the night. But the phone rang and rang and nobody answered. I stood in the booth, holding the phone to my face, until a cross man with a bulging brief-case banged on the glass. There was nobody else I knew well enough to ask; there was nowhere else to go. I dithered on the street for a few minutes, then told myself not to be so stupid. I walked back to the front door, opened it, picked up the junk mail, the gas bill, and the postcard from my aunt, and went upstairs. There were no hand-delivered let-ters. The windows were all locked. The peppermint liqueur stood on the table, top off. Nobody was there.

NINE

I really think he's interested."

"Who? Fred?"

"No. This man who's coming back to see the flat. God knows why, but I think he might like it. If only he did. I hate it here, you know, Louise. Really hate it. I dread coming back at night. If I could only get out of here, maybe all the letters would stop and he'd go away."

Louise looked round the room.

"What time is he coming?"

"About nine. Strange time to be viewing flats, don't you think?"

"That gives us nearly two hours."

"Are you sure you want to give up your precious Thursday evening like this, Louise?"

"I was only going to sit eating chocolate and flick through the TV channels. You've saved me from myself. Anyway, I like a challenge."

I looked grimly around the flat.

"It's certainly a challenge," I said.

Louise rolled up her sleeves, looking, rather alarmingly, as if she were going to scrub the floor.

"Where shall we start?"

I love Louise. She's down-to-earth and generous; even when she's acting outrageous and reckless, I know she's got her feet on the ground. She gets the giggles. She cries at soppy films. She eats too many cakes and goes on mad, hopeless, completely unnecessary diets. She wears skirts that make Pauline raise her beautifully shaped eyebrows, and high platform shoes, T-shirts with strange logos on them, huge earrings, a stud in her navel. She is small, stubborn, sure of herself, dogged, with a sharp, determined chin and a turned-up nose. Nothing seems to get her down. She's like a pit pony.

When I arrived at Laurier School, Louise took me under her wing, for all she had been there only a year herself. She gave me teaching tips, warned me which parents were troublesome, shared her sandwiches with me at lunch when I forgot to bring any, lent me tampons and aspirins. And she was my one point of stability in the whole fluid mess that was London. Now here she was, putting my life in order.

We began in the kitchen. We washed the dishes and put them neatly away, scrubbed the surfaces, swept the floor, cleaned the tiny window that looked over the pub's back garden. Louise insisted on taking down the pots and pans I'd hung above the stove.

"Let's open up the space," she said, squinting around her as if she had turned into an unimpressed interior decorator.

In the living room, twelve foot by ten, she emptied ashtrays, pushed the table under the window so the peeling wallpaper was partly obscured, turned over the stained sofa cushions, vacuumed the carpet, while I stacked bits of paper and mail into piles, threw away junk.

"Are those all the letters?" asked Louise, pointing at the cardboard box.

"Yep."

"Creepy. Why don't you throw them away?"

"Shall I? I thought the police might need them."

"Why? You've got the perv's letters separate anyway. Chuck them. Treat it all like the trash it is."

So she held the neck of a bin bag wide open and I shoved the lavender envelopes, green-ink letters, instruction manuals on self-defense, sad biographies, into it. My spirits rose. Louise went down Holloway Road to buy some flowers while I cleaned out the bath with an old washcloth. She returned with yellow roses for the living room, a potted plant with fleshy green leaves for the kitchen.

"You should have classical music playing when he arrives."

"I don't have anything to play music on."

"We can make coffee at the last minute. Bake a cake. That's meant to be good."

"I've only got instant coffee and even if I had all the ingredients, which I don't, I'm not going to start baking a bloody cake."

"Never mind," she said, a bit too brightly, cutting the stems off the roses. "Just put some perfume on yourself instead. Can I use this jug for a vase? There, doesn't that look better?"

It did. It felt better, too, now that Louise was with me, with her spiky eyelashes, scarlet mouth, vermilion nails, tight green dress. Just an ordinary mediocre room backing on to a pub, not a coffin after all.

"I've been really thrown by all this," I said.

Louise filled the kettle. "Where the fuck does this plug in, anyway? There's no spare socket. That's the other thing your flat needs—total rewiring. Top to bottom." She pulled out another plug with a flourish. "You can always come and stay at my place, if it would help. I haven't got a spare bed but I've a spare bit of floor. Come this weekend, if you want."

I had to stop myself from emitting a sob in response.

"That's nice of you" was all I managed.

The bedroom looked more or less okay, except I hadn't made the bed and the laundry basket was nearly full. We put the basket in the wardrobe, plumped up my pillow on the bed. Louise turned back the corner of the sheet, like my mother used to do. Wandering around, she paused and looked at objects on top of my chest of drawers.

"What on earth is this strange collection?" she asked.

"Things people sent me."

"What, as well as letters?"

"Yes. The police wanted to look at them."

"Bloody hell," she said, picking them up and examining them.

There was a whistle, that I should wear round my neck at all times as an alarm. A pair of tiny silk knickers. A round smooth stone that looked like a bird's egg. A small brown teddy bear.

"Why on earth has someone sent you this?" asked Louise, picking up a slightly grubby pink comb.

"It came with instructions. The point is to scrape it against someone's nose, well, the bit between their nostrils. Apparently it makes murderers go away."

"If they keep still while you get your comb out. This is pretty, though." She was looking at a dainty silver locket on a thin chain. "It looks like it might be valuable."

"If you open it up, there's a piece of hair inside as well."

"Who sent it?"

"Dunno. It arrived wrapped in a newspaper article about have-a-go heroes. It's beautiful, isn't it?"

"And these are exciting." She was looking at a pack of pornographic playing cards. She inspected the picture of a woman cupping her pneumatic breasts. "Men," she said.

I shivered in the heat.

Nick Shale arrived just after nine, by which time I had had a bath and changed into jeans and a yellow cotton shirt. I wanted to look neat and clean, to go with my flat. I piled my hair on top of my head and dabbed perfume behind my ears.

He was wearing running shorts, and when he took off his canvas backpack, I saw there was a dark V of sweat down the back of his jersey.

"Here we are—I bought you these." He handed me a brown paper bag. "Apricots from the stall down the road. I couldn't resist them."

I flushed. It was like giving me flowers. I didn't think prospective flat buyers were meant to give presents to the owner. The apricots were golden and downy, almost luminous.

"Thank you," I said self-consciously.

"Aren't you going to offer me one?"

So we ate them, standing in the narrow kitchen, and he said he'd bring me strawberries next time. I pretended not to notice the bit about next time.

"Don't you want to look round the flat again?"

"Sure."

He wandered from room to room, staring up at ceilings as if he could see interesting patterns on their surfaces. There were several cobwebs that Louise and I hadn't noticed drifting in the corners. In the bedroom, he opened the fitted wardrobe and gazed for a moment into my laundry basket, a funny little smile on his face. Then he straightened up and looked at me.

"I could do with a glass of wine."

"I don't have any."

"Then it's lucky I brought my own."

He stooped down and opened the backpack, bringing out a slim green bottle. I touched it: It was still cold, dribbles of moisture running down its neck.

"Do you have a corkscrew?"

I wasn't feeling especially pleased about this, but I gave him one. He turned his back to me to open it. I handed him a glass and a tumbler and he poured the wine into both, with a very slow and steady hand so that none spilled. He told me he lived in Norfolk but needed to buy a flat in London because he often stayed for two or three nights during the week.

"So my flat could become a pied-à-terre," I said. "What an honor."

"Cheers."

"I've got to go out now," I said, lying of course. My weekend appointment book was empty.

"It's a bit late, isn't it?" he said, draining his glass.

I didn't reply. I didn't see why I needed an excuse for a man I didn't know.

"You should take your bottle," I said.

"No, you keep it," he said, turning to leave.

"What about the flat?"

"I like it," he said. "I'll be in touch."

I heard the door close downstairs. I liked him well enough. I wondered what his handwriting looked like.

TEN

The next day I felt like a robot in class. I was doing a pretty reasonable impersonation of a primary school teacher. The robot got on with a whole-class lesson on letter formation while somewhere inside I was going over things in my mind. I needed to get rid of the flat. That came back and back the way a tune does, nagging at you. I had the tantalizing sense that if I could close the door on that unlovable bit of living space hacked out of an unpleasant house on a noisy road, then I would be able to close the door on other things as well. What I really ought to do was make the flat more secure, but that seemed wrong, like washing a broken bottle. The way to make that flat better and safer was to leave it. Nothing else would do. Starting next weekend I would start seriously looking at other flats.

I'd been too young when I'd bought this one. The money I'd been left by Dad when he died had felt like Monopoly money. There was too much of it to be real. He had said to me to buy somewhere to live; it was almost like a dying command. He was a man who thought that if you owned your own property, then you were safe; the world couldn't touch you, no matter what happened. So I was a good daughter—although of course I wasn't a daughter at all anymore, since I had no parents left; I was just me and very lonely and scared—and I did as he had told me. Very quickly. And since I'd moved to London from a quiet village, my only impulse had been to buy something that was in the *real* city, where things were happening, where there were shops, markets, people, noise. I'd certainly found that.

"Zoe?"

I was woken up out of what felt to me like sleep, and what to an observer would have looked like feverish activity (I was almost surprised to look at my hand and see a piece of chalk and at the blackboard to see a large *b* and *p* that I had carefully and unconsciously traced). I looked round. It was Christine, one of our special-needs teachers. The needs in our school were very special. You would see Christine sitting at improvised desks in the corridor with children suffering from an educational disability: abuse, malnutrition, having recently arrived from a war zone in eastern Europe or central Africa, that sort of thing.

"Pauline asked to see you," she said. "It's urgent. I'll take over here."

"Why?"

"There's a mother with her. I think she's very upset about something."

"Oh."

I felt a dull ache in my stomach, that sense of an imminent blow. I looked at the class. What could it be? The turnover in our class was amazing. People moved their children away, sometimes out of the country, often without a word of warning. Other troubled children quickly took their place. We had children under court orders, with social service files. I made a quick count. Thirty-one. They were all here. No toddler had wandered off home without my noticing. There was no medication I should have administered. Nobody was foaming at the mouth. I felt better. How bad could it be?

As I walked the short distance to Pauline's office, I thought how, if I hated my flat, at least I loved the school. In the small vestibule there was a pool of water made out of bricks with big fat fish in it. I dipped my fingers in it for luck, as I always did when I passed. The school was by the side of another of London's arterial roads. It was shaken all day by lorries making their way up toward East Anglia or down across the river to Kent and the south coast. To get to the nearest bit of scrubby park, you had to lead a crocodile of children along the road and across two dangerous junctions. But that was what I loved about it. It was something from another world, like a monastery, in the middle of the noise and dust. Even when the children were running around screaming it felt like a refuge.

Maybe it was just those stupid fish that made me feel like that, and I'd probably got it all wrong anyway. I remembered some book of facts I'd read as a child on how water conducted sound better than air. The fish probably spent their entire lives moaning about the noise of the traffic and wishing they were somewhere more desirable. I tried to remember what it was like when I lay submerged in the bath rinsing my hair. Could I hear the lorries hurtling past outside? I didn't remember.

Pauline was standing by the half-open door with a woman I recognized. They weren't speaking or doing anything. They had obviously just been waiting in silence for me to arrive. I saw the woman every day at the end of school, hovering at the door of the class. Elinor's mother. I nodded a greeting at her, but she didn't catch my eye. I tried to picture Elinor this morning. Had she been upset? I didn't think so. I tried to picture the girl in the class I had just left behind. Nothing unusual occurred to me.

"Shut the door behind you," Pauline said, leading me in. The mother stayed outside. She waved me to a chair in front of her desk. "That was Gillian Tite, the mother of Elinor."

"Yes, I know."

I noticed that Pauline was white-faced, trembling. She was either deeply upset or so angry that she could barely control herself.

"Did you give the class homework last week?"

"Yes. If you can call it homework."

"What was it?"

"It was just for fun. We'd been talking about stories and I asked them to draw a picture of one of their favorite stories in their art book."

"What did you do with the homework?"

"I'm trying to get them used to doing homework on time and giving it in. So I collected the books up on Wednesday—I think it was Wednesday. I'm pretty sure. I looked through them immediately." I remembered doing it—sitting there while that peculiar man who came to view the flat went through my knicker drawer. That was the day I'd found the letter on the doormat. "I wrote nice comments on them and gave them back on the next morning. I don't know if Elinor's mother expected a mark out of ten. They're too young for that sort of homework."

Pauline ignored me.

"Do you remember what Elinor drew?"

"No."

"Does that mean you didn't look at the drawings?"

"Of course I looked at them. I checked when they began them in class and I wrote a title for each one at the bottom of the page. Then I looked at them all when they were finished. I took them home. I didn't exactly spend hours on each picture, but I looked at them all and wrote something."

"Elinor's mother came in to see me in tears," said Pauline. "This is Elinor's drawing. Take a look."

She pushed a familiar large-format exercise book across her desk. It was open and I recognized my writing at the bottom of the page. Sleeping Beauty. Elinor had made a pretty dismal attempt at copying the words herself. The *p* was the wrong way round and the second word dribbled away as if it had run out of energy. The drawing was different, though. It wasn't like a toddler's drawing. Actually there were traces of Elinor's scratchy drawing here and there, but it had been embellished and drawn over and filled out. The girl was now lying in a carefully rendered room. More than that, I could see what Pauline couldn't. It was *my* room. My *bedroom*. At least bits of it were. There was the picture of the cow on the wall that I had lived with all my life and the mirror with a string bag hanging from its edge. I'd always meant to put it away and hadn't got around to it.

On the bed, Sleeping Beauty wasn't asleep and she wasn't Sleeping Beauty. She was me. At least she had my glasses on. The bed looked more like a mortuary slab. I mean that there were huge incisions in the body, with bits of internal organ, guts, trailing out. Parts of the body, especially around the vagina—*my* vagina—were so mutilated as not to be recognizable. Suddenly I started to be sick; bitter bile came up in my mouth, and I managed to hold it down, swallow it. But it burned the back of my throat and made me cough. I took a tissue from my pocket and wiped my mouth. I pushed the book back to Pauline. She looked at me earnestly.

"If you have done this as some very strange kind of joke,

then you'd better tell me straightaway. Just tell me: Did you do this?"

I didn't speak. I couldn't speak. Pauline rapped on the table as if trying to awaken me.

"Zoe. Do you realize the position you're in? What do you expect me to do?"

My eyes were burning. I had to stop myself from crying. I had to be strong, not collapse.

"Call the police," I said.

ELEVEN

Pauline was dubious and reluctant at first, but I insisted. I wasn't going to leave her office without something being done. Carthy had given me his card, but my hands were shaking so much that I had to fumble in my purse to get it out. Pauline looked visibly surprised as I laboriously dialed the number while looking at the card. I suppose she thought I was going to dial 999 in some hysterical way.

"It's happened before," I said to her in explanation. "In a way."

I asked for Carthy. He was away. So I was put through to Aldham as a pretty poor second best. I was wild on the phone. I said he had to come over now, here, to the school, right away. Aldham was reluctant but I said if he didn't come then I would make an official complaint and added to this any threat that came into my mind. He agreed and I gave him the address of the school and quickly put the phone down. I lit a cigarette. Pauline started to say something about no smoking being allowed except in the staff room, but I said that I was very sorry but this was an emergency.

"Are you going back to your class?" she asked.

"It's not a good time," I said. "I'd better talk to the police. I need to see what they say. I'll wait for them here."

There was quite a long silence. Pauline stared at me as if I were an unpredictable wild animal that needed careful handling. At least that's what I felt she was doing. I felt I would bristle at the slightest touch. Finally she gave a shrug.

"I'll talk to Mrs. Tite outside," she said quietly.

"Yeah," I said, hardly taking in what she was saying.

Pauline stopped at the door.

"Are you saying that someone else did that? That picture?"

I stubbed out my cigarette and started to light another.

"Yeah," I said. "Something horrible's going on. Horrible. I've got to get it sorted out."

Pauline started to say something, then stopped and left me alone in her office. I was hardly aware of the time. I smoked cigarettes one after another. I picked up a newspaper from Pauline's desk but I wasn't able to concentrate on it. It must have been half an hour later that I heard voices outside and Aldham came in, escorted by Pauline. She had already told him as much as she knew. I didn't bother with any greeting.

"Look," I said, pointing at the art book, which was still open where I had left it. "That's me. That's a fucking exact copy of my bedroom. You can't see *that* from the fucking pub."

Maybe Pauline had alerted him to my agitated state, because he didn't warn me or even snap back at me. He just looked at the drawing, and then muttered something under his breath. He looked stunned.

"Where was this done?" he said, looking up.

"How do I know?" It took an effort to slow myself down, to make myself concentrate. "It was just in a pile of schoolbooks. I had it in school last week on Friday when I collected it from the class."

"Where were they kept?"

"In the classroom. I took them home last Wednesday and brought them back the following morning."

"Were they ever out of your sight?"

"Of course they were. What do you think? I didn't sit and guard them all night. Sorry. Sorry sorry sorry. It's just— oh Christ. Sorry. Let me think. Yes, I went out to see a film with some friends. I must have been out for two, nearly three hours, I guess. It was the day I found the letter on my doormat. I told you about it. The first letter—or I thought it was the first letter. I threw it away."

Aldham wrinkled up his nose and nodded.

"So," he said. He looked baffled and anxious. He didn't meet my eye. "When did you return the books?"

"I told you, the following morning. I just had it for that evening. I'm sure. Completely sure."

"And it wasn't discovered until today?"

Pauline stepped forward.

"The mother only looked this morning," she said.

"Have any other books been tampered with?" Aldham asked.

"I don't know," I said. "I don't think so. I don't know, though. I . . ."

"We'll check the other art books," Pauline said.

I lit another cigarette. I could feel my heart beating fast. My pulse seemed to be everywhere, in my face and arms and legs.

"So what do you think?" I said.

"Wait," he said.

He took a mobile phone from his pocket and retreated into a corner. I heard him ask for DI Carthy and then begin a murmured conversation. Clearly there were different de-

grees of being unavailable. I heard fragments of one side
of the conversation.

"Shall we talk to Stadler? Right, Detective Inspector
Cameron Stadler. And Grace Schilling? . . . Can you give
her a bell? And send an officer along with the file. Send
Lynne—she's good at this kind of thing. We'll meet her
there. . . . Right, see you later."

Aldham put the phone away and turned to Pauline.

"Is it all right if Miss Haratounian comes with us for a
while?"

"Of course," Pauline said. She looked at me with a new
concern. "Is everything all right?"

"It'll be fine," Aldham said. "We just need to go through
some routine procedures." He took a handkerchief from his
pocket and used it to pick up Ellie's art book. "All right?"
he said.

It was quite a long drive across London. The permanent
traffic jam was even worse on a Friday and a lorry had got
stuck turning into a builder's yard, and Aldham took a
shortcut that got caught in a residential traffic system off
the Ball's Pond Road.

"Are we going to the police station?" I asked.

"Later, maybe," he said, in between cursing other vehi-
cles. "We're seeing a woman who knows about psycho
stuff like this."

"What did you think of the drawing?"

"Some people, eh?"

But it wasn't clear whether he was talking about the artist
or an old woman crossing the road very slowly. I didn't follow it up.

After almost an hour we drove along a residential street
and arrived at what looked like a school but had a sign
outside identifying it as the Welbeck Clinic. A female of-

ficer was sitting in reception reading a file. When she saw us she snapped it shut and came forward. She handed it to Aldham.

"You stay here," he said to me. "Officer Burnett will stay with you."

"Lynne," she said to me with a reassuring smile. She had a purple birthmark on her cheek and big eyes. On another day, I would have liked the look of her.

I started to light another cigarette but this really was verboten, so Lynne and I stood out on the step and she had one of my cigarettes as well, like a good girl. She didn't seem very used to it and kept coughing and spluttering. I think she did it to keep me company. And she didn't speak, which was a relief. It was just ten minutes before Aldham emerged. With him was a tall woman in a long gray coat. She had blond hair tied up on her head casually. She was carrying a leather briefcase and a khaki canvas shoulder bag. She didn't look all that much older than me. Early thirties maybe.

"Miss Haratounian, this is Dr. Schilling," Aldham said.

We shook hands. She looked at me with narrowed eyes, as if I were an unusual specimen that had been brought in for examination.

"I'm really sorry," she said. "I'm already late for a meeting, but I wanted a quick word."

I suddenly felt crushed. I'd been driven across London to talk to a woman as she accelerated past me on the steps of a clinic.

"So what do you think?"

"I think this should be taken seriously." She gave a sharp look across at Aldham. "Maybe it should have been taken seriously a bit more quickly."

"But it could be a joke, couldn't it?"

"It *is* a joke," she said, and looked troubled.

"But he hasn't done anything. I mean, he hasn't done anything to hurt me physically." In the face of her grave attention, I wanted to turn the whole thing back into a stupid prank.

"Exactly," said Aldham, a bit too enthusiastically.

"The problem with that argument," Schilling said, more to Aldham than to me, "is that . . ." She paused and collected herself. What had she been going to say? She swallowed. "It's not much protection for Miss Haratounian."

"Call me Zoe," I said. "It's less of a mouthful."

"Zoe," she said. "I want us to have a proper meeting on Monday morning to go over this in considerable detail. I'd like to see you here at nine o'clock."

"I've got a job."

"*This* is your job," she said. "For the moment. I've got to go now but . . . That drawing, that really is your bedroom?"

"I've already said that."

Dr. Schilling was fidgeting, moving from one foot to the other. If she had been a child in my class, I would have sent her to the lavatory.

"You've got a boyfriend, right?" she asked.

"Yes, Fred."

"Do you live together?"

I forced a half smile. "He doesn't spend the night."

"What, never?"

"No."

"This is a sexual relationship?"

"Yeah, we've gone all the way to ten or whatever it is, if that's what you mean."

She looked at Aldham.

"Talk to him."

"If you're thinking it might be Fred," I said, "you can stop right now. Apart from the fact that it can't be him, because, oh well, just because, you know." She nodded, kind but quite unconvinced. "Well, he was away the night it must have happened. He was in the Dales, digging a garden with several other people. He didn't come back till the following evening. I think you'll find he's even caught on camera by Yorkshire TV to prove it."

"You're quite sure?"

"Yeah. One hundred percent."

"Talk to him anyway," she said to Aldham. Then to me: "I'll see you on Monday, Zoe. I don't want to panic you and it may well be nothing. But I think it would be a good idea if you didn't spend the night alone at your flat for a while. Doug"—that must be Aldham—"look at her locks, all right? Bye, see you Monday."

Aldham and I walked back to his car.

"That was . . . er, quick," I said.

"Don't worry about her," Aldham said. "She's ten percent bullshit and ninety percent covering her arse."

"She said you should talk to Fred. You don't want to do that, do you?"

"We've got to start somewhere."

"Now?"

"Do you know where he is?"

"He's working on a garden."

"*In* a garden, you mean."

"No, Fred says he's working *on* a garden. I think it's meant to sound more artistic. Where are we now?"

"Hampstead."

"I think he's fairly nearby. He said north London."

"Good. Do you know the address?"

"I could ring him on his mobile. But can't it wait?"

"Please," said Aldham, offering me his phone.

I found the number in my appointment book and started to dial.

"If you go and see him, can I talk to him first?"

Aldham looked disconcerted.

"What for?"

"I don't know," I said. "Out of politeness maybe."

I saw Fred before he saw me. He was at the far end of the long back garden of an amazingly grand house. He was moving sideways along a border with a trimmer that was suspended from his shoulders by straps. He was wearing a baseball cap with the peak backward, torn jeans, a white T-shirt, heavy work boots. He also had an eye visor and ear protectors, so that the only way I could make myself known to him was to tap him on the shoulder. He started slightly, even though I had rung ahead to warn him I was coming. He switched off the machine and unclipped the straps. He pulled off the visor and the ear protectors. He seemed dazed by the noise, even though it had stopped, and by the bright light. We were standing in bright sunshine by a border of lilies. Fred was soaked in sweat.

He stood back and stared at me in surprise and even anger. He's one of those people, I thought, who like to keep everything in their separate compartments: Work and relationships were absolutely separate, like sex and sleep were. I'd leaked over. He wasn't pleased.

"Hello," he said, making the greeting into a question.

"Hello," I said, kissing him, touching his wet cheek. "Sorry. They said they wanted to talk to you. I told them it wasn't necessary."

"Now?" he said warily. "We're in the middle of a job. I can't just stop."

"That's nothing to do with me," I said. "I just wanted to say to you face-to-face that I was sorry you're being dragged in."

He seemed suddenly unyielding.

"What's all the fuss about?"

I gave him a potted version of what had happened at school, but he didn't seem to be taking it in. He was like one of those awful people at parties who glance over your shoulder at a better-looking girl over by the drinks. In this case Fred kept looking at Aldham, who was hovering over at the other end of the garden by the door into the house.

"And so she said I should stay away from my flat for the next few days."

There was a pause and I looked at Fred. I waited for him to speak, to commiserate, to say that of course I could stay with him until all of this had been sorted out, if I would like to. I waited for him to put his arms round me and tell me everything was going to be all right and he was here for me. His face, under the sheen of his sweat, was like a mask. I couldn't tell what he was thinking at all.

Then his eyes dropped to my breasts. I felt myself beginning to flush with humiliation and the first stirrings of a hot anger.

"I . . ." he began and then stopped, looking around. "All right. I'll talk to them for a minute. Nothing to say, though."

"Another thing," I said, without even knowing I was going to. "I think we should stop seeing each other."

That stopped his wandering, mildly lecherous eyes; his vague and disconnected air. He stared at me. I could see a vein throbbing in his temple, the muscles of his jaw clenching and unclenching.

"And why would that be, Zoe?" he said at last. His voice was icy.

"Maybe it's not a good time," I said.

He unstrapped the huge trimmer and laid it on the grass.

"Are you breaking off with me?"

"Yes."

A flush spread over his handsome face. His eyes were

completely cold. He looked me up and down, as if I were on display in a shop window and he was deciding whether he wanted to buy me or not. Then he allowed a little sneer to twitch at his mouth.

"Who the fuck do you think you are?" he said.

I looked at him, his sweaty face and bulging eyes.

"I'm scared," I replied. "And I need help, and I'm not going to get it from you, am I?"

"You cunt," he said. "You stuck-up cunt."

I turned and walked away. I just wanted to get out of here, to be somewhere safe.

Her hair is hanging loose on her shoulders. It needs washing. The parting is dark, a bit greasy. She has aged in the past week. There are lines running from the wings of her nostrils to the corners of her mouth, dark shadows under her eyes, a faint crease in her brow as if she has been frowning for hours on end. Her skin is looking slightly unhealthy, pale and a bit grubby underneath the tan. No earrings today. She wears an old pair of cotton trousers, oatmeal I think you would call the color, and a white short-sleeved shirt. The trousers are loose on her and they need pressing. There is a button missing on the shirt. She chews the side of her middle finger on her right hand without realizing. She looks around a lot, eyes never resting on one person for more than a second. Sometimes she blinks, as if she is having trouble focusing. She smokes all the time, lighting one cigarette from another.

The feeling inside me is growing. When I am ready, I will know. I will know when she is ready. It is like love; you just know. There is nothing more certain. Certainty fills me up, it makes me strong and purposeful. She gets weaker and smaller. I look at her and I think to myself, I did this.

TWELVE

I banged at the door. Why didn't she come? Oh please come quickly, now. I couldn't breathe. I knew I had to, everyone had to breathe, but when I tried, I couldn't, not properly, though an unbearable pressure was growing in my chest. I took some shallow gasps, sounding as if I had been on a desperate crying jag. There was a tight band of pain round my head and everything was out of focus. Please help me, I couldn't say, couldn't shout. There was a boulder in my throat, in my lungs, stopping me from taking a breath. I couldn't stand up any longer; everything was going blurred and gray-black. So I sank to my knees at the door.

"Zoe? Zoe! For chrissakes, Zoe, what's happened?" Louise was on her knees beside me, wrapped in a towel and with wet hair. She had her arm around my shoulder and the towel was slipping away but she didn't mind, darling Louise, and she didn't mind that people were passing and giving us very strange looks and probably crossing the road to avoid us. I tried to speak, but I couldn't get any words out, just a strange, stuttering sound.

She took me in her arms and rocked me. Nobody had done that to me since Mum had died. I was like a little girl again, and someone else was taking care of me at last. Oh, how I'd missed that; how I'd missed having a mother. She was whispering things that didn't make sense, and telling me that everything was going to be all right, everything was going to be just fine, there, there, sssh, that's right. She was telling me to breathe in and out, calmly. In and out. Gradually I started to be able to breathe once more. But I couldn't talk yet. Just whimper, like a baby. I felt warm tears slide under my closed lids, onto my hot cheeks. I never wanted to move, not ever again. My limbs felt heavy, too heavy to stir. I could sleep now.

Louise lifted me to my feet, holding her towel round her with one hand. She led me up the stairs into her flat and sat me on the sofa and sat beside me.

"It was a panic attack," she said. "That's all, Zoe."

The panic was gone, but I was left with the fear. It was like being in a cold shadow, I said to Louise. It was like looking off the edge of a tall building, so tall that I couldn't see the bottom.

I wanted to curl up, sleep until it was over. I wanted someone else to take charge and make everything all right again. I wanted to go put my hands over my ears and close my eyes and it would all go away.

One day, said Louise, trying to be reassuring, you'll look back on all this and it will be something horrible that happened and went away. You'll be able to turn it into a story that you tell people about yourself. I didn't believe her; I didn't believe it would ever go away. The world had become a different place for me.

I stayed with Louise at her flat in Dalston, near the market. There was nowhere else for me to go. She was my friend and I trusted her and while she was around, small and sturdy and kind, I felt less scared. Nothing would happen to me while Louise was with me.

First I had a bath, much better than if I had taken it in the bathroom in my flat. I lay in the hot water and Louise sat on the toilet seat and drank tea and washed my back for me. She told me about her childhood in Swansea, her single mother and her grandmother, who was still alive; rain, gray slates, massed clouds, hills. She always knew she'd come and live in London, she said.

And I told her about the village I came from, which was more a straggle of houses with a post office. About my father driving cabs at night, sleeping in the day, dying in a quiet, modest kind of way, never wanting to draw attention to himself. And then I told her about my mother dying when I was twelve; how for the two years before she died she had drifted farther and farther away from me, in her own land of pain and fear. I used to stand by her bed and hold her cold, bony hand and feel that she'd become a stranger to me. I would tell her about the things I'd done during the day, or give her messages from friends, and all the time I'd be wanting to be out with my friends, or in my room reading and listening to music—or anywhere that wasn't here, in this sick room that smelled odd, with this woman whose skull poked through her skin and whose eyes stared at me. But as soon as I'd left her I'd feel guilty and odd and dislocated. And then, when she died, all I wanted was to be back in her bedroom, holding her thin hand and telling her about my day. Sometimes, I said, I still couldn't believe I would never see her again.

I said that after that I'd never really known what I wanted to do or where I wanted to be. Everything became vague, purposeless. I'd just ended up as a teacher in Hackney. But one day I'd leave, do something else. One day I'd have children of my own.

Louise phoned out for a pizza to be delivered. I borrowed her bright red dressing gown, and we sat on the sofa and ate dripping slices of pizza and drank cheap red wine and watched *Groundhog Day* on video. We'd both seen it before, of course, but it seemed a safe choice.

A couple of times, her phone rang and she answered it and spoke in a low voice, hand over the receiver, glancing at me occasionally. Once, it was for me: Detective Sergeant Aldham. For a stupid moment, I thought perhaps he was going to say that they had caught him. Desperate hope. He was just checking up on me. He reiterated that I shouldn't go back to the flat unaccompanied, that I shouldn't be on my own with any man I didn't know well, and he told me that they would want to talk to me again on Monday, with Dr. Schilling. Extensive interviews, he said.

"Be alert, Miss Haratounian," he said, and the fact that he'd managed to get my name right scared me almost as much as his earnest and respectful tone. I'd wanted them to take me seriously. Now they were serious.

Louise insisted on giving me her bed, while she rolled herself up in a sheet on the sofa. I thought I wouldn't be able to sleep, and it is true that I lay for a while with thoughts whirring like bats that had lost their radar in my head. The night was hot and heavy and I couldn't find a cool patch on the pillow. Louise's flat was on a quiet street. There was a cat fight, a dustbin lid clanged, a solitary man went down the street singing "Oh Little Town of Bethlehem." But I must have gone to sleep quite soon, and the next thing I remember is the smell of burned toast, and day flooding in through the striped blue curtains, dust motes shimmying in the rays of light. The phone rang in the living room and then Louise poked her head round the bedroom door.

"Tea or coffee?"

"Coffee, please."

"Toast or toast?"

"Nothing."

"Toast then."

She disappeared and I struggled out of bed. I didn't feel too bad. I didn't have anything to wear except for the clothes I'd taken off last night, so I pulled them on, feeling a bit grubby.

After I'd eaten toast and drunk coffee, I phoned Guy to find out if anything was happening with the flat. He sounded self-conscious and warily solicitous, not a bit like his usual chirpily ingratiating self.

"I hear you've been having a bad time," he said. Of course, the police would have interviewed him by now.

"Not brilliant. Any news on the sale?"

"Mr. Shale wants to see the house again. Definitely serious. I think we've got him sniffing our hook. It's just a matter of landing him."

"What are you talking about?" I asked wearily.

"I think he's ready to make an offer," Guy said. "The point is, he wonders if today, midday, would be at all convenient."

"Couldn't you just show him round yourself?"

The irritating laugh again.

"I could, but there are some questions. I'll be there as well."

"Yes. No more strange men."

So we arranged to meet at the real estate agent's office at midday, Guy and me and Nick Shale. Safety in numbers. Then the three of us could walk up the road to my flat, whiz round it, and be gone in minutes. Louise insisted on calling a cab to take me there, and we sat for half an hour in traffic, cursing the heat, and arrived late. Both men were waiting for me, Guy in a thin blue suit and Nick in a white T-shirt and jeans. We shook hands formally.

When we reached the flat, Guy opened the door with

his set of keys and went in first. Nick stood back to let me enter. There was a funny smell. Sweet but with just a touch of something unwholesome underneath it. Nick wrinkled up his nose and looked at me questioningly.

"I must have left something out," I said. "I haven't been here for a bit."

It was coming from the kitchen. I pushed open the door. The smell was stronger but still nothing I could identify. I looked on the surfaces. Nothing. I looked in the bin but it was empty. I opened the fridge.

"Oh, God," I said.

The light didn't come on. It was warm. But it wasn't too bad. The milk was sour but there wasn't much else the matter. But I knew where the bad bit would be. I opened the small freezer on top of the fridge. All I could do was groan. It looked as if everything had got mixed with everything else. A tub of coffee ice cream lying on its side had spewed its contents out over an opened packet of prawns. The smell and sight of day-old prawns and melted ice cream in my hot kitchen almost made me gag.

"Fucking hell," I said.

"Zoe." Guy put his hand lightly on my shoulder and I jumped back from him. "It was just a stupid accident, Zoe."

"Wait," I said. "I've got to call the police."

"What?" he asked, his expression puzzled, almost embarrassed.

I turned on him.

"Shut the fuck up. Just shut up. Don't come near me, keep off."

"Zoe—"

"Shut up."

I was practically screaming at him now. He started to speak and then put up his hands in surrender.

"All right, all right."

He glanced across at Nick with the apprehensive expression of a man watching a sale ooze away between the floorboards. It didn't matter. All I cared about now was staying alive. I knew the number by heart. I dialed and asked for Carthy, and this time he came to the phone. No more messing about. He said he would be over right away. And he was there in less than ten minutes, with Aldham and another man who was carrying a large leather bag, and started pulling on thin gloves as soon as he got through the door. They stared at the mess, muttered things to each other in the corner. Carthy was asking me questions, but I couldn't seem to understand them. He said something about police protection. The other two were in the kitchen. Guy said that they ought to leave and Carthy said no, could they wait out on the stairs.

"He's been here again. I can't bear it."

Aldham came back into the room and looked over at me with concern.

"So what are you going to do?" I asked.

Aldham walked over to Carthy and muttered something in his ear. He looked a little shaken. Then he walked over to me, and when he spoke it was very calmly and quietly.

"Zoe," he said. "There was no note, was there?"

"I don't know. I didn't see one, but I didn't look."

"We've looked. We haven't found one."

"So?"

"We checked the fridge. It had been unplugged and the kettle had been plugged into the socket."

"Why would he do that?"

"I think it was a mistake. It's easy to do."

"But I wouldn't—" And then I stopped myself and remembered Louise making me tea, pulling out a cord to plug in the kettle. Oh fuck. I felt my face going red.

There was a silence. Aldham looked at the carpet, Carthy looked at me. I stared back.

"You told me to be alert," I said eventually.

"Of course," Aldham said gently.

"It's easy for you," I said. "I keep thinking I'm going to die."

"I know," said Aldham, his voice almost a whisper now. He put his hand tentatively on my shoulder.

I shook myself free.

"You . . . you . . ."

But I couldn't think of anything rude enough. I turned and ran out, weirdly conscious as I did so that I was leaving them all in my flat.

THIRTEEN

Louise was waiting for me when I got back to her flat. She had a face pack on, so her skin was dead white, except for a naked pink ring round each eye, which gave her a surprised look. As I was telling her what had happened, I realized I was assuming she would let me stay with her. But she made it easy for me.

"Stay as long as you like."

"I'm taking the sofa, though."

"Whatever."

"And paying rent."

She raised her eyebrows at me, so the wrinkles on her forehead cracked the mask.

"If it makes you feel better. You don't need to, though. Just water my plants. I always forget."

I was feeling better. The gripping fear of yesterday was loosening. I never needed to sleep in my flat again, never needed to set eyes on Guy again or show strange men round the rooms, letting them poke in my drawers and stare at my breasts; never needed to lie there in the darkness, listening, waiting, trying to breathe normally. I never needed to see Fred again, either, or his laddish friends. I felt as if

I'd shed a dirty, suffocating skin. I'd stay with Louise; we'd eat supper in front of the TV in the evening, paint each other's toenails. On Monday, I'd see Dr. Schilling. She'd know what to do. She was an expert.

Louise insisted that she had no plans for the weekend, and although I suspected that she had actually canceled everything for me, I was too relieved to make any but the feeblest protest. We bought French baguettes filled with cheese and tomato and walked to the nearby park, where we sat on the dry, baked-yellow grass. The sun was fierce, the air hot and heavy, and the park was crowded. Groups of teenagers playing Frisbee or snuggling in the shade of the trees; families with picnic hampers and balls and skipping ropes; girls in halter tops sunbathing, people with cans of beer, dogs, cameras, kites, bikes, bread for the ducks. They all wore bright, light clothes, had smiles on their faces.

Louise tucked her shirt into her bra and lay back, arms pillowing her head. I sat beside her, smoking cigarette after cigarette, and watched the streams of people as they passed. I waited to glimpse a face I knew, or a face that was looking at me as if it knew me. But I saw no one like that.

"You know what?" I said.

"What?" she said dreamily.

"I've been passive," I said.

"No you haven't."

"I have," I said. "I've wanted other people to sort this out for me. I couldn't be bothered."

"Don't be silly, Zoe."

"It's true. I think it was to do with being in London. I wanted to be lost. I didn't want anyone to notice me. I've got to look at myself. That's what I've got to do. I've got to look at myself and think why somebody would pick on me. Who would do it."

"Tomorrow," said Louise. "Look at yourself tomorrow. Today just look after yourself."

I let the sun soak into my skin, under my grubby clothes. I was tired. More tired than I had ever been, with gritty, aching eyes, limbs that felt too heavy to move. I wanted to have deep baths, sleep for hours on clean sheets, eat healthy food, raw carrots, green apples, drink orange juice and herbal tea. I couldn't imagine that I would ever want to go to a club again, get drunk or stoned again, be touched by a man again. The hot, sweaty, frantic life I had led in London filled me with vague, pervasive horror. All that noise and effort. Maybe, I thought, I'd even give up cigarettes. Not yet.

We passed a cheery shop selling things for children—bright cotton dungarees and stripy tops, bomber jackets in red and pink and yellow—and Louise dragged me in.

"You're a child size," she said, looking at me. "You've lost too much weight; we've got to fatten you up again. But in the meantime, let's buy you a couple of things." So, while the salesgirl looked on rather disapprovingly, I selected a few objects off the rack and took them into the changing room. I pulled the ribbed gray shift, aged thirteen, over my head and examined myself in the mirror. Fine. It made me look flat-chested and sexless. That would do me. Then I took it off and put on a lovely white T-shirt, decorated with tiny stitched flowers.

"Let's have a look," shouted Louise. "Come on, you can't go shopping with a friend if you don't make it into a fashion show."

I pulled the curtains open, giggling, doing a turn for her. "What do you think?"

"Take it," she ordered me.

"Isn't it too small for me?"

"It will be after you've been staying with me for a few days, and sharing my slobby habits. But now, no, it looks lovely on you." She put a hand on my shoulder. "Like a flower, sweetheart."

Later, Louise and I went in her rattling car to the supermarket to stock up. I had gone for a long time living hand to mouth, chips here, a bar of chocolate there, ready-made sandwiches in the smoke-filled staff room. It had certainly been weeks, probably months, since I had actually cooked anything, with a recipe and real ingredients that you have to put together.

"I'll make us a meal tonight," I said boldly. I felt as if I was playing at domesticity. I put fresh pasta into our trolley, Spanish onions, large garlics and Italian plum tomatoes, a little screw-top jar of dried mixed herbs; lettuce hearts, cucumber, mangoes, and strawberries. A tub of single cream. A bottle of Chianti. I bought an economy pack of knickers, some deodorant, a washcloth, a toothbrush and toothpaste. I hadn't cleaned my teeth since yesterday morning. I'd have to collect stuff from the flat.

"Tomorrow," said Louise decisively. "Leave it for now. We'll go together tomorrow morning, in my car. You've got your children's clothes till then."

I picked up some cellophane-wrapped yellow roses from the checkout area, which I added to our trolley.

"I don't know how to thank you, Louise."

"Then don't."

A friend of Louise's, called Cathy, came round for supper. She was extraordinarily tall and thin, with an aquiline nose and tiny ears. Louise had obviously told her about me, for she treated me very carefully, kindly, as if I were an invalid. I overcooked the pasta but the tomato sauce was fine, and anyone can chop up mangoes and strawberries and mix them together in a bowl. Louise lit candles and melted them onto old saucers. I sat at the kitchen table, in my new gray shift, light-headed, unreal. There was a hollow feeling in my stomach, but I couldn't eat very much. I couldn't speak very much, either. It was enough to sit there, listening to them; words buzzing lightly over the surface of my mind. We drank my Chianti, then most of the white wine that Cathy had brought, and watched an old film on TV. A thriller of some kind but I wasn't able to concentrate on the details of the plot. My mind would drift away in one scene so in the next scene I didn't know why the hero was breaking into that warehouse, what he was planning or what he was hoping to find. Outside, it started to rain, and the rain clattered on the roof and rattled on the window. I went to bed before Cathy left. Lying curled up on the sofa in the tiny sitting room, wearing Louise's skimpy nightdress, I could hear them talking in the kitchen, the comforting hum of conversation, occasionally a peal of laughter, and I drifted off to sleep feeling safe.

The next morning, after breakfast, we went to my flat to collect a few clothes. I wasn't going to pack everything just yet, although I had no intention of ever living in the flat again, just some basic essentials. It was still raining steadily. Louise couldn't find anywhere to park near the flat so she stopped on a double yellow line a few yards down from the front door and I said I'd run up.

"I won't be more than a couple of minutes," I said.

"Sure you don't want me to come with you?"

I shook my head and smiled.

"I'm just going to say good-bye."

There was an air of general squalor and neglect about the place, though I'd only been gone one day, as if the flat

knew that nobody cared about it. I went into my bedroom
and gathered a few dresses from the wardrobe. Two pairs
of trousers, four T-shirts, several knickers, bras, and pairs
of socks. Some trainers. That would do for now. I shoved
them all in a large hold-all. Then I went into the bathroom,
took off the dirty clothes I was wearing, and threw them
into a corner. I would collect all my laundry later. Another
time.

I heard a click, like a cupboard door closing. It's nothing, I said to myself. Imagination plays nasty tricks. Back
in the bedroom I found some clean underwear. I closed the
curtains and stood in front of the mirror to put them on. I
saw my face reflected there, smudges under my eyes. My
naked body, tanned arms and legs, white belly. I pulled my
knickers on and took my new T-shirt—the one Louise said
made me look like a flower—out of the bag I had brought
with me and pulled it over my head. It was stupid, but I
couldn't quite face wearing anything that smelled of the
flat, of my old life. I wanted to be clean and new.

As I pulled the shirt over my breasts, without any warning at all, I felt a grasp around my neck, around my body,
and a weight on my back, someone on me. I lost my balance and fell hard with the weight on me, pushing my covered face hard into the carpet. I was stunned, in pain. I felt
the hand through the shirt holding my mouth, a warm hand
smelling of soap, apple soap from my bathroom. An arm
wrapped round my rib cage, just under my breasts.

"Bitch, you bitch."

I started to writhe, twisting my limbs this way and that,
trying to scream, to howl. I couldn't reach anything—my
arms were held—couldn't do anything. He made no sound,
just breathed his hot soft breath into my ear. At last I
stopped struggling. Outside someone shouted, the wail of

a siren came closer, then faded away. Going somewhere else.

The grip on my neck slackened, I tried to move and to scream, but then it was on my throat. There was nothing I could do. Couldn't move. Couldn't fight. Couldn't scream. I thought about Louise sitting in the car outside, waiting for me, though she didn't seem near to me now; she seemed a long long way off. Soon maybe she would come to find me. Not soon enough. How stupid, to die like this, before I'd even begun. Before I had had a life. How stupid.

Very slowly, the floor came up to meet me. I felt my head bounce on floorboards, my feet slide across the wood. I heard the rain on the window, pattering gently. I couldn't speak, no words left to be said now, no time to say them anymore, but somewhere deep inside a voice that was saying: No, please no. Please.

PART TWO

Jennifer

ONE

Everything seemed to be happening, but then our house at breakfast time always seems to be rather like one of those medieval castles with donkeys and pigs and all the serfs coming in for shelter at the first sniff of trouble. In the weeks since our move, it had got even more chaotic, if that's possible, and the medieval castle had a building site slap bang in the middle of it.

Clive had left the house at six, which is even earlier than usual because at the moment he's working on some sort of horrific takeover bid. Just before eight Lena drags the two older boys into the Espace for the school run. Lena's our nanny-slash-au-pair thing; lovely-looking girl, Swedish, infuriatingly blond and slim and young, though she has this thing through her nose that makes me wince every time I see it. Goodness knows what it must feel like when she blows her nose.

Then people started arriving. Mary, of course, our priceless cleaner, who came with us to Primrose Hill. She's a treasure, except that I have to spend so much time standing over her and telling her what to do and then checking she's done it that I've said to Clive I might as well do the cleaning myself. And then there's all the rest of the people who were meant to be improving the house but instead have been reducing it to a slum full of brick dust. The rewiring and replumbing had been finished at the end of the week before, and the best that could be said about the house at that point was that anything from then on had to be an improvement.

I was satisfied, though, despite everything. This was what I had always wanted, what Clive had always promised me. A project. The house was down to bare boards and walls, back to the beams and rafters, practically. Now I was going to turn it into a home we could be proud of. I know you're supposed to fall in love with a house but this house wouldn't be worth falling in love with for another six months at least. There had been two old dears living there before in what looked like a secondhand bookshop that nobody had gone into since the fifties. The question wasn't what to change, but what on earth one could possibly keep.

I spent four months with Jeremy, our clever architect, head down over plans, tanking him up with espressos. It was just a matter of being simple. Rip out everything. Put new roof on. Then kitchen and dining room in the basement, living rooms on the ground floor, Clive's study on the first floor at the back, then bedrooms all the way up. Attic conversion for nanny to get up to whatever nannies get up to without scaring horses. Lavatories left, right, and center. A suite for Clive and me. Power shower for the boys in hopes it might persuade them to wash occasionally.

So this morning Jeremy popped in at around half past eight with Mick to go over a problem with an arch or beam or something. Closely followed by Francis, who we've brought with us to do—by which I mean completely *redo*—what passed for the garden. Hundred and twenty foot, which isn't bad for London, but it looked like a giant rabbit run until Francis got at it. The ruck of electricians and plumbers have gone, thank God, but Mick comes with his entourage. Tea and coffee all round, of course, as soon as Lena gets back to make it. Somewhere in the middle of it I pop Christo—who's four—along to his play-school thing, which he'd joined when we moved in. I'd become a bit dubious about it: no proper uniform, just blue sweatshirts, and wall-to-wall sandboxes and finger painting. But it was hardly worth chopping and changing. He'd be at Lascelles Pre-Prep in September anyway and, what is more, off my hands, which would be something of a relief.

Then it was back to the house and finally a sit-down, a coffee, and the quickest of glances at the paper and the mail before getting down to work—i.e., walking around stopping people knocking through the wrong wall and doing some liaising. Leo, my faithful handyman, was going to be dropping in and I'd been sweating over a list of things that needed doing. And I needed a serious discussion with Jeremy about the kitchen. That had been the really hard part of our planning. The thing is, in any other part of the house, if you get something wrong, you can live with it. But if the fridge door opens and blocks the cutlery drawer, you're going to be irritated by it twenty-five times a day until you're old and gray. What you ought to do ideally is build the kitchen, live in it for six months, then do it again properly. But even Clive isn't rich enough for *that*. Or at least not patient enough.

Lena wandered in and I gave her some instructions. Then, while she got going properly, I sipped some coffee and finally got down to the paper and the post. I have a strict rule of never giving the paper more than five minutes, if that. There's nothing *in* the papers anyway. Then the mail. In general, ninety percent of the mail is for Clive. The remaining ten percent is divided among children, pets, and me. Not that we've got any pets just at present. Our grand total of pets for 1999 consisted of one cat, missing and presumed dead, or having a better time in someone else's house somewhere in Battersea. One hamster, buried in unmarked grave at end of Battersea garden. I'd been thinking of getting a dog. I'd always said that London wasn't a place to keep dogs, but now that we were two minutes from Primrose Hill I can sometimes be caught with a wistful expression on my face considering it. Haven't mentioned it to Clive yet, though.

Hence, mail was speedily dealt with. Immediate pile of anything with Clive's name on it or variations thereof. All bills ditto. I can spot a bill at fifty feet, usually without even needing to open it. Anything addressed to Mr. and Mrs. Hintlesham, ditto. As usual, I put these letters in a pile, carried them upstairs, and deposited them on the desk in Clive's sanctum for him to deal with when he got home or, more likely, over the weekend.

That left two letters to Josh and Harry, duplicated messages from Lascelles about sports day; various advertisements and solicitations that I filed straight in the bin. And then after all that there was one letter, addressed to me. Now, whenever there's a letter addressed to me it almost always turns out to be a bill from a mail-order company that goes straight into Clive's pile. If not that, then it's a letter from a mail-order company who have obtained my address from another mail-order company.

But this was different. The name and address were neatly handwritten. And I couldn't recognize the handwriting. It wasn't Mummy's or a friend or relative. This was interesting and I almost wanted to savor it. I poured another cup of coffee, took a sip, and then opened the envelope. It contained a folded slip of paper that was much too small for the envelope, and I could see straightaway that it didn't have much writing on it. I smoothed it out on the table:

> Dear Jenny,
>   I hope you don't mind if I call you Jenny. But you see I think you're very beautiful. You smell very nice, Jenny, and you have beautiful skin. And I'm going to kill you.

It seemed like the silliest thing. I tried to think if someone was playing a practical joke. Some of Clive's friends have the most awful sense of humor. I mean, for example, he once went to this stag night for a friend of his called Seb and it really was awful, with two stripper-grams and lipstick on everyone's collar. Anyway, Jeremy came down and we started talking about some of the problems with the kitchen. In these last horribly hot days I'd been worrying about the Aga and I wanted to see if the skylights above could be made to open. There were these funny window catches I'd seen in *House and Garden* that could be opened with string. I showed the picture to Jeremy but he wasn't impressed. He never is unless he's thought of it himself. So we had a big bust-up about that. He was very funny about it, really. Stubborn, though. Then I remembered the letter and I showed it to him.

He didn't laugh. He didn't find it funny at all.

"Do you know who might have done this?" he said.

"No," I said.

"You'd better call the police," he said.

"Oh don't be so silly," I said. "It's probably just someone playing a joke. I'll make a fool of myself."

"Doesn't matter. And it doesn't matter if someone's playing a joke. You must call the police."

"I'll show it to Clive."

"No," Jeremy said firmly. "Call the police now. If you're too embarrassed then *I'll* do it for you."

"Jeremy . . ."

He was an absolute pig about it. He rang directory inquiries himself and got the number of some local police station and not only that—he then dialed the number himself and then handed me the phone as if I was a toddler talking to her granny.

"There," he said.

The phone rang and rang. I put my tongue out at Jeremy.

"Probably nobody's home. . . . Oh, hello? Look, this is going to sound really stupid, but I've just been sent this letter."

TWO

I spoke for a few minutes to a girl who sounded like one of those people who rings you up and tries to give you a quote for some dreadful metal window frames. I was dubious and she sounded bored and she said she'd arrange for somebody to call round, but there might be a bit of a delay and I said it didn't matter to me and I ended the conversation and thought nothing more of it.

I went back to Jeremy, who was helping himself to more coffee from the Hintlesham self-service canteen, as Clive has christened the commune we're perched in at the moment. The old dears had knocked through left, right, and center, replaced all the paneled doors, hacked out every chimney piece, and hunted every surviving cornice into extinction. I know that everybody was doing that in the sixties, but it looked as if they were trying to pretend they lived in a council flat at the top of an apartment block rather than in a semidetached house on the end of an early Victorian terrace.

Much of the job was restoring the house to a style that suited its history. The only place where I drew the line was in the kitchen. The Victorian kitchen was a place for scullery maids and cooks, and we hoped to do ourselves a little better than that, but I still wanted a period atmosphere. The tricky bit was not to end up with the style that Jeremy calls farmhouse Ikea. I'd made Jeremy redo the plans about eight times. There also happened to be a tricky pillar that we had to work around. I wanted just to take the wretched thing away, but Jeremy said the back of the house would fall down.

We were right in the middle of discussing his latest bit of cleverness when there was a ring at the door. As usual I left it to Lena, since the only people coming into the house were carrying pots of paint or radiators or strange copper pipes. I heard her yelling for me at the top of the stairs. Being shouted at in my own house is an experience I rank alongside chewing tinfoil. I walked up to the ground floor. Lena was standing at the open front door.

"If you've something to say to me, could you come and tell me?"

"I did tell you," she said in an innocent tone.

I gave up and walked toward her. I saw now that there were two policemen in uniform standing on the front step. They looked young and uneasy, like a couple of Boy Scouts who were asking to wash a car and weren't sure what reception they'd get. My heart sank.

"Mrs. Hintlesham?"

"Yes, yes, it's very nice of you to come round. But I can't think that it's necessary." They looked even more awkward. "But come in. Since you're here."

They both wiped their feet with immense care on the mat before following me inside and down the stairs to the rudiments of our kitchen. Jeremy made a face at me that basically meant, Should I make myself scarce? I shook my head.

"This will only take a minute," I said. I pointed out the

letter where it still lay by the stove. "You'll see it's just something stupid. It's really not worth any trouble. Can I get you some tea or something?"

One of them said, "No, madam," and the two of them looked down at the note while I got back to work with Jeremy. After a few minutes I looked up and saw that one of the officers had stepped just outside the French windows into the garden and was talking into his radio. The other was looking around at the room.

"New kitchen?" he said.

"Yes," I said and pointedly turned back to Jeremy. I wasn't in the mood for a conversation about interior decoration with a junior police officer. The other one stepped back inside. I don't know whether it was the uniform, or their black boots, or that they'd removed their caps, but they made this really rather large basement room feel small and cramped. "Are you finished, then?" I asked.

"No, Mrs. Hintlesham. I've just been talking to someone back at the station. Someone else is going to come over."

"What for?"

"He wants to have a look at your note."

"I was actually planning to go out later this morning."

"He'll only be a minute."

I gave a sort of huffing sigh.

"Really!" I said in a reproving tone. "Isn't this just a waste of everybody's time?" They answered only with lumpish shrugs that were difficult to argue with. "Are you waiting here?"

"No, madam. We'll be in the car outside until the detective sergeant arrives."

"Oh, all right."

They shambled out shamefacedly. I went up with Jeremy, which was just as well because a tin of National

Trust paint in entirely the wrong shade had arrived. One of my main discoveries during this whole horrific process has been that to make sure that the actual things you've ordered actually arrive, and then that the actual things you've asked to be done with them are actually done, is more than a full-time job. While I was on the phone trying to sort it out with a gormless female at the other end, I heard the doorbell ring and while I was still talking a ratty-faced man in a gray suit was shown into the room. I gestured toward him while trying to get some sense out of, or, to be more accurate, *into*, the woman on the phone. But it's embarrassing to get cross with somebody you've never met while someone else you've never met stands right next to you looking expectant. So I brought the call to a close. He introduced himself as Detective Sergeant Aldham and I took him down to the basement.

He also looked at the note and I heard him swear under his breath and he leaned down very close to it as if he were desperately short-sighted. Finally he gave a grunt and looked up.

"Have you got the envelope?"

"What? Er, no, well, I think I chucked it in the bin."

"Where?"

"It's in the cupboard there, by the sink."

I couldn't believe it, but he went and pulled the bin out, lifted the top off, and started rummaging in it like some down-and-out.

"I'm sorry. I think there may be tea and coffee grounds in there as well."

He lifted out a scrunched-up envelope that looked a bit damp and brown and generally worse for wear. He held it very delicately, by a corner, and put it on the side near the letter.

"Excuse me a moment," he said, and took out a mobile phone.

I retreated across the room and put the kettle on. I heard fragments of his conversation: "Yes, definitely" and "I think so" and "I haven't talked to her yet." Apparently from then on it was bad news for Sergeant Aldham. Because his side of the conversation turned into squeaked questions: "What?" "Are you sure?" At last he gave a resigned sigh and replaced the phone in his pocket. His face was red and he was breathing heavily as if he had just jogged here. He was silent for a while.

"Two other detectives are on their way," he said in a sullen tone. "They would like to interview you, if that's possible." Aldham was mumbling now. He looked miserable, like a dog that had been kicked.

"What on earth's going on?" I protested. "It's just a silly note. It's just like an obscene phone call, isn't it?"

Aldham perked up for a moment.

"Have you had any phone calls?"

"You mean obscene ones? No."

"Can you think of anything that might be connected with this letter? Other letters maybe, or someone you know—anything?"

"No, of course not. Unless it's some stupid joke."

"Can you think of anyone who might play a joke like that?"

I was nonplussed.

"I'm not very good on jokes," I said. "That's more Clive's subject."

"Clive?"

"My husband."

"Is he at work?"

"Yes."

Things were a bit sticky after that. Aldham hung around

looking embarrassed. I tried to get on with things, but his doleful, drab face put me off. It was quite a relief when the front doorbell rang, not much more than a quarter of an hour after Aldham had first arrived. I went to answer it and Aldham trailed me in a slightly absurd way. This time the front door was positively crowded. At the front were two slightly more upscale-looking detectives and with them were a couple more uniformed officers and two other people, one of them a woman, coming up the steps behind them. In the street I could see two police cars and two other cars with them, all double-parked.

The older man was balding, with gray hair cut very short. "Mrs. Hintlesham?" he said with a reassuring smile. "I'm Detective Chief Inspector Links. Stuart Links." We shook hands. "And this is Detective Inspector Stadler."

Stadler didn't look like a policeman at all. He looked more like a politician, or one of Clive's colleagues. He had a smartly cut dark suit, a discreet tie. He was rather striking looking, in a way. A bit Spanish, maybe. He was tall, well built, and had very dark hair that was almost black, combed back. He shook hands as well. He had a curious soft handshake that pressed my palm with his fingers as if he were finding out something about it. It was rather disconcerting. At any minute, I thought, he would lift my fingers to his lips and kiss them slowly.

"There are so many of you," I said.

"Sorry about that," Links said. "This is Dr. Marsh. He's from our forensic department. And he's brought his assistant, Gill erm . . ."

"Gill Carlson," said the woman gamely. She was a pretty little thing, in an un-made-up sort of way. Dr. Marsh looked like a scruffy schoolteacher.

"You're probably wondering why there are so many of us," Links said.

"Well . . ."

"A letter of the kind that you have received is a kind of threat. We need to assess its seriousness. In the meantime we have to ensure your safety."

Links had been looking me in the eyes. But with that he slowly shifted his gaze toward Aldham, who began to look even more abjectly embarrassed.

"We'll take over from here," he said quietly.

Aldham mumbled something to me. I think it was good-bye. Then he eased his way past us and was gone.

"Why did he come?" I asked.

"A misunderstanding," said Links. He looked around. "You've recently moved in?"

"In May."

"We'll try not to cause too much disturbance, Mrs. Hintlesham. I'd like to see the letter and then I'd like to ask you one or two questions and that will be all, I hope."

"Downstairs," I said faintly.

"Beautiful house," he said.

"It will be," I said.

"Must have cost a bit."

"Well . . ." I said as a way of not getting into a discussion about property values.

And so, a few minutes later, I found myself sitting at my table with two detectives in the middle of a half-completed kitchen. For reasons that I didn't remotely understand, the two uniformed officers were wandering around the house and garden. The letter had been read by everybody and then lifted with tweezers and inserted into a transparent plastic folder. The crumpled, sodden envelope was put into a small polyethylene bag. There was one item for each scientist, and they left clutching them.

Before speaking to me the two men whispered to each

other, which I found mildly irritating. Then they turned to me.

"Look," I said. "Can I just say that I don't think there's anything remotely I can tell you? It's a horrible silly letter and that's all there is to it. I don't know anything about it."

The two men looked thoughtful.

"Yes," said Links. "We'll just ask a couple of routine questions. You've just moved into this house. Did you live in this area before?"

"No. We lived miles away, south of the river, in Battersea."

"Do you know a school called Laurier?"

"Why?"

Links sat back.

"One of the things we try to do is to establish connections with other threats that may have been made. Do you have children?"

"Yes. Three boys."

"Laurier is a state primary school just off Kingsland Road in Hackney. Is it possible you ever considered it for your children?"

I couldn't suppress a smile.

"A state primary school in Hackney? Are you serious?"

The two men exchanged glances.

"Or maybe you've met one of the teachers. A woman called Zoe Haratounian, for example."

"No. What can the school have to do with this letter?"

"There were . . . er, incidents associated with the school. There may be a connection."

"What sort of incidents?"

"Letters like the one you received. But can we continue with our questions? Has this letter come out of the blue?

You don't connect it with anything else, or any other person, no matter how remotely?"

"No."

"I would like to assess how many people have access to this house. I see that you're having work done."

"That's right. It's like Waterloo Station here."

He smiled.

"Which estate agent did you use?"

"Our house was sold by Frank Dickens. Bunch of sharks."

"Have you ever used Clarke's?"

I shrugged.

"Maybe," I said. "I was looking for ages. I must be on the books of almost every estate agent in London."

They looked at each other again.

"I'll check it out," Stadler said.

One of the officers came down the stairs. Yet another woman was with her. Tall, with long blond hair, some of it up on top of her head, looking as if it had been pinned up by a blind man in a dark room. She was wearing a business suit that looked as if it could do with a run-over from an iron. She was carrying a case and had a raincoat over one arm. She looked harassed and out of breath. Both detectives looked round and nodded at her.

"Hello, Grace," said Links. "Thanks for coming so quickly." He turned back to me. "This may seem strange to you. Somebody has picked on you. We don't know why. We don't know who this person is, or anything about him. But we have you. We can't look at his life but we can look at *your* life."

I felt suddenly alarmed and irritated. This was becoming tiresome.

"What do you mean, look at my life?"

"This is Dr. Grace Schilling. She's a very distinguished

psychologist and she specializes in the psychology of, well, of people who do things like this. I'd be very grateful if you'd talk to her."

I looked at Dr. Schilling. I expected her to be blushing or smiling at Links's flattery. She wasn't. She was looking at me with narrowed eyes. I felt like something stuck to a card with a pin.

"Mrs. Hintlesham," she said. "Can we go somewhere quiet?"

I looked around.

"I'm not sure there *is* anywhere quiet," I said with a forced smile.

THREE

"Sorry about the mess," I said as we tiptoed across the room between packing cases toward a sofa. "This is going to be a drawing room in about twenty years."

She took off her crumpled linen jacket and sat down in the uncomfortable old basket-weave chair. She was tall and slim, with dark blond hair, long thin fingers. No rings.

"Thank you for giving me your time, Mrs. Hintlesham." She put on a pair of spectacles, the kind with no frames at all. She took a notepad and a pencil out of her bag and wrote something at the top. Underlined it.

"As a matter of fact, I haven't got a great deal of time to give. I'm very busy, as you can see. I've a lot to get through before the boys get back." I sat down and smoothed my skirt over my knees. "Do you want coffee or tea or something?"

"No, thanks. I'll try to be quick. I just wanted us to meet."

I was feeling agitated. I wasn't quite sure what was going on, why she seemed so serious.

"Quite honestly, I think the police have got themselves in a bit of a sweat about it all, haven't they? I mean, it's just a stupid letter. I wasn't going to call them at all and then suddenly it's like Piccadilly Circus in here."

She looked thoughtful. So thoughtful that she hardly seemed to be paying proper attention to what I was saying.

"No," she said. "You did the right thing."

"I'm terribly sorry, but I can't remember your name—my mind's like a sieve. Early senility, I expect."

"Grace. Grace Schilling. This must all be strange for you."

"Not at all, actually. I told the police, I just thought it was a joke."

Dr. Schilling was the one with the suit and notebook; she was the doctor. Yet she was shifting uncomfortably in her seat as if she didn't know quite what to say. Of course that wretched chair is enough to make anybody uncomfortable, but I still didn't know what she was playing at.

"I don't want to give you a psychology lecture. I just want to do anything I can to help you." She paused as if she was trying to make up her mind. "Look, as you know, there are men who just attack women at random. This letter you received is obviously something different."

"I can see that," I said.

"He's seen you. Chosen you. I wonder if this person has been close to you. He says that you smell nice. That you have beautiful skin. How does that make you feel?"

I laughed a bit self-consciously. But she didn't. She leaned closer and looked at me.

"You do have beautiful skin," she said.

She didn't say it as if it was a compliment but just as if it were an interesting scientific observation.

"Well, I try hard enough with my skin, for goodness' sake. I have this special cream."

"Are you often aware of people finding you attractive?"

"What a question. I can't think how this is going to help you. Let's see. Some of Clive's friends are awful flirts. I suppose there are men who look at me, you know the way men do." Grace Schilling didn't say anything, just gazed at me with that calm and mildly anxious expression on her face. "I'm nearly forty, for goodness' sake," I said, to break the silence. My voice came out louder than I had intended.

"Do you work, Jenny?"

"Not in the way *you* mean," I said, almost belligerently. "I don't have a job the way you do. I have children, and this house." Take that, I thought to myself with some satisfaction. "I haven't worked since I got pregnant with Josh, fifteen years ago now. Clive and I always agreed that I would give up. I used to be a model. Not in the way you probably think. I modeled hands."

She looked baffled. "Hands?"

"You know, in posters for nail varnish and things like that, consisting of nothing but a giant hand. In the early and mid-eighties lots of those hands were mine."

We both looked at my hands, lying in my lap. I try to keep them nice. I have a manicure once a week, and get the cuticles seen to, and I rub this expensive lotion on them that I've always used, and I never wash anything up without wearing gloves. But they're not like they were. They're plumper, for a start. I can't take off my engagement and wedding rings any longer, not even when I use butter. Dr. Schilling smiled for the first time.

"It's a bit like someone's fallen in love with you," she said then. "From afar. Like in a story. Or someone close to you. It might be somebody you've never seen before or someone you see every day. It would be useful if you could think about men you meet, if any of them act strangely, inappropriately, towards you."

I gave a grunt.

"The boys, for a start," I said.

"Maybe you could describe your life to me."

"Oh dear, you mean a day in the life?"

"I want to get an idea of the things that are important to you."

"This is ridiculous. You can't catch somebody by finding out what I think about my life." She waited, but this time I beat her at her own game. I just stared back. In the background, I could hear a great crash, as if somebody had dropped something heavy. Probably some oafish policeman.

"Do you spend a lot of time with your sons?"

"I'm their mother, aren't I? Though sometimes I feel more like their unpaid chauffeur."

"And your husband?"

"Clive is madly busy. He's—" And then I stopped myself. I didn't see why I should give this woman a detailed explanation of something I didn't understand myself. "I hardly see him at the moment."

"You've been married how long? Fifteen years?"

"Yes. Sixteen this autumn." God, was it that long? I gave an involuntary sigh. "I was very young."

"And would you describe it as a happy marriage, close?"

"I wouldn't describe it to you at all."

"Jenny." She leaned forward in her chair and for one horrible moment I thought she was going to take hold of my hands in some touchy-feely way that would make me sick. "There is a man out there who says he wants to kill you. However ridiculous this sounds, we have to take it seriously."

I shrugged.

"It's a marriage," I said. "I don't know what you want me to say. We have our ups and downs, our silly squabbles, like everybody."

"Have you told your husband about the letter?"

"The detective asked me to. I left a message at work; he'll phone later."

She looked at me as if she could see through me. It made me feel uncomfortable. There was a long pause.

"Jenny," she said finally. "I know that one of the things that you feel, or will feel, is violated. And what's worse is that some of our efforts to help you may feel like a violation as well. There are things I need to know about." She looked around at the chaos of the house and gave her knowing smile again. "Think of me as like your surveyor going round the house looking for bits where the water might get in."

"Tell me about it," I said in mock bitterness.

She leaned forward again.

"Has your husband been faithful, Jenny?"

"What!"

She repeated the question, as if there was nothing strange about it.

I glared at her and felt my face going red. My head was starting to hurt. "I think you should ask him," I said as coolly as I could.

She made a mark on her notepad.

"What about you?"

"Me?" I snorted. "Don't be stupid. When on earth would I find time for an affair, even if I wanted one, unless it was with the gardener or the odd-job man or the tennis coach? I virtually never meet anybody else. Look, you say you are just doing your job and you have to ask about these things, but really, you've done it and now I just want to get on with my day, whatever is left of it, that is."

"Do you find these questions intrusive?"

"Of course I do. I know it's an unfashionable view, but I like to keep private things private."

She stood up at last, but she wasn't ready to leave quite yet.

"Jenny," she said. I was irritated by the way she kept using my first name. I hadn't told her she could. It felt like an insurance salesman keeping his foot in the door. "All I want, all any of us want, is to put a stop to this and get out of your life. If anything comes into your mind that seems significant in any way, let the police know or let me know. Let us decide what is or isn't important. Don't be embarrassed to tell us, will you?"

She almost seemed to be pleading with me. It made me feel better, more in control.

"All right," I said. "I'll put on my thinking cap."

"Do that." She turned to go. "And Jenny."

"Yes."

She hesitated, then thought better of it. "Nothing. Take care."

Later, they all went—except that Stadler man, the one with the bedroom eyes. He told me they would be opening my mail in the morning, just to be on the safe side.

"No more nasty shocks for you," he said, and gave me a smile that was perilously close to a leer. Honestly! I glared at him. "And," he added, as if it was an afterthought, "we're leaving a couple of police officers outside the house."

"This is getting beyond a joke," I said.

"Just a precaution," he said soothingly, as if I were a horse. "And during the day there will be a woman officer who'll be here most of the time." He smiled. "Continuity for you."

I opened my mouth to say something but couldn't think of anything that wasn't obscene, so I just glared.

"She's here now. Hang on a minute." He strode to the

door and shouted: "Lynne! Lynne, can you come in here for a minute? Mrs. Hintlesham, this is Officer Burnett. Lynne, Mrs. Hintlesham."

The woman was almost as small as me, but much younger, almost young enough to be my daughter, with light brown hair, pale lashes, and a birthmark on her left cheek that made her look as if she'd been smacked in the face just before she came in. She smiled at me but I didn't smile back.

"I'll try and keep out of your way," she said.

"Do," I snapped. I pointedly turned my back on her and Stadler until they had both left the room and I was blessedly alone again.

The kitchen was full of empty mugs, and there were a couple of cigarette butts by the back door. You would have thought the least they could do was clear up after themselves. I rang Clive again, but he still wasn't available.

Lena brought Chris and Josh back. Harry was being dropped off by another mum after football practice. I told Josh, in vague and reassuring terms, about a stupid note and there being policemen outside. I thought he might be a bit alarmed, or impressed. But he just leaned against the kitchen door, chewed his lower lip, and shrugged before loping off to his bedroom with two peanut butter sandwiches and a tankard of milk; I don't know where all the food goes.

I dread to think what he gets up to in his room. He closes the curtains and there's loud music, and bleeps and shrieks from his dreadful computer games, and incense, probably to cover up the cigarettes he smuggles in. I make sure it's always Mary who tidies up in there and changes his sheets. I don't go in his room, I just shout through the door for him to do his homework, practice his saxophone, turn down the music, bring down his dirty washing. He's grown up all of a sudden. His voice has broken, he's got little pimples on his forehead, soft hair on his upper lip. And he's so tall. Much taller than me. He's got that odd, man's smell about him, as well, underneath all the lotions and gels that he and his friends seem to wear nowadays. Not like when we were young.

Chris is too young to understand, of course; I didn't say anything to him, just gave his squashy little body a hug. He's my baby.

Then I drove to the reclamation center but it had just closed so I didn't get the hooks, which was the last straw.

Clive rang to say he wouldn't be home until late, so after Harry got back, and after I had put Chris to bed with a story, I had supper with Josh and Harry. Lasagne that I'd taken out of the freezer earlier, with peas, and for pudding ice cream with chocolate sauce. No one spoke much. I watched them shovel food down their throats as if it were fuel. I didn't eat very much. It was too hot.

The boys drifted off into their own rooms again, so I poured myself a glass of white wine and sat downstairs with the TV on, leafing through magazines. We needed a dining room table. I knew what I was looking for, something in grainy dark wood, long and simple, a refectory-type table. I'd seen one I quite liked recently with little mosaics of different-colored wood set into the surface, like coasters. Jeremy said I ought to find the perfect chairs first, since they are always more difficult. He told me about a client of his who had waited eight years for the perfect chairs. I told him I wasn't that patient.

Clive still hadn't come home. From Josh's room came a booming bass note from the awful electronic music he listens to. I drew the curtains, seeing as I did so the two policemen sitting in their car. We should have a dinner party as soon as we buy the table, I thought. I could wear my black dress and the diamond choker Clive had given me for our fifteenth wedding anniversary. I picked up a cookbook and thumbed through the summer recipes. Champagne to begin with. Then iced chervil and cucumber soup, tuna scented with coriander, apricot sorbet, cold white wine, on the table those peachy roses from the garden that Francis planted when we arrived. I put my glass against my forehead. So hot.

I heard the key turn in the door. Clive kissed me on the cheek. He looked gray with tiredness.

"God, what a day," he said.

"There's lasagne if you want some."

"No, I ate with some clients."

I looked at him: expensive charcoal-gray suit; black shoes, well polished; purple and gray tie I'd given him for Christmas; slight paunch beneath his well-ironed white shirt; little threads of silver in his dark hair; a hardly discernible double chin; frown marks just beginning to appear in his high forehead. A distinguished man. I always thought that in a strange way he looked at his best when exhausted, late at night, just after walking through the door. First thing in the morning he was busy, fussy, nervous, distracted, before he put on his lawyer's mask and went to work. He took off his jacket and hung it carefully on the back of a chair, then lowered himself onto the sofa, sighing. There were circles of sweat under his arms. I went to the kitchen and came back with two glasses of white wine, very cold from the fridge. My head was still sore.

"I've had an extraordinary day," I began.

"Oh yes?" He kicked off his shoes, loosened his tie, changed the channel on the TV with a flick of the remote control zapper. "Tell me."

I think I told it badly. I couldn't convey how strange it

felt, how seriously the police had taken it. When I finished he took a sip of wine and looked away from the screen.

"Well, it's nice that someone appreciates your skin, Jens." Then: "I'm sure it's just some crank. I don't want crowds of policemen running all over the house."

"No. Mad, isn't it?"

FOUR

I never go downstairs before I put my makeup on, not even on the weekend. It would be like going down without clothes. As soon as I hear Clive leave in the morning, the front door clicking behind him, I get out of bed and have a shower. I scrub my body down with a loofah to get rid of any dead skin. I sit at my dressing table, which Clive says looks like something in a starlet's trailer. There are pitiless lights all the way round the mirror, and I examine myself. I found a few gray hairs in my eyebrows yesterday. There are lines I didn't have last year, horrible little ones above my upper lip, ones that run down toward the corners of my mouth and give my face a droopy, depressed look when I am tired, slight pouches under my eyes. Sometimes my eyes ache; probably it's from all the dust in the house. I have no intention of wearing glasses yet.

My skin no longer has the bloom of youth, whatever that stupid man wrote in his letter. I used to have beautiful skin. When Clive first met me, he told me I had skin like a peach. But that was a long time ago. He doesn't say things like that any longer. I sometimes think it's more important to say things like that when they're not true. Looking in the mirror I sometimes feel my skin is more the texture of a grapefruit now. The other day, when I put on my green dress to go out to the school fete, he told me to put on something that the children wouldn't be embarrassed by.

I make sure there are no stray hairs between my eyebrows or, God forbid, on my chin, then I start with foundation, which I mix with moisturizing cream so it goes on smoothly. Then I put this wonderful wrinkle concealer round my nose and under my eyes. My friend Caro told me about it. It is unbelievably expensive. Sometimes I try to calculate how many pounds I'm wearing on my face. In the day, everything has to be invisible. A tiny smudge of beige eye shadow, the smallest trace of eyeliner, mascara that doesn't clog the lashes, maybe lip gloss. Then I feel better. I like the face that looks back at me, small and oval and bright, ready to face the world.

Breakfast was awful as usual. In the middle of the chaos there was a knock on the door. Officer Lynne Burnett, except today she was in her ordinary clothes. She was wearing a gray skirt, blue blouse, and woolen top. She looked quite smart, in a drab kind of way, but for some reason I was irritated by the idea that this was what she had worn for hanging around with Mrs. Hintlesham. To blend in with the landscape, no doubt. "Call me Lynne," she said. Everybody says that. Everybody wants to be your friend. I wish they'd just get on with their job. She told me that her first task was to look at my mail when it arrived.

"Will you be tasting my food as well?" I asked sarcastically.

She blushed so her birthmark became livid. The phone rang and it was Clive, who was already at work. I started to describe what was going on but he interrupted me to say that Sebastian and his wife were coming to dinner on Saturday.

"But we haven't got a dining table," I protested. "And we've only got half a kitchen."

"Jens, the documentation we're preparing for next month's merger is over two thousand pages long. If I can coordinate that, I think you can organize a dinner party for a client."

"Of course, I'll do it, I was just saying . . ." Mary came in through the door with a mop and started ostentatiously cleaning round my feet. By the time I'd started speaking again, Clive had rung off. I put the phone down and looked around. Lynne was still there, of course. Well, obviously, but it was a bit of a disappointment all the same. There was a part of me that hoped she would have gone away, like a headache. But now, after that phone call, I had a headache and I had Lynne.

"I'm going out to talk to my gardener," I said frostily. "I suppose you'd like to come and meet him."

"Yes," she said.

With his long plaited hair down his back, Francis may look like he should be in a caravan heading for Stonehenge, but in fact he's an absolute genius. His father was actually something grand in the navy and he went to Marlborough. If you look at him with narrowed eyes you could sort of imagine him working in the city like Clive, except that apart from his three-foot-long hair he's also an alarmingly deep shade of brown and has those strong sinewed arms you get from lugging heavy things around all day. Some people would probably say that he's rather good-looking. I don't want to know about his personal life, which I gather is rather busy, but he's one of the few people I trust absolutely.

I introduced him to Lynne, who blushed. But then she seems to blush all the time.

"Lynne is here because someone's written me a mad letter," I said. Francis looked puzzled, as well he might. "And Francis is here full time for the next month at least," I said.

"What are you doing?" Lynne asked.

Francis looked at me. I nodded and he gave a shrug.

"First we dumped concrete and rubble into a skip," he said. "We've brought soil in. Now we're doing some landscaping and laying paths."

"Are you doing this on your own?" Lynne asked.

Francis smiled.

"Of course not," I said. "Francis has got his collection of lost boys who come and work for him when he needs them. There's a whole subculture of gardeners drifting around London. They're like the pigeons and the foxes."

I gave a nervous glance at Francis. Maybe I'd gone too far. People can be so touchy. Lynne actually got out her notebook and started asking about working hours and firing questions about the fence and access to the house. She wrote down the names of all the casual workers he used.

All in all, it was a relief to leave the house, however late. Or that's what I thought, until Lynne told me that she would be coming with me.

"You're not serious."

"Sorry, Jenny." Yes, she calls me Jenny, although I haven't told her she could. "I'm not sure about the level of support we're providing, but for today I've got to stick with you."

I was about to get cross when the doorbell rang. It was Stadler, so I protested to him instead. He just gave me his smile.

"It's for your own safety, Mrs. Hintlesham. I'm just here

to touch base and make a couple of routine checks. Do you have any objection to us monitoring your telephone calls?"

"What does that involve?"

"Nothing that you need bother about. You won't even notice it."

"All right," I grumbled.

"We want to compile a register of people you have dealings with. So over the next day or so, I'd like you to sit down with Lynne and go through things like your address book, appointment book, that sort of thing. Is that all right?"

"Is this really necessary?"

"The more effective we are now, the quicker we can wind all this up."

I'd almost stopped being angry. I just felt a mild disgust.

First stop was at the reclamation center for the brass hooks. I nearly bought a round stained-glass window that had come out of an old church but at the last minute changed my mind. At least Lynne didn't come into the shop.

She did come into the shops in Hampstead, or at least stood just outside staring neutrally into windows full of women's clothes. God knows what the shop assistants made of her. I pretended to ignore her. I needed something for Saturday. I took an armful of clothes into the changing room, but when I came out wearing a beaded pink top, wanting to see myself in the long mirror, I caught sight of Lynne's face, staring through the window at me. I left empty-handed.

"Find what you wanted?" she asked as we left. As if we were friends on a spree together.

"I wasn't actually looking for anything," I hissed.

I popped into the butcher's to buy the sausages the boys like so much, and then wandered round the next-door antique shop. I had my eye on a mirror there, with a gilt frame. It cost £375, but I thought I might be able to get it for less. It would go perfectly in the hall, once we had it painted.

I had arranged to meet Laura for lunch, so after I had picked up Christopher's name tags for all his Lascelles school clothes, I drove down the hill, Lynne's car in my rearview mirror. Laura was already waiting. It should have been fun, but it wasn't. Lynne sat in the car outside eating a sandwich. I could see her as I fiddled with my arugula and roasted red pepper salad. She was reading a paperback. If an axman came into the room she probably wouldn't even look up. I couldn't quite concentrate on anything Laura was saying to me. I cut the lunch short, saying that I had to dash.

Next stop, Tony in Primrose Hill. Normally I love having my hair done. It makes me feel cosseted sitting in the little room full of mirrors and steel, trolleys laden with colored lotions, the smell of steam and perfume, the lovely crisp sound of scissors cutting through locks of hair.

But today nothing worked. I felt hot, cross, out of sorts. My head banged and my clothes stuck to me. I didn't like the way I looked after the cut. The new shape of my hair had a peculiar optical effect that made my nose too big and my face too bony. In the traffic on the way home a kind of road rage engulfed me, so that I revved impatiently at traffic lights. Lynne kept patiently behind me. Sometimes she was so close that I could see her freckles in the mirror. I stuck out my tongue in the mirror, knowing she couldn't see it.

For the rest of the day, she followed me like a faithful dog—the kind you want to kick. She followed me when I took Chris to play with a chum of his down the road, a scrawny little boy called Todd. What kind of parent calls her child that? Then I had to collect the boys, because it was Lena's night off. Wednesdays are always a nightmare. Josh was at the school after-hours computer club, which was always held in a trailer that stank of boys' sweaty feet. Usually when I come to collect him he is paired with another boy called Scorpion or Spyder or whatever stupid nickname they've chosen. Josh used to call himself Ganymede, but last week he decided that was too effeminate and changed it to Eclipse. That's his password. His best friend is called Freak, spelled with a Ph: Phreek. They're all madly serious about it.

But this evening Josh was sitting slumped in a chair and the rather sweet young man who came in to teach them every week was crouched down beside him, talking to him intently. I remember that when I'd first met him a few weeks earlier, he told me that everybody in the club called him Hacker. I think I'd pulled a face and he'd said that that wasn't his real name and I could call him Hack. "Is *that* your name?" I'd asked, but he only laughed.

All the boys were still in their uniforms but Hack was wearing ancient torn jeans and a T-shirt with lots of writing in Japanese on it. He was pretty young himself, with long, curly dark hair. He could almost have been one of the sixth-formers. At first I thought Josh must have had an accident, or a nosebleed, but as I drew nearer they both looked up and I saw that he had been crying. His eyes were red-rimmed. This startled me. I couldn't remember when I last saw Josh actually cry. It made him look much younger and more vulnerable. How bony and pale he was, I thought, with his bumpy forehead and his protruding Adam's apple.

"Josh! Are you all right? What's wrong?"

"Nothing." The tone was cross rather than miserable. He

stood up abruptly. "I'll see you next term, in September, Hack."

Hack. Honestly. No wonder Josh was such a mess.

"Or lose you. To a summer love," said Hack.

"What?" I said.

"It's a song," he said.

"Is everything all right?"

"What, that?" he said, gesturing at Josh. "It's no big deal, Mrs. Hintlesham."

"Jenny," I corrected him, as I do every week. "Call me Jenny."

"Sorry. Jenny."

"He seemed upset."

Hack looked unconcerned.

"It's probably school, summer, all that stuff. Plus he just got whipped on-screen."

"Maybe his blood sugar's low."

"Yeah, that's right. Give him some sugar. Jenny."

I looked at Hack. I couldn't tell if he was laughing at me.

Harry was round the other side of the school, in the large and drafty hall that doubled as the theater once a year for the school play. When Josh and I went in, he was standing by the side of the stage with a yellow dress over his trousers and a feather boa round his neck. His face was scarlet. The sight of him seemed to cheer Josh up considerably. Up on the stage was a motley crew of boys, a couple of whom were also wearing frocks.

"Harry," called a man with a small mustache and a bullet-shaped head with hair cut brutally short. Probably gay. "Harry Hintlesham, it's your entrance. Come on! 'Ill met by moonlight, proud Titania.' You should be walking on as Roley says that."

Harry struggled onto the stage, tripping over the dress. "'What jealous Oberon,'" he muttered under his breath. His hair looked sticky with sweat. "'Fairies, skip off, I have long—'"

"'Skip hence,'" roared the mustache-man. "Not 'off,' boy, 'hence'—and speak louder for goodness' sake. Rehearsal's over anyway, can't have parents seeing it in this state. It won't be ready till Christmas. And speaking of parents, your lovely lady mother has arrived, Titania. Skip hence. Good evening, Mrs. Hintlesham. You light up our dingy hall."

"Jenny. Good evening."

"Try and get your son to learn his lines."

"I'll try."

"And get him to wear deodorant, will you?"

She's dead. Of course. As I wanted. Of course. And I feel cheated of her. Of course. Forget it. Another one. Another she.

She wears too much makeup. It is like a mask, smoothed over her face. Everything about her face is glossy and cared for—shining lips, dark lashes, creamy skin, neat and glossy hair. She is a picture that is constantly being touched up and polished. An image presented to the world. She can't hide from me. I imagine her face stripped down. There would be lines round her eyes, her nostrils, her mouth; her lips would be pale, soft, nervous.

Walking down a street, she glances constantly at her reflection in the shop windows, checking that everything is still in place. And it always is. Her clothes are ironed, her hair fits her like a cap. Her nails are manicured and painted a pale pink; her toenails are pink too, in their expensive sandals. Her legs are smooth. She holds herself straight, shoulders back and chin up. She is clean, neat, bright with energy and purpose.

Yet I have watched her. I see beyond her smile that is not a real smile, and her laugh that, if you listen carefully, very carefully, is forced and brittle. She is like a string on a violin that has been tightened to the thin screeching point. She is not happy. If she was happy, or wild with fear, or with desire, she would become beautiful. She would be liberated from her shell and become her true self. She does not realize she is not happy. Only I realize. Only I can see inside her and release her. She is waiting for me, sealed up inside herself, still untouched by the world.

Fate smiles on me. I see that now. At first I did not understand that I had become invisible. Nobody can see me. I can go on and on.

FIVE

It's very late, almost midnight, but it's still almost indecently hot. Even though I've opened the windows upstairs, the wind that blows in is warm as well, as if it had blown across a desert. Clive isn't back. His secretary, Jan, phoned and told Lena he wouldn't be back until very late and now it's very late and indeed he's not back. As usual I left him some sandwiches in the fridge and had one of them myself, so that's all right.

The house is quiet now. Lena's out doing God knows what until God knows when. The boys are asleep. Just after eleven I went round and switched their lights out. Even Josh was asleep, exhausted by the rigors of an evening spent on the phone. Everything's done. I've started to pack for Josh and Harry, who are catching the plane tomorrow. It's going to be quiet in the house over the next few weeks, for various different reasons.

I'm not in general especially keen on alcoholic drinks. Clive's terribly clever about wine, but it's not something I would ever bother about if it were just me. But that night it was so incredibly stifling and I felt a bit on edge so that suddenly the idea of a gin and tonic came into my head as if it were in a magazine advertisement. I imagined a beautiful sultry woman, darkly tanned, in an exotic location with a drink that was so cold the glass was glistening with moisture. She would be sweating in a sexy way and in between sips she would press the cold glass to her forehead. She would be sitting alone but you would know that she was waiting for some pretty amazing man to arrive.

So I had to have one, of course. Unbelievably, there was no lemon in the house except for a rather dry leftover slice in the door of the fridge, which would just about do. I made the drink and I felt I needed a snack. All that I could find was one of the packets of cheese puffs that I put in Chris's packed lunch. So I sat and nibbled my way through the packet, which took only a minute, and I was almost shocked to discover that the drink was finished. I had made it with very little gin, so I thought I could manage just one more to take upstairs to the bath.

I wasn't sweating prettily and sexily like the girl in my magazine advertisement. My blouse was wet in the back. My bra was damp, there were dark patches of moisture around the edges of my knickers. My skin was clammy everywhere. I could smell myself. I thought I was going to rot.

The bath was warm and foamy and blurry. By the time I was halfway through the second drink, nothing seemed to matter as much as it had. For example, although I had mixed this rather pungent bath foam into the water, I then washed my hair as well and then rinsed it out in the bathroom without even showering separately. That's not the normal way I behave. Did I mention that a second note had arrived?

Just after lunch today there was delivery after delivery: the right kind of paint, kick-space heaters that should have arrived a month ago. It was like a rugby team marching in and out, and at the end of it all, Lena found an envelope addressed to me lying on the doormat. She brought it to me. I knew what it was straight away but I opened it anyway.

> *Dear Jenny,*
>
> *You're a beautiful woman. But not when you're with anyone. When you're just alone, walking down the street. You bite your top lip sometimes when you're thinking. You sing to yourself.*
>
> *You look at yourself and I look at you. We've got that in common. But one day I'll look at you when you're dead.*

It gave me the creeps a bit, naturally, but mainly I was cross. No, not cross: furious. I'd had days now, two days of Lynne hovering about, being nice enough in a statuary sort of way but always hovering, always being just a bit irritating, a bit ingratiating, a bit too determined not to be offended when I snap at her. And then the police car parked outside. People always watching me, keeping an eye on my day. And this was all the good it had done. So when I had read the letter I went off in search of her. She was on the phone. I stood in front of her, waiting until she got embarrassed and hung up.

"I've got something you might be interested in," I said, handing her the letter.

That lit a rocket under her. It was barely ten minutes before Stadler was sitting in my kitchen, staring at me across the table.

"On the mat, you said?" he asked in a sort of mumble.

"That's where Lena found it," I said tartly. "Clearly he's making private arrangements for his mail. To be honest, it

makes me wonder what the point is of all this disruption
if he can still walk up to the house and deliver a letter."

"It's disappointing," Stadler said, pushing his hands
through his hair. Handsome—and he knows it, my grandmother used to say with disapproval of men like that. "Did
you see anybody approaching the house?"

"People have been approaching the house all day, tramp-
ing in and out."

"Was anything else delivered?"

"Yes, lots of things."

"Could you describe the people who delivered them?"

"I didn't meet any of them. You can talk to Lena about
that."

I was walking busily around the kitchen. Stadler was sitting at the kitchen table looking gloomy, poor thing.

"Tell me what you're actually *doing* about all of this,"
I demanded.

"Doing?" he repeated, as if the question didn't make
sense.

"Yes, you know, forgive me for being stupid, but just
spell it out for me, will you?"

He put his hand on mine and I let it lie there, hot and
heavy. "Mrs. Hintlesham, Jenny, we're doing everything
we can. We're doing forensic tests on all the letters, we're
trying to find out where the paper came from, we're looking at the fingerprints in your house in case he should have
broken in. As you know"—he attempted a rueful smile but
it didn't suit him—"we're going through all your friends,
acquaintances, contacts, people who work or have worked
for you, to try and establish any connections between you
and the, er, the other people who have been targeted by
the writer of these letters. And then, of course, until he is
caught, we are making quite sure you are safe and protected."

I took my hand away.

"Is there really any point in carrying on with all this?" I asked.

"What?" said Stadler.

"All this ridiculous fuss about opening letters and hanging around the house."

There was quite a long silence. Stadler seemed to be finding it hard to make up his mind what to say. Then he looked up at me with his very dark eyes, almost too dark.

"This is serious," he said. "You've read the letters. This man has threatened to kill you."

"Well they're pretty nasty," I admitted. "But really it's the sort of thing you have to put up with living in London, like obscene phone calls and traffic and dog mess on the streets and all that."

"Maybe," said Stadler. "But we need to take it seriously. I'm going to liaise with DCI Links in a minute, but what I'm going to suggest—and I'm sure he'll agree with me—is that we need to make this environment more secure."

"What do you mean?"

"All the work being done here must stop. Just for the time being."

"Are you crazy?" I was aghast. "These builders have a six-month waiting list. Jeremy's off to Germany next week. The plasterers are arriving at the beginning of next week. Do you want to see my folder? This isn't something I can just shut down and start up again when you feel like it."

"I'm sorry, Mrs. Hintlesham. But it's essential."

"Essential for who? Is it just going to help you because you aren't doing your job properly?"

Stadler stood up.

"I'm sorry," he said. "Sorry we haven't caught this lunatic. But it's difficult. Normally there's a procedure, knocking on doors, looking for witnesses. But when a madman picks on somebody at random, there's no normal procedure. You just have to hope that you get a break."

I almost laughed, but I stayed coldly silent. This ridiculous man wanted my sympathy. He wanted me to say "There, there" because it was so hard to be a policeman. I felt like throwing him out, him and the rest of them.

"What we have to consider," he continued, "is that he has made a serious threat on your life. We want to catch him, but our first priority is your safety. I don't feel we can take any more risks with that. The alternative would be for you to move away from this house to somewhere more protected."

I'd felt like there was a volcano trying to erupt deep in my stomach. The second prospect was even worse, so I had agreed, in a sort of cold fury. I asked when he wanted them to leave and he said straightaway, while he was in the house. So I stomped around like a nightclub bouncer and briskly ejected everybody. Then there was an awful hour of phone calls and half explanations to baffled people and attempts to make vague commitments for the future.

I drank the last of my gin and tonic and got out of the bath and wrapped myself with the big soft towel. It was so hot and so steamy in the bathroom that my skin remained clammy however much I rubbed it, so I walked through to the bedroom. The doors on the fitted cupboards had full-length mirrors on them. They were to have been ripped out next week. I stood in front of one of them and watched myself as I dried my hair and then my body. Even then I still felt damp in the heat of the evening, so I tossed the towel down on the carpet and stood and looked at myself. It was something I hardly ever did, not naked, without makeup.

I tried to imagine what it would be like to be unfamiliar with that body, to see it for the first time and to find
it attractive. I narrowed my eyes and tilted my head to one
side, but it seemed almost too much of an effort. I suppose it happens with all married couples after years together and children and all that, and hard work—you just
become part of the furniture, something you hardly notice
except when it starts to go wrong. Maybe that's why other
things—I mean other people—might seem more enticing.
I tried to imagine what it was like when Clive and I had
first seen each other in, well, in that sort of way, and the
funny thing was that I absolutely couldn't. I could remember
our first time. At his first flat in Clapham. I could remember
all the details. I could remember the play we had been to
see beforehand, what food we had eaten afterward. I could
even remember what clothes I was wearing, which he had
then taken off, but what it had felt like, to see each other's
flesh for the first time—that had gone.

I'd had only one serious boyfriend before that. Well,
fairly serious, to me at any rate. He was a photographer
called Jon Jones. He's pretty famous now. You see his name
in *Harper's* and *Vogue*. He did a nail-varnish commission
using my hands, and one thing led to another. I was quite
nervous really, about sex, I mean, that sort of thing. I wasn't
sure what to do. I was obedient, really, more than anything.
I'm not sure how exciting it actually was technically, but
the idea of it—of him—was exciting.

I was almost in a dream and then I realized I was standing naked in my room with the light on. The curtains were
open. The windows were open. I walked to the window
quickly to close the curtains and then stopped. What did it
matter after all, to be looked at? Was it so bad? I stood
there for a moment. The wind blew in hotly. I felt as if I
would have given anything for a breath of cool breeze. It

was too hot to close the window but I turned and switched off the light. That amounted to the same thing.

I lay down on the bed, on my back with the covers off. Even a sheet would have been agony. I touched my forehead and my breasts. I was already sweating again. I moved my fingers down across my stomach and between my legs. I felt warm and wet. I touched myself gently and looked up at the ceiling. What would it be like to be looked at for the first time? What would it be like to be wanted? To be lusted after. To be looked at. To be wanted.

SIX

I'm good at packing. I always pack for Clive when he has to go away for a few days. Men are hopeless at folding their shirts properly. Anyway, now I was packing for the boys, who were off into the wilds of Vermont for their summer camp. We'd heard about it years ago from a friend of a friend of a friend at Clive's work. Three weeks of rappelling and windsurfing and sitting round campfires and, in Josh's case, probably eyeing up nubile young girls in skimpy shorts. I said as much to him as I was carefully laying the T-shirts, shorts, swimming things, and trousers into his case. He just looked glum.

"You just want us out of the house," he muttered.

Everything he says now is in a mutter that I can't quite catch. It makes me feel as if I'm going deaf.

"Oh, Josh, you know you loved it last year. Harry doesn't think it's too long."

"I'm not Harry."

"Don't say you're going to miss me," I said teasingly.

He gazed at me. He's got huge dark brown eyes, and he can use them to look pathetically reproachful, like some fuzzy donkey. I noticed how bony and pale he was looking; his collarbones jutted out like knobs; his wrists were a mass of tendons. When he took off his shirt to put on his clean clothes for the flight, his ribs were like a pair of ladders climbing up his skinny body.

"You could do with some fresh air. As could this room. Don't you ever open your windows?"

He didn't answer, just stared moodily out at the street below. I clapped my hands to wake him up.

"I'm in a hurry. Your father is taking you to the airport in about an hour."

"You always think you're in a hurry."

"I'm not going to have an argument with you just before you go off on holiday."

He turned and looked at me.

"Why don't you get a proper job?"

"Where's your deodorant? I've got a job. Being your mother. You'd be the first to complain if I didn't drive you around to your parties and clubs, and cook your dinner and wash your clothes."

"So what do you do while Lena's doing your job?"

"And I'm doing up this house. Which you seem happy enough with. Okay, what are you going to do in the short time you've got before you leave? Why don't you go and see Christo—he's going to miss you."

Josh muttered something and sat down at his computer. "In a minute. I want to look at this new game. It's only just come."

"That's why it's good you're going away. Otherwise you'd spend two weeks in the dark in front of a screen. Anyway, while you're here you might as well strip your sheets and put them out for Mary." Silence. I started to leave the room and then stopped. "Josh?" Silence. "Will you miss me? Oh, for God's sake, Josh." I was shouting now.

He turned sulkily. "What?"

"Oh, nothing."

I left him locked in a form of unarmed combat in which every blow sounded like a falling tree.

I hugged Harry, though he seems to think that eleven is far too old to be hugged and he stood stiffly in my arms. He's an eager boy, none of Josh's moodiness, thank God. He's like me, not one to brood. You can tell just by looking at him, with his brown curly hair and his snub nose and his stocky legs. Josh looked spindly beside him, his skinny neck sticking out of his new, too-big shirt. I kissed him on the cheek.

"Have a wonderful time, Josh; I'm sure you will."

"Mum . . ."

"Darlings, you've got to go. Clive's in the car. Be good—don't get in trouble. See you in three weeks' time. Bye, darlings. Bye." I waved to them until they were out of sight.

"Come on then, Chris, it's just you and me for the next three weeks."

"And Lena."

"Well, yes, of course, Lena too. In fact, Lena's going to take you to the zoo soon, with a picnic lunch. Mummy's got a busy day."

A busy day cooking for this wretched dinner party that Clive had foisted on me. I couldn't remember the last time I had been alone in the house. It was oddly quiet, echoey. No Josh and Harry, no Chris and Lena, no Clive, no Mary or Jeremy or Leo or Francis; no banging of hammers, whistling of workmen as they slapped paint onto plaster; no ringing of the doorbell as gravel, or wallpaper lining, or electric cables got delivered. Well, almost alone. Lynne was always around somewhere, like a bumblebee that occasionally buzzes into the room and then out again.

This house used to be a building site, which was bad enough. Now it's a building site that's been abandoned: wallpaper half put up in the spare room, floorboards ready to be laid in the room that will be the dining room one day, dust sheets in the living room, all ready for the painting that isn't going to happen, the garden full of weeds and holes. The police may not be able to find the person bothering me but they've certainly blocked *my* plans. And that Schilling woman had got quite angry with me.

She came around again. More of that irritatingly grave and attentive expression, which I bet she practices in front of her mirror. Pushing and pushing, into my life, about Clive, men, generally, scratch, scratch. She says it's a standard part of the investigation. I sometimes feel she doesn't really care about the criminal at all. What she really wants is to solve my other problems. To change me into something else. What? Her, probably. I keep wanting to tell her that I'm not a door that will one day open onto some enchanted garden inside me. Sorry. This is who I am: me, Jenny Hintlesham, wife of Clive, mother of Josh, Harry, Chris. Take me or leave me. Actually, just leave me, leave me alone, to get on with my life again.

I don't enjoy cooking that much, but I do like preparing dinner parties, if I've got plenty of time, that is. Today I had loads of time. Lena wouldn't be back till teatime and Clive was going straight from the airport to a golf course. I had been through my recipe books, which are still all in a cardboard box under the stairs. Because of the heat I had decided to go for a real summer meal: fresh, crisp, clean, with lots of good white wine. The canapés with wild mushrooms I'd have to do at the last minute, the gazpacho I had made late last night, while Clive was sitting in front of the TV. The main course—red mullet in a tomato and saffron sauce, to be served chilled—I could do now. I made the sauce first, just a rich Italian goo, made with olive oil, onions, herbs from the garden (at least Francis had put in the herb garden before everything was put on hold), lots of garlic, seeded and skinned plum tomatoes. And when it's really nice and thick, you add red wine, a touch of balsamic vinegar, and a few strands of saffron. I do adore saffron. I laid the six mullet into a long dish and poured the sauce over them. They only had to cook at a moderate heat for about half an hour and then I could put them in the larder.

For pudding I was doing a huge apricot tart. It always looks spectacular, and apricots are gorgeous at this time of year. I rolled out the puff pastry (I'd bought it ready-made: there *are* limits) and laid it in a dish. Then I made the frangipane with ground almonds and icing sugar and butter and eggs, and poured it over the pastry. Finally, I halved the apricots and popped them on top. There; just a hot oven for twenty-five minutes. Perfect with gobs of cream. The wine and the champagne were already in the fridge. The butter was cut into little knobs. The brown rolls I was going to pick up this afternoon. The green salad I would do just before we ate.

We were going to have to eat in the kitchen, never mind Clive's important client, but I pulled out the Chinese screen so the room was divided in half, and covered the table with our white lace tablecloth, the one my cousin gave us for a wedding present. With our silver cutlery and a mass of orange and yellow roses in a glass vase, it was a brilliant improvisation.

I had invited Emma and Jonathan Barton along as well. God knows what this Sebastian and his wife would be like.

I had a picture of a fat City of London type, with a paunch and broken veins in his nose, and a hard-bitten, ambitious, power-dressing wife, bottle-blond and heavy round the hips. I don't envy women like that, even though sometimes they patronize people like me.

I wanted to look good this evening. Emma Barton has got round hips and big breasts and full lips that she paints bright red, even in the morning for the school run. She seems a bit obvious to me, but men certainly seem to like her. The trouble is, she's getting on a bit now; she's probably my age, maybe a little bit older. And pouting and wriggling is all very well when you are twenty, or thirty, but it starts to look ridiculous when you're forty, and when you're fifty it looks positively pathetic. We've known the Bartons forever. Ten years ago he was all over her, furiously possessive, but now I've seen his eyes stray to women who look just like Emma used to look then.

At six o'clock I had a long bath and washed my hair. Downstairs, I heard the door open and Lena come in with Chris. I put on a dressing gown and sat in front of my mirror. Lots of makeup this evening. Not just foundation, but blusher on my cheekbones, gray-green eye shadow, dark gray eyeliner, my beloved wrinkle concealer, plum-colored lipstick, my favorite perfume behind my ears and on my wrist—I'd splash more on later as well. Usually, between courses, I come up to my bedroom to repair my face and put on perfume. It gives me courage.

I put on a long black dress with spaghetti straps, and over it a delicate maroon lace top with black velvet around the neck and cuffs, which I bought for a small fortune in Italy last year. High-heeled shoes. My diamond choker, my diamond earrings. I examined myself in the long mirror, turned slowly round so I could see myself from every angle.

Nobody would think I was nearly forty. It takes a lot of effort, to stay young.

I heard Clive come in. I must go and say good night to Chris, make sure he's properly settled before everyone arrives. Had I remembered to put the chocolates on the sideboard?

Chris was sunburned and fretful. I left him listening to a Roald Dahl tape with the night-light on, and prayed he wouldn't make a fuss during the meal. Clive was in the shower. Downstairs I put a voluminous apron over my glad rags, and spooned the wild mushrooms over the canapés, shredded lettuce into the salad bowl: just a green salad with the fish. Elegance lies in simplicity. The sky outside the kitchen window was the color of raspberries. Red sky at night, shepherd's delight. Josh and Harry would be at their camp by now, American time.

"Hello," said Clive. He looked bronzed and gleaming in his suit; there was a sheen of success about him.

"You look smart. But I haven't seen that tie before," I said. I wanted him to tell me how chic I looked tonight.

He fingered the knot of the tie.

"No, it's new."

The doorbell rang.

Neither Sebastian nor his wife, Gloria, was the least bit like I had expected. Sebastian was tall, with a startlingly bald head. He would have been rather distinguished-looking in a sinister, Hollywood way if he hadn't been so obviously on edge. There was a faint air of contempt in Clive's manner toward him, a touch of the bully. With a sudden flash of intuition, I realized that Clive was going to shaft Sebastian in his wretched takeover bid, and this dinner party was a cruel charade of friendliness. Gloria, the City headhunter, was much younger than her husband—in her late twenties, I would have guessed. And her blond, almost silver hair didn't come from a bottle after all. She had pale blue eyes, brown slim arms, neat ankles with a thin silver chain around one of them, and she wore a perfectly simple white linen shift and very little makeup. She made me feel overdressed; she made Emma look blowsy.

All three men were attentive to her, turning their bodies subtly toward her as we stood on the half-built patio and drank champagne. She knew how pretty she was too. She kept lowering her lashes and giving secretive smiles. Her laugh was a little silvery peal, like a delicate bell.

"Nice tie," she said to Clive, giving him that smile. It made me want to spill wine on her dress.

They had obviously met before; well, I suppose they would have, given their jobs. She and Sebastian and Clive and Jonathan stood in a group and talked about the Footsie and the futures market, while Emma and I stood by like gooseberries.

"I always think the Footsie index is such a comical name," I said loudly, determined not to be ignored.

Gloria turned politely toward me.

"Do you work in the City too?" she asked, although I knew she knew I didn't.

"Me? Goodness, no." I laughed loudly and took a gulp of champagne. "I can't even add up my bridge hand. No, Clive and I decided that when we had children I would stop working outside the home. Do you have children?"

"No. What did you do before?"

"I was a model."

"A hand model," said Emma. My friend, Emma.

"They are nice hands," said Sebastian, rather stiffly.

I waved them in front of everyone. "These were my fortune," I said. "I used to wear gloves all the time, even during mealtimes. Sometimes I even wore them in bed. Mad, eh?" Jonathan poured more champagne in our glasses. Gloria was saying something softly to Clive, who was smiling down at her. Upstairs Chris started crying. I poured the champagne down my throat.

"Excuse me, everybody. Carry on. Duty calls. I'll tell you when dinner's ready. Please have some more canapés."

I turned over the tape for Chris and kissed him again, and told him if he called downstairs again I'd be annoyed. Then I went into our room. I put on more lipstick and brushed my hair and splashed perfume down my cleavage. I felt the teeniest bit tipsy. I wanted to be lying in bed, between clean, ironed sheets. Alone, thank you very much.

I drank fizzy water with the soup, but then I had some lovely Chardonnay with the fish, a glass of claret with the Brie, a rather nice dessert wine with the apricot pudding, and the coffee was like a little jolt of clarity in between the alcohol fuzz.

"What a manipulative girl," I said to Clive, afterward, when I was wiping off my makeup with a cotton pad and he was cleaning his teeth.

He rinsed his mouth carefully. He looked at me, with my one eye on and one eye off. "You're drunk," he said.

I had a sudden, utterly disconcerting fantasy of slapping him, plunging my nail scissors into his stomach. "Nonsense." I laughed. "I'm just tipsy, darling. I think it all went quite well, don't you?"

SEVEN

~

My big vice is catalogs, mail order. That's mad in a way because it's not me at all. If there's one thing I believe in it's that the objects in your home have to be exactly right. The thought of having the second-best object, that you chose because it was a little bit—or a lot—cheaper, and having it squatting there in the corner of the room year after year, accusing you, well, that's my idea of torture. You need to touch things before you buy them, walk around them, get a feeling of how they would look in the particular space you've envisaged.

So I shouldn't bother with catalogs. The towels that look fluffy in the picture may feel synthetic when they arrive and be just a different enough shade to clash with the wooden frame of the wonderful mirror you found in that market last summer. The salad spoons may look heavy but feel tackily light when they arrive. And I know that theoretically you can return them and get your money back, but somehow you never get around to that. It's indefensible and Clive is pretty contemptuous of it, if he happens to notice it, but then he's got his wretched wine catalogs, which he pores over late into the night.

So when catalogs arrive I can't resist flicking through them, and there'll always be something that catches my eye: trainers or a baseball jacket for the boys, or a clever pencil holder or a slotted spoon or an amusing alarm clock or a wastepaper basket that might look good up in the den. As often as not they'll end up stuffed in the loft or the back of a cupboard, but sometimes they'll turn up trumps. In any case, it's such fun when they arrive, brought by special delivery that you have to sign for. It's like an extra birthday. Better in some ways. If I were being sarcastic, I might say that while boys—and certain men who shall remain nameless—might forget a birthday, at least overnight delivery doesn't fail to deliver the lampshade you ordered, even if you don't care for it quite as much as you expected to.

Slightly naughtily, these mail-order companies then pass your name on to other companies, especially when their computers have probably cottoned on to the fact that you're pathetically likely to buy things you don't really need. It's a bit like being the most popular girl in the school. Everybody wants to be your friend and you don't always want to be theirs. I mean honestly, sometimes I get advertisements from the most extraordinary people. Just last week I got a brochure from a company that makes ponchos out of llama hair. Twenty-nine pounds ninety-nine, and you could get two for thirty-nine ninety-nine, as if anybody who wasn't living in the Andes would even want *one*. I didn't consider it for a second.

All of which is a prelude to what happened on the Monday when I came downstairs in the middle of the morning and saw the normal dross on the mat. Not real mail, of course. Just the usual bunch of silly colored flyers offering to deliver pizza with a free Coke and clean our windows and give a valuation for a house and pull out our original window frames and replace them with metal and double glazing. And among them was one that said "Special Offer Victorian Interiors." So I opened it.

I bet you don't know how you open a letter. You do it every day but you never think about it. I know because I've been forced to dwell on it. You pick up the letter, turn the front of it, the address side, away from you. If it's stuck firmly down, you pry away one corner of the stuck-down flap and tear it slightly. The point is to make space so you can insert your second finger and push it along the fold, tearing it all the way along. That's what I did and the curious thing was that I didn't feel any pain. I opened the envelope and saw a dull glitter of metal and that the envelope seemed to be wet in places, wet and spotted with red.

It was only then that I felt not pain exactly but a dull ache in my left hand. I looked down and it took a strangely long time for me to take in what I was seeing. There seemed to be blood everywhere, splashes across my fawn trousers, drip-dripping on the floor; my fingers were wet with it. I still didn't properly understand, so I looked stupidly into the envelope as if it might have been spilling warm red paint onto the floor. I saw the dull metal. Flat pieces stapled in a line along a piece of card. I didn't see at first what they were and then suddenly I thought of my father, sitting on the edge of the bath when I was a little girl watching him with white foam on his face like Father Christmas. Old-fashioned razor blades.

I looked at my fingers. A steady stream of blood was trickling down onto the bare board. I lifted up my hand and inspected it. There was a deep livid cut in the second finger. I could feel it pulsing, oozing out blood. That was when it began to hurt and I felt dizzy and cold and hot all at once. I didn't scream or cry. I wasn't sick. Instead my legs gave way and I slipped down onto the blood and half-lay there. I don't know how long I was like that. Just a few minutes, probably, before Lena came down and ran to get help, and Lynne appeared with her mouth in the shape of a perfect O.

She is wearing cream slacks and a maroon shirt. Her hand is bandaged, and every so often she holds it in her healthy hand, carefully, as if it was a wounded bird. Her hair is pushed behind her ears in a way that makes her face look even thinner, her cheekbones more gaunt. She looks older already. I am putting on the years.

No earrings today. No perfume. Reddish lipstick that makes her face look pallid. Powder too thickly applied, so I can see specks of it on her cheek, her forehead. She walks as if she is in a dream, her feet scuffling the floor. Her shoulders are slumped. Every so often she frowns, as if she is trying to remember something. She puts her hand against her heart. She wants to feel her life beating against her palm. The other one did that too.

She was so carefully held together and now she is coming apart. Bit by bit, the shell is cracking open. I can see her. The bits of her that she never wanted to show anybody. Fear turns people inside out.

Sometimes I want to laugh. It has turned out so well. This can be my whole life. This is what I have been waiting for.

EIGHT

Does it hurt?"

Detective Chief Inspector Links leaned toward me. Too close. But at the same time he seemed far away.

"They gave me pills for that."

"Good. We need to ask you some questions."

"Oh, for goodness' sake."

The police have been good for some things. They can get you to the front of the queue in the casualty department and they give you a lift to the hospital and back and make you tea. It's the other stuff that's been a problem.

"I know it's a difficult time. We need your help."

"Why? I've had enough of your questions. It seems simple enough to me. There's a man out there who seems to keep coming to the house. So can't you just arrest him while he's posting envelopes through the door?"

"It's not that easy."

"Why not?"

Links took a deep breath.

"If someone really sets his mind on doing something, then—" He stopped abruptly.

"Then what?"

"We want to go through some names."

"Go on, then. Do you want a cup of tea? It's in the pot."

"No, thank you."

"Do you mind if I have one?" I poured myself a cup, but then, somehow, I put the teapot down on a plate and very slowly it toppled and crashed to the quarry-tile floor, shattering. Boiling tea splashed everywhere.

"Sorry. It must be my hand. How clumsy."

"Let me help." Links started picking up broken pieces of china. Lynne mopped the floor, making herself useful for a change. Then we sat down again at the kitchen table. Lynne passed a file over to Links, who opened it up. There was a list of names, with photographs attached. There were teachers, a gardener, a real estate agent, an architect, all sorts; suits, T-shirts, clean-shaven, stubble. The pain or the pills or the shock had made me feel slow and dreamy. It seemed almost funny to be looking at this list of drab people I'd never met.

"Who are they? Criminals?"

Links looked uncomfortable.

"I can't tell you everything," he said. "For legal reasons. But what I can say is that we're trying to establish any possible connections there may be between you and, er . . ." He seemed to be searching for the right word. "Areas where similar problems have been reported. Anything here that rang any kind of bell could be useful. However remote. I mean, this estate agent, Guy Brand. To take just one example. I'm not suggesting anything, but an estate agent has access to many properties. And you have recently moved house after looking in many areas of London."

"Yes, I met hundreds of estate agents. But I've got the most dreadful memory for faces. Why don't you ask him?"

"We have," said Links. "They couldn't find you on their

books. But their record-keeping seemed to be pretty hap-hazard."

I looked again.

"He might be familiar. But then estate agents have a sort of look in common, don't they?"

"So you might have met him?"

"I don't know about *that*," I said. "I just mean that if you proved that I *had* met him, then I wouldn't think it was impossible."

Links didn't look very satisfied with that answer.

"I can leave these pictures with you, if you like."

I shrugged.

"Why would he do this?" I asked. "Go to all this trouble for something so nasty?"

Links caught my eye and for the first time he looked distressed and unable to conceal it.

"I don't know."

"Well, I hardly need reminding of that, do I?" I responded tartly. At this very moment there were about eight of them, crawling round the house like ants, taking things away in small boxes and plastic bags, muttering to each other in corners, looking at me as if I were a wounded animal. I couldn't go anywhere without bumping into them. They were very polite, in their way, but still there was practically nowhere I could go to be on my own. I raised my voice. "What I want to know is what your lot are doing while I'm working away, racking my brains to help you?"

"I can assure you that we are all working hard too," he replied. Actually, he did look a bit weary, now I came to think about it.

As I went upstairs I passed an officer coming down with a stack of papers. I went into the bathroom and locked the door, leaning on it for a moment. I splashed cold water on my face with one hand. Blood was starting to seep through the muslin wrapped around the other. Afterward I sat at my dressing table and applied more makeup with my inept left hand. I was looking a bit ragged, what with one thing and another. My hair could do with washing. In this heat you almost need to wash your hair every day. I rubbed cream into the smudges below my eyes and put on some lip gloss. I had to admit that this was getting me down. I wished Clive would ring back so I could speak to someone who wasn't a policeman. I had already told him about my hand and he had been very shocked and insisted on talking to Stadler on the phone, barking questions at him, but he hadn't come rushing back, as I had hoped, bearing flowers.

Then Detective Inspector Stadler wanted to talk to me about the details of my daily life. We had to retreat into the sitting room because Mary wanted to wash the kitchen floor.

"How's your hand, Mrs. Hintlesham?" he asked in that soft, deep, insistent voice of his.

On this hot day he had taken his jacket off and his shirtsleeves were rolled up to just below the elbows. There were beads of sweat on his forehead. When he asked me questions, he always looked me directly in the eyes, which gave me the feeling that he was trying to catch me out.

"Fine," I replied, which wasn't exactly true. It stung. Razor cuts are always horrible, that's what the doctor had said when she strapped it up.

"This person," he said. "Obviously knows that you used to be a hand model."

"Maybe."

He picked up two books, and I saw for the first time that they were my appointment book and my address book.

"Can we go through some things?"

I sighed. "If we have to. As I told that senior officer of yours, I'm very busy."

He looked evenly at me in a way that made me flush.

"This is for your benefit, you know, Mrs. Hintlesham."

And so I watched my life passing before my eyes. We started with my appointment book. He leafed through each page and fired questions at me about names, places, appointments.

That was my hairdresser, I said, and that was a checkup with the dentist for Harry. That was lunch with Laura, Laura Offen. I spelled out initials, described shops, explained arrangements with handymen and French tutors and tennis coaches, lunches, coffee mornings, reminders. We went farther and farther back, through events I had forgotten, couldn't even remember when he reminded me of them: all the negotiations for the house, the real estate agents and surveyors and the tree surgeons and planners. The school year. My social life. All the details of my days. He kept asking where was Clive when this happened, when that happened.

Finally we got back to New Year's Day and Stadler closed the date book and picked up my address book. We went through every blessed name. I took Stadler through the old neglected dusty attic of my social life. So many who had moved away or died. Couples who had separated. And those friends I had just lost touch with—or who had lost touch with me. It made me think about how much of a social asset I'd been over the last few years. Could this person really be one of those names?

As if that wasn't enough, he produced Clive's accounts for the house. I tried to tell him that I didn't deal with any of that, it was all up to Clive, that I have no head for figures. But he didn't seem to hear. £2,300 for the living room curtains, which we hadn't hung yet. £900 for the tree surgeon. £3,000 for the chandelier. £66 for the front door knocker that I fell in love with in Portobello Market. The numbers started to blur. I couldn't make head or tail of them. I certainly couldn't remember the quarry tiles being that expensive. Dreadful how it all adds up.

When we'd finished, he looked at me and I thought, This man knows more about me than anyone in the world except Clive.

"Is this all relevant?" I asked.

"That's the problem, Mrs. Hintlesham. We don't know. For the moment we just need information. Lots of it."

Then he told me to be careful, just like Links had said. "We don't want anything else happening, do we?"

He sounded reasonably cheerful about it.

Outside, the leaves on the trees had turned dark, dirty green. They hung limply from the branches, hardly stirring in the sluggish warm breeze. The garden looked like a desert, the earth was baked hard and was run through with cracks, like an old piece of china; some of the plants that Francis had recently planted were beginning to droop. The new little magnolia tree would never survive. Everything was parched.

I rang Clive again. His secretary said he'd popped out. Sorry, she said, though she didn't sound sorry at all.

Dr. Schilling was different. She didn't march into the room with a pile of names to check and bark questions at me. She looked at my hand, unrolling the bandage and holding my fingers in her slim, cool ones. She said she was very sorry, as if she was personally apologizing for it. To my horror, I suddenly wanted to cry, but I certainly wasn't going to do that in front of her. There was nothing she would like better.

"I want to ask you some questions, Jenny."

"What about?"

"Can we talk about you and Clive?"

"I thought we'd done that already."

"There are some more details. Is that all right?"

"I suppose so, but look . . ." I shifted uncomfortably. "This doesn't feel quite right. I just want to be sure that your questions are just about catching the person doing this. You probably think I'm completely mad and have an awful life, but I'm happy with it. Is that clear? I don't need your help. Or if I *do* need it, I don't *want* it."

Dr. Schilling gave an embarrassed smile.

"I don't think any of that," she said.

"Good," I said. "I just wanted to be clear."

"Yes," said Dr. Schilling. She looked at a notebook that was open on her lap.

"You wanted to ask about Clive and me."

"Do you mind that he's away so much?"

"No." She waited, but I didn't say anything else. I knew her tricks by now.

"Do you think that he's faithful to you?"

"You asked me that before."

"But you didn't answer."

I gave a huffy sigh.

"Since Detective-whatever-he-is Stadler now knows when my next period is due, I suppose I may as well tell you about my sex life as well. If you really want to know, just after Harry was born he had a—a thing."

"A thing?" She raised her eyebrows at me.

"Yes."

"How long for?"

"I'm not exactly sure. A year, maybe. Eighteen months."

"So it wasn't just a thing, was it? It was rather more serious than that."

"He was never going to leave me. She was just extra. Men are such clichés, aren't they? I was tired, I had put on some weight." I touched the skin beneath my eyes. "I was getting older."

"Jenny," she said gently, "you were only, let's see, in your late twenties when Harry was born."

"Whatever."

"How did you feel about it?"

"Don't want to talk about that. Sorry."

"All right. Have there been others?"

I shrugged.

"Perhaps."

"You don't know?"

"I don't want to know, thank you very much. If he has some stupid fling, I'd prefer he kept it to himself."

"You think he does have affairs?"

"I've just said: maybe, maybe not." The unbidden image of Clive looking down at Gloria entered my mind. I pushed it away.

"And you don't?"

"As I told you last time you asked: no."

"Never?"

"No."

"Not close to it?"

"Oh, stop it, for goodness' sake."

"Do you and your husband have a satisfactory sex life?"

I shook my head at her.

"Sorry," I said. "I can't."

"All right." Once again, she was unexpectedly gentle. "Do you think that your husband loves you?"

I blinked.

"Loves me?"

"Yes."

"That's a big word." She didn't reply. I took a breath. "No."

"Likes you?"

I stood up.

"I've had enough," I said. "You're going to walk away from this conversation and write it up in concise notes, but I'm going to live with it, and I don't want to. Clive isn't sending me razor blades, is he, so why do you want to know all this?" I stood at the door. "Has it ever occurred to you that what you do is rather cruel? Now, I'm rather busy, so if you'll excuse me."

Dr. Schilling left and I stood alone in the sitting room. I felt as if I had been turned upside down and emptied all over the floor.

NINE

I could hear the wind rippling in the trees outside. I wanted to open the windows, let the night breeze blow through all the rooms, but I couldn't. I mustn't. Everything had to be closed and locked. I had to be secure. The air inside was stale, secondhand. Heavy, hot, dead air. I was shut up in this house, and the world was shut out of it, and I could feel it all returning to chaos and to ugliness: wallpaper hanging off the walls, plasterwork abruptly stopping, floorboards torn up so you could see the dark, grimy holes beneath. The dust and bits and pieces of years and years working their way back onto the surface. All the unfinished work, all my dreams of perfect spaces: cool white, lemon yellow, slate gray, pea green, the stippled hallway, a fire in the grate throwing shadows across the smooth cream carpet, the grand piano with gladioli on top, the round tables for drinks in cut-glass tumblers, my prints hanging under picture lights, long views through the windows of green lawns and graceful shrubs.

I was sweating. I turned my pillow over, to find a cooler patch. Outside the trees rustled. It wasn't quite dark; the street lamps cast a dirty orange stain across the room. I could see the shapes of my surroundings, my dressing table, the chair, the tall block of the wardrobe, the paler squares of the two windows. And I could see that Clive still wasn't here. What time was it? I sat up in bed and squinted across at the luminous numbers on the alarm clock. I watched a seven grow into an eight and then shrink into a nine.

Half past two and he hadn't come home. Lena was out till tomorrow morning, staying with her boyfriend, so it was just me in the house, me and Chris, and all those empty disintegrating rooms, and outside a police car. My finger throbbed, my throat hurt, my eyes stung. It was quite impossible to sleep anymore.

I stood up and saw myself dimly reflected in the long mirror, like a ghost in my white cotton nightdress. I padded across to Chris's room. He was sleeping with one foot tucked under the other knee and with his arms thrown up like a ballet dancer. The duvet was in a heap on the floor beside him. His hair was sticking to his forehead. His mouth was slightly open. Maybe, I thought, I should take him to Mummy and Daddy's house down in Hassocks. Maybe I should go there myself, get away from all this ghastliness. I could just leave, get in the car and drive away. Why not? What on earth was there to stop me and why hadn't I thought of that before?

I walked to the top of the stairs and looked down. The light was on in the hall, but all the rooms were dark. I gulped. Suddenly it was hard to breathe. Stupid. This was stupid, stupid, stupid. I was safe, absolutely safe. There were two men outside, all the doors and windows were locked, double-locked. There were ugly iron grilles on the downstairs windows. A burglar alarm. A light that turned on in the garden when anyone passed it.

I went into the room that would be a spare bedroom,

and turned on the light. Half a wall was papered, the rest just lined. The rolls of wallpaper were stacked in the corner, waiting beside the stepladder and the trestle table. The brass bed was in pieces on the floor. The room smelled musty. There was a hot bubble of rage in my chest; if I opened my mouth it would come out as a scream. A scream that would go on and on, ripping into the silent night, waking up everyone in the city, telling them to beware. I pressed my lips together. I had to put my life in order. Nobody else was going to do it for me, that was clear. Clive wasn't around. Leo and Francis and Jeremy and all the rest of them had gone, as if they'd never been here. Mary crept round me as if I was contagious, and I was lucky if she emptied the wastepaper baskets nowadays. Tomorrow I would tell her I didn't need her anymore. The police were all stupid, incompetent. If they had been my workmen, I would have fired them by now. I would just have to rely on me. It was just me, now. I felt a tic start up under my right eye. When I put my finger there, I could feel it jumping, like an insect under my skin.

I picked up the box of wallpaper paste and read the instructions. It all seemed simple enough. Why did everybody make so much fuss about it? I would start with the room and then I'd move through my life, putting it all back together again, just like it was before.

Clive arrived home about half an hour later. I heard the key in the door and froze for an instant, until I heard him take off his shoes and pad into the kitchen, where he turned on the tap. I didn't stop what I was doing. I didn't have time. I was going to finish this before morning.

"Jenny," he called when he went into our bedroom. "Jens, where are you?"

I didn't reply. I slapped the paste onto the wallpaper.

"Jens," he shouted, from our bathroom this time, the one that was going to have Italian tiles one day. The hem of my nightdress was sodden with paste, but that didn't matter. The bandage on my hand was soaked as well, and my finger throbbed harder than ever. The most difficult part was putting the paper on straight, and without any bubbles. Sometimes I put on too much paste and it stained through the paper. That would dry, though.

"What on earth do you think you're doing?" He stood in the doorway in his white shirt and red boxer shorts and the socks that bloody Father Christmas had given him last year.

"What does it look like?"

"Jens, it's the middle of the night."

"So?" He didn't say anything, just stared around the room as if he didn't quite know where he was. "What does it matter if it's the middle of the night? What does it matter what time it is? If nobody else is going to do it, I'm going to do it myself. And you can be pretty sure that nobody else is going to do it. If there's one thing I've learned it's that if you want something done, do it yourself. Mind where you step, for goodness' sake. You'll ruin everything and then I will have to do it all over again and I don't have time for that. Had a good day, did you? Good day at the office till three in the morning, darling?"

"Jens."

I climbed up the ladder, holding up the sticky paper, which twisted round on itself.

"I blame myself," I said. "I've let everything go to pieces, that's what. I didn't notice at first, but now I see. A few silly letters, and we let the house fall down, fill up with dirt. Stupid."

"Jens, stop this now. It's all crooked anyway. And you've got glue in your hair. Come off that ladder now."

"The master's voice," I hissed.

"You're behaving in an unbalanced way."

"Oh really! How should I be behaving? I'd like to know. Take your hand off my ankle."

He backed off. A violent ache sprang up behind my eyes.

"Jenny, I'm going to phone Dr. Thomas."

I looked down at him.

"Everyone uses that tone of voice with me, as if there was something the matter with me. There's nothing the matter with me. They just need to catch this person and we'll be back to normal. And you"—I flourished my gluey brush at him so a drop fell on his frowning, upturned face— "you're my husband, in case you had forgotten, darling. For better or for worse, and this is for worse."

I tried to smooth the paper onto the wall, bending down at a painful angle with my damp nightdress slapping against my shins, and prickles of dust and grime on my feet, but it creased terribly.

"It's hopeless," I said, staring round the room. "It is all completely hopeless."

"Come to bed."

"I'm not in the least bit tired, thank you." And indeed I wasn't. I was fizzing with energy and rage. "But if you want to do anything to help, you can phone Dr. Schilling and tell her it is at the very best dull, thank you very much. She'll understand what I mean. You look pathetic in your socks," I added spitefully.

"All right. Have it your own way." His tone was a mixture of indifference and contempt. "I'm going to bed now. You do what you want. That strip is on back to front, by the way."

At six, Clive left for work. He called good-bye as he left, but I didn't bother to reply. Chris got himself up that day.

I shouted at him to get his own breakfast. He stood and watched me for a few minutes, looking as if he was about to cry. Just the sight of him, standing in his blue pajamas with teddy bears, looking sad, with his thumb in his mouth, made me feel scorched with anger and impatience. When he tried to hug me, I shrugged him off, telling him I was all sticky. When Lena arrived, he ran to her as if I were his wicked stepmother. A new sidekick and pretend-best-friend, a small woman with a face like a fox who introduced herself as Officer Page, marched round the house, checking all the windows. She came into the spare room and said good morning to me in a careful voice, as if she was pretending that it was quite normal to find me decorating in my nightclothes. I ignored her too. Idiot. I had no use for any of them, no confidence in them at all.

When I had finished the walls, I had a bath. I washed my hair three times, waxed my legs, shaved under my arms, plucked between my eyebrows. I applied new varnish on my nails and put on more makeup than usual, lots of foundation because my skin looked oddly blotchy, a bit of blusher to give me color, eyeliner. My face was a mask. But I couldn't keep my hand steady. The lipstick kept going outside my lips, which gave me the look of a drunken old woman. I got it right eventually: discreet plum color, hardly noticeable. It was me again in the mirror. Jennifer Hintlesham: immaculate.

I chose a thin black skirt to wear, with black mules and a crisp white shirt. It was meant to look businesslike, chic, cool. But the skirt hung off my waist. I must have lost weight. Well, every cloud has a silver lining.

I told Lena to take Chris to the London aquarium and then buy him lunch. Chris said he wanted to stay with me, but I blew him a kiss and told him not to be silly, he would have a lovely day. I gave Mary a week's wages and told her she shouldn't bother to return. I ran a finger over the top of the microwave and showed her the dust there. She put her hands on her hips and said she never wanted to come back anyway; the job gave her the spooks.

I made a list. Two lists. The first was of things to do in the house and didn't take me long. The second was for Links and Stadler and was more complicated, and I drank four cups of strong coffee while I was doing it. They had said anything I could remember might be relevant, hadn't they?

Dr. Schilling and Stadler arrived together, looking grave and mysterious. I asked them both to come into Clive's study.

"It's all right," I said to them. "Don't look so anxious. I've decided to tell you everything. Do you want some coffee? No, then do you mind if I have some more? Oops."

I spilled a large splash on the desk, and wiped up the puddle with a document that was lying near the computer that said "Without Prejudice" at the top.

"Jenny . . ."

"Hang on. I made a list of things I thought you should know. I tried ringing the Haratounian woman, you know."

Grace looked at Stadler, stared at him as if she was ordering him to tell me something. Stadler frowned back.

"I've met lots of strange men, if you want to know," I said. "In fact, as far as I'm concerned, you're all strange. No one sticks out as odd because everyone sticks out." I laughed and drank some more coffee. "My first boyfriend, in fact my only boyfriend if you don't count Clive, was called Jon Jones. He was a photographer—still is, maybe you know of him, he takes pictures of models wearing almost no clothes—and I met him when I was a model, only a hand model, of course, so I didn't have to take my top off, or not in public, but he took loads of pictures of me in private. When we broke up, except that's not what it felt like, breaking off—it felt as if he just ever so slowly withdrew his interest so that one day I couldn't be sure if we were going out any longer. Yes, well, when that happened, and that's about when I met Clive, I asked for the pictures back and he laughed and said he had copyright, so he must still have them somewhere."

"Jenny," interrupted Grace. "Would you like something to eat?"

"Not hungry," I said, taking a violent slurp of coffee. "I was putting weight on my hips, anyway, before all of this. I don't think I'm a very sexual woman, actually." I leaned forward and hissed under my breath: "The earth doesn't move for me."

Grace took the coffee cup out of my hand. I noticed I'd left a ring on Clive's desk. Never mind. I'd put that wonder polish on it later and it would vanish, like magic. I'd clean all the windows too, so that it would look as if there was no barrier at all between me and the outside world.

"That's not what I wanted to say, though, except she keeps on asking about my sex life. I've made a list of men who I think act oddly towards me." I waved it at them. "It's rather long, I must say. But I've put asterisks by the side of the oddest ones, to help you." I squinted at the list. My writing was rather erratic this morning, or maybe I was just too tired to see straight, except I didn't feel tired.

Stadler took the list out of my hand.

"Can I have a cigarette?" I asked him. "I know you smoke, even though you don't smoke in front of me, because I've watched you out of the window. I watch you, you know, Detective Inspector Stadler. I watch you and you watch me."

He took a packet out of his pocket, took out two cigarettes and lit both, then handed me one. It felt oddly intimate, and I jumped away from him and giggled.

"Clive's friends are odd," I said, coughing extravagantly. The ground swam when I took a puff, and my eyes watered. "They look respectable, but I bet they all have affairs, or want to have them. Men are like animals in a zoo. They have to be put into cages in order to keep them from running all over the place. Women are the zookeepers. That's what marriage is, don't you think, we try and tame them. So maybe it's like a circus, not a zoo. Oh, I don't know.

"I tried to think of everyone who had come to this house, even those people who weren't in my address book or date book. I don't know where to start. Obviously there's all the men working in the garden and in the house. Everybody knows the way that sort of men behave. But to be honest it's the same everywhere I go. I mean everywhere. When I see the fathers at Harry's nursery school, or when I've gone into Josh's computer club. There are some pretty odd fish there. And . . . there was something else I was going to say."

Grace laid a hand on my shoulder.

"Jenny, come with me and I'm going to make you some breakfast," she said.

"Is it still only breakfast time? Goodness. Well, at least I've got plenty of time to clean the boys' bedrooms. But I haven't gone through the list properly."

"Come on."

"I got rid of Mary, you know."

"Did you?"

"So now it's just me left. Well, me and Chris and Clive. But they don't count."

"How do you mean?"

"They're not going to help me, are they? Men don't, in general. That's been my experience, anyway."

"Toast?"

"Whatever. I don't care. God, this kitchen's in a mess, isn't it? Everything is in such a mess. Everything. How on earth am I going to do it all, with nobody to help?"

TEN

Things got a bit misty after that. I said I wanted to go out shopping and I think I even started looking for my coat. But I couldn't find it and people all around me kept telling me not to. Their voices seemed to be coming in at me from all directions, and also scratching at me from the inside as if there were wasps inside my skull crawling around my brain and waiting to sting me. I started to shout at them to get them to go away and leave me alone. The voices stopped, but I felt them gripping my arm. I was in my bedroom and Dr. Schilling was so close to me that I could feel her breath on my face. She was saying something I couldn't understand. I felt a pain in my arm and then everything faded very slowly into darkness and silence.

It was as if I was at the bottom of a deep, dark pit. Every so often I would emerge and see faces, which would say things I couldn't make out, and I would sink back into the comforting darkness. When I woke up it felt completely different. Gray and cold and generally horrid. A police-woman was sitting by the bed. She looked at me and got up and left the room. I wanted to go back to sleep, just be unconscious, but I couldn't make it happen. I thought of what I'd done and then tried not to think of it. I don't know what had become of me, but there was no point in dwelling on it.

After a time Dr. Schilling and Stadler came into the room. They looked a bit nervous, as if they were coming into the headmistress's study. It seemed funny until I remembered that they probably just thought I would carry on behaving stupidly. I must have been feeling better because then I felt irritated by these people in my bedroom. I looked down and saw I was wearing my green nightie. Who had got me out of my own clothes and into this? Who had been present when it was being done? Another thing to try not to think about.

Stadler stayed just inside the door, but Dr. Schilling came forward clutching one of my French earthenware mugs that are really for the children. People didn't understand. The Hintlesham kitchen was a complicated operation and nobody had it in their head except for me. God knows what else was being done down there.

"I brought you some coffee," she said. "Black. The way you like it." I sat up to take the warm mug in the hollow of my hands. The bandage made it a little awkward but protected me against the heat. "Would you like your dressing gown?"

"Please. The silk one."

I put the coffee down on the bedside table and got into the dressing gown with much wriggling. I thought of being thirteen years old and wriggling into my bathing costume on the beach while tightly bandaged in a towel. I was being as stupid now as I had been then. Nobody cared whether they saw me or not. Dr. Schilling pulled a chair up closer and Stadler stepped forward to the end of the bed. I was determined not to speak. I had nothing to apologize for and

I just wanted them to go away. But I never have been able to bear silences, so I did speak.

"It feels like visiting time in hospital," I said with more than a trace of sarcasm. Neither of them spoke. They just kept looking at me with ghastly expressions of sensitivity and sympathy. If there's one thing I cannot stand, it is the idea of being pitied.

"Where's Clive?"

"He saw you during the night. It's Tuesday. He had to go to work but I'll ring him in a minute and tell him how you are."

"You must be pretty sick of me," I said to Dr. Schilling.

"That's funny," she said. "Because I've just been thinking the same. I mean the opposite, I suppose. I think you must be pretty sick of me. We've been talking about you."

"I bet you have," I said.

"Not in a bad way, I hope. One of the things we've been arguing about. Or, rather, talking about." She gave a glance across at Stadler as she said this, but he was fiddling with the knot in his tie and didn't seem to be paying any attention. "I feel, we feel, that we may not have been open enough with you and I want to do something to correct that. Jenny . . ." She paused for a second. "Jenny, firstly I want to apologize if you feel that I've been intrusive. I think you know that in my day job I'm a psychiatrist treating patients. But here my job is to do anything I can to help the police catch this dangerous person." She was talking to me very gently now, as if she was a doctor talking to a child in bed with a temperature. "You have become an object of somebody's obsessive attention. One of the ways of catching the person is to find out what it is that has attracted the attention, and that can sometimes mean that I become pretty intrusive myself. But I just want to say that I know that you already have a perfectly good doctor and I don't want to replace him. Nor do I want to tell you how to run your life."

I gave her a sort of sarcastic frown, if such a thing is possible. I suddenly had this image of the two of them deciding to come in and treat me delicately and "sensitively." That funny Jenny Hintlesham who needs careful handling.

"I suppose you've discovered that I'm completely batty," I said. This was planned to be a crushing put-down but it came out all wrong. Dr. Schilling didn't smile.

"You mean yesterday?" she said. I didn't say anything. I wasn't going to talk about anything that had happened with her. "You're under a great deal of pressure. We're all here. We're trying to do something to help. But the pressure is on you. You're the one it's hard for. I want you to know that we appreciate that."

I held up my bandaged hand and looked at it. Maybe it was just my silly imagination, but it seemed to hurt more when I looked at it.

"You feel my pain, do you?" I said with some bitterness. "I don't want you to be sympathetic with me," I added quietly. "I want you to make all this go away."

I expected Dr. Schilling to get cross or flustered, but she hardly reacted at all.

"I know," she said. "Detective Inspector Stadler is going to talk to you about that."

She moved her chair to the side, but still close to me. Stadler shuffled forward. He had the expression of a kindly local constable who had come to a primary school to give the little tots some road-safety advice. It looked very odd on his libertine's face. He pulled up a chair.

"All right, Jenny?" he said.

I was slightly shocked by his using my name just like

that, but I just nodded. He was very close. I saw for the first time that he had one of those dimples in his chin. They almost tempt you to put your finger into them.

"You're wondering why we can't just catch this man, and I know what you mean. It's supposed to be our job, isn't it? I'm not going to give you the standard lecture, but the fact is that most crimes are bloody easy to solve. Because most people don't put much effort into their crimes. They hit somebody or steal something and somebody sees them do it and that's it. We just pick them up. But the sort of person who does this is different. He's not a genius but this is his hobby, and he puts a lot of effort into it. He could just as well have been wearing an anorak and spotting trains. But he's picked on you instead."

"Are you saying you can't catch him?"

"He's difficult to catch in the normal way."

"He's come to the house. Under your noses."

"Give us a break," Stadler said with an embarrassed smile.

"But that's crucial," Dr. Schilling interrupted. "He could just attack women if he wanted. But for him the point is to demonstrate his power and control."

"I don't care about his psychology," I said irritably.

"I do," said Dr. Schilling. "His psychology is one of our main ways of catching him. We can use it. And one of the main ways of doing that is to see you the way he does. That's not nice for you, I'm afraid."

"We're depending on you," Stadler said. "It puts even more pressure on you, but we'd like you to think about your own life and to let us know if there is anything out of the ordinary."

"This isn't just an ordinary Peeping Tom," said Dr. Schilling. "It could be somebody you bump into in the

High Street more often than you expect. It could be a friend who's suddenly a bit more attentive to you, or a bit less attentive. He wants to show his power, so the main thing is to be aware of your surroundings, for anything new or out of place. He wants to show he can get things to you."

I gave a snort.

"It's not so much a matter of new things arriving," I said. "It's more the old things disappearing."

Stadler looked up sharply.

"What do you mean?"

"Nothing that will be of any help to you. Have you never moved house? It took two moving vans to shift us and I'm convinced that there is a small van somewhere going round the M25 with all the objects that didn't make it. Shoes, bits of food mixers, my favorite blouse—you name it."

"This was all during the move?" asked Stadler.

"Don't be ridiculous," I said. "This man couldn't have stolen all of that unless he'd pulled up with a van and four helpers. Even you would have noticed that."

"Still . . ." said Stadler, looking lost in thought. He leaned over to Dr. Schilling and whispered to her, as if anything they were saying could be interesting enough to be secret. Then he looked up. "Jenny, could you do us a favor?"

It looked like a rummage sale organized by a blind madman. After phoning ahead, the two of them had taken me to the police station and to a special room where, Stadler told me, there would be objects on display. In the car, Dr. Schilling put her hand on mine in a gesture that gave me the creeps and said that I should just look at the objects and say whatever came into my mind. The only thing that came into my mind was what a wretched lot of hocus-pocus it all sounded.

The stuff itself almost made me laugh. A comb, some rather tacky pink knickers, a fluffy teddy, a stone, a whistle, some definitely pornographic playing cards.

"Honestly," I said. "I can't see what you expect—"

And at that very moment I felt as if I had been punched in the stomach and given an electric shock all at the same time. There it was. The funny little locket. I remembered different things at the same time. A day and a night in Brighton on our first anniversary. We'd gone to better places in later years, but that had been the best. We walked in all those little dinky shopping streets just away from the front and we'd laughed at the awful souvenir shops, and then at the same moment we'd spotted that in a jeweler's and Clive had walked in and bought it just like that. And another stupid thought had come into my mind: That night in the hotel Clive took all my clothes off but left the pendant on. It had hung down between my breasts. He had kissed it and then kissed my breasts. It's mad, the things that stick in your mind. I felt myself blushing and almost had to stop myself from crying. I picked it up, felt the familiar weight in my palm.

"Nice, isn't it?" said Stadler.

"It's mine," I said.

The most idiotic expression came over his face. It was almost comic.

"What?" he said, almost in a gasp.

"Clive gave it to me," I said, as if in a dream. "It was lost."

"But . . ." said Stadler. "Are you sure?"

"Of course," I said. "There's a fiddly clip at the back that opens it up. There's a lock of my hair inside. Look, there."

He stared.

"Yes," he said. Dr. Schilling was gawking as well. They were looking at each other, open-mouthed. "Wait," he said. "Wait."

And he ran, ran, out of the room.

ELEVEN

I didn't understand. I didn't understand at all. Not anything. I felt as if I were looking at one of Josh's wretched computer games that get posted through our front door and that make his grumpy face light up, but I didn't even know the language, the alphabet it was written in. It was just dots and dashes and signs and codes to me. I looked over at Dr. Schilling, as if she could tell me what was going on, but she just offered me her meaningless reassuring smile, the one that gave me the shivers. Then I looked at the locket again, sitting among the curious pile of objects. I reached over and touched it with one finger, lightly, as if it could blow up in my face.

"I want to go home," I said, not really meaning it but needing to say something to break the silence in the drab little room.

"Soon," said Dr. Schilling.

"I want to have something to eat. I'm hungry."

She nodded, but in an absentminded way. She had a little frown on her face.

"When did I last eat? It must have been ages ago." I tried to remember back through the last few days, but it was like peering into inky darkness. "Is anybody going to tell me how my locket got here?"

"I'm sure they'll—"

But then she was interrupted by Stadler coming back into the room with Links. They both looked intensely agitated as they sat down opposite me. Links picked up the locket by its chain.

"You are quite sure this belongs to you, Mrs. Hintlesham?"

"Of course I'm sure. Clive's even got a photo of it somewhere for our insurance."

"When did you lose it?"

Now I had to think.

"It's hard to say. I remember wearing it to a concert. That was on the ninth of June, the day before my mother's birthday. A couple of weeks later I wanted to wear it to Clive's work's bash, but I couldn't find it."

"What date was that?"

"You've got my date book, for goodness' sake. But it was in June sometime, the end of June."

Stadler looked down at a notebook in his lap and nodded as if he was satisfied.

"What's important about it? Where did you find it?"

Stadler looked into my eyes and I made myself not look away. For a second I thought he was going to tell me something, but the moment passed, and he looked down at his notebook once more with that secret satisfaction on his face.

There was a brief, strange hush in the room, then I raised my voice:

"Won't someone please tell me what is going on, for goodness' sake?" But my heart wasn't in it. My anger seemed to have all seeped away. "I don't understand."

"Mrs. Hintlesham," said Links, "can we just establish—"

"Not now," said Dr. Schilling suddenly. She stood up. "I'm taking Jenny home. She's been under great strain; she has been unwell. Later."

"Establish what?"

"Come on, Jenny."

"I don't like secrets. I don't like people knowing things about me that I don't know. Have you caught him? Is that it?"

Dr. Schilling put a hand under my elbow and I stood up. Why on earth was I wearing these cotton trousers? I hadn't worn them for years; they didn't suit me at all.

Everybody was behaving oddly. The house was full of a new kind of energy, as if the curtains had been pulled back, the windows thrown open. Nobody told me anything, of course, but Dr. Schilling came back with me and a bored-looking woman officer. Links and Stadler pitched up soon afterward. They were all beckoning to each other and muttering things to each other and looking at me, then looking away when I caught their eye. Dr. Schilling didn't seem as happy as the others.

"Do you think you could phone your husband, Mrs. Hintlesham?" asked Stadler, following me into the kitchen.

"Why can't you phone him yourself?"

"We want to talk to him. We thought it might sound more civilized from you."

"When?"

"Straightaway."

"What on earth for?"

"We need to clarify a couple of points."

"We've got a drinks party this evening. An important one."

"The quicker we can talk to him, the quicker he'll be free."

I picked up the phone.

"He's going to be irritated," I said.

He was very irritated.

The phone rang. It was Josh and Harry, calling from America, early morning for them, although they sounded as if they were just round the corner and at any moment would come charging into the house. Harry told me he had caught a pike, whatever that is, in the lake and he had learned how to sailboard. Josh asked me how things were at home; his voice jumped from boy's to man's, the way it does when he's overemotional.

"Fine, darling."

"Are the police still there?"

"I think they're making progress."

A little gust of hope blew through me.

"Do we have to stay out here another two weeks?"

"Don't be silly, darling, you're having a lovely time. Have you got enough money to last?"

"Yes, but—"

"And did I pack the right clothes? Oh, and remember to tell Harry that there are spare batteries for his Walkman in your backpack."

"Yeah."

I put the phone down feeling the conversation hadn't been a success. Christo trailed past, dragging a blanket after him. I felt a sharp pang of guilt when I saw his blotchy, sullen face.

"Hello, Christo," I said to him. "Can Mummy have a hug?"

He turned to me.

"I'm not Christo," he said. "I'm Alexander. And you're not my mummy." Lena called to him from his room in her singsong Swedish accent and he raised his yellow head. "Coming, Mummy," he shouted, darting a glance of triumph at me as he went.

I changed my trousers for a yellow, low-waisted sundress and threaded earrings into my lobes. I looked in the mirror. I wasn't wearing any makeup. My face was thin and pale, my hair was a mess, my eyes were oddly bright although the skin under them was all papery and frail, and there was a long red scratch on my cheek. How had that got there? I hardly recognized myself anymore.

Dr. Schilling ordered me to eat the omelette that she made, using the herbs I'd been saving for dinner after the drinks party. Never mind. I ate it in a few forkfuls, hardly chewing it, stuffing in brown, slightly stale bread after each rapid mouthful. I hadn't realized how famished I was. She watched me as I ate, leaning her chin on a hand, staring at me as if I puzzled her. Soon, I thought, I would get control back, clean the house, bring back the workmen, the gardener, the cleaner, take a deep breath and find the energy to be Jenny Hintlesham all over again. Tomorrow. I would begin again tomorrow. But just for this once, there was something pleasantly anesthetizing about being looked after. It no longer felt like my own house, just a place I was sitting in, waiting for something to happen; everyone was waiting for something to happen.

My eyes clicked open. A key in the lock, a door slamming loudly, heavy footsteps in the hall.

"Jenny. Jens, where are you?"

Grace Schilling stood up at the same time as me. Stadler

and Links were there before us. We all converged by the staircase.

"What's going on?" Clive scowled; his voice was loud and abrupt; it made my head ache. At that moment he saw a box of his precious documents on the hall floor. I saw a vein pulsing angrily in his forehead.

"Mr. Hintlesham," said Stadler. "Thanks for coming." He was much taller than Clive, who looked square and hot next to him.

"Yes?"

He was talking to Stadler as if he were a particularly low-grade functionary.

"We'd prefer it if you could come with us," said Links.

Clive stared.

"What do you mean?" he said. "Why not here?"

"We want to take a statement. It would be better."

Clive looked at his watch.

"For God's sake," he said. "This had better be important."

"Please," said Stadler, holding open the door for Clive, who turned to me before leaving.

"Phone Jan and tell her something," he snapped at me. "Anything that doesn't make us both look stupid. And Becky. Go to that party and make sure you are jolly, as if everything is perfectly normal, do you hear?" I put a hand on his arm but he shook it off violently. "I am sick of this," he said. "Utterly sick."

Grace Schilling went too, buttoning up her long jacket purposefully before striding out the door.

I rang Clive's office and told Jan that Clive had a bad back. "Again?" she said sarcastically, which I didn't understand at all. I told Becky Richards the same, two hours later, and

she laughed sympathetically. "Men are such hypochondri-
acs, aren't they?" She sniggered.

I looked round the room, at all the women in their black
dresses and all the men in their dark suits. I knew most of
them by sight, at least, but suddenly I couldn't summon
up the energy to talk to them. I couldn't think of a single
thing I had to say. I felt quite empty.

TWELVE

Clive didn't arrive and I felt more and more out of place standing there fiddling with the glass in my hand, looking at pictures in hand, walking from one room to another as if I were urgently on my way to meet someone, somewhere. I realized, almost with a feeling of horror, that being at a party on my own had become an utterly unfamiliar experience. It felt wrong, too. I've sometimes joked with Clive that when I go out to a party with him I know that it's really him people want to see and that I'm really there as Mrs. Clive.

So it was a relief rather than a hideous embarrassment when Becky told me there was someone at the door for me.

"A policeman," she said with awkward puzzled delicacy.

Because we all know what the idea of a policeman at the door means for ordinary people like us: There's been an accident, a death, a disappearance. But I wasn't an ordinary person like them anymore. I went to the door feeling unworried. Stadler was there on the doorstep with a uniformed officer I hadn't seen before. Becky hovered for a moment, helpful and nosy. The officer didn't speak and I turned and looked questioningly at Becky.

"If there's anything I can do, I'll be inside," she said and moved back, reluctantly.

I turned back to the officer.

"Sorry to bother you," he said. "I was sent to tell you that your husband won't be along. Mr. Hintlesham's still being interviewed."

"Oh," I said. "Is anything the matter?"

"We're just trying to clear up some details."

We stood there on Becky's doorstep looking at each other.

"I don't really want to go back to the party," I said.

"We can run you back home, if you like," Stadler said. Then he said: "Jenny," and I blushed violently.

"I'll get my coat."

Nobody spoke to me on the short drive back. Stadler and the officer murmured to each other once or twice. Back at the house, Stadler walked up the steps with me. As I turned the key in the lock it felt for an absurd moment as if the two of us were coming back from an evening out together and we were saying good night.

"Will Clive be back this evening?" I said firmly as if to show myself how stupid that was.

"I'm not sure," Stadler said.

"What are you talking to him about?"

"We need him to corroborate some details of the investigation." Stadler looked around casually while speaking. "Oh, and there's one other thing. As part of this extra push in the inquiry, we would like to conduct a more detailed search of your house tomorrow morning. Do you have any objection to that?"

"I don't suppose so. I can't believe there's anything left to look at. Where do you want to search?"

Stadler looked casual again.

"Different places. Some of the upstairs. Maybe your husband's study."

* * *

Clive's study. It had been the first room we made habitable in the new house, which was a bit rich because nobody inhabited it except Clive. Wherever we had lived, Clive always insisted on that: a room that was his private lair, for his own stuff. When we were planning the rooms for the new lair, I remember protesting with a laugh that I didn't have a sanctum and he said that didn't matter because the whole house was my sanctum.

The room wasn't exactly kept locked and bolted, but it hardly needed to be. The boys were strictly forbidden on penalty of torture and death from even entering the room. I wasn't absolutely excluded, obviously. I'd sometimes go in while Clive was working on the accounts or writing letters and he wouldn't get cross with me or tell me to go away. But he would turn toward me, take the coffee or hear what I had to say, and then wait until I was finished and started to go. He always said that he couldn't work if I was in the room.

So there was a feeling of something forbidden when—after checking round the house, getting undressed, and putting on my nightie and dressing gown—I went into the study. I put the light on and straightaway felt guilty, walking across the room and pulling the curtains shut so that I truly felt alone there, at almost midnight.

The room was Clive. Neat, precise, well ordered, almost bare. There were just a few pictures. A small blurry watercolor of a sailing boat he had inherited from his mother. An old etching of his public school that he'd been given as a boy. There was a photograph of Clive with a group of his colleagues at a celebration dinner, all cigars and red shiny faces and empty glasses and arms round shoulders, with Clive looking just a little hunted and awkward. He was never happy being touched, especially by other men.

My husband's study. What was there here that could possibly be of any interest? I wasn't going to search through his things, of course. The idea of doing that while he was away at the police station would have seemed terribly disloyal. I just wanted to have a look. It might be important if I had to speak on his behalf. That's what I told myself.

The study contained two filing cabinets, one tall and brown, the other short, stubby gray metal. I opened them both and flicked through the folders and papers, but they were incredibly boring. Mortgage documents, instruction booklets, endless receipts and bills and guarantees, invoices, accountants' letters. It made me feel a small glow of love for Clive. This was what he did so that I didn't have to. He let me do just the interesting, creative part, and he did all this. And it was all done, all arranged. There was nothing pending, no bill unpaid, no letter unanswered. What could I ever have done without him? I didn't look at the individual pieces of paper. I just wanted to check that there was no file containing anything that wasn't boring.

I closed the second filing cabinet. It was all so stupid. There was nothing here that could possibly be of any interest to the police unless they wanted to read through our mortgage agreement. Just more misdirected effort. I could have told them if they'd only asked me.

I rolled back the top of the desk. It made a horrible noise and I looked round nervously. I was careful not to do anything that couldn't be undone in a few seconds if the front door were to ring. Nothing of interest, needless to say. Clive always said that one of his strictest rules was always to clear his desk before he got up from it. There was nothing on the work surface but pens, pencils, erasers, a rather expensive electric pencil sharpener, rubber bands, paper clips, all in some container or dish specially meant for them. There were pigeonholes with envelopes, notepaper, cards, labels. If nothing else, the police would certainly be impressed.

All that remained were the drawers. I sat at his chair. Above my knees was a shallow drawer. Picture postcards. I examined them. All blank. Then the drawers on either side. Checkbooks, new and empty. Holiday brochures for the winter. A whole lot of paperwork from Matheson Jeffries, where Clive works. All blessedly tedious.

The bottom right-hand drawer contained some large, bulky, brown envelopes. I examined the top one. It was full of handwritten letters. The same handwriting. I looked at the end of one of them. It was a long letter on three sheets of paper. Signed Gloria. I knew that one of the wrongest things you can do is to read anybody's private letters without their permission. "Nobody ever overhears good about themselves" was a saying that came into my mind. I knew I mustn't read them and what I really ought to do was to put them back and go to bed and put all this out of my mind. At the same time it occurred to me that in the morning the police might be reading these letters for reasons of their own. Shouldn't I have some idea of what they contained?

I compromised by skimming the letters and looking at a phrase here and a word there. It may seem difficult to make sense of letters in that way, but words seemed to jump up off the page at me: darling . . . I miss you desperately . . . thoughts of last night . . . counting the hours. Funnily enough, my initial feeling was not anger against Clive or even against Gloria. At first I just felt contemptuous at the triteness of her letters. Do people having secret affairs have to express themselves in the same old hackneyed phrases? Couldn't Clive do better than that?

Then I thought of her at dinner when I had last seen her, leaning over to whisper something to him, looking over the table at him, and my cheeks burned. I carefully put the letters back in the envelope. The last letter was the most recent. I shouldn't have read them; it would do nothing but harm, cause more pain, more humiliation.

Just one more bit. One paragraph, not just a phrase. I would allow Gloria a paragraph to do herself justice. The last one of that most recent letter. I needed to know where I stood.

"And now I must close, my darling. I'm writing this at work and it's time to go home. I can't bear not seeing you, but in September we'll have Geneva." Geneva. A business trip. He hadn't mentioned that yet. "It seems awful to admit, but sometimes I hate her too, nearly as much as you."

I laid the letter down for a moment and swallowed hard, but the lump in my throat wouldn't go away. Hated me. So he hated me. Not loved. Not even liked. Not indifferent. Hated. I looked down at the letter again. "But we mustn't. We'll work things out and be together somehow. We will find a way, I trusted you when you said that. All my loveliest love, Gloria."

I folded the letter and slipped it into the large brown envelope carefully, at the bottom, where it was meant to be. I looked at the other stuffed envelopes in the drawer, and even the thought of what they contained filled me with such desolation. I lifted the top one and underneath it was a photograph. It was a woman but it wasn't Gloria. She looked as if she was at a party. She was holding a drink and she was raising it to the photographer in a jokey way and laughing. She looked different from any woman I knew. Fun. Small and slim and very young. Dark blond hair, short skirt, strange all-over-the-place blouse. But all quite casual-looking. I thought for a mad moment that she looked nice, that she could have been my friend, and then I felt angry and sick and I couldn't bear any more. I put the photograph back under the second bundle and closed the drawer. I left the room, remembering to switch off the light.

THIRTEEN

❧

I was in the dark. My life was the dark place. Everything I had once taken for granted now loomed over me, horrible. I had thought there was someone out there who wanted to harm me, and that had seemed terrifying enough, but now I realized nowhere was safe. Not out there, not in here, not with the person I had been married to for fifteen years, not in my own house, my own room, my own bed. Nowhere.

Josh and Harry were in America, in some tent up a mountain, far from home. Christo was pretending I wasn't his mother at all. And Clive hated me; that's what he had said to Gloria. Lying in bed that night, I tested that word, like testing a battery by laying the tip of your tongue against it. Hated. Hated. Hated. The word stung in my brain. My husband hated me. How long, I wondered, had he hated me? Since Gloria, or for years and years? Always?

Outside, there was a faint sigh of wind in the limp trees. I imagined eyes out there, watching my window.

Maybe my husband wanted me dead.

I sat up in bed, turned on the light beside me. That was

ridiculous. Mad, a mad thing to think. Except, why were the police holding him for so long?

At dawn, after a night of jumbled dreams, I went into Christo's room and sat beside him while he slept. Light was filtering in through his fish curtains; it was going to be another scorching day. He had thrown off his covers and his pajama top was unbuttoned. The fluffy dolphin that Lena had bought him at the zoo was clasped in one fist. His mouth was slightly open and every so often he mumbled something incomprehensible. Today, I thought, I would arrange to send him with Lena to my parents. I should have done it before. This was no place for a child to be.

The police arrived early, three of them, who moved into Clive's study like a task force. I pretended they weren't there.

I made Christo and Lena a cooked breakfast, though Lena, who never ate anything, merely picked at the grilled tomato with her fork and tried to push the rest of it into a pile so it would look as if she'd eaten some. And Christo, after piercing the yolk of the fried egg and smearing it round his plate, said it was all yuck and couldn't he have his chocolate flakes instead? What was the magic word? I asked automatically. Please. Please could he not eat this disgusting mess.

The police left, carrying boxes. It was just a few months since they'd all been brought in and piled high at random by a group of surly and resentful removal men. Christo didn't ask where his father was, because Clive was usually gone before he woke up anyway. Gone before he woke up, back after he had gone to sleep. Hated. My husband hated me.

The kitchen was a mess. The whole house was a mess

now that I'd sent Mary off. I'd clean it tomorrow. Not today. I looked down at my bare legs. They needed waxing again, I thought, and my nail varnish was beginning to chip.

"Are you all right, Mrs. Hintlesham?" Lena asked me in her singsong voice. What a pretty girl she was, so blond and slim in her tiny sundress, her delicate arms tanned from the summer. Maybe Clive had thought so too. I stared at her until her face swam.

"Mrs. Hintlesham?"

"Fine." I put my fingers against my face; my skin felt thin and old. "I slept badly. . . ." I trailed off.

"I want to watch the cartoons."

"Not now, Christo."

"I want to watch cartoons!"

"No."

"You're a bumhole."

"Christo!" I seized his upper arm and pinched it fiercely.

"What did you say?"

"Nothing."

I let go of his arm and turned to Lena, who was looking demure.

"Today is a bit complicated," I said vaguely. "Maybe you and Christo could go to the park, take a picnic, go to the bouncy castle."

"I don't wanner picnic."

"Please, Christo."

"I wanner stay with you."

"Not today, darling."

"Come on, Chrissy, let's choose your clothes." Lena stood up. No wonder Christo loved her. She never got cross, just chanted things at him in her funny voice.

I put my head in my hands. Dust and dirt everywhere. Ironing to be done. No one to help me. Clive in the police station, answering questions. What questions? Do you hate your wife, Mr. Hintlesham? How much do you hate her? Enough to send her razor blades?

They left together, hand in hand. Christo wore red shorts and a stripy shirt. I stared at the congealing food on their plates. I stared at the window, which needed washing. And there was a spider's web on the light above me. Where was the spider, I wondered.

The doorbell rang and I jumped. It was Stadler, crumpled and sweaty, with stubble on his face. He looked as if he hadn't gone to bed.

"Can I just ask a couple of questions, Jenny?" He always called me Jenny now, as if we were friends, lovers.

"More questions?"

"One," he said, with a tired smile.

We walked downstairs, where he turned down offers of coffee and breakfast. He looked around.

"Where's Lynne?" he asked.

"Sitting outside in her car," I said. "You must have passed her."

"Right," he said dully. He hardly seemed awake.

"You wanted to ask a question?"

"That's right," he said. "It's just a detail. Can you remember where you were on Saturday July seventeenth?"

I made a feeble attempt to recall and gave up.

"You've got my appointment book, haven't you?"

"Yes. All you wrote on that day was 'Collect fish.'"

"Oh, yes, I remember."

"What were you doing?"

"I was at home. Cooking, preparing things."

"With your husband?"

"No," I said. Stadler gave a visible start, then a smile

of suppressed triumph. "I don't see why you need to look surprised. As you know, he's hardly ever here."

"Do you know where he was?"

"He had to go out, he told me. Urgent business."

"Are you sure?"

"Yes. I was cooking a meal for us. He told me in the morning he had to go out."

I remembered the day clearly. It had been Lena's day off. Harry and Josh had lounged around and squabbled, before going out with separate friends; Christo had watched television most of the day, and played with his Legos, and gone to bed early, worn out by heat and bad temper, and I had sat in the kitchen with the ruined day behind me and my beautiful meal spread out on the table, long-stemmed wineglasses and flowers from the garden, and he hadn't come back.

"He was out the whole day then?"

"Yes," I said.

"Can you be precise about times?"

As I spoke I could hear my own voice, flat, sad.

"He left too early to be able to go to the fishmonger's. He came back at about midnight. Maybe a bit later. He wasn't there when I went to sleep."

"Are you willing to make a statement repeating all that?"

I shrugged.

"If you want. I assume you're not going to tell me why it matters."

Stadler startled me by taking hold of my hand and holding it.

"Jenny," he said softly, his voice like a caress. "All I can tell you is that all of this will soon be over, if that is of any comfort to you."

I felt myself going red.

"Oh" was all I could manage in response, like some village idiot.

"I'll be back soon," he said.

I didn't want him to go, but I couldn't say that, of course. I pulled my hands away.

"Good," I said.

I lay on my bed in a puddle of sunlight. I couldn't move. My limbs felt weighted down and my brain sluggish, as if I were under water.

I lay in a cool bath and closed my eyes and tried not to think. I wandered from room to room. Why had I ever liked this house? It was ugly, cold-hearted, unsatisfactory. I would move from here, start again.

I wished Josh would call me. I wanted to tell him that he didn't need to stay there if he hated it so very much. It wasn't worth the wretchedness; I saw that now.

I went into the boys' rooms and fingered the clothes in their wardrobes, the trophies on their shelves. We were all so very far from each other. I caught sight of myself in the long mirror in the hall—a thin, middle-aged woman with greasy hair and bony knees, wandering about like a lost thing in a house that was too large for her.

Outside, the sky was hazy with heat and fumes.

Maybe we could move to the country, to a small cottage with roses round the door. We could have a swimming pool and a beech tree the boys could climb.

I opened the fridge and stared inside.

The doorbell rang.

I was unable to speak. It was just not possible. It wasn't real. I just shook my head as if I could clear the confusion away. Links leaned closer, as if I were short-sighted and deaf as well as mad.

"Did you hear what I said, Mrs. Hintlesham?"

"What?"

"Your husband, Clive Hintlesham," he said, as if it had to be spelled out, detail by detail. "An hour ago. We charged him with the murder of Zoe Haratounian on the morning of July seventeenth, nineteen ninety-nine."

"I don't understand," I repeated. "This is mad."

"Mrs. Hintlesham, Jenny . . ."

"Mad," I repeated. "Mad."

"His solicitor is fully involved. He will appear at Saint Steven's Magistrate's Court tomorrow morning. They will make a bail application. Which will be refused."

"Who is this woman, anyway? What's she got to do with Clive? With me and the letters?"

Links looked uneasy. He took a breath and spoke in a slow, patient voice, quietly, even though there was nobody around to hear.

"I can't tell you in detail," he said. "But because of the special circumstances I thought I should prepare you. It seems that your husband was having an affair with her. We believe he gave her your locket. Her photograph was among his possessions."

I remembered the photograph I had seen last night: an eager, laughing face, a glass in her hand lifted in a toast to the future she didn't have. I gulped, and a wave of nausea swept over me.

"That doesn't mean he would kill her."

"Miss Haratounian also received letters like yours. Written by the same person. We believe that your husband threatened her, and then killed her."

I gazed at him. A jigsaw was beginning to click together, but the picture that emerged made no sense, it was just a scribble of violent images. A bad dream.

"Are you saying that Clive was the person writing those letters to me?"

"All we are saying at the moment is that your husband is charged with the murder of Miss Haratounian."

"Tell me what you think."

"Mrs. Hintlesham . . ."

"You must tell me. It doesn't make any kind of sense."

Links was silent for some time, visibly trying to make up his mind.

"This is very painful," he said. "I wish you could be spared it. But it is possible that he wanted to rid himself of this woman, for whatever reason. Then, having done that, it seemed that nobody knew that he had met her. For that reason, if you were . . . well, targeted by the person who did that murder, he wouldn't be a suspect." Another long silence. "It's one way of looking at it," he said uneasily. "I'm sorry."

"Could he loathe me that much?"

Links didn't speak.

"Has he admitted it?"

"He still denies even knowing Miss Haratounian," Links said dryly. "Which is a bit rich."

"I want to see him."

"That's your right. Are you sure?"

"I want to see him."

"You don't believe this, Jenny? Jens. You can't possibly believe this ludicrous charge?" In his voice I heard a mixture of anger and fear. His face was red and unwashed, his clothes were stained. I gazed at him. My husband. Jowly cheeks, a thickening neck, eyes that were slightly bloodshot.

"Jens," he said.

"Why shouldn't I believe it?"

"Jens, it's me, Clive, your husband. I know things have been shaky recently, but it's me."

"Shaky," I repeated. "Shaky."

"We've been married for fifteen years, Jens. You know me. Tell them it's ridiculous. I was with you that day. You know I was. Jens."

A fly settled on his cheek and he brushed it away violently.

"Tell me about Gloria," I said. "Is it true?"

He flushed and tried to speak and then stopped.

I looked at him, the hairs in his nostrils, the grime of dirt on his neck, the flaky skin by his ears, dandruff in his hair. He looked good only when he was carefully groomed. He wasn't one of those people, like Stadler, for example, who actually look better after staying up all night. Who could stay up all night and still seem sexy.

"I don't think there's anything more to talk about, do you?"

"Yes," he said. "Yes, I do."

"Good-bye."

"You'll see," he shouted. "You'll see and then you'll be sorry. You are making the biggest mistake of your whole stupid, little life." His fists came down on the table between us, and the moon-faced policeman at the door stood up. "I will make you suffer for it, see if I don't."

There was only one police officer outside my house now, and he lay in the car, half asleep behind a paper. Clive's office looked like a burglar had been in there. The house was a building site of half-finished rooms. The garden was a wasteland; nettles grew in the beds that Francis had prepared for the flowering, sweet-smelling shrubs; the grass was yellow.

I opened a bottle of champagne and drank a glass of it,

but it made me feel violently sick. I ought to eat something, but that didn't seem possible. I wanted Grace Schilling to come in and make me another herb omelette, runny and good. I wanted Josh to call me and say he was coming home.

I sat alone in the kitchen. I was shamed and I was free.

FOURTEEN

❦

A day of frenetic activity calmed me down. That was what I needed. It stopped me from dwelling on things too much; it muffled the jangling in my head that I couldn't make go away whatever pills I took for it. The morning was sunny and it hadn't yet got horribly hot, and as I sat at the kitchen table with Lynne, I felt almost calm. She was wearing her uniform again. There was a feeling of things being over and winding down and farewells. We had worked our way through almost a whole cafetière and I'd made some toast that we both nibbled. Lynne asked if she could smoke and not only did I say she could but I asked for a cigarette myself and went and found a saucer we could use as an ashtray.

My first puff felt sinful, as if I was fourteen years old, and then I felt soothed. Maybe in my new life I'd start smoking again.

"I used to do this to lose weight," I said. "At least it was a welcome by-product. I gave up when I was pregnant with Josh. My bottom and thighs have never been the same."

Lynne smiled and shook her head.

"I wish I had your figure," she said.

I looked at Lynne with a critical eye.

"You wouldn't like it," I said. "You haven't seen it the way I see it."

We both took puffs from our cigarettes. Mine felt amateurish after all these years. I would need a lot more practice.

"So you've been busy?" Lynne asked.

"An awful lot of things need sorting out."

"When do you leave?"

"I'm flying to Boston this evening."

"Do the boys know yet?"

I very nearly laughed at this.

"The idea of informing Josh over the phone that his father—well, it didn't seem such a good idea. No, I'm sure that Dr. Schilling would recommend doing it face-to-face."

"It's probably better."

"And I spent most of the afternoon on the phone to my architect and my various builders and Francis, my brilliant gardener. We're flying back at the beginning of next week and then we can get going on the house."

Lynne lit another cigarette and then caught my eye and lit me one.

"Won't that feel strange?" she said. "Starting all that again?"

"It's different this time," I said. "That's why it took so long on the phone. They're going to come and patch things up, slap some white paint on the walls, put some shrubs in the garden. Then I'm putting the house on the market."

Lynne's eyes widened in surprise.

"Are you sure?" she said.

"What I'd really like is to burn the house down with everything inside it and make a run for it. But selling it will have to do."

"You've only just moved in."

"I can hardly bear the sight of it. I've been unhappy here. I suppose it's not the house's fault, but still . . ."

"Have you talked to Dr. Schilling?"

"Why should I talk to her?" I said, a bit belligerently. "Grace Schilling's job was to use her professional skill to catch the man harassing me. Well, he's caught." I stopped myself. "I'm sorry. I didn't mean to shout. Again."

"That's all right."

"In fact, all in all, this probably hasn't been the most enjoyable job you've ever had to do."

"Why?"

"Trying to look after a bad-tempered, miserable woman." Lynne looked serious.

"You shouldn't say that. It was awful. We all felt terrible for you. We still do."

"Still?"

"Look, we're glad we caught the person who did this. We're not glad for you that it was Mr. Hintlesham."

I took some time to reply. I was looking over Lynne's shoulder at the garden. It was difficult to believe that even Francis could get this into a salable shape within a fortnight. We'd see.

"I just keep remembering details of our marriage and wondering how it could have happened. I know we had difficulties, but I don't see why he had to hate me so much. What had I done to him, what had that poor girl, Zoe, done except climb into bed with him?" Lynne looked me in the eyes. She didn't turn away, I'll say that for her. But she didn't reply. "And even if he hated me so much, would he have wanted to kill me? And to make me suffer? Well, could he? Say something."

Lynne looked a bit shifty.

"I've got to be careful," she said. "With the committal

hearing and everything. But people do things like that. Mr. Hintlesham had met somebody else. He knew that you wouldn't give him a divorce." She gave a shrug. "The last murder I dealt with, a fourteen-year-old boy killed his granny because she wouldn't lend him the money to buy a lottery ticket. It's like one of my sergeants used to say: You don't need qualifications to be a murderer."

"So he *could* have done it. Do you think he'll be found guilty?"

Lynne paused before speaking.

"The Crown Prosecution Service say that we've got to be confident of a seventy-five percent chance of conviction before we charge anybody. As far as I know, there was no hesitation about charging your husband. We've got the clear connection with the dead girl, Zoe, and his attempts to lie about it. There's the lack of an alibi. His threats against you, his affair and motivation. We've got a good case."

"What if the murder is tried separately?" I asked cautiously.

"No chance," said Lynne. "The identical notes to the two of you make the cases inseparable."

"Half the time I think that he's innocent and will be found guilty. The other half I think he's guilty and that he'll go free. He's clever. He's a lawyer. I don't know what to think."

"He won't get off," said Lynne firmly.

We drank up our coffees and finished our cigarettes.

"Have you packed?" she asked.

"That's on my list," I said. "I'm only taking a small bag."

She looked at her watch.

"I think I'd better go," she said.

"I'll feel strange being unsupervised," I said.

"You won't be entirely unsupervised. We'll keep an eye."
I pulled a slightly sarcastic face.
"Does that mean you're not entirely sure?"
"Just to see you're all right."
And she was gone.

I didn't have lunch. No time. Packing was a little more complicated than I had suggested to Lynne. Normally I'm a world champion at packing exactly the right amount, but I was feeling a bit strange and I felt I was doing everything a little bit slowly, as if I were underwater or on the moon. And even though I was doing things more slowly, I also had to think about them more carefully.

The phone kept ringing, as well. I had rather a long conversation with Clive's lawyer. It consisted of us slightly dancing around each other. I wasn't at all clear that we were on the same side, and by the end of it I was wondering whether I oughtn't to think of getting my own lawyer. Several people rang for Josh: his violin teacher, that fellow Hack from the computer club who said Josh had asked him to drop a game round, and Marcus, one of his friends. And a couple of *my* friends—or Clive's friends—called who had clearly heard that something funny was going on. In each case I put them off with a series of excuses that didn't quite amount to bare-faced lies.

With the state I was in, I thought I'd better leave in hugely good time for the plane, so I ordered a cab and ran around the house in a frenzy of closing windows and half-closing curtains. I had phoned Mary. She would come in and switch on lights in the evening. Anyway, what was there to steal? They were welcome to it. One thing more. Long transatlantic flight. Soft shoes. I had a pair of nice blue canvas slip-ons. Where were they? Had I even un-packed them since the move? I remembered. Bedroom cupboard. At the top. I ran upstairs. In the bedroom—*our* bedroom I would once have said—I looked around. I could see nothing I'd forgotten.

There was a knock at the door. I don't mean the front door. A rap at the bedroom door.

"Mrs. Hintlesham?"

"What?" I said, startled.

A face peered round the door. I was completely baffled for a moment. You know when you see a face completely out of its normal setting. A good-looking young man in jeans and a T-shirt and a black work jacket. Long dark hair. Who was he?

"Hack. What are you—"

"That's not my real name. That's just something that impresses the boys."

"What's your real name?"

"Morris," he said. "Morris Burnside."

"Well, Morris Burnside, I'm in a bit of a rush. I'm off to the airport."

"The game," he said, brandishing a gaudy package. "I rang, remember? Sorry, the door was open and I wandered in. I shouted from downstairs."

"Oh. Well, you're lucky you caught me. The cab will be here at any moment."

He was actually panting, as if he'd been running.

"Yes, I'm really glad because . . . It's not just the game. I saw the evening paper. There's something in it about your husband being charged."

"What? Oh, God. I thought that might happen."

"I'm really sorry, Mrs. Hintlesham. And I know how difficult it will be for Josh."

"Yes, I know. Hang on, I'm just reaching down these shoes. There."

"That's why I wanted to come and see you right away.

You see, I've been thinking about it, and Mr. Hintlesham couldn't have done it."

"That's very nice of you, er, Morris, but . . ."

I slipped my shoes on. It was almost time to go.

"No, it's not just that. I know how your husband can prove that he's innocent."

"What do you mean?"

"It's absolutely foolproof. When they find your body they'll know he can't have done it."

"What?" I asked dully and felt a wave of alarm.

He was close to me and there was a very sudden movement, something flashing over my head and drawn tight around my neck. He was now right against me, his breath hot on my face, and looking down on me.

"You can't speak," he said to me almost in a whisper. His face was so close to mine he could have kissed me. "You can hardly breathe. One pull on this and you'll be dead." His face had gone red now, gorged with blood, his eyes staring at me, but his voice when it came was almost gentle. "It doesn't matter now. There's nothing you can do."

I lost control. I felt warm and wet between my legs. I was peeing myself. I heard it trickle and splash on the floorboards. I thought of my waters breaking. That was a good thing. Christo was away. Christo was with my parents. Josh and Harry were far far away. That was good.

His face crinkled in disgust.

"Now look what you've done," he said. "With your clothes on as well."

This was the last thing I was ever going to see, his face, and I wanted to ask why and I couldn't.

"Pity about the cab," he said. "I thought I'd have a long time. I wanted time to show my love for you but now I've only got a little time."

He tightened the cord again and held it in place with one hand. He reached to one side and the other hand reappeared. I saw a blade.

"I love you, Jenny," he said.

All I wanted was blackness, to sink into numbness. But I didn't. I couldn't.

PART THREE
Nadia

ONE

I was in a hurry. Well, I wasn't in a hurry at all. But I thought if I created an impression of hurry, I might trick myself into getting something done. By the time I realized my mistake, it would be too late. I would be back in control of my life.

I found an old cotton skirt under my bed and pulled that on, with a black sleeveless T-shirt over the top so the chocolate stain was hidden. An overexcited child must have rammed into me holding a Mars bar or something. I glanced at myself in the mirror. My hair looked like a cartoon of a swarm of bees and I still had a smear of face-paint on my cheek.

Coffee. That would be a start. I found a cup and rinsed it out in the bathroom, where I also filled the kettle. The sink in the kitchen was unreachable: a tower of encrusted dishes and pans. When I'd completed my tax return, I'd wash them. That was another good idea. That obnoxious unsanitary pile of dirty crockery would be my way of blackmailing myself into getting things in order.

I took my coffee over to my desk, along with a half a bar of chocolate. I'd also start having breakfasts of muesli and chopped-up fresh fruit. Four servings of vegetables and six servings of fruit. That was what I was meant to have every day. Chocolate came from a bean, didn't it?

I might as well get this over with. The final demand from the Inland Revenue lay on top of the computer keyboard. It had been sent several weeks ago, but I'd put it in the drawer with all my other unopened letters and tried not to think about it. Max used to say that I should go to see a therapist, just about my inability to open my mail. Sometimes I let it go for weeks. I don't know why. I know I'm stacking up trouble for myself. And it's not as if it is all stuff I don't want, like bills and library fines. I also leave unopened checks, letters from friends, invitations to jobs that I could certainly do with at the moment. Later, I tell myself. I'll do it later. When the drawer's full up.

This was the moment when later had arrived. I swept a packet of biscuits and a straw hat off the chair and sat down; turned on the computer and watched the screen glow green. I clicked the mouse on "Accounts," and then on "Expenses." It was good. It was very good. I worked for an hour. I rummaged around my desk, behind the desk, in pockets of jackets. I opened envelopes. I unscrewed old receipts and invoices. My life was taking shape. I decided to print it out to be on the safe side. A small window appeared: "Unknown error, type 18." What did that mean? I clicked again, but the cursor didn't move. Everything was frozen. I jabbed at the keys furiously, really hard, as if I could move the cursor by physical force. Nothing happened. Now what? Now what was I supposed to do? My life, my new ordered life, was there somewhere behind the screen, and I couldn't get at it. I put my head in my hands and cursed and whimpered. I banged the top of the monitor. I stroked it pleadingly.

"Please," I said. "I'll be good from now on."

I needed to look at the manual, but I didn't have a manual. The computer had been bequeathed to me by a friend of Max's. Then I remembered the card that had been slid under my windscreen wiper last week. Help with your computer. At the time I had laughed and tossed it aside. But where had I tossed it? I opened the top drawer of my desk: tampons, chewing gum, leaking pens, cellotape, wrapping paper, a travel Scrabble set, a handful of photographs I didn't even recognize. I tipped out the contents of my shoulder bag: lots of spare change, a scrumpled ball of tissues, an old key, a pack of playing cards, a couple of marbles, one earring, several rubber bands, a lipstick and a juggling ball and a few pen tops. I looked through my wallet, among the credit cards, the receipts, the foreign bank notes and the photo-booth snap of Max. I threw away the photo. No card.

Nor was it under the sofa cushions, or in the chipped teapot I use to store odd things, or in my jewelry drawer, or in the pile of papers on the kitchen table. I'd probably used it as a bookmark. I went in the bedroom and leafed through the books I'd read or looked at recently. I found a dried four-leaf clover in *Jane Eyre*, and a flyer for take-away pizzas in a guide to Amsterdam.

Or had I stuffed it contemptuously in my pocket? What had I been wearing that day? I started riffling through my jackets, trousers, shorts, all the clothes that were lying about my bedroom and bathroom, waiting for wash day. I discovered it inside a suede boot under an armchair. It must have landed there like a fallen leaf when I had tossed it aside. I straightened it out and looked at the writing: COMPUTER TROUBLE? it read in bold type. BIG OR SMALL, CALL ME AND I'LL SORT YOU. In smaller type was the phone number, which I immediately dialed.

"Hello."

"Are you the computer thing?"

"Yeah."

He sounded young, friendly, highly intelligent.

"Thank the Lord. My computer is paralyzed. Everything's there. My whole life."

"Where do you live?"

I felt my spirits lift. Great. I had pictured myself carrying it across London.

"Camden, quite near the tube station."

"How about this evening?"

"How about now? Please. Trust me. I wouldn't ask unless it wasn't a major emergency."

He laughed. It was a nice laugh, boyish. Reassuring. Like a doctor.

"I'll see what I can do. Are you in during the day?"

"Always. That would be great." I quickly gave him my address and phone number before he could make an excuse. Then I added: "By the way, my flat's a complete tip." I looked around. "I mean, really a tip. And my name's Nadia, Nadia Blake."

"See you later."

TWO

L ess than half an hour later, he knocked on the door. It was almost insanely convenient. He was like one of those handymen my dad's always going on about, who used to exist in the great old days of lamplighters and chimney sweeps. He was the sort of person who comes straight around to your house and fixes something. Even better, he wasn't really from the old days. He wasn't one of these middle-aged men in a uniform who calls you madam and has a clipboard and a van with the name of his company written on the side and then gives you an invoice at the end for an amount that makes you realize it would have been cheaper to replace the toilet rather than have it unblocked.

He was just one of us, except a bit younger. A bit younger than me, anyway. He was tall, casually dressed in sneakers, gray trousers, a T-shirt, and a battered jacket that must have been hot in this tropical weather. He had pale skin, long dark hair that reached his shoulders. All-right-looking, and not actually tongue-tied at all, like computer nerds are supposed to be.

"Hello," he said, holding out his hand. "I'm Morris Burnside. The repairman."

"Fantastic," I said. "Fantastic. I'm Nadia."

I showed him inside.

"Burglars?" he said, looking around.

"No, I told you on the phone it was a tip. Doing a cleanup is at the top of my priority list."

"Can't you take a joke? I think it's nice. Lovely big doors leading out into the garden."

"Yes, very horticultural. The garden is also on the list. A bit lower down."

"Where's the patient?"

"Through here." The offending machine was in my bedroom. You actually have to sit on the bed to operate it. "Do you want some tea?"

"Coffee. Milk, no sugar."

But I hung around, waiting for his response to my problem. In a perverse way, it was like going to the doctor with some small ache. If it turns out to be something reasonably serious, you feel quite proud, as if you've offered the doctor something worthy of his attention. On the other hand, if you turn out to be almost not ill at all, you feel rather ashamed. I wanted to have a healthy computer and yet at the same time I wanted to have something that provided a challenge for Morris the Nerd and made his journey worthwhile. It wasn't to be.

He took off his jacket and tossed it on the bed. I was surprised. I expected thin, stringy arms, but they were muscled and sinewed. He had a large chest. This was a man who worked out. With my five-foot-nothing height and general wispiness, I felt puny next to him.

"Space Buddy," I said.

"What?" he said, and then looked down and smiled. "My shirt? I don't know who makes these slogans up. I reckon it's a computer in Japan where somebody joined up the wrong wires."

"So," I said. "As you can see, it's just frozen. Usually I can just tap on the keyboard and in the end *something* will happen, but I've bashed and bashed and nothing has any effect." He sat on the bed and looked at the screen. "I mean, it says that there's a type-eighteen error, as if that means anything to anybody. I was wondering whether it would just be best to pull the plug out and try to restart it. But maybe that would damage it."

Morris leaned forward slowly. With his left hand he held down several of the larger keys on the left of the keyboard, then with his right hand he pressed the Return key. The screen went black and then the computer relaunched itself.

"Is that it?" I asked.

He stood up and grabbed his jacket.

"If it happens again, press these three keys together and the Return. If that doesn't work, there should be a little hole at the back of this unit." He picked it up and blew some dust away. "Here. Push a matchstick in. That will almost always work. If all else fails, pull the plug out."

"I'm so sorry," I said breathlessly. "I'm just hopeless with this stuff, I feel very bad about it. One day I'll learn. I'll go on a course."

"Don't bother," he said. "Women aren't meant to know how to operate computers. That's what men were invented for."

I was in a bit of a rush because I had to get my stuff together, but I didn't feel I could just push him out the door.

"I'll get you the coffee," I said. "If I can find it."

"Can I use your bathroom?"

"Yes, it's through there. Can I apologize in advance for it?"

"How much do I owe you?" I asked.

"Don't worry," Morris said. "I wouldn't take your money for what I did."

"That's ridiculous, you must have a call-out fee."

He smiled. "The coffee will be fine."

"How are you going to make a living if you go around doing things for nothing? Are you some kind of mahatma?"

"No, no, I do lots of computer stuff, software stuff, some schools, whatever. This is just a hobby." There was a pause. "What do *you* do?"

I always had a sinking feeling when I had to launch into this particular explanation.

"It's not exactly a job, and I wouldn't portray it as a career, but just at the moment I'm working as a sort of entertainer. Children's parties."

"What?"

"That's it. Me and my partner, Zach—I mean my *business* partner—we go to parties and do a few tricks, let them stroke a gerbil, tie some balloons into shapes, do a puppet show."

"That's amazing," said Morris.

"It's not exactly rocket science, but it's more or less a living. Hence the need for keeping accounts, et cetera, et cetera. And I really am sorry, Morris; I don't feel good wasting your time like this. I don't expect you to be amused by my impersonation of a helpless female."

"Couldn't your boyfriend fix it for you?"

"What makes you think I've got a boyfriend?" I said with a slightly sly expression.

Morris went red.

"I didn't mean anything by it," he said. "I just saw the shaving foam in the bathroom. Extra toothbrush, that sort of thing."

"Oh, *that*. Max—i.e., this person I've been involved with—left some stuff behind when he scarpered a couple of weeks ago. When I get around to my clear-up, all that will be right at the bottom of the bin bag."

"I'm sorry," he said.

I didn't want to get into all *that*.

"So my computer is fully functional," I said brightly, finishing my mug of coffee.

"What is it? Three years old?" he asked.

"I don't know. It used to belong to a friend of a friend."

"I don't know how you can use it. Isn't it like walking through a swamp wrapped in cotton wool?" Morris said. He looked at it with narrowed eyes. "You need some memory. Faster hamsters. That's what it's all about."

"I beg your pardon? Faster *hamsters*. What are they?"

He grinned. "Sorry. An expression."

"I had a hamster when I was a girl. It wasn't at all fast."

"All I mean is that your machine is a Stone Age implement, anyway."

"That doesn't sound good."

"For a grand you could have a machine that was a thousand times more powerful. You could be on-line. You could have your own Web site. There's a spreadsheet that could handle all your own accounts. I could set it up for you if you like. You could see me being a grown-up computer consultant."

I started to feel a little dizzy.

"That's fantastically nice of you, Morris, but I think you may have got me mixed up with a woman who can cope with the world."

"No, Nadia, you're wrong. A proper system will make everything easier for you. It will put you in control."

"Stop," I said firmly. "I don't want a computer that can do more; I want one that can do less. I don't want a Web site. I've got six months' ironing to do."

Morris looked disappointed. He put his coffee mug down on the table.

"If you change your mind," he said. "Then you've got my card."

"I certainly have."

"And maybe, we could, you know, maybe we could meet for a drink sometime."

There was a ring on the front doorbell. Zach. Thank God. It is a statistical fact that seventy-nine percent of male people I meet ask me out. Why don't I intimidate men more? I looked at him. The harps were not playing. No.

"That's my partner," I said. "I'm afraid we're going to rush out. And . . ." I gave a sensitive pause. "I'm feeling a bit wobbly at the moment. I'm not quite ready. I'm sorry."

"Of course," Morris said, not meeting my eyes. "I completely understand."

That was nice of him. He followed me to the door. I introduced Morris to Zach as they passed in the doorway.

"This is a man," I said, "who comes and fixes computers for nothing."

"Really?" said Zach, looking interested. "I'm totally baffled by mine. Any chance of taking a look?"

"Sorry," said Morris. "It was a once-only offer. Never to be repeated."

"That's what I always seem to find," said Zach bleakly.

Morris nodded at me pleasantly and was gone.

I have found her. My perfect third. She is small, like the others, but strong, full of energy. She glows with it. Skin like honey, glossy chestnut hair, but all in a tangle, green-brown eyes the color of a walnut, copper-colored freckles scattered over her nose and cheeks. Autumn colors for the end of the summer. Firm chin. White teeth. She smiles easily, tips her head back a bit when she laughs, gestures when she speaks. Not shy, this one, but at ease with herself. Like a cat by the fire. Her skin looks warm. Her hand was warm and dry when I shook it. I knew as soon as I saw her that she was right for me. My challenge. My sweetheart. Nadia.

THREE

We ought to have another trick or something." Zach frowned at me over his frothy pink milk shake. "Something new, anyway."

"Why?"

"If we get invited back to a house."

I have two magic tricks (three if you count the wand that collapses into segments when I depress a little lever at the base, amazing to anyone under the age of four). The first one involves putting a white silk scarf into an empty bag—the children know that it is empty because several of them have put their grubby little hands in it before I start—and then, hey presto, when I pull it out it's turned a tie-dyed pink and purple. In the second, I make balls disappear and reappear. They're basic tricks. Extremely basic. Rudimentary. But I've perfected them over the years. The point is to make the audience look in the wrong direction. Then if they gasp, resist the temptation to repeat it. And don't tell anybody—even curious parents—how they're done. I once told Max. I did the balls and he was amazed. And curious. How d'ye do it? How d'ye do it? He went on and on. So I showed him and I watched his face fall in disappointment. Was that all? What did he expect? I shouted at him. It's a fucking trick.

I can juggle, too. Only with three balls, like everybody else. Nothing hard. But I don't use just multicolored bean-bags; I can juggle with bananas and shoes and mugs and teddy bears and umbrellas. Kids love it when I break eggs juggling. They assume that I do it on purpose, that I'm just clowning around.

Zach is much better at the puppet shows than I am. I can only do two different voices and they sound exactly the same. Sometimes we do cook-a-meal parties—you come along with all the ingredients and teach a group of children how to make fairy cakes and sticky icing and ham-burgers and how to cut circular ham sandwiches with pastry cutters. Then they eat everything while you clear up the mess. And if you're lucky the mother makes you a cup of tea.

I'm the clown, the jester, noisy and bright and chaotic and falling over my own feet. Zach's the glum, serious sidekick. We'd just been to the party of a five-year-old called Tamsin—a roomful of tyrannical little girls in dresses that looked like meringues—and I was sweaty and ex-hausted after all my animated screeching. I wanted to go home, have a nap, read a newspaper in the bath.

"Insects," Zach said suddenly. "I heard of a guy who takes bugs and reptiles to children's parties and the children just touch them. That's all there is to it."

"I'm not keeping insects and reptiles in my flat."

He slurped his milk shake and looked wistful.

"We could get some sort of insect that would bite the children. No, that wouldn't work. We'd be prosecuted. What would be better would be one that passed on a serious dis-ease to the children, so that they got very ill, but only much later."

"Sounds good."

"Don't you hate 'Happy Birthday'?" he said.

"Hate it."

We grinned at each other.

"And you were terrible at juggling today."

"I know. I'm out of practice. They'll never invite us back. But that's fine, because Tamsin's dad put his arm around me." I stood up to go. "Do you want to share a cab?"

"No, it's okay."

We kissed each other and wandered off in our separate directions.

Going back to the flat has been strange for the past few weeks, since Max left. I had only just got used to him being there: the toilet seat up instead of down, the wardrobe full of his suits and shirts, freshly squeezed orange juice and bacon in the fridge, another body in the bed—at night telling me I was beautiful, and in the morning telling me to get the fuck up because I was late again—someone to make meals for, someone to make meals for me and rub my back and order me to eat breakfast. Someone to make plans with and alter my life for. I had occasionally resented it, the limiting of my freedom. He'd nagged at me to be neater, more organized in my life. He thought I was a slob. He thought I was too dreamy. The things he had once found charming about me had begun to irritate him. But now I found that I missed sharing my life. I needed to learn to live alone once more. The delights of selfishness: I could eat chocolate in bed again, and make porridge for supper, and see *The Sound of Music* on video, and blue-tack notes to the wall, and be in a bad mood without worrying about it. I could meet someone new and begin the whole dizzying, delicious, dismaying round again.

All around me, friends were beginning to settle down. They were in the jobs that they had trained for, with pensions and prospects. They had mortgages, washing machines, office hours. Lots were married, several even had babies. Maybe that was why Max and I had separated. It had become obvious that we weren't going to open a joint bank account and have children with his hair and my eyes.

I was beginning to make convoluted scary calculations about how much of my life I had already lived, and how much time I had left; what I've done and will do. I am twenty-eight. I don't smoke, or hardly ever, and I eat lots of fruit and vegetables. I walk up stairs instead of taking the lift, and I have been known to go running. I reckon I've got at least fifty years to go, maybe sixty. That's enough time to learn how to develop my own films, to go whitewater rafting and see the northern lights, to meet the man of my dreams. Or the men of my dreams, more like. Last week I read a newspaper story about how women will soon be able to have babies when they're in their sixties, and I caught myself feeling relieved.

Probably, I thought, Max would be at the party I was going to tonight. I promised myself, as I went home through the clogged traffic, that I was going to make myself look lovely. I would wash my hair and wear my red dress and laugh and flirt and dance and he'd see what he had walked out on, and he would see that I didn't give a damn. I am not lonely without him.

I did wash my hair. I ironed my dress. I lay in a bath full of oils, with candles all round the edge, although it was still bright daylight outside. Then I ate two pieces of toast and Marmite and a cool, gleaming nectarine.

In the end, Max wasn't even there, and after a bit I stopped looking round for him every time someone new walked through the door. I met a man called Robert, who was a lawyer with thick eyebrows, and a man called Terence, who was a pain. I danced rather wildly with my old mate Gordon, who had introduced me to Max all those months ago. I talked for a bit with Lucy, whose thirtieth birthday party this was, and her new boyfriend, who was about seven feet high with bleached hair. He had to lean right down to me; it made me feel like a dwarf, or a child. And at half past eleven, I left and went out for a meal at a Chinese restaurant with my old friends Cathy and Mel and got mildly drunk, but in the nicest way possible. Spare ribs and slimy noodles and cheap red wine, until I started feeling cold in my thin red dress. Cold and tired and I wanted suddenly to go home and climb into my large bed.

It was past one when I came back to the flat. Camden Town comes alive after midnight. The pavements were crawling with strange people, some languorous and some rather frenzied. A man in a green ponytail tried to grab me, but shrugged and grinned when I told him to piss off. A beautiful girl, wearing almost nothing, was twirling round and round on the pavement near my road, like a spinning top. Nobody seemed to be taking any notice of her.

I stumbled in through the front door and turned on the hall light. There was a letter on the doormat. I picked it up and looked at the handwriting. I didn't recognize it. Neat black italics: *Ms. Nadia Blake.* I slid my finger under the gummed flap and slid out the letter.

FOUR

Did he ransack the flat as well?"

"What's that?"

Links gestured at the mess, the cushions on the floor, the papers piled up on the carpet.

"No," I said. "It's just me. I've been a bit busy. I'm going to deal with it."

The detective looked nonplussed for a moment, as if he had just woken up and wasn't exactly sure where he was.

"Er, Miss er . . ."

"Blake."

"Yes, Miss Blake. Do you mind if I smoke?"

"Go ahead."

I rummaged around and found an ashtray, carved, as it happened, in the shape of the island of Ibiza. I suddenly started worrying about possible drug connotations, but Detective Chief Inspector Links apparently had more urgent things on his mind. He didn't look a well man. I've got an uncle who's had three heart attacks and still smokes, even though he has difficulty exerting enough suction to keep the cigarette alight. And a friend of Max's is recovering from a major nervous breakdown that involved him being institutionalized. That was a year ago but he still talks in the quavery voice of somebody trying not to cry. Links reminded me of both of them. Watching him light his cigarette was an exercise in suspense. His fingers shook so much that he could barely get the match together with the end of the cigarette, and then only for an inadequate microsecond. He looked as if he were trying to light it in the crow's nest of a North Sea trawler rather than in my relatively draft-free living room.

"Are you all right?" I asked. "Can I get you something? Would you like some tea?"

Links started to speak but was seized with a fit of bronchitic coughing that sounded very painful. All he could do was shake his head.

"Some honey and lemon?"

He carried on shaking. He took a dirty-looking handkerchief from his side pocket and wiped his eyes. When he spoke it was in quite a low voice, so I had to lean forward to catch what he was saying.

"It's a matter of . . ." He paused for a moment. He kept losing the thread of what he was saying. "Of establishing access. That is, who has access."

"Yes," I said wearily. "You already said that. It seems like a lot of trouble to go to over one sick letter. It'll be a big job. I have people to stay quite often. My boyfriend was here a lot. There are people in and out all the time. I was just away for a couple of months and a girlfriend of mine stayed here. Apparently it was virtually open house while she was here."

"Where is she now?" Links asked in what was not much more than a miserable gasp.

"I think she's in Prague. She was doing some work there on her way back to Perth."

Links looked round at his colleague. The other policeman, Detective Inspector Stadler, looked a better insurance risk than Links. A bit wasted maybe, in an oddly attractive way. He was just completely impassive. He had straight hair combed back over his head, prominent cheekbones, and dark eyes, which he kept focused on me every second as if I were very very interesting but in a slightly odd way—I felt more like a car crash than a woman. Now he spoke for the first time:

"Have you any idea who the note may have come from? Have you had anything similar? Any threatening calls? Any strange encounters with people?"

"Oh, endless strange encounters," I said. Links perked up and looked very slightly less like one of the undead. "My job involves going into different houses every week. I should explain that I'm not a burglar." They didn't smile at all. Not remotely. "Me and my partner, we entertain at children's parties. The people you meet—honestly, you wouldn't believe it. I can tell you that being hit on by the father of the five-year-old you've just done a show for while the mother is in the kitchen lighting the candles on the cake—well, it lowers your view of human nature."

Links stubbed out his cigarette, which he'd only just half smoked, and lit another.

"Miss, erm . . ." He looked down at his notebook. "Miss, erm." He seemed to be having trouble reading his notes. "Erm, Blake. We have, erm, reason to believe that, currently, or as of the more recent, er, months, there may have been, er, other women also targeted by this person." He kept darting glances toward Stadler, as if in search of moral support. "So one aim of our inquiries will be to establish, or, that is, to attempt to establish, possible connections between them."

"Who are they?"

Links coughed again. Stadler made no attempt to fill in for him. He just sat and stared at me.

"Well," he said finally, "it may not be appropriate, as of this stage of the inquiry, to, erm, furnish precise details. It may hinder aspects of the investigation."

"Are you worried I might try to get in touch with them?"

Links took out his handkerchief and blew his nose. I looked across at Stadler. For the first time he wasn't looking back. He seemed to be finding something of great interest in a notebook.

"We'll keep you as in touch with our progress as we can," Links said.

"Investigation?" I said. "It's just a letter."

"It's important to take these matters seriously. Also, we have a psychologist, a Dr. Grace Schilling, who is an expert on, er . . . She should be here"—he looked at his watch—"at any minute, really."

There was a silence.

"Look," I said. "I'm not stupid. I had a break-in about a year ago—well, nothing was taken. I think I disturbed them. But it took the police about a day to get here and they did sod-all about it. Now I get a single nasty letter and it's a major operation. What's going on? Don't you have real grown-up crimes to solve?"

Stadler snapped his notebook shut and put it in his pocket.

"We've been accused of not being sufficiently sensitive to offenses targeted against women," he said. "We take threats of this kind very seriously."

"Oh, well," I said. "That's good, I suppose."

Dr. Schilling was the kind of woman I rather envied. She'd obviously done really well at school, got fantastic grades, and still looked rather intelligent. She dressed pretty elegantly as well, but even that was in an intelligent sort of way. She had this long blond hair that looked great but that she'd obviously pinned up in about three and a half seconds to show that she didn't take it all *too* seriously. She certainly wasn't the sort of person you'd catch standing on her head in front of a group of screaming tots. If I'd known she was coming I really would have tidied up the flat. The only thing that irritated me was that she had this air of extremely serious, almost sad, concern when she addressed me, as if she were presenting a religious TV program.

"I understand you've been in a relationship which ended," she said.

"I can tell you that that letter wasn't written by Max. For all sorts of reasons, including the fact that he would have trouble composing a letter to the milkman. Anyway, he was the one that walked out."

"All the same, that might mean you were in a vulnerable state."

"Well, a pissed-off state, maybe."

"How tall are you, Nadia?"

"Don't rub it in. I try not to think about it. Just a little over five foot. An emotionally vulnerable dwarf. Is that the point you're trying to make? *You* should be all right, then."

She didn't even smile.

"Should I be worried?" I asked.

Now there was a very long pause. When Dr. Schilling spoke, it was with great precision.

"I don't think it would be . . . well, productive, to get alarmed. But I think you should behave as if you were worried, just to be on the safe side. You have been threatened. You should act as if the threat means what it says."

"Do you really think somebody just wants to kill me for no reason?"

She looked thoughtful.

"No reason?" she said. "Maybe. There are a lot of men

who feel they have very good reasons for attacking or killing women. They may not be reasons that would convince you or me. But that isn't much comfort, is it?"

"It's not much comfort to *me*," I said.

"No," said Dr. Schilling, almost inaudibly, as if she were talking to somebody else, somebody I couldn't see.

FIVE

They stayed and stayed. After a couple of hours Links received a message and shambled away, but Stadler and Dr. Schilling remained. While Schilling talked to me, Stadler went out and came back with sandwiches, cartons of drink, milk, fruit. Then, while he took me through the flat examining my security arrangements (to be substantially upgraded), she retreated into my kitchen area, made some tea. I even heard the rattle and clink and splashing of washing-up being done. She returned clutching mugs. Stadler took off his jacket and rolled up his sleeves.

"There's tuna and cucumber, salmon and cucumber, chicken salad, ham and mustard," he announced.

I took the ham, Dr. Schilling took the tuna, which made me think the tuna must be vastly healthier and that there was something slightly squalid and frivolous about my choice.

"Are you some kind of medical policewoman?" I asked.

Her mouth was full, so she could only shake her head while laboriously attempting to swallow her sandwich. I felt a moment of triumph. I'd caught her looking undignified.

"No, no," she said, as if I'd insulted her. "I do consulting work for them," she said.

"What's your real job?" I asked.

"I work at the Welbeck Clinic," she said.

"What as?"

"Grace is being too modest," Stadler said. "She is eminent in her field. You're lucky to have her on your side."

Schilling looked sharply round at him, and went red, almost in anger or distress, I thought, rather than embarrassment. All these looks and whispered asides. I felt like an intruder into a group of old friends who had their own special catchphrases, jargon, their shared happy history of working together.

"What I really meant," I was saying, "is that I'm a children's party entertainer. I often don't have much pressure on my time during the weekdays when everybody else is in their offices. But you, Dr. Schilling . . ."

"Please, Nadia, call me Grace," she murmured.

"All right, Grace. I know that doctors are incredibly busy people, which I've discovered every time I've wanted to see one. I freely confess that this is very pleasant sitting here and chatting, and I'm extremely willing to talk about my life in whatever detail you want. But I was just thinking why a grand psychiatrist like you is sitting here on the floor of a crappy bedsit in Camden Town eating a tuna sandwich. You're not looking at your watch, you're not receiving calls on your mobile. It seems strange to me."

"It's not strange," Stadler said, wiping his mouth. He'd had the salmon. I bet the ham sandwich was the cheapest as well as being the most unhealthy. "What we want to do is to make a plan of how to proceed. We want to give you informal protection, and the purpose of this meeting is to decide what kind. As for Dr. Schilling, she is an authority on harassment of this kind and she has two objectives. Most important, of course, is to help us to find the person who has sent you this threat. To do that she needs to look at you and your life, to get a sense of what has attracted this madman."

"It's my responsibility, is it?" I said. "I've led him on?"

"It's not your responsibility in any way," Grace said urgently. "But he chose you."

"I think you're being daft," I said. "This is a guy who gets off on sending rude letters to women because he's scared of them. What's the big deal?"

"You're not right," Grace said. "A letter like that is a violent act. A man who sends a letter like that has—well, he may have—crossed a boundary. He must be considered dangerous."

I looked at her, puzzled.

"Do you think I'm not getting frightened enough?"

She drained her mug of tea. She almost looked as if she were playing for time.

"I may advise you what you should do," she said. "I don't think I should tell you what to feel. Here, give me your mug. I'll get some more tea."

Subject closed. Stadler gave a cough.

"What I'd like to do," he said, "if it's all right, is to talk to you a bit about your life, who your friends are, the kind of people you meet, your habits, that sort of thing."

"You don't look like a policeman," I said.

He gave a slight start. Then he smiled.

"What's a policeman meant to look like?" he asked.

He was a difficult man to embarrass, or at least for me to embarrass. I had never met anyone before who looked me in the eyes the way he did, almost as if he were trying to look inside. What was he trying to see?

"I don't know," I said. "You just don't have a police look about you. You look, er—"

And I ground to a halt because what I was feeling my way toward saying was that he was too good-looking to be a policeman, which was both a deeply foolish comment and miles away from being remotely appropriate to the situation and, in any case, Grace Schilling had just come in with more tea.

"Normal," I said, belatedly ending the sentence.

"That's all?" he said. "I thought you might say something nicer than that."

I made a face.

"I think it's nice not to look like a policeman."

"Depends what you think policemen look like."

"Am I interrupting something?" Grace asked with a touch of irony.

Then the phone rang. It was Janet. She was checking about our arrangement to meet. I covered the mouthpiece.

"It's one of my best friends," I said in a stage whisper. "I arranged to meet her for a drink early this evening. By the way, she definitely didn't write the note."

"Not today," said Stadler.

"Are you serious?"

"Indulge us."

I pulled another face and made an excuse to Janet. She was very understanding, of course. She wanted to chat, but I wound the conversation down. Grace and Stadler seemed a bit too interested in what I was saying.

"Is this some kind of joke?" I said.

"What do you mean?"

"I'm beginning to feel persecuted," I said. "But not by the sad bastard who wrote that letter. I feel like something lying on a card with a pin through me. I'm still wiggling around and somebody's looking at me through a microscope."

"Is that what you feel?" asked Grace earnestly.

"Oh, don't start," I said hotly. "For God's sake, don't tell me that that's significant."

Anyway, it was only half what I felt. We sat there for the afternoon and I made tea and then coffee and found biscuits in a tin. And I dug out the scraps of paper that I call an appointment book, and I went through my address book and I held forth about my life. Every so often one of them would ask a question. It started to rain for the first time in days and days, and all of a sudden I didn't feel like a rare specimen being examined prior to dissection, but instead like someone spending time with two rather strange new friends. Sitting on the floor with rain running down the windows, it just felt reassuring as much as anything.

"Can you really juggle?" Stadler asked at one point.

"Can I juggle?" I said pugnaciously. "You watch this." I looked around the room. There was some fruit in the bowl.

When I grabbed two wrinkled apples and a tangerine, a puff of tiny flies flew up into the air. Something was going off in there.

"I'll deal with that," I said. "Now look."

I started juggling with them, then, rather carefully, walked up and down the room. I stumbled on a cushion and they fell to the floor.

"That gives you a general idea," I said.

"Can you do more than that?" he asked.

I made a scoffing sound.

"Juggling with four balls is very boring," I said. "You just hold two in each hand and throw them up and down with no interchanges."

"What about five?"

I made my scoffing sound again.

"Five is for mad people. To juggle five balls you need

to sit in a room alone for three months and do nothing else. I'm saving up five balls for when I get sent to prison or become a nun or get stranded on a desert island. They're only toddlers, and in any case it's only a phase I'm going through while I work out what I'm going to do with the rest of my life."

"That's no excuse," said Stadler. "We want to see five balls, don't we?"

"Minimum," said Grace.

"Shut up," I said. "Or I'll show you my magic tricks."

SIX

I can't explain what happened next. Or at least I can't explain it so it makes proper sense.

Grace Schilling left. She put her hands on my shoulders when she said good-bye and stared at me for a moment, as if she were going to kiss me, or cry. Or say something deeply serious. Then Stadler told me that they had arranged for a policewoman, Officer Burnett, to keep an eye on me.

"She's not going to stay here, is she?"

"No, I wanted to explain this to you. Lynne Burnett will be the officer primarily assigned to your protection. At night she or, more often, other officers will be placed outside your house, mainly in a car. Not a police car. During the day she may spend some time inside, but that's a matter for you and her."

"At night?" I said.

"It'll just be for a while."

"What about you?" I said. "Will you be around?"

He looked at me for just a couple of seconds too long, so that I almost started thinking about saying something else, and then the doorbell rang. I started, blinked, smiled blearily at him.

"It'll be Lynne," he said.

"Aren't you going to answer it, then?"

"It's your flat."

"It'll be for you."

He turned on his heel and opened the door. She was younger than me, although not much, and rather lovely. She had a large purple birthmark on her cheek. She didn't dress like a police officer. She was wearing jeans and a T-shirt, and carrying a light blue jacket in her hand.

"I'm Nadia Blake," I said, holding out my hand. "Sorry about the mess, but I wasn't exactly expecting visitors."

She smiled and blushed.

"I'll keep out of your way as much as possible, unless you want me for something," she said. "And I'm rather good at tidying up. Only if you want things tidied," she added hurriedly.

"Everything's got a bit out of hand," I said. I glanced across at Stadler and smiled, but he didn't smile back, just looked at me thoughtfully. I went into my bedroom and sat on the bed, waiting for him to go. I felt tired and odd. What was going on? What was I supposed to do all evening with Lynne hanging around? I couldn't even feel relaxed going to bed early with cheese on toast.

It could have been worse. We ate fried eggs and baked beans for supper, and Lynne told me all about her seven brothers and sisters, and her mother, who was a hairdresser. She did some tidying up, almost as if she needed something to do with her hands. Then she left. Not to go away, of course. She went and sat outside in the car. After tonight, she said, there would be other officers instead; after all, she had to sleep sometimes. I had a long bath, until the tips of my fingers were shriveled, and when I got out I looked out between the crack in the curtains. I could see her silhouette in the car. Was she reading or listening to the radio? I couldn't tell. Probably nothing distracting was allowed. I wondered if I should go out with soup or coffee. I went to bed.

The next day Lynne followed me to the shops; she sat around while I wrote letters. There was a hint of embarrassment when Zach rang up and arranged to come round to go through the appointment book. I put the phone down, looked round at her, and said: "Um . . ."

She instantly responded: "I'll wait outside."

"It's just that—"

"That's fine."

Early in the evening the doorbell rang and she went to answer it. It was Stadler. He was carrying a very serious briefcase, I saw, and wearing a somber suit.

"Hello there, Detective," I said sweetly.

"I've taken over from Lynne for a spell." His expression was impassive. No smile. "Everything all right?"

"Just fine, thanks."

"I thought I'd ask some questions."

He sat on the sofa, and I sat opposite him in the armchair.

"What are your questions, then, Detective?" He had lovely hands. Long, with smooth nails.

He opened his briefcase and fumbled with some papers.

"I wanted to ask you about previous boyfriends," he said.

"You've done that already."

"I realize that, but—"

"You know what? I think I'd prefer talking about my past relationships with Grace Schilling."

He took a deep breath. He seemed ill at ease. I didn't mind that.

"You might find it useful—" he began, but I interrupted him.

"I don't really want to tell you any more details of my sex life."

He gazed at me then, and didn't look down at his notes anymore. I stood up and turned away from him.

"I'm going to have a glass of wine. Do you want one? And don't say, Not while I'm on duty."

"Maybe a very small one."

I poured us both a glass of white wine, neither of them small. We walked out into what there was of the garden. My yard backs onto an industrial unit where containers are stored, but it made a change from being trapped indoors. The rain of yesterday and today had stopped and the air felt fresher than it had for weeks. The leaves of the pear tree glistened.

"I'm going to do lots of work out here soon," I said, as we stood among the bolted plants. "It's like *The Day of the Triffids*. The weeds are taking over."

"It's private, though. No one can see in."

"True."

I took a sip of my wine. He knew a lot about me. He knew about my work, my family, my friends, and my boyfriends; my exam results and my affairs. The things I wanted, like an open-top sports car and a better singing voice and more dignity, and the things I was scared of— like lifts and heights and snakes and cancer. I had talked to him, and to Grace, in the way I would talk to a lover, lying in bed after sex, with quiet dark outside, telling secrets and intimate nonsense. Yet I knew nothing about him, nothing at all. It made me feel giddy.

We began to lean toward each other. Here I go, I thought: another big mistake about to happen. But as I leaned I caught my foot on a thick bramble and stumbled badly. I dropped my glass and landed on my knees in the long, wet grass. He knelt down beside me and put a hand under my elbow.

"Come on, get up," he said in a hoarse voice. "Come on, Nadia."

I put my arms around his neck. He didn't look away. I couldn't tell what he was thinking, what he wanted. I kissed him full and hard on his mouth. His lips were cool; his skin was warm. He didn't push me away and he didn't kiss me back at first. He just knelt there letting me hold him. I saw the lines on his face, the wrinkles round his eyes, and the grooves round his mouth.

"Help me up then," I said.

He pulled me to my feet and we stood together in the wild garden. He was much bigger than me, wide and tall, blotting out the low sun.

I ran a thumb across his lower lip. I held his heavy head in my hands. I kissed him again, harder, for longer. I felt completely tipsy, as if I'd drunk not half a glass but six glasses of wine. I put my hands on his back, beneath his shirt, and pressed myself against him. He felt solid and huge. His arms hung by his sides. I picked up one of his hands, laid it against my hot cheek, then led him back through the double doors and into the sitting room again.

He sat himself in a chair and watched me. I unbuttoned my shirt and then I sat astride him.

"Stadler," I said. "Cameron."

"I shouldn't do this," he said. He burrowed his head between my breasts and I put my hand in his hair. "I really shouldn't." His eyes were closed at last. Then he was on top of me, on the floor, and there was a shoe under my back and an old hairbrush spiking my left foot, and dust everywhere, and he pulled up my skirt and came into me, there on the dirty old floor. Neither of us said a word.

Afterward, he rolled off me and lay on his back beside

me, arms under his head. We spent about ten minutes just lying there, side by side, staring at the ceiling and saying nothing at all.

When Lynne came back, Cameron was on the phone, very businesslike, and I was reading a magazine. We said good-bye to each other quite formally, but then, muttering to Lynne that there was something he had forgotten to check, he followed me into my bedroom with his file under his arm, and closed the door and laid me back on the bed and kissed me again, pushed his head into my neck to muffle his groans, and told me he would be back as soon as he could manage it.

I spent the rest of the evening on my bed, tingling, pretending to read and not turning a single page and not reading a single word.

SEVEN

What's the plan?" I said to Lynne over breakfast.

I think I'm a woman of some degree of resource, but this was more than my brain could deal with. I'd had sex the day before with a man I hardly knew. Now I was having breakfast not with the man but with a woman I hardly knew.

This morning I'd woken out of a turbulent dream that I instantly forgot, and then I remembered what had happened the day before and the day before that. It felt incredible, a violent cartoon of reality, but I looked out of the window and there was Lynne sitting in the front seat, looking dully ahead. What a job. It made being me seem intellectually demanding. I washed and dressed and brushed my hair and teeth in about two minutes and then walked outside and tapped at the window of her car, giving her a start. Some protection.

I said I'd go and get us something for breakfast and she said she'd come with me. She insisted. We bought some croissants in the bakery. She paid half. I toyed with the idea of making her pay for the whole lot since I generally don't have breakfast at all except on special occasions.

We came back, I made coffee and found a jar with about a millimeter of strawberry jam left and we sat down for breakfast. And I asked what the plan was.

"We're taking responsibility for your protection," she said, as if by rote.

I took a big munch of my croissant and washed it down with a swill of coffee. Once I've broken my rule about not eating breakfast, I make sure that I break it properly. There was a long pause, not for reflection but for consumption. I was like a python swallowing a deer. Finally I managed it.

"All the same," I said. "Don't you feel this is all a ridiculous overreaction?"

"It's for your benefit," she said.

"Someone sent me a letter," I said. "Are you going to guard me for the rest of my life?"

"We want to catch the person who's sending the letters," she said.

"What if you don't? You can't carry on like this."

"We'll see," she said. "When the time comes."

In the face of nonsense like that, there was nothing more to be said on the subject.

"I'm embarrassed as well," I said. "My life's ridiculous enough with just me here. You seem great, Lynne, and I'm not criticizing you, but the thought of doing everything I do with a policewoman staring at me doesn't seem cheering."

"We'll talk about that," Lynne said with an earnest expression, as if I'd raised some important point about policy. But we were interrupted by the doorbell. I went over to the door and Lynne hovered in the background. It was Cameron. He looked over my shoulder and nodded toward Lynne.

"Good morning, Miss Blake," he said.

"Oh, please call me Nadia, Detective," I said. "We're very informal here."

"Nadia," he said in a sort of feeble mumble. "I've stopped in to relieve Lynne for a couple of hours."

"Fine," I said, trying to sound bright and casual.

"And make some plan for the day," he continued. "I don't know if you've got any arrangements."

"Yes," I said. "At half past four me and Zach have to be at a children's party in Muswell Hill. And there are two more on the weekend. Maybe more if anybody else rings up."

"That's no problem," said Cameron. "Lynne can accompany you to those."

"It might be a bit obtrusive," I said.

"I'll sit outside," Lynne said. "I can give you a lift."

"Better and better."

Lynne still had a half-full cup of coffee and half a croissant.

"There's no hurry," said Cameron, unnecessarily.

It turned out that there really wasn't any hurry. Lynne sipped her coffee slowly and only toyed with her croissant. She was in the process of buying a flat herself and she started to ask about what it had been like buying mine. Had I sold a flat of my own before buying this one? It was quite a long story and the shorter I tried to make it, the longer it got. Meanwhile Stadler walked around the room scrutinizing it in some supposedly expert and dispassionate way, picking up objects, opening drawers. I couldn't help feeling that he was looking at me as he did it, finding out more things I wanted to keep to myself. Finally we exhausted the subject of flat-buying. Lynne turned to Cameron.

"Nadia has certain concerns about our plans."

"Basically, I don't know what they are," I said.

"I'll discuss it with her," said Cameron dismissively, and turned away, not continuing the conversation.

She continued holding her coffee. Hadn't this woman had enough of me? Didn't she have a job to do?

"So I'll see you back here about one?" said Cameron.

"Are you going out?" she asked.

"Whatever we do, we'll be here at one."

She nodded.

"Fine. See you later, Nadia."

"See you, Lynne."

She was out of the door. I saw her legs going up the steps outside and reaching the pavement. The legs walked away. Safe. I turned toward Cameron.

"About yesterday . . ."

And he was on me, holding me as if I was unbearably precious, his hands touching my face, stroking my hair. I pushed him away slightly and looked him in the eyes.

"I . . ." I stammered. "I'm not . . ."

"I can't . . ." he murmured, and kissed me again.

I felt his hands behind me now, on my back, then under my T-shirt, feeling for my bra, discovering there wasn't one.

"Do you want me to stop?"

"I don't know. No."

He took my hand and led me into my bedroom. It was different from the day before: more relaxed, more deliberate, slower. I sat down on the bed. He walked to the window and pulled the blind down. Then he closed the bedroom door. He removed his jacket, loosened his tie, and took that off too. It occurred to me that sex with a man who needed to remove a suit and tie was almost a unique experience.

"I can't stop thinking about you," he said, as if it were a symptom. "I see you when I close my eyes. What shall we do?"

"Take your clothes off," I said.

"What?" He looked down, almost as if it were a surprise to see he was still dressed.

He took his clothes off as if in a dream, tossing his trousers into a heap on a chair, looking at me all the time. I reached out my arms toward him.

"Wait," he said. "Wait. Let me. Nadia."

I lay in a fog of pleasure, and then at last he was inside me and later, when it was over and we lay there entwined, he was still looking at me, stroking my hair, saying my name as if it were some kind of magic spell. After a time we moved away from each other and I propped myself up on a pillow.

"That was lovely," I said.

"Nadia," he said. "Nadia."

"And I feel confused," I said.

A spell had been broken. He moved back slightly; a shadow crossed his face; he bit his lip.

"Can I be honest with you?" he said.

Suddenly I felt like shivering.

"Please," I said.

"This job is my whole life," he said. "And this . . ."

"You mean *this*," I said, gesturing at the bed.

He nodded.

"It's so not allowed," he said. "It is so fucking not allowed."

"I won't tell anyone," I said. "Is that it?"

"No," he said bleakly.

"What is it?" I asked. He didn't reply. "Fucking what is it?"

"I'm married," he said. "I'm so sorry. I'm so so sorry."

And he started crying. I was lying there with a naked detective crying in my bed. About eighteen hours of the relationship and we'd already moved from first lust to the weeping and recrimination. I felt sour inside. I didn't say anything. I didn't pat him and stroke him and say that everything was all right, there, there. Finally he gave a huge sigh, as a sign that he was pulling himself together.

"Nadia?"

"Yes?"

"Say something."

"What do you want me to say?"

"Are you furious with me?"

"Oh, Cameron," I said. "Just fucked off. And I suppose your wife doesn't understand you."

"No, no, I don't know. I just know I want you. I'm not messing you around, Nadia, I promise you that. I want you so much. It means so much to me I don't know what to do. Is that all right? What do you think? Nadia, tell me what you think."

I swung round and looked at my frog-shaped clock on the bedside table. Then I leaned over and kissed Cameron's chest.

"What do I think? I have a rule not to sleep with married men; it makes me feel bad. I can't stop thinking about the wife. But I mainly think this is your problem, not mine. And I think that Lynne is due back in about seven minutes."

The speed of putting clothes on was almost amusing. It felt companionable.

"I wonder if I should put different trousers on," I said. "Just to test Lynne's detective skills."

"No, no," said Cameron, looking alarmed.

"Oh, all right," I said.

And we kissed, smiling at each other through the kiss. Married. Why did he have to be married?

* * *

That was on the Wednesday. On Thursday he only had time to talk to me on the phone, while Lynne was in the room, a strange conversation with passionate protestations on his part and blank statements on mine: Yes. Yes. Of course. Yes. I feel that as well. All right. On Friday morning, a team of men moved into my flat and fitted new locks on every door and iron grids over each window. And after lunch he came, and Lynne was needed to provide a report. We had time for a bath.

"I'd like to see your show," he said. "I'd like to see you perform."

"Come tomorrow," I said. "We're performing for a group of four-year-olds just up the road in Primrose Hill."

"I can't," he said, looking away.

"Oh," I said primly, hating myself. "Family business."

"I can't get out of it," he said. "I would if I could."

"That's quite all right," I said. This was why I didn't sleep with married men—the shame and the pain and the guilt of it.

"Are you cross?"

"Not at all."

"Are you sure?"

"Do you want me to be cross?"

He picked up my hand and held it to his cheek. "I'm in love with you, Nadia. I've fallen in love."

"Don't say that. It frightens me. It makes me feel too happy."

She thinks they are invisible. I see them. Kissing. My girl and the policeman kissing. Crashing to the floor. As he stands at the window to close the blinds, I see on his stupid face the besotted, thickened look of a man in love.

I love her more. Nobody can love her the way that I love her. Everyone looks in the wrong direction. They look for hate. Love: That's the key.

EIGHT

Five- and six-year-old girls make the best audiences. They are sweet and admiring, and sit in decorous rows in their silky pastel dresses, with their hair in plaits and their feet in patent leather shoes. When I call one of them up to the front to help me, she'll put her finger in her mouth and speak in a whisper. Eight- and nine-year-old boys are the worst. They jeer at us, and shout out that they know the disappeared object is in my pocket, and they push each other about and surge forward to inspect my box of tricks. They snigger when I drop a ball. The puppet show is for sissies, they say. They sing "Happy Birthday" in a sarcastic shout. They burst all the balloons. And Zach and I have an unbreakable rule: Nobody in double figures.

This party was for five-year-old boys, with a few girls drifting round the edges. It was in a large and handsome house in Primrose Hill that had steps leading up to the front door, an entrance hall you could turn several cartwheels in before reaching the other side, a kitchen the size of my flat, a living room filled with children that stretched back, across a pale, deep carpet, to French windows. The garden was long and well tended, with a patio, a goldfish pond, a series of trellised arches, clipped box hedges, white roses.

"Blimey," I whispered at Zach.

"Just don't break anything," he whispered back.

The birthday boy was called Oliver, and he was small and plump; his cheeks were blotchy with excitement; his friends raged round him like random atoms while he ripped wrapping paper off presents. His mother was called Mrs. Wyndham, and she looked very tall and very thin and very rich and already seemed terminally irritated by the party that was just beginning. She looked doubtfully at me and Zach.

"There are twenty-four of them," she said. "Rather boisterous. You know what boys are like."

"We do," said Zach, dolefully.

"No problem," I said. "If the children go into the garden for a few minutes, we can set up in the living room." I walked into the living room and clapped my hands. "Kids, run outside now. We'll call you when the show is about to begin."

There was a stampede through the French windows. Mrs. Wyndham ran after them, wailing something about her camellia.

Zach and I had made the puppet theater together. We had sawed and nailed. On a canvas sheet we had painted blue mountains, a green forest, the inside of a cottage. We had even made one of our puppets, a lion, out of papier-mâché. It was messy, took ages, and looks like a lump of dried plasticine with a wonky face painted on its knobbly, asymmetrical surface. We bought the rest from a specialist shop. We have a couple of short plays, which Zach wrote. After all, he's the writer. That's what he says he does when anyone asks him. "I write novels," he says firmly, maybe adding as an afterthought that he subsidizes his writing with other things, like being a children's entertainer.

His puppet shows are short and complicated and involve too many different voices. Today's had a boy, a girl, a wizard, a bird, a butterfly, a clown, a fox. I always feel very sweaty afterward.

Zach already knew about the letter, of course, and the police, and all of the precautions they were taking. He'd met Lynne today, for we had given him a lift to Primrose Hill, and he'd sat in the front beside her and talked to her about chaos theory and how the population of India was about to pass one billion while she maneuvered through the traffic, looking dazed.

As we were slotting together the theater, he asked me if I was at all scared by the business.

"No." I hesitated as I hooked the curtains across the miniature stage. But I had to tell someone. "More excited, as a matter of fact."

"That sounds a bit perverse."

"The thing is, Zach, can you keep a secret?" I didn't wait for him to reply. I knew he couldn't. He's famous for being like a sieve. "I'm having a thing with one of the policemen."

"What?"

"I know. It's a bit weird, but—"

"Nadia." He took hold of my shoulders so I had to stop what I was doing. "Are you insane? You can't do this."

"Can't?"

Zach gestured wildly, as if he couldn't show by words alone how badly I was behaving.

"It's not on. It's wrong. It's like having an affair with your doctor. He's taking advantage of you, of your vulnerability. Can't you see? Look, I'm sure that you see it as something beautiful and pure and important, but you've just split up with Max and you're jumping into bed with someone who's supposed to be protecting you."

"Shut up, Zach."

"Father figure. You have to stop it, Nadia."

"He's married," I added miserably. Just saying it made my chest hurt.

Zach gave a sarcastic snort. "But of course."

"He's very attractive. I mean I'd never have thought . . ." I shivered as I remembered that morning, just a few hours ago, when he'd taken over from Lynne for an hour, and we'd made love in the bathroom, up against the tiled wall, fumbling at each other's clothing, desperate.

"Nadia," Zach said urgently. "Oh fuck, here they come."

The boys had returned from the garden.

After the show, I got Oliver to help me do my pathetic magic trick, and the wand collapsed every time he touched it, and all the children shouted "Abracadabra!" as loudly as they could, and Mrs. Wyndham winced in the doorway. Then I asked them to give me strange objects that I could juggle with. One vile child, called Carver, presented me with a cheese grater he had found in the kitchen, but I didn't think Mrs. W wanted blood on the carpet. I chose a melon, a napkin ring, and a drumstick, and I didn't drop any of them. Zach blew up long balloons and twisted them into animal shapes. Then the children bolted into the kitchen for sausages on sticks and jam-filled biscuits and a birthday cake in the shape of a train. And it was over. Zach was desperate for his cigarette, so I pushed him outside.

"Do you mind?" he asked. "Clearing up the stuff?"

"No, go on, scarper."

"Remember what I said, Nadia."

"Sure, sure. Now push off, partner."

"You're not going to stop, are you?"

I shut my eyes for a moment, felt in my imagination his mouth against my throat.

"I don't know. I can't say."

Parents and nannies started arriving—I can tell the difference between the two a mile off. I dismantled the theater and started to stack it into its box. A pretty young woman came up to me with a cup of tea.

"Mrs. Wyndham asked me to bring you this." She had silver-blond hair and a funny, lilting accent.

I took it gratefully.

"Are you Oliver's nanny?"

"No. I came to collect Chris. He lives just down the road." She picked up a puppet and examined it, put it on her hand. "It must be hard, your job."

"Not as hard as yours. Do you have just the one?"

"There are two older ones, but Josh and Harry are at school. Does this go in the bag?"

"Thanks." I gulped at the tea and started loading up. I had this down to an art. She stayed, looking at me. "Where do you come from? Your English is fantastic."

"Sweden. I was meant to go home but there was a bit of fuss."

"Oh," I said vaguely. Where was that wand? I bet Oliver had wandered off with it and worked out how to bend it into segments. "Well, thanks, er . . ."

"Lena."

"Lena."

She disappeared back into the kitchen, where the other nannies were gathered round their charges, watching them stuff chocolate pieces of train into their mouths and talking about boyfriends and nightlife. Children started leaving. "Say thank you," I heard, and "Where's my party bag?" and "Harvey's got a blue one—I want a blue one too."

I picked up all my stuff. Thank God Lynne was out there with her car. There were some advantages to being followed around by a blushing, stubborn policewoman. A small fair-haired boy bumped into me in the hall. He had violet smudges under his eyes and a chocolate smear round his mouth.

"Hi," I said brightly, determined to make a quick exit.

"My mummy's dead," he said, fixing me with his bright gaze.

"Oh well," I said, looking around. The mother was probably in the kitchen somewhere.

"Yup. Mummy died. Daddy says she's gone to heaven."

"Really?" I said.

"No," he said, taking a suck of his lolly. "I don't think she's gone *that* far."

"Well . . ." I said.

"A man killed her dead."

"That can't be true."

"In true life," he insisted.

Lena returned, carrying his jacket. "Come on, Chris, home," she said.

He took her hand.

"I want my party bag first."

"He says his mother was killed," I said.

"Yes," she said simply.

"What? Really?"

I put down the box and bent down to Chris again. "I'm very sorry," I said again, ineptly. I couldn't think what to say.

"Can I have my party bag now?" He tugged on Lena's hand impatiently.

"When did this happen?" I asked Lena.

"Two weeks," she said. "It's a terrible thing."

"Christ." I looked at her with fascination. I'd never been

near someone who'd been near someone who was murdered. "What happened?"

"Nobody knows." She shook her head from side to side so her silver hair swung. "It happened in the home."

I gawked at her.

"How terrible. How terrible for everyone."

Mrs. Wyndham came up with a party bag for Chris. It looked three times as big as everyone else's.

"There you are, darling," she said, and planted a kiss on the top of his head. "If there's anything I can do . . ." She sighed, as if it hurt her just to look at him. "Little lamb." She glanced round at me. "I'll get you your money, Miss Blake. I won't be a minute—it's all ready."

"I've got two packets of sweets and Thomas only got one," said Chris triumphantly. "And I've got a slime ball."

"Here's your money, Miss Blake."

From her tone of finality, it didn't sound as if we would be asked back.

"Thanks." I shouldered all my gear again and turned to go.

"Good luck," I said to the young nanny.

"Thank you."

We lingered in the hall together. I couldn't leave yet. Zach was going back on his own. I had to say good-bye to him.

"Was it a robbery?"

"No," she said.

"He wrote letters," Chris said brightly.

"What?"

Lena nodded and sighed.

"Yes," she said. "It was horrible. Letters saying that she would be killed. Like love letters."

"Like love letters," I repeated dully.

"Yes." She picked up the little boy and he wrapped his legs round her waist. "Come on, Chris."

"Wait. Wait one minute. Didn't she call the police?"

"Oh yes. There were many police."

"She still died?" I said, feeling icy cold.

"Yes."

"What were they called?"

"What?"

"The policemen. What were their names?"

"Why do you want to know?"

"Can you remember their names?"

"Remember? I am seeing them every day. There is Links, Stadler. And a psychologist: Dr. Schilling. So. Why? What is it?"

"Oh, nothing important." I smiled at her while my insides burned. "I thought I might know them."

NINE

"You all right, Nadia?"

"What?"

I looked round, startled, hardly knowing where I was. I was sitting next to Lynne in her car. She was leaning across to me with the concerned look of a friend.

"You look pale," she said.

"I've suddenly got a blinding headache," I said. "Is it all right if we don't talk for a while?"

"Can I get you anything?"

I shook my head and lay back in the seat with my eyes closed. I didn't want to look at her. I couldn't trust myself to speak. Lynne started the car and began the drive home. I felt as if my skull were full of boiling liquid and I had to hold it tight in my hands to stop it bursting apart. I suddenly remembered I'd forgotten to say good-bye to Zach. I'd left him there in the wreckage of the party. Well fuck it.

I'd been dropped into a new world, a horrible dark world, and I needed to work out where I was, but before that I would have to wait for the boiling buzzing in my head to die down. Most of all, on the short car journey home, I had to concentrate on not throwing up all over Lynne's nice new metropolitan police-issue vehicle. I thought of the moment when you spill boiling water on your hand. There is no pain but you know that in about one second you are going to have to deal with a current of scouring agony tearing up through your hand and arm. I knew that I was going to have to settle down and properly experience what it was that I had heard. For the moment there was just a voice, somewhere far away, deep in my mind, telling me over and over again that another woman had received letters like mine, that she was dead, murdered. A woman had gone through what I'd gone through, and at the end of it she'd been killed. And just a couple of weeks ago. When I'd last been squabbling with Max she had been alive and worried about the threat and wondering when it would end and now there were children who didn't have a mother.

The car stopped. I was taking deep breaths now.

"We're home," a voice said in my ear. "Do you want some help?"

"I think I'll just go and lie down for a while."

"Would you rather I stayed outside in the car?"

Abruptly, I felt as if my face had been plunged into ice-cold water. My mind was clear now. From now on I would just be pretending to be ill.

"No, no, definitely not. I want you inside where you can do some good."

"If you're sure?"

"It's just that I won't be very sociable. I think I may have a migraine."

"Do you need to take anything?"

"I just need to lie down in a darkened room."

We went inside and I left her and retreated to my bedroom. I shut the door. And I checked that the window was firmly closed. And I pulled the blind down. Like Cameron.

Like fucking Detective Inspector Cameron Stadler. I lay on the bed, facedown. I felt like I was five years old. I wanted to climb into the bed, to pull the covers over my head, so that I would be safe, so nobody could find me. Except that I wouldn't be safe. He could find me. For the first time in my life, lying in the bed I didn't feel safe. I needed to be able to see. I pulled the pillow up against the headboard so I could lean back on it. I could see every part of the room. But what good was that? Maybe it was just better to be killed and not see it.

I tried to go over the conversation I'd had with Lena. I had difficulty reconstructing it. For a feverish few minutes I tried to construct an optimistic version of it. Maybe she was mad. But even in my feverish state, I wasn't able to convince myself of that. She had named Links, Grace Schilling, Cameron. She'd lived nearby, hadn't she? That was a thought.

A strange free local paper is pushed through my door every Friday. I never even look at it. I'm not interested in new one-way streets, inquiries in the social services department of the local council, and I put it straight into a cupboard under the sink ready to be used for things like screwing up and shoving into wet shoes. My shoes hadn't got wet for some time, so the last couple of months of them would still be in the pile. I walked out of my bedroom and told Lynne I was feeling a bit better. I'd go and make some tea for us both. I filled the kettle and switched it on. That would give me the couple of minutes I needed.

I started five issues earlier. Nothing there and nothing in the following issue either. Just a drugs raid in the market, a fire in a warehouse, and articles marked "Advertising Feature." But in the following issue, which was just over two weeks ago, there it was, small and on an inside page, and my hands started to shake so much that I thought Lynne's attention would be attracted by the rustling.

The headline was PRIMROSE HILL MURDER. I quickly tore out the page of the newspaper. The kettle had boiled. I poured water over the tea bags.

"Biscuit, Lynne?"

"Not for me, thanks."

I had another couple of minutes. I smoothed out the article on the work surface: "A mother of three was found murdered in her £800,000 Primrose Hill home last week. Police announced that Jennifer Hintlesham, 38, was found dead on August 3rd. Police suspect that she stumbled on an intruder in the late afternoon. 'It's a tragedy,' said Detective Chief Inspector Stuart Links as he announced the setting up of a murder inquiry this week. 'If anybody has any information I would urge them to contact us at Stretton Green Police Station.'"

That was it. I read it and reread it, as if I could suck out some more information through sheer desperation. No mention of any letters. Again I tried to cobble together a version in which the nanny and I had been talking at cross purposes. But then the truth forced itself on me with a bleakness that I could almost taste—dry, metallic. Lena had volunteered the information. I had told her nothing. The policemen were the same.

I picked up the two mugs of tea, but my left hand was compulsively shaking. Scalding tea splashed on my hand. I had to put them down and fill the mug again. I carried one mug through to Lynne and then returned with another for myself, and a shortbread biscuit as well. I sat down near Lynne and looked at her. Had they brought her in to look after me because she hadn't known the previous woman or because she had? Had she sat like this with Jennifer Hintlesham, drinking tea, pretending to be her friend, saying that everything would be fine, that she was safe? I took a sip of my tea. It was too hot and I burned my tongue and started to cough. When I had recovered I dipped the biscuit in the tea and bit off the warm soft edge. When I spoke, I tried to imitate a woman making conversation.

"It still seems strange to me," I said. "I get one letter and a policewoman stays with me for days and days. Do you do this every time anybody gets a threatening letter?"

Lynne looked uncomfortable. Or it may have been that, to me, now, Lynne's imperturbable expression seemed a camouflage.

"I'm just following routine," she said.

"And if somebody came into the house to attack me, you'd protect me?" I said with a smile. "That's the idea, is it?"

"Nothing like that will happen," she said, and for a moment I hated Lynne in a way I've never hated anybody in my life. I wanted to fly at her like a madwoman and claw bloody furrows into her face. Whose feelings was she trying to protect here? But the hatred subsided into nothing more than a dull ache. I gulped down the hot tea as quickly as I could. I needed time to go over things in my mind. The phone rang and it was Zach. I told him I had a migraine.

"A migraine?" he said. "How do you know?"

"Because it feels like one. I've got to go and lie down."

I did go and lie down again. I tried to remember everything I could from the previous few days, which I had taken so lightly. Every memory was like an object in a house that I was wandering around. I picked up the object and examined it and it looked different. Above all, I thought of Cameron. Cameron sitting in the corner looking at me, almost hungrily. Cameron taking my clothes off as if I were a precious beautiful object that might break. Cameron

stroking me tenderly with infinite care and precision.
Cameron with his head between my breasts. What was it
he had said? I have to be honest with you, that was it.
Honest.

In the evening I wandered out with Lynne and we bought
fish and chips. I picked at them, drank a bottle of beer,
and hardly spoke a word. Lynne kept darting glances at
me. Did she suspect I suspected? Then I went to bed, although it was still early; not yet getting dark. I lay there
listening to the noises of the street, of Saturday night in
Camden Town. I thought and thought and the more I thought
the more I became afraid, like damp rising in a house,
weakening and undermining it. Finally I slept and had frag-
mented dreams.

When I woke I forgot my dreams instantly, as I always
do. I forget them utterly, but I was also grateful to have
forgotten them, as if a part of me knew what they had been
and wanted them gone. The phone was ringing. I crawled
out of bed and answered it. It was Cameron. He was whispering.

"I just grabbed a moment," he said. "I miss you so much."

"Good," I said.

"I'm desperate to see you," he hissed. "I can't not be
with you. I've arranged that I can get away in the late afternoon. Can I come and see you around four?"

"Oh, yes," I said.

I spent the day in a sullen fog. Lynne and I went out for
a couple of hours, walking around the market at Camden
Lock, but that was just because it made it easier not to
speak, or at least not to speak about anything important,
and not to listen to any more lies. Cameron arrived at exactly four o'clock. He was wearing jeans and a loose blue
shirt. He hadn't shaved. He looked more rumpled than

usual. I could see that he was even more handsome than ever, less buttoned up. He told Lynne he'd take over for a couple of hours. There were some matters about the upcoming week he wanted to discuss with me. Lynne hung around as she always did. Did she guess what was going on? How could she not? But on this occasion I found the delay almost unbearable. I felt I could hardly restrain myself, that I would damage myself. Finally her feet clattered up the steps to the pavement and disappeared. Cameron gently closed the front door behind her and turned to me.

"Oh Nadia," he said.

I walked toward him. I had prepared myself for this moment for the whole day since I had talked to him on the phone. He reached his arms out toward me. I clenched my fist as hard as I could. When I was a foot away I looked him in the eyes and then, with all my strength, I punched him in the face.

TEN

He lifted his hands to his face. Was it in self-defense or to hit back? I stood with my chin up, almost daring him to strike. But then he lowered his hands and took a pace backward.

"What the fuck?" His voice wasn't loud, but it was cold. His eyes were cold. His handsome face looked heavy and stupid and vicious. I saw with satisfaction that blood trickled down from his nostril, where my ring had nicked it.

"I know, Detective Inspector Stadler."

"What?"

"I know everything."

"What are you going on about?"

"Did it turn you on?"

"What?" he said again. "What?" He wiped the blood away from his nose and examined his fingers.

"It did, didn't it? It turned you on, thinking that you were fucking a woman who was going to die."

"You're hysterical," he said, voice flat with contempt.

I jabbed him in the chest with a forefinger.

"Jennifer Hintlesham. Does that name ring any bells for you?"

His expression changed; the first glimmering of comprehension crept across his features.

"Nadia," he said. He took a step toward me and put out his hand, as if I were a wild animal that needed coaxing. "Nadia, please."

"Stay where you are, you . . . you." I couldn't find a word that was nasty enough. "What were you *thinking*? How could you do that to me? Did you think of me dead?"

His face shut down.

"We told you we were taking the threat seriously," he said blankly.

"You fucking hypocrite. You were fucking me there, in the bathroom, and on the floor there in the living room, and in my bed."

"I didn't notice you resisting."

I slapped him across the cheek. I wanted to hurt him, mutilate him, pulverize him.

"I can't believe it," I said. "I can't believe I did that with you." I looked at him, disgusted. "A married man who gets turned on by having sex with someone he's supposed to be protecting."

"We are protecting you."

I shocked myself then by bursting into tears.

"Nadia." His voice was soft, with a hint of triumph in it. "Darling Nadia, I'm sorry. I hated not telling you."

I felt his hand on me and it made me jump.

"Fuck off," I screamed through my tears. "I'm not fucking crying because of you. I'm scared, don't you see? I'm so scared I feel like there's a great hole in my chest."

"Nadia."

"Shut up." I pulled a tissue out of my pocket and blew my nose. Then I looked at my watch. "Lynne's back in an hour. I need you to answer some questions. I'm going to wash my face."

"Wait," he said. "I won't touch you, I promise, but can I just say that what happened between us, it wasn't, I mean it's not, I wouldn't want anyone . . ." He ground to a halt and looked at me with an expression that was both obsequious and resentful. He was scared of me now.

In the bathroom I washed my hands and face, and cleaned my teeth. There was a nasty taste in my mouth. I watched myself in the mirror. I didn't look any different from usual. How was it possible that I looked the same? I smiled and my reflection smiled back happily.

The heat had gone out of my hatred. I felt cold and calm and ghastly. Cameron seemed dulled too. We sat across the table from each other, like indifferent strangers. It seemed impossible that a couple of days ago he was holding my head between his hands as if I were the most adored object in the world, feeling for me beneath my clothes. I shuddered at the memory.

"How did you find out?" he asked.

"North London's a small place," I said. "Especially rich north London. I met the nanny, Lena." He didn't reply but I saw a slight nod of recognition. "She told me about the notes. And you. Are you sure they're from the same person?"

He didn't meet my eyes.

"Yes," he said.

"He wrote letters to her, like the one he wrote to me, and then he killed her."

"Yes."

"But weren't you guarding her?"

"We had been. There were complicating factors."

"But he still got into the house and murdered her."

"We weren't exactly guarding her at that point."

"Why not? Didn't you take it seriously?"

"Not at all," he replied, stung. "We took it very seriously, after all—" He stopped abruptly.

"What?"

"Nothing."

"What?"

"Nadia, you should understand that we are taking every precaution to protect you."

"What? After all, what? Tell me."

"We knew how serious the letters to Mrs. Hintlesham were," he muttered, so quietly I had to strain to hear him.

"Why?" He caught my eye and then I realized. The new knowledge flooded over me so I could scarcely breathe. I stared at him. My voice came out in a hoarse whisper. "She wasn't the first, was she?"

Cameron shook his head.

"Who else?"

"A young woman called Zoe Haratounian. She lived over in Holloway."

"When?"

"Five weeks ago."

"How?"

Cameron shook his head again. "Please, Nadia. Don't. We're looking after you. Trust us."

I couldn't suppress an ugly laugh.

"I know how you must be feeling, Nadia."

I sank my head into my hands.

"No, you don't," I said. "I don't know what I feel. How do you know?"

"What are you going to do?"

I lifted up my head and glared at him. He meant: Was I going to tell on him? What a baby; a cruel, vain baby.

"I'm going to live," I said.

"Of course you are." His voice was placatory and saccharine. He sounded like a doctor talking to a dying patient.

"You think I'm going to die, don't you?"

"Not at all," he said. "No way."

"A madman," I said. Fear rose in my throat, like bile. Blood roared in my ears. "A killer."

The doorbell rang. Blushing, smiling, lying Lynne. Cameron said in a low voice: "Please don't tell anyone about us."

"Fuck off. I'm thinking."

ELEVEN

In a twisted way, I almost enjoyed my meeting with Lynne. She had tried to ask Cameron some technical questions about next week's roster, but he was scarcely able to speak or catch her eye—or my eye. He just stroked his cheek lightly as if he was trying to detect with his fingertips whether there was a revealing mark where I'd hit him. Then he mumbled something about having to get away.

"We'll talk tomorrow," I said.

"What?" he said miserably.

"About arrangements," I said.

He looked sharply at me, then gave a shrug and left. Almost with surprise, I found myself alone with Lynne. I hadn't even thought of what I would say to her after speaking to Cameron.

"Want a drink?" I asked.

I'm not the sort of person who ever needs a drink, but God, I needed a drink.

"Tea would be great."

So I bustled off and put the kettle on. I seemed to be always making tea for her, as if I was her grandmother. Just a mug and tea bag for her. In the back of a cupboard

I found a bottle of whiskey that somebody had once bought in duty-free for me as a present. I splashed some into a tumbler and topped it up from the cold tap. We walked out into the garden. Although it was now the early evening, it was still fiercely hot.

"Cheers," I said, clinking my whiskey against her mug and taking a sip of my drink, which stung the back of my throat and I could feel sizzling all the way down the inside of my body into my tummy. The garden was a disaster, of course, but just because it *was* so overgrown, it felt like a refuge from all that horrible stuff outside, which I could still hear: the traffic, music from a sound system in a flat along the road. We walked across to a corner where there was a plant that looked like a bush trying to become a tree. It was covered in cone-shaped clusters of purple flowers. White and brown butterflies were fluttering around it like tiny scraps of paper blown about by the wind.

"I love to stand out here in the evenings," I said. Lynne nodded back at me. "I mean in the summer. I don't do it in the rain. I like looking at the flowers and wondering what their names are. Do you know anything about gardening?" Lynne shook her head. "Pity." I took another sip. Now for it. "I owe you an apology," I said, just as she was lifting the mug to her lips, testing the heat of the liquid with that delicate first sip. She looked puzzled.

"What for?"

"Yesterday I was asking you whether all this—I mean all the protection—wasn't a bit much. I wondered why you were doing this. But in fact I knew."

Lynne froze in the act of lifting the mug of tea to her mouth. I continued.

"You see, a funny thing happened. Yesterday at the children's party I got talking to the nanny of one of the children. And then completely by chance I discovered something. She worked for, I mean used to work for, a woman called Jennifer Hintlesham." I had to give Lynne credit. She gave no visible reaction at all. She wouldn't catch my eye, that was all. "You have heard of her?" I said.

Lynne took some time to answer. She looked down at her tea.

"Yes," she said, so quietly I could hardly catch the words.

A thought—actually more a feeling than a thought—occurred to me. I remembered that strange sensation when I'd gone somewhere with Max and he would say something that would make me realize that he'd been there before with an earlier girlfriend. And, although I knew it was stupid, things would go a bit gray and sour.

"Did you do this with her? With Jennifer? Did you stand in her garden with her, drinking tea?"

Lynne looked trapped. But she couldn't run away. She had to stay here, looking after me.

"I'm sorry," she said. "It felt bad not telling you, but there were strict instructions. They thought it might be traumatic for you."

"Did Jennifer know about the one before?"

"No."

I felt that my mouth was flapping open. I was aghast. I just couldn't think what to say.

"I . . . you lied to her as well" was all I finally managed.

"It wasn't like that," said Lynne, still not catching my eye. "It was a decision made from the beginning. They thought it would be bad to panic you."

"And to panic her. I mean Jennifer."

"That's right."

"So—let me get this straight in my mind—she didn't know that the person sending her letters had already killed somebody."

Lynne didn't reply.

"And she couldn't make decisions about how to protect herself."

"It wasn't like that," Lynne said.

"In what way wasn't it like that?"

"This wasn't my decision," Lynne said. "But I know that they've been acting for the best. What they thought would be the best."

"Your strategy for protecting Jennifer—and the first one as well, Zoe—it didn't quite work out." I took a gulp of the whiskey, which made me cough. I wasn't really used to spirits. I felt so miserable and frightened and sick. "I'm sorry, Lynne, I'm sure that this is awful for you, but it's worse for me. This is my life. I'm the one who's going to die."

She moved closer toward me.

"You're not going to die."

I recoiled. I didn't want these people to touch me. I didn't want their sensitivity.

"I don't understand, Lynne. You've been sitting here with me for days. You've been here in the house, drinking my tea, eating my food. I've talked to you about my life. You've seen me barefoot, slouched on the sofa; half-naked, wandering around. You've seen me believing you, trusting you. I can't understand it. What were you thinking?"

Lynne stayed silent. I didn't speak, either, for a time. I reached for my whiskey and sipped at it.

"Do you think I'm being stupid?" I said. "It's just that I have this problem with everybody knowing something about me and me not knowing it. What would you feel, if it was you?"

"I don't know," she said.

I took another sip of the drink. It was starting to work on me. I have a startlingly low resistance to any kind of drug. I would like it to be because I have a perfectly attuned body, but I think it's just a weak head. It was getting harder to maintain my feeling of fury, although the fear was still throbbing away somewhere deep inside. But I could feel the alcohol all over my body and outside it as well, making the world seem softer, fuzzier in the golden light of this summer evening right in the middle of north London.

"Did you look after the first one?"

"Zoe? No. I only met her once. Just before . . . well . . ."

"And Jennifer?"

"Yes. I spent time with her."

"What were they like? Were they like me?"

Lynne drained her mug of tea.

"I'm sorry," she said. "I'm sorry you were kept in the dark like this. But it's completely forbidden to divulge details of that kind. I'm sorry."

"Don't you understand what I'm saying?" I raised my voice in some bitterness. "I've never met these two women. I don't even know what they look like. But I've got something very big in common with them. I'd like to know about them. It might help."

Lynne's face had gone blank now. She suddenly looked like a bureaucrat behind a desk.

"If you've any concerns, you'll have to raise them with DCI Links. I'm not authorized to make any disclosures." There was a flash of human concern on her face. "Look, Nadia, I'm not the one to ask. I haven't seen the files on the case. I'm just on the edge of it, like you."

"I'm not on the edge," I said. "I wish I were. I'm in the black hole at the center. So that's it? You just want me to trust you, to have faith that you're getting better at this?"

Fuck her, I thought. Fuck all of them. We walked in-

side, hardly looking at each other. She made some sandwiches with bits of ham that were left in the fridge and
we sat watching the TV and not talking. I hardly noticed
the program. At first I thought angrily, playing through
scenes from my recent life, conversations with Lynne,
Links, Cameron. I remembered lying in bed with Cameron,
the way he gazed at me. I tried to imagine the erotic charge
of a naked body like mine, the body of a woman who was
going to die soon and didn't know it. What was it like to
be a lover whose only rival was a murderer? Did that make
sex more exciting? The more I thought of it, the thought
of him nuzzling my body made me want to vomit, as if
there had been rats gnawing at my breasts and between my
legs.

I hadn't ever really been scared before. I don't think I
am someone who scares easily. I fall in love easily, and
get angry quickly, and happy too, and irritated, and excited.
I shout, cry, laugh. These things lie close to my surface,
and they bubble up. But fear is deep down and hidden.
Now I was scared, but the feeling didn't obliterate all other
emotions the way rage does, for instance, or sudden desire. It felt more like walking out of the sunlight into the
shadow: stony cold, eerie. A different world.

As the night wore on, I realized that I didn't know who
to turn to. I thought about my parents but quickly dismissed
them. They were old and nervous. They had always been
anxious about me, before there was any real need for anx-
iety. Zach, darling glum Zach. Or Janet, maybe. Who would
be calm, strong, a rock? Who would listen to me? Who
would save me?

And then, without meaning to, I started to think about
the women who had died. I knew nothing about them except their names, and that Jennifer Hintlesham had had
three children. I remembered her little son's belligerent

cherub's face. Two women. Zoe and Jenny. What had they looked like, how had they felt? They must have lain awake in their beds in the dark, as I was doing now, and felt the same icy fear flowing round their bodies that I was feeling now. And the same loneliness. For now of course it was not two but three women, joined together by one madman. Zoe and Jenny and Nadia. Nadia: That was me. Why me? I thought, as I lay there and listened to the sounds of the night. Why them, and why me? And just why?

But even as I lay there, curled up in my covers with my heart thumping and my eyes stinging, I knew I was going to have to move on from this blind and helpless state of terror. I couldn't just huddle up and wait for something to happen, or for other people to rescue me from the nightmare. Crying under the sheets wasn't going to save me. And it was as if a small part deep inside me clenched itself in readiness.

I fell asleep in the early hours, and the following morning, when I woke dazed with tiredness and strange dreams, I didn't exactly feel braver or safer. But I did feel steelier. At ten o'clock I asked Lynne if she could leave the room because I had a private phone call to make. She said she'd wait in the car, and when she had gone, pulling the door firmly shut behind her, I phoned Cameron at work.

"I'm feeling desperate," he said as soon as he came on the line.

"Good. So am I."

"I'm so sorry that you feel betrayed. I feel terrible."

"That's all right," I said. "You can do something for me."

"Anything."

"I want to see the files on this case. Not just about me, about the other two women as well."

"That's not possible. They're not available to the public."

"I know. I still want to see them."

"It's completely out of the question."

"I want you to listen to me very clearly, Cameron. In my opinion you behaved badly about the whole sex thing. Presumably the thought of having sex with a potential victim is some kind of sicko turn-on. But I enjoyed it as well and I'm a grown-up and all that. I'm not interested in punishing you. I just want to make that clear. But if you don't bring me the files I will go and see Links and I will tell him about our sexual relationship and I'll probably cry a bit and talk about having been in a vulnerable state."

"You wouldn't."

"And I'll contact your wife and tell her."

"You wouldn't—that would be . . ." He made a coughing sound, as if he was choking. "You mustn't tell Sarah. She's been depressed; she couldn't deal with it."

"That doesn't matter to me," I said. "I'm not interested. Just get me the files."

"You wouldn't do it," he said in a strangled voice. "You couldn't."

"Listen carefully to what I'm saying. There is a man who has killed two women and is now going to kill me. Just at this moment, I don't care about your career and I don't care about your wife's feelings. If you want to try playing poker with me, try it. I want the files here tomorrow morning and enough time to read through them. Then you can take them away again."

"I can't do it."

"It's your choice."

"I'll try."

"And I want everything."

"I'll do what I can."

"Do," I said. "And think of your career while you're doing it. Think of your wife."

When I put the phone down I expected to cry or feel ashamed, but I surprised myself by catching sight of my reflection in the mirror above the fireplace. At last, a friendly face.

TWELVE

❦

I cleared my big living room table but there still wasn't enough space. After Cameron had got rid of Lynne, it took him three trips to bring in the files from his car. There were two bulging cases and two cardboard boxes. He unloaded the red, blue, and beige files onto the table-top and, when there was no more room, onto the carpet as well. When he had finished, he was panting, his face pale and slimy with sweat. His skin had a tired gray deadness.

"Is that all?" I asked ironically as the final pile was dumped at my feet.

"No," he said.

"I said I wanted everything."

"You'd need a small van for everything," he said. "These are the active files from the office, and the others that I've got direct access to. Anyway, I don't know what good you think this will do you. You'll find most of it incomprehensible." He sat in the uncomfortable wicker chair in the corner. "You've got two hours with this. And if you mention to anybody that you've seen any of this at all, then that's my job."

"Hush," I said, picking up files at random. "How are these arranged?"

"Don't get them out of order," he said. "Mostly the gray files are for statements. The blue files are our own reports and documents. The red files are forensic and crime scene. It's not completely consistent. Anyway it's all written on the outside."

"Are there photographs?"

"There are pictures of the crime scenes in the albums on the floor by your feet."

I looked down. It seemed strange that police would put pictures of murders into the same sort of album that people use for their holiday snaps. I felt cold suddenly. Was this a good idea?

"Maybe in a minute. I just wanted to see what they looked like."

Cameron came forward and started rummaging on the table, muttering to himself.

"Here," he said. "And here."

As I reached for it he took my hand.

"Sorry," he said.

I pulled away from him. I was in a hurry.

"Go away," I said. "Go into the garden. I'll call you when I'm ready."

"Or what?" he said wearily. "Or you'll ring my wife?"

"I can't read with you here."

He paused. "It doesn't make nice reading, Nadia."

"Leave me."

Slowly and reluctantly, he left the room.

I had a moment's hesitation in opening the first file, in even touching it, as if there were an electric current protecting it. I was going to open a door and go into a room and somehow things would always be different. *I* would be different.

I opened the file and there she was. A snapshot was pinned to a piece of paper. Zoe Haratounian. Born February 11, 1976. I looked closely at the picture. She must have been on holiday. She was half sitting on a low wall with an intensely blue sky behind her. The fierce sunlight was making her squint slightly (she was holding a pair of sunglasses in her hand) and she was also laughing, saying something to whoever was taking the photograph. She was wearing a green vest and floppy black shorts. She had blond hair that came down to her shoulders. Was she lovely looking? I think so, but it was difficult to tell. Certainly she looked nice. It was a happy picture, the sort that should have been pinned on a cork notice board in the kitchen next to the shopping list and the card of the local taxi firm.

Also in the file were some typed notes. This was what I'd been looking for. Boyfriend, friends, employer, references to other files, contact numbers, addresses. I had a notebook ready for this. I jotted down some names and numbers, looking round to check that Cameron couldn't see me. I flicked through the files. There was another photograph, a black-and-white portrait that looked as if it had been taken for some kind of identification. Yes, she was lovely. I'd seen in the previous picture that she was slim but there was a slight roundness to her face. She looked very young. Although she had a basically serious expression, there was a glint of something in her eyes as if, the very moment that the picture had been taken, she was going to break out into a naughty smile. I wondered what her voice had sounded like. Her name sounded foreign but she had been born somewhere near Nottingham.

I closed the file and put it carefully to one side. Now for the second. Jennifer Charlotte Hintlesham, born 1961, looked completely different from Zoe. Admittedly, it was a more formal photograph, taken in a studio. I could imagine it standing on a dressing table in a silver frame. She was more striking-looking than Zoe. She wasn't exactly beautiful, but she was a woman who would catch your attention. She had large dark eyes and prominent cheekbones that were made more prominent by her long, thin face. There was something old-fashioned about her: She was wearing a round-necked sweater with a necklace of small pearls. Her dark brown hair was brushed so that it shone. She reminded me of one of those minor British movie stars of the fifties who were a bit left behind when the sixties started.

I had felt that Zoe was much younger than me; Jennifer Hintlesham seemed a generation older. It wasn't that she had an older-looking face than me. The only faces that look more haggard than mine, especially first thing in the morning, have been dug out of a peat bog after two thousand years of mummification. She just seemed grown-up. I felt I'd like to have met Zoe. I wasn't sure I'd have been Jennifer's type. I looked at the file again. Husband and three children, names and ages. Fuck. I wrote down details.

Something occurred to me. I looked in the pile of files where these two had come from. As I thought, there was a file with my name on it. I opened it and was looking at a picture of myself. Nadia Elizabeth Blake, b. 1971. I shivered. Maybe in a few weeks this file would be fatter and another would have been opened.

I looked at my watch. What on earth next? And what was the point of this, apart from curiosity? When I was eleven years old there was a five-meter board at our local swimming pool. I never dared jump from it until one day I just climbed the steps as if I happened to be climbing a ladder for no reason and stepped over the edge of the board without thinking and I'd done it. I did this now.

I reached down for the first album of pictures, bound in

gaudy red plastic. It should have contained pictures of little girls blowing out candles and people kicking balls along
the beach. I opened it and mechanically turned the pages
one after another. Not that much to see, really. I turned
back to the beginning to check. Yes, this was the scene of
the murder of Zoe Haratounian. Her own flat. And then
there she was. She was lying facedown on a carpet. She
wasn't naked or anything like that. She was wearing knickers and a T-shirt. And she didn't look dead. She could have
been asleep. There was a ribbon or tie or something pulled
tight around her neck and there were photographs showing it from various angles. I just kept looking at the knickers and the shirt. It was the thought of her putting on those
clothes that morning and not knowing that she'd never take
them off. It's the sort of stupid thought you can't get out
of your mind.

I put it down and picked up the second book. The crime
scene at Jennifer Hintlesham's house. I began to flick du-
tifully through it as I had the previous one, but then I
stopped. This looked completely different. It was a single
photograph, it was a single scene, but I saw it in fragments:
staring open eyes, wire around the neck, clothes ripped or
slashed off, legs splayed, and something like a metal bar
pushed into her, I couldn't see into what bit of her. I threw
the book down and ran to the sink. I got there just in time,
vomit spluttering out of my mouth. My stomach heaved
and heaved, painfully emptying itself. I looked down and
it was almost funny. The sink was full of dirty dishes. Even
dirtier dishes.

I washed my face in warm and cold water and then em-
barked on the most disgusting washing-up of my life, and
I'm speaking as someone who shared a house with a girl
and two boys at college. The activity made me feel stead-

ier. I was able to walk back to the table and close the photograph album without looking at it.

I didn't have much time. I would have to be selective. I rummaged through the files quickly, checking their contents. I saw plans of Zoe's flat and Jennifer's house. I skimmed through witnesses' statements. They were so long, rambling, and diffuse that it was almost impossible to extract any sense from them. Zoe's boyfriend, Fred, talked about the increasing fear she had felt and his efforts to calm her. Her friend, Louise, seemed distraught. She had been the one who had actually been sitting outside the flat in her car while Zoe had been strangled. The witness statements for Jennifer's murder filled ten bulky files. I could do little more than identify the interviewees, mainly people who worked for her. The Hintleshams seemed to have been major employers.

I paid a little more attention to the pathologist's reports on the two dead women. Zoe's was much simpler: ligature strangulation with the belt of her dressing gown. There were some minor contusions, but these were only related to the force required to hold her down while she was strangled. Vaginal and anal swabs showed no sign of sexual assault.

The report on Jennifer's death was far longer. I did nothing more than note details: ligature strangulation, a thin deep furrow on the neck consistent with the use of wire; incised wounds and stabbed wounds; blood splashes, pools, smears, trails; tearing of the perineum; a copious amount of urine. She'd pissed herself.

There was a fat file dealing with the analysis of the letters. They included photocopies of the letters sent to Zoe and Jennifer, and I read them with a macabre guilty sense that I was reading stolen love letters. But they *were* love letters, with their promises and their vows. And there was a drawing as well of a mutilated Zoe. Strangely, of all the horrors I saw that day, it was that vile, crude drawing that made me cry. It was the one that made me dwell on the crazed ingenuity that one person was putting into destroying another. I skimmed through the analysis of the documents. There had been attempts to associate the letters with people Zoe knew: her boyfriend, Fred; an ex-boyfriend; a real estate agent; a potential buyer of her flat. However, incised marks on the drawing (confirmed, a note added, by injuries inflicted on Jennifer Hintlesham) showed conclusively that the murderer was left-handed. The above suspects were all right-handed.

There were files of crime-scene reports on dust and fabric and hair and much else. Many of them were so technical that I couldn't work out whether anything significant had been found. It didn't look like it. There was a single-page summary report at the front, which was copied to Links, Cameron, and other members of the murder inquiry. What was clearly stated was that no significant links had been found among the forensic traces recovered from the two murder scenes. The hair and fiber samples found on the clothes that the dead Zoe was wearing, and also found on the carpet, bedclothes, and other items of clothing, were only those of the recent inhabitants of the flat: namely her boyfriend, Fred, and Zoe herself. The hair and fiber analysis of the Jennifer Hintlesham crime scene was more complicated. There were numerous unidentified samples due to the sheer number of people who had been on the premises. There was, however, no forensic link between the two scenes, apart from Jenny's locket found in Zoe's flat, and Zoe's photograph found in Jenny's house. More awful news.

I also read through a bundle of internal memos, which outlined the various stages of the inquiry, including the result of an informal internal inquiry that was marked "Most Secret." It was there I learned that Jennifer Hintlesham's guard had been removed because her husband, Clive, was in the process of being charged with the murder of Zoe Haratounian. What a fuck-up.

Just as I was about to call Cameron back I started flicking through a routine-looking file. It consisted of rosters, minutes of meetings, holiday assignments. But then at the bottom a photocopied memo caught my eye. It was from Links to a Dr. Michael Griffen, with copies to Stadler, Grace Schilling, Lynne, and a dozen other names I didn't recognize. It began by apparently responding to a complaint by Dr. Griffen that the two murder scenes, especially in the flat of Zoe Haratounian, had been compromised by faulty procedures by the first officers on the scene:

> I will make every effort to ensure that the scene of any future scene will be swiftly and effectively sealed. I realize that in all probability, and in no small part because of the practical difficulties of personal protection, the solution of this case will lie in the hands of the forensic scientists and we will furnish you with all possible cooperation.

I shouted for Cameron and he was in the room in a few seconds. Had he been watching through the window? What did it matter?

"Look," I said, handing him the note. "'Any future scene.' Not exactly a vote of confidence in your own abilities."

He looked at it, then replaced it in the file.

"You asked to see the files," he said. "Obviously we have to plan for every eventuality."

"Maybe it looks different from where I'm standing," I said. "That's me: any future scene. Me."

"So what did you think?"

"It was horrible," I said. "And I'm glad I know."

Cameron started gathering up the files, putting them in boxes, cramming them into the briefcases.

"We're not very alike," I said.

He paused.

"What?"

"I thought we'd all be the same type. I know it's hard to tell from photos and a few particulars, but we seem completely different. Zoe was younger, sweeter than me, I bet. Also, she had a real job. And as for Jennifer, she looks like a member of the royal family. I don't think she'd have had much time for *me*."

"Maybe not," said Stadler wistfully, and at that moment I felt a stab of jealousy. He'd seen her, talked to her. He knew what her voice sounded like. He had seen her funny little gestures, the sort that would never get written down on a form.

"You're all small," he said.

"What?"

"You're all short and light," he said. "And you live in north London."

"So that's where you've got to," I said. "Nearly six weeks and two women dead and you know that this murderer doesn't choose six-foot bodybuilders and he doesn't choose women who live randomly all over the world."

He was finished packing up.

"I've got to go," he said. "Lynne's about to arrive."

"Cameron?"

"Yes."

"I won't tell your wife, or Links or anyone."

"Good."

"But I would have done."

"That's what I thought."

We were both acting a bit embarrassed with each other now. For me it was that embarrassment of being with someone who you've been naked with and now don't fancy in the very least. Added to it was a very strong feeling that all I wanted to do was retreat into my bedroom and cry and think about dying for a few hours.

"Nadia?"

"Yes?"

"I'm sorry about everything. It has all been so . . . so." He stopped and rubbed his face, then looked around as if he thought Lynne might already be in the room without either of us knowing. "I've got something else."

"What?" I could tell from the tone of his voice that it wasn't good news.

He reached inside his jacket and took out a paper. In fact it was two sheets of paper. He unfolded them and flattened them on the table.

"We intercepted these in the last few days."

"How?"

"One was sent as a letter. I think the other was pushed through the door."

I stared at them.

"This was the first," he said, pointing at the sheet on the left.

It read:

Dear Nadia,
  I want to fuck you to death. And I want you to think about that.

"Oh," I said.

"This came two days ago," Stadler said.

Dear Nadia,

I don't know what the police are saying to you. They can't stop me. They know that. In a few days or a week or two weeks you'll be dead.

"I wanted to be honest with you," he said.

"You know, it had been a very small comfort to me that there was just the one letter. I thought maybe he was going to kill someone else."

"I'm sorry," he said, looking around. "I've got to get this stuff into the car. But I'm very sorry."

"I'm going to die, aren't I?" I said. "I mean, at least that must be what you think."

He already had a box in his hand.

"No, no," he said, moving toward the door. "You'll be fine."

THIRTEEN

"I'm going to Camden Market," I said. "Straightaway."

Lynne looked confused. It was Saturday and only just past nine o'clock, and I guess she'd got used to my staying in my bed till late, trying to find ways of being alone. For the past two days I had been locked into my nightmare, seeing those photographs over and over again in my mind. Zoe, looking as if she had simply gone to sleep; Jenny, obscenely mutilated. Yet here I was, washed and dressed and strangely friendly, and ready to go.

"It'll be crowded," she said doubtfully.

"Just what I need. Crowds, music, cheap clothes and jewelry. I want to buy lots of useless things. You don't need to come with me."

"I'll come, of course."

"You've got to, haven't you. Poor Lynne, trailing round after me, having to be polite all the time, having to lie. You must miss your normal life."

"I'm fine," she said.

"I know you don't wear a wedding ring. Do you have a boyfriend?"

"Yes." Her familiar blush spread over her pale face, her birthmark flamed.

"Hmmm. You must be wishing this was all over. One way or another. Come on. It's only five minutes' walk away."

Lynne was right. It was a hot day, the sky a faded dirty blue, and Camden Market was packed. Lynne was wearing long woolen trousers and heavy shoes. Her hair hung down her face in sweaty little tails. She must be sweltering, I thought to myself with satisfaction. I had put on a lemon-yellow sundress and flat sandals; my hair was tied back. I felt cool, light-footed. We pushed our way through the crowds, and the heat rose from the pavements. I looked round as we walked and felt a wave of euphoria rise in me, that I was among this great sea of people again. The dreadlocks, the punks, the bikers, the girls in bright dresses or tie-dyed skirts, the men with pitted faces and watching eyes, the teenagers slouching by and being cool in that self-conscious kind of way you lose, thank God, as you get older. I tipped back my head and breathed in the patchouli oil and dope and incense and scented candles and good honest sweat.

There were stalls selling freshly squeezed juices on the corners and I got us each a tumbler of mango and orange and a pretzel. Then I bought twenty thin silver bangles for £5, and slipped them onto my wrist, where they clinked satisfyingly. I bought a floaty silk scarf, a pair of tiny earrings, some flamboyant clips for my hair. Nothing I couldn't put on immediately. I didn't want to be carrying anything. Then, while Lynne was examining wooden carvings, I slipped away. It was as easy as that.

I went quickly down the staircases that led to the canal and ran along the path until I got to the main road. It was still crowded and I was just another body in the crowd. I ducked and weaved between them. If Lynne came this way, looking for me, she wouldn't be able to see me now. Nobody would be able to see me. Not even him, with his X-ray eyes. I was on my own at last.

I felt free, quite different, as if I'd shaken off all the rubbish that had been clinging to me over the past weeks: The fear and the desire and the irritation fell away. I felt better than I had in days. I knew where I was going. I had planned the route last night. I had to be quick, before anyone worked out where I was.

I had to ring the bell several times. I thought maybe he had gone out, although the curtains in the upstairs windows were still closed. But then I heard footsteps, a muffled curse.

The man who opened the front door was taller and younger than I had expected, and more handsome. He had pale hair flopping over his brow, pale eyes in a tanned face. He was wearing jeans and nothing else. He looked bleary.

"Yes?" His tone wasn't exactly friendly.

"Are you Fred?" I tried to smile at him.

"Yes. Do I know you?" He spoke with a languid self-assurance. I imagined Zoe beside him, her eager, pretty face looking up at his.

"Sorry to wake you up, but it's urgent. Can I come in?" He raised his eyebrows at me.

"Who are you?"

"My name's Nadia Blake. I'm here because I am being threatened by the same man who killed Zoe."

I thought this would surprise him, but it clearly hit him like a physical blow. He almost fell backward.

"What?" he said.

"Can I come in?"

He stepped back and held the door open. He looked utterly dazed. I was past him before he could say anything more. He followed me upstairs to a small cluttered living room.

"I'm sorry about Zoe, by the way," I said.

He was looking at me intently.

"How did you hear about me?"

"I saw you on a list of witnesses," I said.

He ran his hand through his tousled hair and then rubbed his eyes.

"Want some coffee?"

"Thanks."

He went into the adjoining kitchen and I stared around me. I thought there might be a photograph of Zoe, something that would remind me of her, but there was nothing. I picked up some of the magazines lying on the floor: horticultural manuals, a guide to London club life, a TV guide. There was a heap of round stones on one of the shelves and I picked up a marbled one that looked like a duck's egg and held it in the palm of my hand. I put it carefully back and picked up a brown felt hat that was hung on the edge of the chair, swung it round on my forefinger. I wanted to feel close to Zoe, but she felt utterly absent. I picked up a carved wooden duck from a shelf and examined it. When Fred came back into the room I hastily restored it to the shelf.

"What are you doing?" he asked suspiciously.

"Just fidgeting. I'm sorry."

"Here's your coffee."

"Thanks." I had forgotten to tell him I don't like it with milk.

Fred sat on a sofa that looked as if it had been retrieved from a dump and motioned me into the chair. He held his mug in both hands and stared into it. He didn't speak.

"I'm sorry about Zoe," I said again, for want of anything better.

"Yeah," he said.

He shrugged and looked away. What had I been expecting? I had felt that there was a bond between us, because he had known Zoe and that made him, in a quite irrational way, closer to me in my imagination than any of my friends.

"What was she like?"

"Like?" He looked up sulkily. "She was nice, attractive, happy, you know, all that, but what do you want from me?"

"It's stupid, I know. I want to know silly things about her: her favorite color, her clothes, her dreams, what she felt like when she got the letters, everything . . ." I ran out of breath.

He looked uncomfortable, almost disgusted.

"I can't help you," he said.

"Did you love her?" I asked abruptly.

He stared at me as if I had said something obscene.

"We had good fun."

Good fun. My heart sank. He hadn't even known her, or didn't want me to know her through him. Good fun: what an epitaph.

"Don't you wonder, though, all the time what she must have felt like? When she was being threatened, I mean, and then when she died?"

He reached across for a packet of cigarettes and a box of matches on a low table by the sofa.

"No," he said, lighting a cigarette.

"The photograph I saw of her looked quite old. Do you have a more recent one?"

"No."

"Not one?"

"I don't take photos."

"Or any things of hers that I could look at? There must be something."

"What for?" he said, his face hard and unyielding.

"I'm sorry. I must seem like a ghoul. It's just that I feel a connection to these two women."

"What do you mean *two* women?"

"Zoe and then Jenny Hintlesham, the second woman he killed."

"What?" he said, leaping forward. He put the mug on the table, spilling quite a lot of the coffee. "What the fuck?"

"Sorry, you didn't know. The police have been keeping it a big secret. I only found out by mistake. This other woman got the same letters. She was killed a few weeks after Zoe."

"But . . . but . . ." Fred seemed lost in thought. Then he looked at me with a completely new intensity. "That second woman."

"Jenny."

"She was killed by the same man?"

"That's right."

He gave a low whistle.

"Fuck," he said.

"I know," I said.

The telephone rang, loud as an alarm, and we both started. Fred picked up the receiver and turned his back on me.

"Yeah. Yeah, I'm up." A pause, then: "Come round now and we'll collect Duncan and Graham later."

He put the phone down and glanced over at me.

"I've got a friend coming round," he said in dismissal. "Good luck, Nadia. Sorry I couldn't be any help."

Was that it? That couldn't be it. I gazed at him helplessly.

"Good-bye, Nadia," he said again, almost pushing me to the door. "Take care."

I walked with my head down, making my way blindly toward the underground. Poor Zoe, I thought. Fred had struck me as a man almost entirely without imagination, handsome and heedless. I couldn't imagine him being very sympathetic toward her while she was receiving the threats, whatever he had told the police afterward. I went over what he had said, which was not very much—nothing that made it worth escaping from police protection. A sudden shiver of fear went through me. I was on my own, nobody looking after me. I imagined eyes in the Saturday crowd looking after me.

Suddenly my way was blocked. A man standing in my path looked down at me. Dark hair, pale face, teeth glinting behind his smile. Who was he?

"Hello there, you look miles away."

I stared at him.

"It *is* Nadia, isn't it? The woman with the ancient computer?"

Ah, now I remembered. Relief flooded through me. I smiled.

"Yes. Sorry. Um—"

"Morris. Morris Burnside."

"Of course. Hi."

"How are you, Nadia? How have you been?"

"What? Oh, fine," I replied absently. "Look, I'm really sorry but I'm in a bit of a hurry, actually."

"Of course, don't let me keep you. You're sure you are okay? You look a bit anxious."

"Oh, just tired, that's all. You know. Well, bye then."

"Good-bye, Nadia. Take care of yourself now. See you."

The house was beautiful. I'd seen it in the photographs of course, but it was grander in real life: set back from the road in its own gardens, steps leading up to its porched front door, wisteria climbing up the tall white walls. Everything about it was substantial and spoke of good taste and wealth. I knew about the wealth of course, but now I could practically smell it. I looked upward to the windows on the first floor. In one of those rooms, Jenny had died. I smoothed back my hair and fiddled nervously with the straps on my cheap cotton shift. Then I walked briskly up to the door and banged the brass knocker.

I almost expected Jenny to open the door herself: to see her narrow face and her glossy dark hair framed in the doorway. She'd be polite to me, in that well-bred and faintly surprised way that says get lost to people like me: the rude and the reckless.

"Yes?" Not Jenny, but a tall and elegant woman with blond hair swept smoothly back, jewels at her ears, wearing a pair of well-cut black trousers and an apricot-colored silk blouse. I had read about Clive's affair in the file and I had a pretty good idea who she was. "Can I help you?"

"I'd like to speak to Clive Hintlesham, please. My name is Nadia Blake."

"Is it urgent?" she asked with chilly pleasantness. "As you can probably hear, we've got visitors."

I could hear the rise and fall of voices coming from inside the house. It was midday on Saturday and the bereaved widower Clive was hosting a small social event with his lover. I could hear the clink of glasses.

"It is urgent, actually."

"Come in, then."

The hall was huge and cool, and from here the sound of voices was louder. She had lived here, I thought, gazing round. This is the house that she had wanted to turn into her dream home, but now Gloria was presiding over the dream home, for the workmen had obviously come back. The room in front of me was full of ladders and pots of paint. There were drapes over the furniture at the end of the hall.

"Would you like to wait here?" she said.

I followed her through anyway. Together, we went into a large living room, obviously freshly painted in slate gray, with large French windows giving out onto a newly dug-over garden. On the mantelpiece there was a photo in a silver oval frame of three children. No Jenny. Was this what would happen to me, if I died—would the waters just close over me like this?

The room had maybe ten or twelve people in it, all holding glasses and standing in clusters. Maybe they had been friends of Jenny's and now they were gathered here to welcome the new mistress of the house. Gloria went up to a solid-looking man with dark, graying hair and a jowly face. She put a hand on his shoulder and murmured something in his ear. He looked up sharply at me and walked across.

"Yes?" he said.

"Sorry to butt in," I said.

"Gloria said you had something to tell me."

"My name is Nadia Blake. I'm being threatened by the same man who killed Jenny."

His face hardly altered. He looked around shiftily as if he was checking whether anybody else was paying attention.

"Oh," he said. "Well, what do you want?"

"What do you mean? Your wife was murdered. Now he wants to kill me."

"I'm very sorry," he said evenly. "But why are you here?"

"I thought you could tell me things about Jenny."

He took a sip of wine and began steering me toward the edge of the room.

"I've told the police everything that's relevant," he said. "I don't quite see what you're doing here. This has been a tragedy. Now I am just trying to get on with my own life as best as I can."

"You seem to be managing pretty well," I said, looking round the room.

His face turned purple.

"What did you say?" he said furiously. "Please leave now, Miss Blake."

I felt in a panic of rage and mortification. I started to make a stammering attempt at self-justification. Even as I spoke, I saw a boy, a teenage boy, sitting alone on the window seat. He was skinny and pale, with greasy fair hair and dark smudges under his eyes, pimples on his forehead. He had about him all the awkward spindly hopelessness of male adolescence; all the messy, terrified confusion of a son who has lost his mother. Josh, the eldest son. I stared at him and our eyes met. He had huge dark eyes, like a spaniel's. Lovely eyes in a plain face.

"I'll go now," I said quietly. "I'm sorry if I disturbed you. It's just that I'm scared. I'm looking for help."

He nodded at me. Maybe his face wasn't so cruel, really, just a bit stupid and complacent. Maybe he was just like everybody else. A bit weaker, maybe, a bit more selfish.

"Sorry," he said with a helpless shrug.

"Thanks." I turned on my heel, trying not to cry, trying not to care that everyone was looking at me as if I was some beggar who had forced her way in. In the hall a little boy on a trike pedaled furiously across my path and stopped.

"I know you. You're the clown," he shouted. "Lena, the clown's come to visit. Come and see the clown."

FOURTEEN

I'll have everything," I said firmly. "Eggs and bacon, fried bread, fried potatoes, tomato, sausage, mushrooms. And what's that?"

The woman behind the counter inspected the contents of the metal container.

"Black pudding."

"All right, I'll have that. And a pot of tea. What about you?"

Lynne had gone slightly pale, maybe at the sight of what was being piled onto my plate.

"Oh," she said. "A piece of toast. Some tea."

We carried our trays out of the café into the sunny garden on the edge of the park. We'd arrived when it opened and we were the first. I chose a discreet table in a corner and we unloaded our plates and cups and metal teapots. I began eating. I attacked the fried egg first, cutting into the yolk so that it spread around the plate. Lynne looked at me with what I took to be fastidious disapproval.

"Is this not your sort of thing?" I said, wiping my mouth with the paper napkin.

"It's a bit early in the day for me." She sipped her tea

delicately and took a caterpillar-sized nibble out of her toast.

It was a beautiful morning. Tame sparrows stalked around the table legs in search of crumbs, squirrels were chasing each other along branches of the large trees on the other side of the wall in the park proper. For a blessed few seconds I just pretended Lynne wasn't there. I took bites of my heart-attack breakfast and washed it down with mahogany-brown tea.

"Do you want me to move away from the table?" Lynne asked. "When your friend arrives."

"Don't bother," I said. "You know her."

"What?" she asked, looking startled.

This was the bit I enjoyed. It must have been the magician in me.

"It's Grace Schilling."

I took a triumphant bite of grilled tomato attached to a piece of bacon.

"But . . ." Lynne stammered.

"Hm?" was all I could manage from my full mouth. I could see she was trying to decide which of fourteen questions she was going to ask.

"Who . . . who arranged it?"

"I did."

"But . . . does DCI Links know?"

I shrugged.

"Dr. Schilling may have let him know. That's not my problem."

"But . . ."

"There she is."

Dr. Schilling had walked into the eating area. There were several tables occupied now—people with children, couples spreading out the Sunday papers—and she hadn't spotted us yet. She was smartly dressed as usual, maybe just a bit more casual. She wore dark blue trousers that came only halfway down her ankles and a black V-necked sweater. And she wore sunglasses. She caught sight of us and walked across. She took the sunglasses off and put them on the table with a bunch of keys and, I was interested to see, a packet of cigarettes. She looked at us warily. She had her normal cool expression and I felt in an amused way as if I had been caught sitting in a pigsty with my head in the trough.

"Do you want some breakfast?" I said.

"I'm not really a breakfast sort of person."

"Black coffee and a cigarette?" I said.

"That's usually all I can manage."

I looked over at the aghast Lynne.

"Could you get Dr. Schilling a coffee?" I asked.

Lynne scampered off.

"It's a bit like having a PA," I said with a smile. "I quite like it. Did you talk to Links?"

She lit a cigarette.

"I told him you had asked to see me."

"Is that all right?"

"He was surprised."

I cleared up the last of the egg yolk with my fried bread.

"Can you be discreet?" I asked.

"What do you mean?"

"I've seen the files," I said. "Well, some of them. It wasn't exactly through the normal channels, so I'd rather you didn't talk about it too much."

She was startled. Of course she was. I was getting used to the look. She took a deep drag of her cigarette and shifted in her chair. She was ill at ease. Did she feel she had lost control? I hoped so.

"Then why did you tell me?"

"I need to ask you some questions. I know that you've

been lying to me solidly." She looked up sharply, opened her mouth to speak but didn't. "It doesn't matter. I'm not interested in that anymore. I want you to realize that I know about Zoe and Jennifer. I've seen the autopsy reports. I've got no illusions. All I want is for you to be frank with me."

Lynne returned with the coffee.

"Do you mind if I sit here?" she asked.

"Sorry, Lynne, but I think this conversation had better be private," I said.

She flushed and moved away to a neighboring table. I turned back to Grace Schilling. "I don't have any opinion one way or the other about the general ability of the police. But obviously you'll understand that I don't have any confidence in their ability to protect me from being killed. You, they, whatever, have had two women under protection and they're both dead."

"Nadia," said Grace. "I can appreciate how you feel, but there were particular reasons for that. In the first case of Miss Haratounian—"

"Zoe."

"Yes. In that case the degree of threat wasn't appreciated until it was too late. In the case of Mrs. Hintlesham, there was a problem . . ."

"You mean the arrest of her husband?"

"Yes, so you should realize that your situation is entirely different."

I poured myself a new cup of tea.

"Grace, you may have misunderstood me. I'm not here to score points against you, or gather information for a complaint, or to get some reassurance. But please don't insult me by saying I shouldn't be worried. I've seen the police memo, which you've also seen, about how the scene of my murder should be dealt with."

Grace lit another cigarette.

"What do you want from me?" she asked impassively.

"There was no report by you in the files I saw. Maybe that's because it says things about me I wouldn't like. I need to know what you know."

"I'm not sure I know anything useful."

"Why me? I hoped the files would show something we had in common. I couldn't find anything beyond the fact that we're all little."

Grace looked reflective. She took a deep drag on her cigarette.

"Yes," she said. "And you're all striking-looking, in different ways."

"Well, that's very nice. . . ."

"You're all vulnerable. Sexual sadists prey on women the way a hunting animal preys on other animals. It chooses ones who hang back, who are unsure. Zoe Haratounian was new to living in London, unsure of herself. Jenny Hintlesham was trapped in an unhappy marriage. You've just split up with a boyfriend."

"Is that it?"

"It may be enough."

"Can you tell me anything about him?"

She paused again for a while.

"There will be clues," she said. "There are always clues. It is just a question of recognizing them as such. A French criminologist, Dr. Locarde, once famously said that 'every criminal leaves something of himself at the scene of the crime—something no matter how minute—and always takes something of the scene away with him.' Until we find out precisely what those clues are—and we will find out—all that I can say is that he's probably white. Probably in his twenties or early thirties. Above average height. Physically strong. Educated, possibly to university level. But I'm sure you've worked most of that out for yourself."

"Do I know him?"

Grace stubbed out her cigarette and started to speak, then stopped and for the first time looked really unhappy. She was having obvious difficulty pulling herself together.

"Nadia," she said finally. "I wish I could say something helpful. I'd like to say it's not somebody you know well, because I hope that the police would have established some connection with the other women. But it might be a close friend, might be somebody you've met once and forgotten about, or it might be someone who just saw you once."

I looked around. I was glad I had chosen to meet her on a sunny morning with children running around making a racket.

"It's not a matter of sleeping," I said. "At the moment I don't dare close my eyes because when I do I see the photograph of Jenny Hintlesham lying dead with . . . well, I'm sure you've seen it. I can't accept that there is someone I have met, who is walking around leading a normal life after having done that."

Grace was running a long, slim finger around the rim of her coffee cup.

"He's highly organized. Look at the notes and the effort taken to deliver them."

"But I still can't believe that the police couldn't have protected these women after he'd said what he was going to do."

Grace nodded vigorously.

"In the last few weeks I've done some research. There have been a number of cases of this kind. One was a case a few years ago in Washington, D.C. A man made murderous explicit threats in notes to women. The husband of the first woman hired armed guards and she was still murdered in her home. The second had twenty-four-hour police guard and was tortured and killed in her own bedroom while her husband was in the house. I'm sorry to talk like this, but you asked me to be frank. Some of these men see themselves as geniuses. They're not geniuses. They're more like men with an obsessive hobby. What they are is motivated. They want to make women suffer and then to kill them, and they devote all their energy and resourcefulness and intelligence to carrying it out. The police do their best, but it's hard to combat such singleness of purpose."

"What happened to that killer in Washington?"

"They finally caught him at the scene."

"Did they save the woman?"

Grace looked away.

"I can't remember," she said. "All I can say is that this isn't a sweating psychopath living in a cardboard box under a bridge. He's probably functioning perfectly well at the moment. Ted Bundy returned from committing two separate murders and, according to his girlfriend, he didn't even seem tired."

"Who's he?"

"Another man who killed women."

"But why go to all this trouble?" I protested. "Why not just attack women in dark alleys?"

"The trouble is part of the pleasure. The point I'm making, Nadia, is that you've got to give up all your commonsense views about character or motive. He's not after your money. He doesn't even hate you. At least, that's not how he sees it. He may see it as love. Think of the letters he sends: They are love letters, in a perverse way. He becomes obsessive about the women he chooses."

"You mean he's the train-spotter and I'm the train."

"Well, sort of."

"But why? I can't understand all this effort, writing notes, doing a drawing, taking terrible risks delivering the notes, and then killing these ordinary women horribly. Why?"

I looked Grace in the eyes. Her face was now almost a mask, expressionless.

"You think because terrible things are happening there have to be big motives. At some point, this person will be in custody and someone—it may be me—will talk to him about his life. Maybe he was savagely beaten as a child, or abused by an uncle, or suffered a head injury which resulted in a brain lesion. That will be the reason. Of course there are plenty of people who were savagely beaten or abused or injured who don't grow up as sexual psychopaths. It's just what he likes doing. Why do we like doing what we like doing?"

"What do you think will happen?"

She lit yet another cigarette.

"He's escalating," she said. "The first murder was almost opportunistic. He probably didn't even look at her face, as if he wanted to eliminate her individuality. The second was far more violent and invasive. It's a characteristic pattern. The crimes become more violent and uncontrolled. The perpetrator gets caught."

I suddenly felt as if a cloud had passed over the sun. I looked up. It hadn't. The sky was a beautiful blue.

"That should be helpful to the person after next that he picks on."

We both got up to leave. I looked round at Lynne and she avoided my gaze. I turned back to Grace.

"How do you feel about the last couple of months?" I asked. "Are you pleased with the way you've conducted the inquiry?"

She picked up her sunglasses, her keys, and her cigarette packet.

"I gave up smoking—when was it?—five years ago, I think. I keep going over and over and thinking what I could have done different. When he's caught, maybe I'll know."

She gave a rueful smile. "Don't worry. I'm not asking for your sympathy." She took something out of her pocket and offered it to me. It was a business card. "You can call me anytime."

I took it and looked at it in the pointless, polite way one does.

"I don't think you'd be able to get there in time," I said.

FIFTEEN

When I was at college, supposedly learning how to be a grown-up and ready for the real world, I had a friend who died of leukemia. Her name was Laura, and she had tiny feet, cheeks like rosy apples, and a dirty laugh. She got ill in her first year and died before her finals. We got used to the fact of her death and her absence from us horribly quickly, remembering her occasionally in jolts of shame and sentimentality, but I thought a great deal about Laura now. In a strange and entirely unwelcome way, I felt closer to her—and to Jenny and Zoe, women I'd never met—than I did to my living friends.

Even Zach and Janet felt distant to me. They seemed appalled, yet almost embarrassed, by my situation. They rang me up too often but didn't come round often enough, and when we did meet there was nothing we could properly talk about, because I was in the shadow and they were in the sunlight. We were self-conscious together. It was as if I had gone beyond them, into some other place that they could not enter and I couldn't exit. I remembered with a shiver that Laura had said the same kind of thing, toward the end, when it was obvious to all of us that she wasn't going to make it. She had said, or shouted, rather, that she felt as if she had gone into a waiting room, and soon the door on the other side of it would open for her and she'd have to go through. I remembered the shudder of terror I had felt when she'd said that. I had imagined the door opening out onto pitch black, and stepping out of a lit and furnished room into the empty abyss.

Laura had gone through all the stages you're supposed to go through when you're confronting the fact of death: disbelief and anger and grief and terror and finally a dazed, numbed kind of acceptance—perhaps because she was so worn down by the treatment and by the lurches between hope and despair. One night after she had died, a group of us had had an ugly argument, fueled by too much to drink, about whether she could have lived, or lived longer, if she had struggled more, rather than giving up and letting go. In the past, the image of letting go had for me been one of a hand gently uncurling from the hand of a beloved; now, after seeing the photos and case notes, it was more of two hands clinging to a ledge until a heavy boot stamps them off. Someone said she should have fought harder, as if it was Laura's fault that she had died, not just brutal bad luck.

I was going to fight. I didn't know if it would make the smallest bit of difference, but that wasn't the point. I wasn't going to cower in blind terror in a fucking waiting room, staring at the door in the opposite wall, feeling only the heart-thumping, mouth-drying, stomach-churning, blinding, dehumanizing dread I'd been feeling for the last few days. I'd seen the photographs, the case notes. I'd talked to Grace. I didn't have much faith in Links and Cameron, partly because I sensed they didn't have much faith in themselves and, without ever admitting it, they were waiting for me

to die. So I was left with me. Just me. And I have always
hated waiting.

One thing was certain. I couldn't go on sitting in my flat
any longer, hiding from Lynne and from my own fear. The
odd thing was that Lynne and I were still not talking about
my possible death. It was a taboo subject. We only discussed plans, functional things like where I was going to
go, and where she should wait for me. We no longer ate
meals together, not even takeaway chips or toast at breakfast. I had stopped treating her like a semi-guest, a nearly-
friend.

The day after I met Grace Schilling I went ice skating
with Claire, who was a resting actress and usually more
resting than acting. She could skate backward and do those
twizzles that make your head spin. Lynne and another policewoman sat morosely on the side and watched me smashing into young children, toppling them like nine pins, and
falling over myself in a wild flailing of arms and legs.
Then, later the same day, I invited myself to Zach's and
told him to get other friends round, which he obediently
did. Lynne waited outside while we ate tacos and I drank
too much red wine and made loud and stupid jokes, and
only tipped myself back into the waiting car at two in the
morning. And all the time, even when I was flooding my
body with alcohol or flirting with a man called Terence
who was clearly gay and embarrassed by me, I was trying
to think what to do next. Grace had said that people like
this man were always several steps ahead: more focused,
more determined, more persistent. I wanted to get a step
ahead of him.

The next morning I woke with a splitting headache and
a dry mouth. I felt queasy, and when I drew the curtains,
the light was like a shaft of pain boring through my eye

sockets. I staggered to the kitchen and drank two tumblers of water, ignoring Lynne's sympathetic, mildly reproachful expression. Then I made a large pot of tea and returned to my bedroom, carrying it. I sat cross-legged on my bed, wearing a tatty gray vest and a pair of sweatpants, and stared at my reflection in the long wardrobe mirror. I was looking at myself much more often these days, I suppose because I no longer took myself for granted. Shouldn't I look different, thinner and more tragic? As far as I could tell, nothing about me had changed from the outside. There I was, just a small woman with freckles over the bridge of her nose, unbrushed hair, and a hangover.

The doorbell rang and I heard Lynne answer. I listened, but I could make out only a few muttered words. Then there was a knock on my bedroom door.

"Yes?"

"There's someone who's come to see you."

"Who?"

There was a fractional hesitation on the other side of the door.

"Josh Hintlesham." Lynne lowered her voice to a stage whisper. "Her son."

"Oh my God. Hang on." I jumped off the bed. "Tell him to come in."

"Are you sure? I don't know what Links would—"

"I'll be through in a minute."

I rushed into the bathroom, swallowed three acetaminophen for my headache, splashed cold water over my face, and scrubbed my teeth vigorously. Josh. The boy on the window seat with teenage acne and Jenny's dark eyes.

I went into the living room and held out my hand.

"Josh, hello."

His hand was cold and limp in mine. He didn't meet my gaze but muttered something and stared at the floor.

"Can you wait outside, in the car, Lynne?" I said.

She left, casting an anxious gaze back over her shoulder as she closed the door behind her. Josh shifted nervously from foot to foot. He was wearing a tracksuit that was a bit too small for him, and his greasy hair flopped over his eyes. Somebody needed to take him shopping, tell him to take a bath and wash his hair and use deodorant. I couldn't see Gloria doing that.

"Coffee or tea?" I asked.

"I'm all right." His voice was a mumble.

"Juice?" Though come to think of it, I didn't have any juice in the fridge.

"No. Thanks."

"Sit down."

I gestured to the sofa.

He perched uncomfortably on one end, while I ground some coffee beans and waited for the kettle to boil. I saw how large his hands and feet were, how bony his wrists. His skin was pale but the rims of his eyes were red. He looked a mess to me, though I hadn't met a teenage boy in ten years. Any boys over nine were a mystery to me.

"How did you find me?"

"I looked in the Yellow Pages, under 'Entertainers.' Christo told me you were a clown."

"Brilliant." I sat opposite him with my cup of coffee. "Listen, Josh, I'm sorry about your mother."

He nodded and shrugged.

"Yeah," he said. Mr. Cool.

"You must miss her."

God, why couldn't I just shut up?

He winced and started to chew one of his nails.

"She didn't really have much time for me," he said. "She was always in a hurry, or cross about something."

I felt compelled to stick up for her.

"I suppose that with three children and the house and stuff," I said, and pretended to take a sip from my empty cup. Nadia the amateur therapist. "Have you got someone you can talk to about all of this?" I asked. "Friends or a doctor or something?"

"I'm all right," he said.

We sat in silence and for something to do I poured myself another cup of coffee and gulped it.

"What about you?" he asked suddenly.

"Me?"

"Are you scared?"

"I'm trying to be positive."

"I dream about her," he said suddenly. "Every night. I don't dream of her being killed or stuff. They're nice dreams, happy dreams all about Mum stroking my hair and hugging me and stuff like that, though she only used to stroke Christo's hair. She said I was too old for all that now." He flushed furiously. "It just makes it worse." Then he said: "Nobody'll tell me exactly how she died."

"Josh . . ."

"I can cope with the truth."

I thought about the photograph of Jenny's corpse and looked at the awkward brave boy in front of me.

"Quickly," I said. "She died quickly. She wouldn't have known what was happening."

"You're lying to me as well. I thought you'd tell me the truth."

I took a deep breath.

"Josh, the truth is: I don't know. Your mother is dead. She's out of pain now."

I was ashamed of myself, but I didn't know how to do any better. Josh stood up abruptly and started wandering around the room.

"Are you really a clown?"

"An entertainer."

He picked up my juggling beanbags.

"Can you juggle?"

I took them from him and started to toss them around. He looked unimpressed.

"I meant, really juggle. I know loads of people who can juggle with three balls."

"*You* try it."

"I'm not an entertainer."

"No," I said dryly.

"I've brought you something," he said.

He crossed the room to his rucksack and fished out a manila envelope.

There were dozens of photographs, most of them taken on holiday over the years. I leafed through them, horribly aware of Josh at my shoulder and of his labored breathing. Jenny very slim and tanned in a yellow bikini on a sandy beach under a slice of blue sky. Jenny in well-pressed jeans and a green polo shirt, in the stiff circle of Clive's arm and smiling prettily for the camera. She was so much better looking than he was. Jenny with a much younger Josh, hand in hand; holding a bald baby who was presumably Chris; sitting on a lawn surrounded by all three sons. Jenny with long hair, bobbed hair, layered hair. Jenny skiing, crouched neatly forward with poles tucked behind her. In groups, alone.

The one that touched me most was a photograph taken when she was obviously unaware of the camera and no longer wore her watchful look. She was in profile and slightly blurred. There was a strand of glossy hair against her face. Her cheek looked smooth; her lips were slightly parted, and her hand was half raised. She seemed thoughtful, almost sad. Armor off, she looked like someone I could have known after all. Something else hit me like a blade pushed into me: There was something interesting about her. I could see what might have caught someone's attention. I could imagine her as a woman people could be fascinated by. Oh God.

I laid them down in silence and turned to Josh.

"You poor boy," I said, and he started crying then, but trying not to: gulping and sniffing and gagging on his grief, and saying "Jesus" under his breath; hiding his head in the crook of his arm. I put a hand on his shoulder and waited, and eventually he sat up, fished in his pocket for a crumpled tissue, blew his nose snottily.

"Sorry," he said.

"Don't," I said. "It's good she has someone to cry for her."

"I ought to go now," he said, gathering up the photographs and pushing them back into the envelope.

"Will you be all right?"

"Yeah." He wiped his nose on his sleeve.

"I'll give you my card so if you want to call me, you don't have to look me up in the Yellow Pages again. Hang on."

I went to my desk in the bedroom and Josh lounged in the doorway. He was so thin. He looked as if he would fall over if he didn't have something to lean on. A pile of bones.

"You're not exactly tidy," he remarked. Lippy sod.

"True. I didn't know you were coming, so I didn't tidy up for you."

He grinned in embarrassment.

"And your antique computer," he observed.

"So I've been told."

I rummaged in the drawers for my business cards.

"Are you on-line?"

"On-line? Not as such."

He sat down and started tapping at the keyboard. He looked at the screen as if it were a porthole with something comical on the other side.

"How big is your hard disk?"

"You've lost me."

"That's what it's all about. You just need more power. This is like a mosquito trying to pull a lorry. You need a system with proper memory."

"Right," I said, hoping he'd shut up.

"Faster hamsters."

I found the card and brought it through, brandishing it.

"Here you are. Nadia Blake, children's entertainer, puppeteer, juggler, magician, and general—" Then I froze. "What? What the fuck did you say?"

"Don't be angry. It's just that a computer is almost useless without proper—"

"No, what did you actually say?"

"I said you needed more power."

"No. What fucking exact words did you say?"

Josh paused and thought for a moment and then for the first time I saw him laugh.

"Sorry, that's just a stupid expression. Faster hamsters. It just means more power."

"Where did you get it from?"

"It's just a metaphor. It must come from hamsters running round on wheels, I suppose. I never really thought about it before."

"No, no, no. Who did you hear it from?"

"Who?" Josh pulled a face. "Just a guy at our school's computer club."

"What? A pupil?"

"No, Hack, one of the guys who helps run it. He's been really nice to me, since Mum died especially."

I was trembling.

"Hack? What kind of name is that?"

"It's his handle. It's his *nom de guerre*."

I tried to control myself. I gripped my hands together.

"Josh," I said. "Do you know his real name?"

He wrinkled his brow. Please please please.

"He's called Morris, I think. He knows about computers, but he'll just say the same thing I've said."

SIXTEEN

$\mathbf{M}$y hands were shaking so much I could hardly punch the numbers on the phone. I got myself put through to Links. I had discovered that if you were insistent enough, he always turned out to be in. He was wary and distant with me on the phone. I don't think he'd quite known how to handle me since I'd absconded. He'd like to have charged me with something, no doubt, but it didn't seem I'd broken any law. Still, he could be grumpy at least, from his position of weakness.

"Yes?" he said.

"I've just been talking to Joshua Hintlesham."

"What?"

"He's Jennifer Hintlesham's son."

"I know that. What are you doing talking to him?"

"He came round to see me."

"How? How does he know who you are?"

If he had been within reach I think I would have leaned over and shaken him and rapped my knuckles on his skull, but he wasn't.

"Don't bother about that. It doesn't matter. The point is, I've found someone we both know."

"What do you mean?"

"The other day something went wrong with my computer and I called a number on some card and this guy called Morris came round and fixed it. It was actually very easy. I actually know sod-all about computers. And the other day, when I slipped away, I bumped into him in the street. He was very friendly. I didn't think anything of it. But I was talking to Josh and he goes to a computer club that's connected to his school. And one of the people who runs it is this guy called Morris."

Now there was a long pause on the phone. That had given him something to chew on.

"Is it the same person?"

"Sounds like it." I couldn't resist adding: "It may not mean anything. Do you want me to do some checking?"

"No, no," he said instantly. "Definitely not. We'll do that. What do you know about him?"

"He's called Morris Burnside. I think he's in his mid-twenties. I can't say much about him. He seemed nice, clever. But then I'm impressed with anybody who can switch a computer on. Josh liked him a lot. He's not like some weirdo. He's good-looking. He wasn't shy or strange with me or anything like that."

"How well do you know him?"

"I don't know him. As I said, I just met him twice."

"Has he tried to get in touch with you?"

I went through our meetings in my mind. There wasn't much.

"I think he was attracted to me. I told him that I'd just split up. He half asked me out and I put him off. But there was nothing nasty about it. He offered to help me buy a powerful new computer. I said no, but that doesn't seem enough reason to kill me."

"Do you know where he lives?"

"I've got his phone number. Is that all right?"

I read it to him off the card, the card I'd been so pleased to find just two weeks earlier.

"Fine, leave it with us. Don't make any attempt to get in touch with him."

"You'll talk to him?"

"We'll check him out."

"It may be nothing," I said.

"We'll see."

"It may not be the same person."

"We'll check."

When I put the phone down I wanted to collapse in a heap, to cry, to faint, to be put to bed and looked after. But there was just Lynne, hovering like an annoying fly that I wanted to swat. She had been listening to my end of the phone conversation with growing interest. Now she looked at me expectantly. She wanted to be filled in. My heart sank. Sometimes it felt like having a live-in au pair without even having a child for her to look after. I needed to get out of here. Quickly, without even giving myself time to speak, I picked up the phone and dialed.

"You met him."

Zach stopped, as if he couldn't walk and think hard at the same time.

"When?"

"The other day. When you came round and this young man had fixed my computer. You met him when he was on the way out."

"The one who wouldn't take any money?"

"That's right."

"Sandy-colored hair."

"No. Quite long dark hair."

"Have you seen *my* hair?"

Zach stepped over and tried to look at his reflection in a shop window. We were walking along Camden High Street, in and out of shops, occasionally trying things on, not buying anything. Lynne was twenty yards behind, hands in pockets.

"It's going," he continued. "What I ought to do is shave it, if I had any integrity. What do you think?"

He turned his anxious face to me.

"Leave it as it is," I said. "I don't think a shaved skull would suit you."

"What's wrong with my skull?"

"As I was saying, it turned out that this guy, who's called Morris, also knew the son of one of the women who was killed."

"You mean he might have killed her?"

"Well, he's the only connection we've found."

"But he couldn't have. I know I only met him for eight seconds, but he just seemed a normal person."

"So? I talked to the psychologist who's an expert on this. She said it probably would be someone who seemed normal. I'm just praying it's him. If he could just be locked away and my life could start again." I reached for Zach's hand. "You know, I was absolutely convinced I was going to die. They tried to protect these other two women and they failed. They were killed. I just keep thinking about dying. About being dead. I've been so scared."

Tears started running down my face. It wasn't precisely the time or the place for that, with shoppers pushing their way past us. Zach put his arms around me and kissed the top of my head. He could be nice sometimes. He pulled some fairly pristine tissues from his pocket and handed them to me. I wiped my face and blew my nose.

"You should have asked for help," he said.

"What would you have done?"

"Something," he said. "For example, about being dead. Think of before you were born. You were dead for millions and billions of years. You don't find that frightening, do you?"

"Yes, I do."

Suddenly there was a presence at my elbow. It was Lynne.

"There's a message from DCI Links. He'd like to see you straightaway."

"What's happened?"

Lynne gave a shrug.

"He just said he wants to see you."

They were so nice to me at the police station. I was whisked straight through and taken into a grander office, set away from all the other desks in the open-plan setting. I was seated in the chair in front of the desk and brought tea and two biscuits on a little saucer and I was told that Links would be along in just a tick. I had managed no more than a couple of sips and a dip of the biscuit into the tea when Links and Cameron came into the room. They both looked serious and formal. Cameron sat on the sofa to one side and Links sat behind the desk. So it was *his* office.

"They got you tea?" he said.

I held up my cup. There wasn't really much to be said.

"I wanted to tell you straightaway," he said. "We've interviewed Morris Burnside and we've now eliminated him from the inquiry."

The room seemed to shift around me, leaving me queasy and dazed.

"What?"

"I want to assure you that this is a positive step."

"But how could you clear him so quickly?"

He had picked up a paper clip from his desk. First he had unwound it so that it was straight. Now he was trying to twist it back into its old shape. I had tried that before. It never works as well again. But as an activity it at least prevented him from having to look me in the face.

"I understand from Dr. Schilling that you have found out that there are two other murders—I mean two murders involved—in this inquiry. Document analysis has shown with complete certainty that the same person was involved in the murders of Zoe Haratounian and Jennifer Hintlesham and in sending you the threats that you have received. It's not just the documents." Links was now talking as if he were in severe pain. "We know that the murderer went to the trouble of placing an object belonging to Mrs. Hintlesham in the flat of Miss Haratounian as a means of er . . . muddying the waters." He untwisted the clip again. "On the morning that Zoe Haratounian was murdered, Morris Burnside was in Birmingham at an information technology conference that lasted all that weekend. He was manning a stall, doing presentations. We made a couple of calls. There are numerous witnesses who can place him there for the entire Sunday, morning till evening."

"Couldn't he have got away?"

"No, he couldn't."

"How did he react to being questioned?"

"He was a bit shocked, of course. But he was perfectly polite and cooperative. Nice young man."

"Was he angry?"

"Not at all. Anyway, we didn't mention you had given us his name."

I leaned forward and put my teacup on the desk.

"Is it all right if I leave that here?"

"Yes, of course."

I had nothing left. Everything seemed to have drained out of me. I'd thought I was safe. Now I had to go back out into it again. I couldn't face it. I was too tired.

"I thought it was all over," I said numbly.

"You'll be fine," Links said, still not looking at me. "The protection will continue."

I got up and looked around for the door, in a daze.

"You must see it as a positive step. We've eliminated one potential suspect. That's progress."

I looked around.

"What?" I said.

"One less person to bother about."

"Only six billion to go," I said. "Oh, I suppose we can eliminate women as well and children. That's probably two billion. Minus one."

Links stood up.

"Stadler will see you out," he said.

It was a matter of half leading, half carrying me out. On the way he stopped in a quiet stretch of corridor.

"You all right?" he said.

I moaned something.

"I need to see you," he said.

"What?"

"I've been thinking about you all the time. I want to help you, Nadia. I need you and I think that you need me. You need me."

He touched my arm.

"Uh?" It took me some time to work out what he was doing. I moaned something again and shook him off me. "Don't touch me," I said. "Don't ever touch me again."

SEVENTEEN

⁓

Fear kicked in. I was legless with it; my insides felt molten with it. I crawled into bed and lay staring up at the ceiling, trying not to think, yet trying desperately to think. A few hours of hope and elation, and what now, then? What now, when I was back at the beginning where I'd begun just a few days, a week or so, ago? Except it didn't seem like days, but months and years, a dreary and ghastly eternity of fear. I slept and woke and slept again, stale and itchy sleep, just under the first level, where dreams lurk and catch you like thick weeds waving under the surface of the water. It was dark and then it was dim and then at last light again, a steely sky outside the window. I lay and listened to a bird singing outside. I peered at my watch. Six-thirty. I pulled the covers over my head. What was I supposed to do with myself today?

The first thing I did was to ring Zach. His voice when he answered was thick with sleep.

"Zach, it's me. Nadia. Sorry. But I had to. It wasn't him after all. It wasn't Morris. He couldn't have been the one."

"Shit," he said.

"Right. What am I going to do now?" I found I was crying. Tears were dribbling into my mouth, itching against my nose, tracking their way down my neck.

"Are they sure?"

"Yeah, it's not him."

"Shit," he said again. I could tell he was trying to think of something to add that wouldn't sound so dismaying.

"I'm back at square one, Zach. He'll get me. I can't do this. I can't go on like this. It's no use."

"Yes you can, Nadia. You can."

"No." I wiped the sleeve of my nightie over my teary, snotty face. My glands ached and my throat hurt. "No, I can't."

"Listen to me. You're brave. I have faith in you."

He kept saying that: I have faith in you; you're brave. And I kept crying and snuffling and saying: I'm just me, and: No, I can't. But somehow the repetitions made me feel a bit better; my protests thinned out. I even heard myself giggle when Zach swore I'd live to be a hundred. He made me promise to make myself some breakfast. He told me he'd ring me in an hour or so, that he would come round to see me later.

I obediently toasted some rather stale bread and ate it with a large cup of black coffee. I sat in the kitchen and stared out of the window. People walked past and I thought to myself: It could be him, with the baseball cap and the wide trousers, lips pursed in a whistle I couldn't hear. Or him with headphones, towing the yappy dog. Or him, with the straggly beard and thinning hair, hunched inside his quilted anorak on a baking late-August day. Anyone. It could be anyone.

I tried not to think about Jenny after she had died. If I called to mind that photograph, panic almost closed my throat. Before I saw the files, the killer had been a lurking menace, something abstract and almost unreal. But there was nothing abstract about Zoe's sweet face, or about Jenny's grotesque corpse, and now there was a stirring, tentative part of me that was starting to feel personal hatred toward him: an intimate, purposeful feeling. I sat at the kitchen table and held on to that feeling, let it take clearer shape in my mind. He wasn't a cloud, a shadow, something dreadful in the air I breathed. He was a man who had killed two young women and wanted to kill me. Him against me.

I found an unopened letter informing me on the outside of the envelope that I had already won a prize and I started to make notes on the back of it. What did I know? He had killed Zoe in mid-July, Jenny in early August. As Grace put it, he was "escalating." A locket of Jenny's, missing for weeks, had been discovered in Zoe's flat, a photograph of Zoe had been found among Clive's possessions, but those were the only things that had been found to connect the two women. The only link—weak and, as it turned out, meaningless—between me and Jenny was Morris. I thought of the other people who had been interviewed: Fred, of course, though never as a suspect since he had been cleared before the murder was even done; Clive; the real estate agent, Guy; a businessman called Nick Shale; a previous boyfriend of Zoe's back from traveling round the world; Jenny's crew of architects and builders and gardeners and cleaners. Now Morris. All the police had achieved, it seemed to me, was to eliminate the obvious suspects.

I sipped my cooling coffee. Where did that leave me? It left me sitting at my kitchen table, pathetically trying to be my own detective, watching men out the window, thinking: him, or him, or anyone at all. I was banging my head against the same wall the police had been banging their heads on for weeks.

I went into my bedroom and found the scrap of paper

on which I'd written the names and addresses I'd filched from the files Stadler had shown me. I stared at them, until the writing blurred. Then, for lack of any better idea, I took a deep breath and picked up the telephone.

"Good morning, Clarke's. Can I help you?" A woman's voice, ringing with fake enthusiasm.

"I heard you're selling a flat in Holloway Road. I wondered if I could have a look at it."

"Hold on, please," she said, and I sat for a couple of minutes listening to Bach played on a child's miniature electric organ.

A male voice announced its presence on the line with a discreet cough.

"Guy here. Can I help you?"

I repeated my request.

"Great," he said. "Superbly located. Extremely convenient for Holloway Road."

"Can I see it today?"

"Definitely. How about this afternoon?"

"Is the owner there?"

"I'll show you round myself."

Lucky me.

I rang another number from my scrap of paper next. I don't really know why. Perhaps because of all the people in the files, she was the only one who had sounded sad.

"Hello?"

How do you begin? I decided to be direct.

"I'm Nadia Blake. You don't know me. I wanted to talk to you about Zoe." There was a silence on the other end of the phone. I couldn't even hear her breathing. "Sorry," I said. "I didn't want to upset you."

"Who are you? Are you a journalist?"

"No. I'm like her. I mean I've been getting letters from the man who killed her."

"Oh, God. I'm sorry. Nadia, you say?"

"That's right."

"Can I do anything?"

"I thought we might meet."

"Yes, of course. I'm still on holiday. I'm a teacher."

"How about at her flat, then, at two?"

"Her flat?"

"I'm being shown round."

"Why?"

"I wanted to see it."

"Are you sure?" She sounded doubtful. Maybe she thought I was mad.

"I just wanted to find out about Zoe."

"I'll be there. This is weird. You've no idea."

I had four hours before the appointment. A different woman police officer was here today. Bernice. I told her I wanted to go and visit a flat on Holloway Road just before two, and she didn't even blink, just nodded impassively and made a mark in the notebook she carried around with her. Perhaps she didn't know Zoe's old address, or perhaps everybody was just getting bored waiting for something to happen. Then I had a long bath, washed my hair, soaked in the sudsy water until the skin on my fingers and toes softened and shriveled. I painted my toenails and put on a dress I'd hardly ever worn. I'd been saving it up for a special occasion, some glamorous party where I'd meet my next Mr. Right, but it seemed stupid to wait for that now. I might as well wear it for Zoe's flat, for Louise and Guy. It was a lovely pale turquoise, tight-fitting with short sleeves and a scoop neck. I put on a necklace, some small earrings, a pair of sandals. I looked fresh and smart, as if I was about to go out to a summer party, drink champagne in some green garden. If only. I put on some lipstick to complete the picture.

At midday, Bernice came in and told me that two young men were here to see me. I peered out the hall window and saw Josh standing fidgeting at the doorway. Beside him stood someone with dark tousled hair, wearing a black cloth jacket. He was holding a packet of cigarettes in one hand and a bunch of flowers in the other and smiling at the doorway I was going to appear in.

When, for a couple of elated hours, I had thought Morris was the killer, the face I had remembered had been a murderer's face: cunning, his eyes dead, like shark's eyes. Now I saw that he was boyish and handsome. He looked rather endearing as he arranged his smile for me, and held up his paper-wrapped bouquet.

"Come in, both of you."

Josh muttered something and stumbled in, tripping over his undone laces. Morris held out the flowers.

"It should be me giving you flowers, to apologize for my suspicions," I said. "But thanks; they're lovely." On an impulse I stretched up and kissed him on his cheek. Bernice closed the door behind us like a jailer.

"I hope you don't mind me turning up like this," said Morris, watching me as I filled a jug with water and stuck the flowers in.

"Hack thought we should all get together," added Josh.

He was doing his restless prowl around the living room again, picking things up and putting them down, running his hands over objects.

"Sit down, Josh. You're making me nervous. It's good to see you both. It feels a bit odd."

"What?"

"Come on, look at us." I started to giggle wretchedly,

and Josh, out of nervous politeness, joined in. Morris stared at us both, frowning.

"How can you laugh," he asked when I'd stopped my hysterical chuckling, "when there's someone out there who wants to kill you?"

"You should have seen me this morning. Or yesterday, when I discovered it wasn't you after all. I hope you won't take it the wrong way when I tell you that I really, really wanted it to be you."

"Hope's a cruel thing," said Morris, nodding his head gravely.

I looked at Josh with concern.

"Are you all right?"

"Yeah, fine."

He didn't look fine at all; he looked dreadful, with a pallor that was almost green and bloodshot eyes. I stood up and steered him over to the sofa, pushed him back into its cushions.

"When did you last have something to eat?"

"I'm not hungry."

"I'm going to make you something to eat. Pasta maybe, if I've got any. Do you want some?" I asked Morris.

"I'll help you," he said. "Just rest there," he said to Josh, giving him a small slap on his shoulder. "Gather your strength."

Josh lolled back and closed his eyes. A pale smile spread over his face.

Morris chopped tomatoes. I found half a bag of pasta spirals. I poured them into a pan with a clatter and put the kettle on.

"Are you very scared?" he asked, just like Josh had done.

"It comes and goes," I said. "I'm trying to stay strong."

"That's good," he said, chopping away. "Are they helping you?"

"Who?"

"The police."

"Sort of," I said dismissively.

I didn't want to get into all of that. I had found a tin of pitted black olives. When the pasta was ready, I tossed a handful over it and sprinkled some olive oil over the top. It looked rather minimalist and elegant. I should have Parmesan cheese and black pepper to finish it off, though. Never mind. Morris was still cutting the tomatoes very slowly and methodically, into tiny cubes.

"How do you imagine him?" he asked.

"I don't," I said, surprising myself by my firmness. "I think about the women. Zoe and Jenny."

He scraped the tomatoes into a bowl.

"If there's anything I can do," he said. "Just ask."

"Thanks," I said. But not too encouragingly. I've got enough friends.

As we ate, I told Josh and Morris about my appointment to see round Zoe's flat. Both of them looked appropriately dumbfounded by the idea.

"Why don't you two come with me?" I asked suddenly, half regretting the suggestion as soon as I'd made it.

Josh shook his head. "Gloria's taking all of us to meet her mother," he said bitterly.

He seemed much better after his pasta, although all the olives were piled in a neat heap on the side of his plate.

"Yes," said Morris with a smile. "I'll come with you."

"I'm meeting a friend of Zoe's there as well," I said. "A woman called Louise."

"That's funny," Morris said.

"Why funny?"

Morris looked a bit taken aback.

"You're getting to know people who knew Josh's mother. And now people who knew Zoe. It seems strange."

"Does it?" I said. "It seems like something I have to do."

He murmured something that sounded like vague agreement. When he had finished his pasta, he stood up and fished a slim mobile phone out of his jacket pocket.

"Checking my messages," he said. He stood by the window and pressed buttons on the phone and listened, frowning. "Shit," he said eventually, buttoning up his jacket. "I've got an urgent call. I'll have to skip the flat. Sorry. I feel awful about that, after promising to help you."

"It doesn't matter."

He took my hand and squeezed it. Then he left. He liked me; I could tell he liked me. He'd liked me the first time he saw me, when he came round to mend my computer. Couldn't he tell I was miles away from things like that now, so far away it seemed impossible that one day I would feel desire again?

Josh left soon after. I kissed his cheek at the doorway and tears welled up in his eyes.

"See you," I said as cheerfully as I could. "Take care of yourself now."

Then, before he slouched off up the road, he blurted out: "You first. I mean you take care of yourself."

EIGHTEEN

Guy wore a chocolate brown suit, a Bart Simpson tie, and a large smile. He had very white teeth and a tan. He shook my hand firmly. He asked if he could call me Nadia and then kept saying my name, as if it was something he had learned at a course. As he unlocked the front door, a voice behind us said:

"Nadia?"

I turned and saw a woman about my size, about my age. She was dressed in a sleeveless yellow top and a very red skirt, which was so short I could almost see the curve of her buttocks; her bare brown legs were strong and shapely. Her glossy brown hair was pulled back from her face in a ponytail; her lips were painted a red to match her skirt. She looked bright, alert, pugnacious. My spirits rose.

"Louise? I'm glad you came."

She smiled reassuringly. Together we went into a dingy entrance hall and up the narrow stairs.

"This is the living room," said Guy unnecessarily as we stepped into a cramped space, which smelled musty and unlived in. A pair of thin orange curtains were half drawn across the small windows, and I stepped forward and opened them. What a depressing little flat.

"Tell you what," I said to Guy, "would it be all right if we just looked round it without you? You can wait outside."

"Don't you . . . ?"

"No," said Louise. Then, as he left, "Creep. Zoe couldn't stand him. He asked her out. Kept hassling her."

We smiled at each other sadly. I felt tears prick the back of my eyes. Zoe with the lovely smile lived here. Through that door, she died.

"I like the sound of her," I said. "I wish—" I stopped.

"She was great," said Louise. "I hate saying 'was.' The kids at the school adored her. Men were smitten too. There was something about her. . . ."

"Yes?"

Louise was walking around looking with eyes that clearly saw things I couldn't. When she talked it was almost to herself.

"She lost her mother when she was young, you know. And somehow she always seemed like that—like someone who didn't have a mother. It made you feel protective towards her. Maybe that's why . . ."

"What?"

"Who knows? Why does a woman get picked on?" She caught my eye.

"I've been wondering about that," I said.

I walked round the room, looking: Nothing had been cleared away yet, although somebody had obviously tidied everything up. Books were neatly stacked on surfaces, a couple of pencils, a ruler and an eraser lay on top of a lined notebook on the small table by the window. I opened it up and there on the first page was a list of lesson ideas, neatly listed and numbered. Zoe's handwriting: small looped letters, neat. On the wall was a framed page from a newspaper, with a picture of Zoe, surrounded by dozens of small children, holding a giant watermelon.

We went into the kitchen. Mugs stood on the draining board; some dead flowers drooped in a vase. A single bottle of white wine stood by the kettle. The fridge was open and gleamingly empty.

"Her aunt owns the flat now," said Louise, as if I had asked her some questions about arrangements.

I picked up a calculator that was lying on the counter surface and idly pressed a few buttons, watched a sum appear on its screen.

"Was she terrified?"

"Yeah. She stayed at my place. She had been completely out of it, but she seemed calmer on that last day. She thought it was going to be all right. I was outside, you know." Louise jerked her head toward the street. "Waiting on a double yellow line in my car along the road. I waited and I waited. Then I tooted the horn and waited some more and cursed her. Then I rang the doorbell. Finally I called the police."

"So you didn't see her body?"

Louise blinked at me.

"No," she said eventually. "They would not let me see it. It was only later they brought me to look at the flat. I couldn't believe it. She just got out of my car and said she wouldn't be a minute."

"Are you ladies all right in there?" called Guy from the stairwell.

"We won't be long," I shouted back.

Together we went through into her bedroom. The bed was stripped and a pile of sheets and pillowcases lay stacked on the chair. I opened the wardrobe. Her clothes were still there. She didn't have many. Three pairs of shoes stood on the wardrobe floor. I put up a hand and fingered the cloth of a pale blue dress, a cotton jacket with an unstitched hem.

"Did you know Fred?" I asked.

"Sure. Very charming. Zoe was better off without him, though. He wasn't exactly supportive. It was a relief to her when she finally told him it was over."

"I didn't know that."

Briefly I closed my eyes and let myself see the photograph of her corpse, peaceful on the floor as if she had gone to sleep there. Maybe she didn't suffer. I opened my eyes and there was Louise, looking at me with mild concern.

"What are you doing here?" she asked. "What's all this for?"

"I don't know," I said. "I hoped I might learn something, but I've no idea what it would be. Maybe I'm just looking for Zoe."

She smiled. "Are you looking for a clue?" she asked.

"Stupid, aren't I? Is anything missing?"

Louise looked around.

"The police wanted to know that. I couldn't really tell. The only thing I noticed was that there was a wall hanging that Fred had given her. That was gone."

"Yes," I said. "I saw that in the file on the murder scene."

"It seems a funny thing to steal. It can't have been worth anything."

"The police assumed that the killer used it to carry stuff away in."

Louise looked puzzled. "Why not just use a plastic carrier bag from the kitchen?"

"I don't know. I don't suppose people are all that rational just after they've killed someone."

"Anyway, she didn't have that many things. Her aunt may have helped herself already. And the police will have removed stuff, of course. Mostly it looks just like I remember it. Dreary place, isn't it?"

"Yes."

"She hated it. Especially by the end. But it doesn't give you any idea of what she was like." Louise went back into the living room and sat down on the sofa. "On her last day, we went shopping together. Just to buy her a couple of things to wear until she collected all her stuff, you know. We got her a pair of knickers and a bra and some socks, and then she said she wanted to buy a T-shirt. Mine were all too big for her. She was a skinny thing, and she'd lost weight with all the fear. So we ended up going to this kids' shop down the road from my flat and she found a light summer dress and a white T-shirt with little embroidered flowers all over it. Size ten to eleven, it said on the label. Ten to eleven: It fitted her perfectly. She tried it on in the fitting room and when she came out wearing it she looked so—so sweet, you know, with her hair all mussed up and her thin arms and her bright face, giggling a bit, in this kids' T-shirt."

Tears were trickling down Louise's face. She made no attempt to wipe them away.

"That's how I think of her," she said. "She was twenty-three, with a proper grown-up job and a flat and all that. But when I think of her, I see her standing giggling at me, wearing clothes made for a child. She was so little, so young." She fished inside her bag and pulled out a tissue, wiped her face. "That's what she was wearing when she was killed. All dressed up in her brand-new clothes. Clean and fresh as a daisy."

"Ladies," called Guy again, putting his head round the door. He looked confused when he saw us hugging in the middle of the room, tears streaming down our faces. I didn't know who I was crying for, but we stood there like that for a while, weeping, and when we left Louise put her hands on either side of my face and held me like that for a moment and stared at me.

"Good luck, Nadia, my new friend," she said. "I'll be thinking of you."

NINETEEN

~ · ೨

Just before seven on the following evening I was lying on the sofa in my flat when the front doorbell rang. Up to that point, the day had gone wrong. In the night I'd been thinking about Zoe and Jenny. I thought of them like friends now. More than that, maybe. I lay in bed that night and thought of myself as walking on a footpath and knowing that Zoe and then Jenny had walked this footpath before me. Sometimes I would see traces showing they had passed and always I knew that they had seen what I was seeing. They had gone ahead, and, in that early morning with the light around my curtain edges, I thought of them waiting for me out there, in the darkness and nothingness.

Had they thought about dying? What had they done? I didn't mean what precautions they had taken. Had they lived their lives in a different way? What do you do when you may have a day or a week to live? It was supposed to make life more precious. I should think clearly, read great books. I wasn't sure I had any great books. After I got up and made myself some coffee, I looked along the shelves and found a book of poems someone had given me for a birthday present. They were supposed to be particularly suited to learning by heart but I couldn't even read them off the page. Something seemed to be wrong with my brain. I couldn't follow the sense of the poems. Their meaning was a song playing in the next house too faintly to make out. I put it back in the shelf and switched on the television.

Just a day earlier I'd been thinking about constructive ways to use the rest of my life. Now I was watching a talk show involving women who'd had affairs with their sister's boyfriend and then a cooking program that was also a game show and then a repeat of a sitcom from the seventies and a rather old-looking documentary about a coral reef somewhere. The divers had sideburns. I saw lots of weather reports.

If I died at twenty-eight and somebody wrote an obituary of me, which they wouldn't, what would they find to say? "In her later years she found her niche as a moderately successful children's party entertainer." Zoe had a job as a teacher, though she was hardly more than a child herself. Jenny had three children. She had Josh, a child who was almost a man.

I fell asleep on the sofa and woke up and watched the end of a western and some indoor bowling and a quiz program and another cookery program, and it was then that the doorbell rang. I opened the door. Josh and Morris were standing there. The damp, warm aroma of Indian food blew in. Morris was in discussion with a policewoman.

"Yes, she does know us. And the other woman who was here already has our names and addresses. I can give it to you again if you want." He turned and saw me. "We bought a takeaway and we were nearby, so we thought we'd drop in."

I looked blank. It wasn't them. It was having spent an entire day in front of the TV screen. I felt tranquilized.

"It's fine," Morris continued. "Don't worry. We can go off with our food and find a bench somewhere or a doorway. Somewhere under a street lamp. In the rain."

I couldn't help smiling. The day was still sunny and bright.

"Don't be stupid. Come in." The policewoman looked reluctant. "It's all right. I know them."

They came in bringing the lovely smell with them and dumped three carrier bags on the table.

"You're probably going out to a dinner party," said Morris.

"As it happens, I'm not," I confessed.

They both took off their jackets and tossed them to one side. They looked very at home.

"I rescued Josh from a nightmarish soiree at home and we went out in search of a woman."

Josh smiled so awkwardly that I almost felt I should give him a hug, except that that would have made things even worse. They started unloading tinfoil cartons.

"We didn't know about your tolerance," said Morris, peeling off the cardboard lids. "So we got everything from extremely mild cooked in cream to meat phal, which is marked dangerously hot, and various things in between and a couple of nans, papadums, dhal, and various veg. Beer for the grown-ups, whereas Josh will have to make do with lager."

I raised an eyebrow.

"Are you allowed to drink, Josh?"

"Of course," he said truculently.

Oh well. I had enough to worry about. I got out plates, glasses, and knives.

"What would you have done if I hadn't been in?" I asked.

"Morris was sure you'd be in," Josh said.

"Oh yes?" I asked, turning to Morris with a mock-ironical expression.

He smiled.

"I wasn't making fun of you," he said. "I thought you might be a bit shaken up."

"I was a bit," I said. "It's not been a good time."

"I can see that," he said. "So eat."

And we did and it was good. I needed a good, messy, undignified meal in which lots of things were piled up together, and I ripped off bits of nan and dipped them in different sauces. We challenged each other to take mouthfuls of the phal with glasses of very cold beer standing by. I think Morris cheated and only took a tiny amount while pretending to be brave, but Josh took a few deep breaths and really did put a substantial spoonful of the fiery meat into his mouth and chewed and swallowed it. We stared at him and beads of sweat started to pop out of pores on his forehead.

"You're going to erupt," I said. "We'd better stand clear."

"No, I'm fine," Josh said in a strangled tone, and we all laughed. It was the first time I'd ever seen him with any expression more cheerful than an awkward self-conscious grimace, and I couldn't remember when I'd last laughed helplessly. There hadn't been anything to laugh about.

"Now you," said Josh.

With exaggerated elegance I took a large spoonful and ate it. They stood looking as if I were a firework taking a long time to go off.

"How do you do it?" Morris asked finally.

"I love hot food," I said. "And I can deal with it like a lady."

"We're impressed," said Josh, awestruck.

I then hastily took a massive gulp of cold beer.

"You all right?" Josh asked.

"Just thirsty," I said casually.

Surprisingly quickly, there was just the cooled wreckage of a meal. While I cleared the table, which meant putting the foil containers one inside the other, the boys wandered over to my notorious computer. They crouched over it and I heard occasional gasps and guffaws. I came back with another glass of beer, sipping it. I felt pleasantly dizzy.

"I know it's comical."

"No, it's great," Josh said, clicking away expertly with the mouse. "You've got all these primeval versions of programs, all these one-point-ones and one-point-twos. It's like a software dinosaur park. Hang on—what's this?"

It turned out that my computer had somewhere embedded in it a solitaire card game that I hadn't even found. Did I know the rules? they shouted at me. No, I didn't. So with much shouting and fighting over the controls, they began playing.

"This is like an evening with two thirteen-year-olds," I said.

"So?" said Josh.

He seemed to be loosening up. He was certainly more relaxed with *me*. There was no longer any of that agonized, embarrassed respectfulness. They shouted for more beer and I brought them two cans, cold from the fridge.

"I feel like I've become the Princess Leia in this scenario," I said.

Josh turned from the screen, looking at me thoughtfully.

"More like Chewbacca, I think," he said.

"Who?"

"Forget it."

Maybe too much fuzziness wasn't entirely a good thing. I went and made a pot of coffee. I poured myself a mug. Very black, very hot.

"There's coffee," I shouted.

Josh was absolutely engrossed. For the moment he didn't know I existed. But Morris wandered over and poured himself a coffee.

"Is there any milk?"

"I'll get it."

"You stay there. I'll find it."

Morris went off to the kitchen and I looked across at Josh, who was staring into the screen with fierce attention. His arms looked surprisingly thin and white. He was still a little boy. While being very big. Morris came back.

"Nice flat," he said. "Very quiet."

"Are you flat hunting?" I asked. "In which case you should take a look at the one I saw yesterday. Not very quiet, though."

"How did that go?"

"I don't know," I said. "I'm not sure what I was doing there. It was probably stupid, but it felt important. I talked to Zoe's friend, Louise. She was nice. It brought me closer to Zoe."

Morris took a sip of coffee.

"Can you really care about somebody you've never met?"

"Well, you know, I feel slightly connected to Zoe and Jenny."

"Did you see the news report about the landslip in Honduras last week?"

"No."

"They recovered more than two hundred bodies. They don't even know how many people are missing."

"That's awful."

"It was a very small news item on the foreign pages of my newspaper. If it had happened in France it would have been a big story. If it had happened to people who speak English it would have been on the front page."

"Sorry," I said. "You'll excuse me if I'm a bit self-obsessed at the moment. It's the constant feeling of fear and nausea all the time. It does that to you."

Morris leaned forward and put his coffee down delicately, on a magazine, as if the value of my crappy table could be reduced any further.

"Do you really feel that?" he said sympathetically.

"Yes," I said. "I try to forget about it or cover it up, but it's always there. You know when you're a bit ill and everything you eat has a slightly curious undertaste? That's what it's like."

"If you want to talk about it, that's all right. You can tell me what you're feeling. Anything."

"That's nice of you, but there's nothing complicated about it. I just want it to be over."

Morris looked around. Josh was still engrossed in the game.

"What are your plans?" he said.

"I don't know. I had some stupid idea that I could try and look for clues myself, but I think it was a waste of time. The police have combed through everything."

"What were you looking for?"

"I've no idea, isn't that the most ridiculous thing of all? Looking for a needle in a haystack is one thing, but what about looking through a haystack without even knowing what you're looking for? Maybe I'm looking for a bit of hay. I had a brief look at some of the police files."

"They let you look at their files?" said Morris sharply. I laughed.

"Well, sort of."

"What were they like? Were there autopsy reports?"

"Mostly bureaucratic stuff. There were some horrible pictures. What was done to Jenny. You don't want to know. I still see it when I close my eyes."

"I can imagine," Morris said. "Did you learn anything?"

"Not really. Oh, lots of information, but nothing that would help me. It was horrible, but it was pointless, really. I suppose I was hoping I would recognize something, some connection, that would link us: Zoe, Jenny, and Nadia, the three strange stepsisters."

"You found *me*," he said with a smile.

"Yes. Don't worry, Morris—I've still got my eye on you. And there was also the estate agent, Guy, who may have been a link between Zoe and Jenny. He seemed pretty weird. But I know a little bit about probability. We all live in north London. It would be strange if there weren't connections between us. We must have gone to the same shops, we must have passed each other in the street. But that's not important. It's just that I keep worrying away at it in my head. There must be something. There *must* be. I talked to this psychologist and she mentioned some principle that the criminal always takes something to the scene of the crime and always takes something away with him. It's a haunting idea, isn't it?"

Morris shrugged.

"Well," I continued. "It haunts *me*. I feel I've got it all in my head. I've got the haystack inside my head and I feel there are two straws in there and if I bring them together, maybe I'll save my life."

"Of course you will," Morris said. "You mustn't give up hope."

"I sometimes think I should. You know what the real pain is? It's the occasional moment when I have a feeling of what it might be like to get through all this and live a normal life and grow old." I had to stop and pull myself together before tears started running down my cheeks. I was aware of a presence next to me. It was Josh. I poured him some coffee. "This evening has been a bit like that," I said. "Something unexpected and casual."

We were silent for a moment. Josh looked grown-up again, sitting on the sofa with two adults. We all sipped our coffee and caught each other's glances and smiles.

"So what you've been doing," Morris said, "is trying to make a connection between you and the other two women, Zoe and . . . er . . . Josh's mum."

"Of course."

"I've been thinking about it—and would you mind if I said something that was really dumb but it was a thought?"

"Go ahead," I said. "It'll make a change from me prattling away."

"It's just that there is an obvious connection between the three of you."

"What?"

"It's a trick question, really, but who are the people you have in common?"

"Who?"

I looked from Morris to Josh. Suddenly Josh's face lit up in a smile. "I know," he said smugly.

"Well who? Tell me then."

"I think you should guess for a bit longer." Josh was actually teasing me now, like an irritating younger brother.

"Fucking tell me, Josh, or I'll tweak your nose." I held up my hand threateningly.

"All right, all right," he said. "The police."

"Has it been the same lot?" Morris asked.

"I think so," I said. "But really . . ."

"Actually," he said, "there's a major flaw in my brilliant theory."

"What's that?"

"The first one, Zoe. The police would only have become aware of her after the first note."

"Oh, yeah."

We relapsed into silence. Suddenly I felt a small charge

in the back of my head. It was the sort of thing I'd been looking for.

"That's not true," I said.

"What?" said Morris.

"What you said, that they only came on the scene after the first note."

"What do you mean? How could they know about her earlier?"

"It was in the files. Zoe was in the papers just before it happened. She tackled a mugger in the street. She hit him with a watermelon. She was famous; she had her picture in the paper. The police *did* know about her."

"I didn't mean it completely seriously," said Morris. "But still . . . It might be worth thinking about whether there's been any strangeness about the way they've treated you. I suppose it's just been the normal detached sort of police style."

I looked up slightly nervously. I must behave as if there were nothing to feel odd about.

"Yes," I said. "Just the normal sort of style." I know I'm not a good liar. Is that what a person would have said who was telling the truth?

"Are you all right?" Morris asked.

"Yes, of course. Why shouldn't I be?" My mind was now racing. There was too much to think about, too much to go over in my mind. "I mean, it couldn't be a police-man, could it?"

"What do you think, Josh?"

Josh was shaking his head in puzzlement. "No, it couldn't be. It's just too weird. Except, I was . . . no, it's stupid."

"What?" I said. "Out with it."

"I don't know if you heard that before my mum . . . well, you know, they actually picked up my dad because of some-thing belonging to my mum that had been planted in the flat of the other woman, Zoe. Who else could have done that?"

There was a silence like a dark cavern.

"I've got to get my head round this," I said. "It's like a crossword puzzle. I'm not intelligent enough."

"I'm sorry," said Morris. "I seem to have started something. I should have kept my mouth shut."

"No," I said. "Don't be stupid. It's worth thinking about. I just can't believe it. What do I do?"

Morris and Josh just looked at each other and shrugged.

"Just look after yourself," Morris said. "Keep your eyes open." He winked at Josh. "We should go," he said.

I walked with them to the door.

"What do I do?" I repeated pathetically.

"You think about things," Morris said. "And we'll think as well. Maybe we'll come up with something. Remember, we're on your side."

I closed the door and I didn't even sit down. I stood there by the door, thinking and thinking, trying to put it into a shape that fitted. My head hurt.

I am there, right at the heart of things. Invisible. I stand in front of her and she smiles at me in that way she has, that crinkles her eyes. She giggles at my jokes. She puts her hand on my shoulder. She has kissed me on the cheek: a soft, dry kiss, burning into my skin. She lets her eyes well up with tears and doesn't wipe them away. There aren't many people she trusts anymore, but she trusts me. Yes, she trusts me perfectly. While I am with her I must not laugh. The laughter builds up inside me, like a bomb.

She is strong, resilient; she bends but she doesn't break. She has not collapsed. But I am strong. I am stronger than she is, stronger than anyone. I am clever, cleverer than those fools who snuffle around for clues that are not there. And I am patient. I can wait for as long as it takes. I watch and I wait and, inside, I laugh.

TWENTY

"You," I said.

"Me," Cameron said. We stared at each other. "I'm Lynne for the day. Orders."

"Oh." I had gone to the door wearing a skimpy robe and with my hair unbrushed, expecting Lynne, or Bernice. I didn't want him seeing me like this. His eyes dropped from my face to my chest, my bare legs. Instinctively I put my hand up to my throat and I saw him give a tiny smile. "I'll get dressed," I said.

I put on jeans and a T-shirt, good and plain. I brushed my hair back from my face and tied it up. It was a cooler day; I almost thought I could smell autumn in the air, a sense of freshness. I wanted to see the autumn: trees turning, fast gray skies, and rain in the winds. Pears on the tree out in the yard, blackberries from the cemetery up the road. I thought about walking through the coppice near my parents' house, boots crunching on leaves. I thought about sitting by a fire at Janet's house and eating buttered toast. Little things.

I could hear Stadler in the kitchen, familiar with all the appliances. I remembered what Morris had said yesterday,

and I thought: Yes, it could be, it could be true. I let myself think about what had happened between me and
Cameron, remember it while he rattled the cups next door.
He had hidden his head between my breasts, groaning;
pinned me down; been savage, brutal, gentle. When he had
stared at me with his hungry eyes, what had he seen? What
did he see now? Should I be scared of him?

I took a deep breath, went to join him in the kitchen.

"Coffee," he said.

"Thanks."

There was a silence. Then I said:

"I've arranged to go and see my parents today. They live
near Reading."

"Fine."

"I'd like you to wait outside. I won't tell them about
you."

"Are they very anxious?"

"Not about this. They don't know. I haven't told them."

They were always anxious, though, I thought. That was
why I hadn't said anything to them. Every time I'd picked
up the phone, I had imagined my mother's mild and fretful voice with its submerged note of panic. She was always waiting to hear bad news from me. Each time she
heard my voice on the other end of the phone, she thought
I was going to break some unwelcome event to her and
her unfocused fears were going to find a point. She had
never been sure about me, I don't know why. She didn't
trust my capacity to look after myself and make a life for
myself. But I was going to tell them today. I had to.

"Nadia, we need to talk. . . ." He put his cup down and
leaned toward me.

"I wanted to ask you something . . ." I told him.

"About us. You and me."

"I wanted to ask you about Zoe and Jenny."

"Nadia, we need to talk about what happened."

"No, we don't." I tried to keep my voice businesslike. I concentrated on holding the coffee steadily in my hands.

"You don't mean that," he said.

I looked at him. Tall and solid, like a wall between me and the rest of the world. He had strong, thick hands with hair on the knuckles. Hands that had held me, touched me, felt for all my secrets. He had eyes that stared at me, undressed me.

"I've fallen in love with you," he said hoarsely.

"Have you told your wife?"

He flinched, then said, "She's got nothing to do with this. This is just about you and me here in your flat."

"Tell me about Zoe and Jenny," I said insistently. "You've never told me about them. What were they like?" He shook his head irritably, but I persisted. "You owe it to me."

"I owe you nothing," he said, but he put his hands up in a gesture of surrender, then closed his eyes for a moment. "Zoe: I didn't know Zoe so well; I hardly got the chance. . . . I saw her first in a huge photograph from a newspaper that was put up on the wall at the station, you know, after she poleaxed a mugger with a watermelon. She was like a heroine to the guys, and a kind of dirty joke too."

"What was she like, though?"

"I never met her."

"What about Jenny? You must have known Jenny well." I watched his face.

"Jenny was something else." He almost grinned at the memory, then checked himself. "Small, too. You're all small," he added musingly. "But strong, energetic, dense, dark, angry. Coiled wire, Jenny was. Clever. Impatient. Seriously insane sometimes."

"Unhappy?"

"That as well." He put a hand on my knee and I let it

lie there for a moment, though his touch sent a wave of repulsion through me. "She'd have bitten your head off for saying it, though. Bit of a dragon."

I stood up, to be free of his hand; poured myself some more coffee, to give myself something to do.

"We ought to go soon," I said.

"Nadia."

"I don't want to be late."

"I lie in bed at night and I see you, your face, your body."

"Keep away."

"I know you."

"You think I'm going to die."

Before we left, I phoned Links, while Cameron was in the room with me, and told him that Detective Inspector Stadler was driving me to see my parents, and that we should be back mid- to late afternoon. I could hear the note of bemusement in Links's voice: He couldn't understand why I should be ringing up and telling him my arrangements. I didn't care, though. I repeated myself loudly and clearly: So he couldn't help but hear, so that Cameron couldn't help but hear, either.

We didn't talk much on the way there, up the M4 then along small lanes. I gave him curt instructions, and he drove and looked across at me with his heavy gaze. I sat with my hands on my lap and tried to look out my window, but I could feel his head turning toward me, his brooding stare.

"What do your parents do?" he asked, just before we arrived.

"Dad was a teacher, geography, but he took early retirement. Mum did odd things, but mostly she stayed at home and looked after me and my brother. Right here, at the T-junction. You're not coming in, remember."

The house was a thirties semi, much like all the others along the cul-de-sac. Cameron drew up outside it.

"Hold on one minute," he said as I reached for the door handle. "There's something I ought to tell you."

"What?"

"There was another letter."

I lay back in the car seat and closed my eyes.

"Oh God," I said.

"You made me promise to tell you everything."

"What did it say?"

"It was short. It just said, 'You're being brave, but it won't do you any good.' Something like that."

"And that was all?" I opened my eyes and turned my head to look at him. "When was it sent?"

"Four days ago."

"Have you got anything from the note?"

"We're using it to augment our psychological evaluation."

"Nothing," I said with a sigh. "Well, I guess it doesn't really change much. We knew he was still out there, didn't we?"

"Yes, we did."

"I'll see you in a couple of hours."

"Nadia."

"What?"

"You *are* being brave." I stared at him. "It's true," he said.

I looked at him.

"You mean brave like Zoe and Jenny?"

He didn't reply.

Mum had made a neck of lamb stew, with rice—overcooked so it stuck together in lumps—and a green salad. I used to love lamb stew when I was a girl. How do you ever tell your mother you've gone off something? It was hard to eat, gristly and with too many sharp splinters of bones. Dad opened a bottle of red wine, although neither of them ever drink at lunchtime. They were so pleased to see me. They fussed over me, as if I were a stranger. I felt like a stranger with these two nice old people, who weren't really old yet.

Always cautious, making their way through life in a gingerly fashion. They were careful with me, as well, waiting up for me every time I went out in the evenings, putting a hot-water bottle in my bed on cold nights, telling me to put on an extra layer when it was cold, sharpening my crayons for me before the beginning of each new school term. It used to drive me insane, their care, the way they thought about every detail of my life. Now the memory made me feel intensely nostalgic: a lump of homesickness beneath my ribs.

I thought I would wait until after lunch to tell them. We drank coffee in the living room, with mint chocolates. I could see Cameron sitting at the wheel of his car. I cleared my throat.

"I've got something to tell you," I said.

"Yes?"

Mum looked at me expectantly, apprehensively.

"I . . . there's a man who—" I stopped and looked at the pleasure flowering on her face. She thought I had a serious boyfriend at last; she had never thought much of Max as a long-term possibility. I couldn't make the words come out of my mouth. "Oh, it's nothing really."

"No, go on. Tell us. We want to hear, don't we, Tony?"

"Later," I said, standing up abruptly. "First I want Dad to show me what's going on in the garden."

The plums were ripening on the tree, and he was growing runner beans, lettuce, and potatoes. There were tomato plants in his greenhouse, and he insisted on giving me a plastic tray of cherry tomatoes to take back with me.

"Your mother's got some jars of strawberry jam she has set by for you," he said.

I took hold of his arm.

"Dad," I said. "Dad, I know we've had our disagreements"—homework, cigarettes, drink, makeup, staying out late, politics, drugs, boyfriends, lack of boyfriends, serious jobs, you name it—"but I just wanted to say that you've been a good father."

He made an embarrassed tutting sound in the back of his throat and patted my shoulder.

"Your mother will be wondering what's keeping us."

I said good-bye in the hall. I couldn't hug them properly because I was holding the tomatoes and the jam. I pressed my cheek against Mum's and breathed in the familiar smell of vanilla, powder, soap, and mothballs. Smell of my childhood.

"Good-bye," I said, and they smiled and waved. "Good-bye."

For just one moment, I let myself think I would never see them again, but you can't be like that; you can't walk down the path and get into the car and smile and keep on going if you let yourself be like that.

All the way home, I pretended to sleep. I told Stadler that he should stay in his car after he had done his check round the flat. I wanted to be alone for a while. He started to protest, but the pager strapped to the belt of his trousers bleeped, and I slammed the door in his face.

I sat on the edge of my bed with my hands on my knees. I closed my eyes and then opened them again. I listened to myself breathing. I waited, not for anything to happen but for this feeling to go away.

Then the telephone rang, as if it was ringing inside my skull. I reached out a hand, picked it up.

"Nadia." Morris's voice was hoarse and urgent.

"Yes?"

"It's me. Don't say anything. Listen, Nadia. I've found something out. I can't tell you over the phone. We've got to meet."

I felt the fear growing in my stomach, a great tumor of fear.

"What is it?"

"Come to my flat, as soon as you can. There's something you've got to see. Is anyone with you?"

"No. They're outside."

"Who is it?"

"Stadler."

I heard the intake of Morris's breath. When he spoke again, he was very calm and slow.

"Get away from him, Nadia. I'm waiting for you."

I put down the phone and stood up, balanced on the balls of my feet. So it was Cameron, after all. My fear ebbed away, and I was left feeling strong, springy, and full of clarity. It had come at last. The waiting was over, and with it all the grief and all the dread. And I was ready and it was time to go.

TWENTY-ONE

As I walked through my front door my head felt very clear. I knew what I was going to do. Matters had become simple for the moment. The layer of fear was still there, but even that had receded a little. Cameron was out of his car and beside me in a second, looking questioning, hopeful even.

"I'm going up the road to get some food for supper," I said.

We walked along together. I didn't speak.

"I'm sorry," he said finally. "For everything. I just want to make it all right. For you and me. Us."

"What are you talking about?" I said.

He didn't reply. We walked across High Street and along the pavement until we were standing outside Marks & Spencer. We mustn't have an argument, nothing to arouse his suspicions. I put my hand on his forearm. Contact but nothing excessive.

"I'm sorry," I said. "I'm not dealing with things in a rational way at the moment. It's not the time."

"I understand," he said.

I turned to go into the shop. I gave a sigh. "I'll be out in a minute."

"I'll wait here."

"Can I get you anything?"

"Don't worry."

The Camden Town Marks & Spencer has a small back entrance. Up the escalator and out, and within a few minutes I was on an underground train. Going down the escalator to the platform, the warm air blowing past me, I had looked back. He was definitely not there.

As I sat on the train for the short journey, I tried to make sense of what Morris had said. I felt as if I had been trapped for weeks in a thick mist and now it was not exactly lifting, but it was becoming thinner and some sort of landscape was starting to become visible. If it had been a policeman, if it had been Cameron, suddenly what had seemed impossible became simple. The police had easy unquestioned access to Zoe's flat, to Jenny's house. My heart sank. To *my* flat. But why would they do that? Why would Cameron do that?

I only had to think of Cameron's gaze and I knew the answer. I remembered my first meetings with the police, Cameron in the corner, his eyes fixed on me. Cameron in my bed. I had never been looked at like that before, never touched like that, as if I were an infinitely attractive and strange object. I'd felt he wanted to look at me and touch me and penetrate me and taste me all at the same time, as if nothing could ever be enough. It had been wonderfully exciting at first and then repellent, and now it seemed appallingly understandable. To be right next to the woman you were terrifying, to fuck her, to find out all her secrets. What a turn-on. And yet, what evidence was there? Had Morris found something I could use?

Morris's flat was only a few minutes' walk from the tube station. The main road itself was packed with crowds of people. He lived in a small alley that was difficult to find.

I walked past it the first time, then asked and found it and walked along and round the corner. The tiny cobbled back-street was deserted on this Saturday evening. At the end I found a door with a little card by the bell: BURNSIDE. I rang the bell. There was silence for a time.

Could he have gone out? Then I heard a series of knobs being turned, levers pulled, and he opened the door. He looked amazing, a live wire. He was wearing bulky trousers with large pockets all over and a short-sleeved shirt. He was barefoot. But there was something about his eyes, bright and alive, that was captivating. He had an energy about him that was like a force field. He was an attractive man, and what was more—here my heart sank a little—he was a man who fancied himself in love. I hoped he hadn't made a mountain out of a molehill, just in the hope of wooing me.

"Nadia," he said with a welcoming smile.

He stood in the doorway and looked over my shoulder. I turned and looked as well. There was nobody there at all, the whole length of the street.

"How did you get away?" he said.

"I'm a magician," I said.

"Come in," he said. "I haven't tidied up."

It looked very tidy to me. We had stepped straight into a small and cozy living room with a doorway at the far end leading into a short corridor.

"Was this a warehouse?"

"Some kind of workshop, I think. I'm just flat-sitting for a friend who's out of the country."

The only thing out of place was an ironing board and iron to one side by the table.

"You've been doing your ironing," I said. "I'm extremely impressed."

"Just this shirt," he said.

"I thought it was new."

"That's the trick," he said. "If you iron your clothes, they look like new."

I smiled.

"The real trick is to wear new clothes," I said.

I walked around the room. I was addicted to looking at other people's houses. I gravitated with the instinct of a master snooper to a large cork board on the wall on which, here and there, were pinned takeaway menus, business cards of plumbers and electricians, and, most interesting of all, little snapshots. Morris at a party, Morris on a bike somewhere, Morris on a beach, Morris and a girl.

"She looks nice," I said.

"Cath," he said.

"Is she someone you're seeing?"

"Well, we had a sort of thing."

I smiled inwardly. She was someone he was seeing. When men said of a girl that they had had a sort of thing with her, it was the equivalent of a man taping over his wedding ring. They wanted to be ambiguous about their state of availability.

"Where are the rest of them?"

"What?"

"The pictures," I said. "Many drawing pins, few pictures." I pointed. There were gaps all over the board.

"Oh," he said. "There were just some I got bored with." He laughed. "You should have been a detective."

"Speaking of which, this had better be good, because Detective Inspector Stadler is going to be very angry. I'll probably be lucky if I get away with a charge of wasting police time."

Morris gestured me to a chair at the table and he sat opposite me. "I've been going over the interview I had with Stadler and—what was the other one?"

"Links?"

"That's right, and I'm convinced that there's something strange about Stadler. The way he talked about those other two women was really strange, and I wanted to go through it with you. And I just felt I had to get you away from him."

"Have you got any evidence?"

"What?"

"I thought you might have found something we could use against him."

"I'm sorry," he said. "I wish I could have."

I tried to think. The mist in my mind that had been clearing suddenly became thicker again. Then suddenly I felt a wave of coldness pass through me.

"It doesn't work anyway," I said dully.

Morris looked puzzled. "What doesn't?"

"The police theory. I got so excited about Zoe and that watermelon and her connection with the police before the notes arrived. But that doesn't explain Jennifer."

"Why?"

"Her locket was planted in Zoe's flat before Zoe died, before Jennifer started getting the notes, before she called the police."

"The police might have faked the planting of the locket."

I thought for a moment.

"Well, maybe," I said doubtfully. "Still, that doesn't explain the connection with Jenny. Why pick on her?"

"Stadler may have seen her somewhere."

"You could say that about anybody. The police theory depended on the fact that they had dealings with all the women."

I felt depressed and sick. "It was all wrong," I said. "I'd better go."

Morris leaned across and touched my arm. "Just stay a bit," he said. "Just a bit, Nadia."

"It would have been so good," I said flatly. "It was such a nice theory, it's a pity to let it go."

"Back to the haystack," Morris said. He was smiling at me as if that was funny. His teeth, his eyes, his whole face, shone.

"You know what?" I said dreamily.

"What?"

"I used to feel strange that I'd never met Zoe and Jenny. It's different now. Sometimes I think of us as sisters, but more and more I think of us as the same person. We've gone through the same experiences. We've lain awake at night with the same fears. And we're going to die in the same way."

Morris shook his head. "Nadia . . ."

"Shhh," I said, as if to a small child. I was almost talking to myself now and I didn't want my reverie interrupted. "When I went to the flat with Louise—that's Zoe's friend— it was amazing. It was almost as if she had already been my best friend, as if we recognized each other. It was so funny when she talked of going shopping with Zoe on that last afternoon; it was almost as if she had been talking of a shopping expedition that *we* had made together. She felt it too. I could tell."

And at that moment, quite suddenly, the fog lifted and the landscape was there—there it was—cold and hard in the sunshine and I could see it. There was no doubt. I had been going over the forensic file in my mind ever since I had seen it.

"What is it?"

I started. I had almost forgotten Morris was there. "What?" I said.

"You don't seem quite here," he said. "What were you thinking?"

"I was thinking," I said, "that when Zoe was killed she was wearing a shirt she had just bought with Louise. Funny, isn't it?"

"I don't know," said Morris. "Tell me why it's funny, Nadia. Tell me."

"Pity to mess it up," I said.

Morris gazed at me as if he was trying to see inside my mind. Did he think I was going a bit mad? Good. I leaned over the table and took his hand. It felt clammy. Mine felt cool and dry. I held his right hand between my two hands and squeezed it.

"Morris," I said. "I'd love some tea."

"Yes," he said. "Yes, of course, Nadia." He was smiling and smiling. He couldn't stop.

He got up and walked out of the room. I looked across at the front door. There were several levers and knobs. Then fifty or sixty yards down the deserted road; no one about. I stood up and walked over to the cork notice board.

"Can I help?" I shouted.

"No," he shouted from the kitchen.

I looked at the notice board. Below it was a writing desk with drawers. As quietly as I could I opened the first. Checkbooks, receipts. I opened the second. Postcards. The third. Catalogs. The fourth. A pile of photographs. I picked up a couple. I knew roughly what I was going to see, but still I gave a shiver of horror. Morris and someone and someone and Fred. Morris and Cath and Fred. Morris and someone and Fred. I put one of them in the back pocket of my jeans. Maybe it would be found on my body. I closed the drawer and went and sat down at the table. I looked around. It would have to do. I cleared my mind. No, that's wrong. I didn't clear my mind; I filled it. I made myself think of the photograph of Jenny dead. I made myself think of every detail. What would Jenny do if she were sitting where I was sitting?

Morris came in, somehow managing to hold a teapot, two mugs, a carton of milk, and a packet of digestive biscuits. He put them on the table and sat down.

"Hang on a second," I said, before he could pour. "I want to show you something." I stood up and walked round the table. "It's a sort of magic trick."

He smiled at me once again. Such a nice smile. He looked happy, excited. The excitement was like a light behind his eyes.

"I don't know very much about magic," I said, "but the first thing you learn is you never tell your audience in advance what you are going to do. If it goes wrong, then you can pretend you did it on purpose. Look." I took the lid off the teapot and then lifted the pot and then very quickly threw it into his face. Some of it splashed on me as well. I didn't even feel it. He let out a howl like an animal. In the same movement I reached for the iron. I took it in both hands. I had one chance and I had to do real damage. He was clutching his face. I lifted the iron up and then brought it down with all my weight on his right knee. There was a cracking crumbling sound and a further scream. He crumpled and slumped off the side of his chair. What else? I thought of the photograph. I felt white hot, glowing, like a poker. His left ankle was exposed. I brought the iron down again. More cracking. Another scream. I moved back but as I did so I felt a hand clutching my trousers. I raised the iron again but as I pulled back the grip fell away.

I moved back out of his reach. He was lying sprawled on the floor, twisted, whimpering. What I could see of his face was a livid blistering red.

"If you move one inch towards me," I said, "I'll break

every fucking bone in your body. You know I'll do it. I've seen the pictures. I've seen what you did to Jenny."

But still I moved backward, never taking my eyes off him. I glanced around quickly and found the phone. Still with the iron in my hand, the cord trailing on the floorboards, I dialed.

TWENTY-TWO

I put the receiver down and stood there, as far away as it was possible to get from him in that room. He was still slumped on the floor groaning and wheezing. I wondered if he was gathering his strength, if he would raise himself to his feet and come at me. Should I go back to him and hit him again? Should I run to the front door and out? I couldn't move my feet. There was nothing I could do. Suddenly I started to tremble in every bit of my body. I leaned back against the wall to try and steady myself.

I saw some traces of movement, tentative at first, then more purposeful. He was pulling himself up, groaning with the effort. I quickly saw that there was no prospect at all of his getting up. His legs were clearly useless. All he could do was drag himself, whimpering with the pain, so he was leaning against the bookshelf. He pushed himself up a bit farther and twisted so he could look at me. He was really badly burned on his face, blistered across his cheeks and forehead. One of his eyes was almost closed. Saliva was spilling out of his mouth, running down his chin. He coughed.

"What've you done?"

I didn't speak.

"I don't understand," he said. "I didn't do it."

I took a firm grip on the iron.

"One move, and I'll smash some other bit of you."

He shifted slightly and cried out.

"Jesus." He panted. "It hurts so fucking much."

"Why did you do it?" I said. "She had children. What had she done?"

"You're mad," he said. "I didn't do it, I swear, Nadia. They told you. I was a hundred miles away when Zoe was killed."

"I know," I said.

"What?"

"I know you didn't kill Zoe. You were going to but you didn't. You killed Jenny."

"You're wrong, I swear it," he said. "Oh God, what have you done to my face? Why did you do that to me?"

He was crying now.

"You were going to kill me. Like you killed her."

I was having difficulty in speaking. My breath was coming in uneven gasps, my heart beating hard.

"I swear, Nadia," he said in little more than a whisper.

"Shut the fuck up. I've seen the pictures. In the drawer."

"What?"

"Of you and Fred, the ones you took down before I arrived."

He didn't miss a beat. "I admit I hid the pictures. I got in a panic because it looked bad. But it doesn't mean I killed anybody."

"The way you panicked when we were due to meet Louise at the flat?"

"No, that was a real message. Nadia, you're all confused here. . . ."

I don't know what I was expecting. Maybe I wanted him

just to admit to what he'd done and to say something, however inadequate, that would make it comprehensible. Now I realized that he would never give up, and that I would never understand. He would lie and lie and maybe even he would grow to believe all his lies in the end. I stared at him, his peeling face, his writhing body, the one eye gazing up at me.

"I ought to kill you," I said. "I should finish you off before the police get here."

"Maybe you should," he said. "Because I didn't do it, Nadia, and there's no evidence against me. And they'll let me go and they'll send you to prison. But could you do it? Could you, Nadia? Could you kill me?"

"I'd like to do it, I promise you."

"Do it then. Come on, darling. Come on." Spittle ran down his face. He tried to smile.

"I'd like to make you suffer the way you made Zoe and Jenny suffer."

"I'll help you," he said, and with much panting and groaning, he started to crawl toward me across the floor like a big fat horrible slug. His progress was very slow.

"Come any closer and I'll smash your head," I said, taking a firm grip on the iron.

"Do it," Morris said. "You're going to prison anyway. They're going to let me go. Even if they don't, I'll be out soon. Wouldn't it be better to get rid of me?"

"Stop it, stop it!" I shouted and started to cry. I felt he was wriggling around in my head as well as on the floorboards. I was about to fling the iron at him when there was a banging at the door and voices shouting my name. I looked around; there were lights outside. I ran across and opened the door. It turned out to be easy. It took no more than a couple of seconds. A blur of figures rushed past me. There were a couple of police officers in uniform and

Cameron. Over his shoulder I could see two police cars, and another was arriving. Cameron looked at the scene. He was sweating, his tie flapping over his shoulder.

"What the hell have you done?"

I didn't speak. I just bent down and placed the iron on the floor.

"Did you call an ambulance?"

I shook my head. He shouted across at one of the officers, who walked out.

"She attacked me," Morris said. "She's gone mad."

Cameron looked from Morris to me and back again in obvious bafflement. "Are you hurt?" he said to Morris.

"Oh yeah," he said. "I'm so fucking hurt. Mad."

Cameron walked up to me and put his hand on my shoulder.

"You all right?" he whispered.

I nodded. I kept looking at Morris slumped on the floor and every time I looked at him he was staring back. Staring at me with an eye that never seemed to blink. The officer bent over and was saying something, but he just kept on looking at me.

"Sit down," Cameron said to me.

I looked around. He had to lead me across the room to one of the chairs by the table. I sat so I didn't have to see Morris. I thought I would throw up if I had to look at him for one more second.

"Now, Nadia, I have to say this before we do anything more, so listen to me. You don't have to say anything. But if you do say anything, then in the event that charges are brought, anything you say may be used as evidence. Also, you have a right to a lawyer. If you wish, we can arrange for one to be provided for you. Do you understand?"

I nodded.

"No, you have to say out loud that you understand."

"I understand. I don't mind talking."

"So what happened?"

"Look in the drawer. Over there."

He went over to the open front door and barked out something about a scene-of-crime officer. An ambulance arrived noisily. A man and a woman in green overalls rushed in and bent down over Morris. Cameron stared at me. From his pocket he took thin plastic gloves that were more like the rubbishy ones they give away in petrol stations than the kind that surgeons use. He opened the drawer and looked at the photographs.

"He knew Fred," I said.

The scene was becoming farcical. Cameron was staring stupefied at the picture. Morris was whimpering in pain as they cut his trousers off him. Then Links arrived.

"What the hell . . . ?" he said, trying to make sense of what happened.

"She attacked Morris with an iron," Cameron said.

"What the fuck—Why?"

"She said he did the murder."

"But . . ."

Cameron handed Links one of the photographs. He stared at it. Then he looked at me.

"Yes, but still . . ." He turned to Cameron. "Have you cautioned her?"

"Yes. She says she's willing to talk."

"Good. What about Burnside?"

"I haven't managed to talk to him."

Links leaned down by Morris and showed him the photograph. In response he just shook his head and groaned. Then he came over and sat by me. I was feeling calm now, clear-headed.

"Did Morris attack you?"

"No," I said. "If Morris had attacked me, I would be dead now. No, not dead. Dying. Being killed."

"But Nadia," Links said in a gentle tone. "You do realize that, well, for example, Morris Burnside couldn't have killed Zoe Haratounian. He wasn't there."

"I know. I know who killed Zoe."

"What? Who?"

"It suddenly came to me. You all got it into your heads that the person who sent the notes must have killed her. But what if somebody else killed her first?"

"Why would anyone else kill her?"

"I was thinking about something that Grace Schilling told me. Something about how the criminal always leaves something of himself at the scene and always takes something away. You've heard that?" I looked up at Cameron, who was busying himself with the contents of the drawer. "I saw the forensic report of the crime scene. Do you remember the report on the shirt she was wearing when she was found?"

"Yes, I do, but how on earth do you—"

"Do you remember what it said?"

"It shared the background traces of the flat in common with her other clothes, the carpets, the beds. Just her and her ex-boyfriend."

"But the shirt shouldn't have had traces of Fred. She came into the flat carrying it in a plastic bag. She had bought it the day before with her friend, Louise." I twisted my head to look over at Morris. He was paying attention. "Fred left traces of hair on Zoe's shirt while he was strangling her."

I thought I almost caught the tiniest trace of a smile on Morris's face.

"You didn't know that, did you?" I said to him. "Your friend killed Zoe before *you* could." I looked at Stadler and

Links. "Two murderers. See? Two. Didn't you think about why the murders were so different? There wasn't any fucking escalation. It was because they were done by different people. Was that why it was so violent, Morris? Did you punish Jenny because you'd missed out on Zoe?"

"I don't know what you're talking about," he said.

"But there was a compensation," I said. "You suddenly found yourself with the perfect alibi. It gave you a chance to get at me from close up, to really watch me suffer."

"But how could Fred have done it?" Links asked. "Miss Haratounian wasn't even intending to return to her flat."

"I don't think he planned it," I said. "That's what I've been puzzling about, sitting here. I was thinking about that strange thing that was stolen, the crappy hanging from the wall that Fred gave her. Why would anybody take that? I don't think it was taken. I think Fred took it *back*. I think he came to collect his stuff. Zoe came back suddenly and he grabbed the cord from her dressing gown and strangled her.

"That's why the forensics were so difficult. The thing he took away was something that had belonged to him. What he brought to the scene was just more of what was already there. More Fred. Too much Fred. And he had the perfect alibi as well. The police knew he couldn't have written the notes. And who else would have killed Zoe but the man who said he was going to? Funny, isn't it, Morris? You and Fred made a great team, if you'd only known it."

The paramedics had lifted Morris onto a stretcher and were inserting a drip.

"Are you going to look in his pockets?"

"Why?"

"I don't know. I think he was going to attack me."

Cameron glanced at Links, who nodded. Morris's nice new trousers were now in halves. They had endless pockets, and Cameron started rummaging in them. I saw something glisten in his hands. He was holding up a wire.

"What's this?" he said to Morris.

"I was doing some repairs," he answered.

"What repairs were you doing that needed piano wire tied into a running noose?"

He didn't reply. He stared at me instead and said in a whisper, "Darling. I'll be back, darling."

The paramedics picked up the stretcher and carried it out. Links shouted at one of the uniformed officers.

"Two of you go with him to the hospital. Caution him on the way. Keep him fully secure—no access."

I watched him go. He looked at me steadily until they turned the corner, with his bright eye, his friendly murderer's face. He was smiling at me through his mask of blood and blisters.

Then: "What about Fred?" I said.

Links gave a sigh. "We'll interview him immediately. Or as soon as we can."

"What about me? Can I go?"

"We'll give you a lift home."

"I'll walk. Alone."

Links stood firmly in front of me.

"Miss Blake, if you refuse to go in a police car and with police protection, I shall have you restrained."

"I think," I said, as coolly as I could manage, "I think I would feel safer on my own."

"Very well," he said heavily. I saw fear in his face: He was looking at public disgrace, a career in tatters.

"I was always safer on my own."

TWENTY-THREE

W hat did I do next? What does one do when a life has been given back?

I spent the first day and night at my parents' house, helping my father paint the garden shed and lying facedown on the faded chenille counterpane in my old bedroom, the smell of mothballs and dust in my nose, while my mother clattered anxiously round the kitchen, making milky cups of tea and baking ginger biscuits that I couldn't eat. Every time she saw me she would gaze at me with her red-rimmed eyes and press my shoulder or put her hand cautiously on my hair. I had told them something of what had happened, but I had left everything out. Everything that mattered.

Then I went back home and I cleaned my flat. My first thought had been that I would move out immediately, pack up my bags and begin again—but what would be the point of that if I couldn't begin again with me? I didn't want to. So I threw open the French windows, and I put on an old pair of cotton dungarees that looked as if they had been given to me as a joke—certainly I couldn't remember buying them. I turned on the radio so it was blaring cheerful, inane music through all the rooms. I went through every

drawer. I filled bin bags with torn tights, old envelopes,
scraps of hard soap, empty toilet rolls, leaking pens, moldy
cheese. I put newspapers in a pile of recycling, bottles in
a large box. I folded clothes or hung them in the wardrobe,
filled a laundry basket with washing, put bills in piles,
poured bleach down the sink and lavatory and anywhere
else that looked like it needed it. I defrosted the fridge,
scrubbed the kitchen floor. I cleaned the windows. I dusted,
for Christ's sake.

It took two days. For two days I just worked, morning
till evening. It was like meditation. I could have thoughts
without really thinking, let memories bob around without
pursuing them, without tracking them down to their source.
I didn't feel euphoric, and I hardly even felt relieved, but
bit by bit I felt I was crossing back over into my life. I
picked up Morris's business card from my desk and remembered his bright eyes watching me as he had been carried away, and put it with the other rubbish in the bin bag.
I screwed up the paper covered with my jottings from the
case files Cameron had filched for me and threw that away
too, though not before copying down Louise's address. I
collected two small buttons from the floor. Cameron's? I
held them for a minute in the palm of my hand before de-
positing them into a shoe box, which from now on would
be where I kept my sewing things.

I screened all my calls—and there were a lot of them,
because the first tremors of the story had reached the media.
There were even pictures of us—Zoe, Jenny, and me, though
I didn't know where they had managed to get hold of the
one of me—in a line across the top of page three of the
Participant, as if we had all of us died. Or all lived. Re-
porters rang, and friends suddenly wanted to get in touch,
and Cameron rang several times with a hissing, secret urgency, and people I had met once or twice in my life rang,

breathless with discovering that they knew someone who was suddenly and briefly a little bit famous. I didn't pick up the phone.

Not until early on the morning of the fourth day after, a blowy beautiful day when the sun was streaming in through the open French windows and the first few autumn leaves were scattering themselves under the pear tree, where I had first put my arms round Cameron and kissed him. I was thinking about beginning on my garden next, hacking down the nettles, when the phone rang and the answering machine clicked on.

"Nadia," said a voice that made me stop in the middle of pouring boiling water over a tea bag. "Nadia, it's Grace. Grace Schilling." Pause. "Nadia, if you're listening to this, can you pick up the phone?" Then: "Please. This is urgent."

I crossed over to the telephone.

"I'm here."

"Thanks. Listen, can we meet? There's something important I need to tell you."

"Can't you tell me over the phone?"

"No. I need to see you."

"Really important?"

"I think so. Can I come to your flat in, say, forty-five minutes?"

I looked round at my gleaming home that smelled of bleach and polish.

"Not here. On the heath?"

"I'll come over to your side. Ten o'clock, by the pavilion."

"Fine."

I was early, but she was already there. It was a warm morning, but she was huddled up in a long coat, as if it were winter. Her hair was pulled back austerely, which made her face look curiously flat, and older and more weary than I had remembered. We shook hands formally and started walking up the hill, where a solitary man was flying a huge red stunt kite, which flapped and jerked in the wind.

"How are you?" she asked, but I just shrugged. I didn't want to be talking about my mental health with her.

"What is it?"

She stopped and took out a pack of cigarettes; struck a match into the cup of her hand and inhaled deeply. Then she looked at me steadily with her gray eyes.

"I'm sorry, Nadia."

"Is that the important thing?"

"Yes."

"Oh, well." I kicked a stone out of our path and watched as it clattered away into the grass. Above us, the red kite swooped and danced. "And what did you want me to say back?"

She frowned but didn't reply.

"Do you want me to forgive you or something?" I asked curiously. "I mean, it's not me who's dead." She winced. "I can't just hug you and say there, there."

She made an impatient gesture with her hand, as if she were swatting a cloud of insects away from the space between us.

"I don't want that. I'm saying sorry because I'm sorry."

"Did they send you, then? Is this a group apology?"

She smiled and took a drag of her cigarette. "God, no. Everybody has been forbidden to have contact with witnesses." Another dry smile. "Pending legal proceedings and internal inquiries. And TV documentaries."

"Are you in trouble then?"

"Oh yes," she said in a vague tone. "That's okay. We should be in trouble, Nadia. What we did was——" She checked herself. "I was about to say unforgivable. It was unprofessional. Stupid. Blind. Wrong."

She dropped her cigarette on the path and ground it out with the toe of her narrow shoe.

"Maybe I should be taping this for Clive's solicitor."

She frowned. "Yes, he's taking legal action. And Zoe's aunt. I don't care, really. I do care about Zoe and Jennifer. And you. I care about what you went through."

We turned off the path and walked down the hill, toward the pond. Ruffles of wind blew across the surface of the water and showers of leaves fell at our feet. A small child stood with his mother, throwing chunks of bread at the fat, indifferent ducks.

"It wasn't really your fault," I said cautiously. "It wasn't your decision, was it? I mean, not telling us what was going on."

She looked at me and didn't respond: She had decided to take the blame full on, not slide away.

"For what it's worth," I plowed on, "I think that within the limits of the situation, you weren't as dishonest as you could have been."

"Thanks, Nadia. But I don't think I'm going to put that on my résumé. It's strange," she continued. "I am always talking about taking control of one's life, but it got out of control. One step taken—to keep the press out of Zoe's death, not to scare the local population, not to make ourselves look incompetent, or worse—which led to the next step, then the next, and before they—we—knew it, we were on this road and couldn't turn back. And we ended up lying and lying and not looking after the people who looked to us." She smiled ruefully at me. "That's not an excuse, by the way."

"All that fear," I said.

"Yes."

"I've never really been able to believe in God. Have you?"

She shook her head.

"There are these two women," I said, "I feel connected to, though I never met them. And then there are these two men, who I did meet, of course. Did you?"

She took a deep breath.

"I met Fred when he was questioned after Zoe, and then I met Morris of course after you had discovered he knew both you and Jennifer Hintlesham."

"I need your help here, Grace. You know about this. They seemed normal. Could you imagine them, you know, when you met them, could you see that they could be killers? Was there anything about them—I mean, Fred, for instance. Did he have a history of violence?"

"He does now."

"I mean . . ."

"I know what you mean. You want me to say that these men are different, don't you? You want to put a label on them: dangerous. Or: mad." We stopped by the side of the pond and she lit another cigarette. "That's what's going to happen, of course. People like me will question Morris and they'll discover that he was abused or neglected, that he was hit or pampered, that he saw a video or fell on his head off a climbing frame. And someone will eventually get in touch with the press to say that Fred hit them five years ago, or whatever. And then there will be politicians and various pundits getting hot under the collar and saying why wasn't it spotted."

"And?"

"There wasn't anything to spot. When people commit murder most of them do it to someone they know. That's what the numbers say. Fred was jilted by Zoe and he was humiliated and furious and then, by bad luck for both of them but especially for Zoe, found himself alone with her. And he killed her. It's as simple as that. It happens all the time. He's probably no more murderous than a lot of people, except he happened to commit a murder that went unnoticed because the woman happened to be receiving threatening letters from somebody else."

"Comforting," I said dryly.

"I didn't think you were asking for comfort. I don't think you have ever asked me for comfort. That's not your style, is it? Morris, well, Morris *is* different, of course, and maybe you could call him mad, in the same way you can call anyone who commits senseless crimes mad. Or evil, if you believe in those kinds of terms. But that doesn't get us anywhere, does it? Because what troubles you is that for all the terror and all the horror and the death, this has no lesson, no label."

"Yes."

"Exactly." We walked on, back to the path we had left, and for a few minutes we didn't speak.

"Can I ask you a question, Nadia?"

"Sure."

"It's been bugging me. How on earth did you get to see all the files?"

"Oh, that. I had sex with Cameron Stadler and then I blackmailed him."

She looked at me as if I had just slapped her face. Her face looked comical.

"Don't ask," I said. "You don't want to know."

She started laughing then, an unsteady and not entirely cheerful sound, but I joined in and soon we were holding on to each other's arms, giggling and chortling like teenagers. Then she suddenly stopped and her expression became grave.

"You can't go round feeling guilty for the rest of your life," I said.

"Want to bet?"

"Not really."

We came to a fork in the path and she stopped. "I go this way," she said. "Good-bye then, Nadia."

"Bye."

She held out her hand and I shook it. Then I started walking back the way we had come, to where the kite still swung in the air.

"Nadia!"

I looked back. "Yes?"

"You saved us," she called. "Us, yourself, the other women who would have come after. You saved all of us."

"It was just luck, Grace. I was lucky."

TWENTY-FOUR

It was too cold for snow. The sky was icy blue and the pavement still sparkled with the frost of the previous night. My breath smoked in the air, my eyes watered, my nose felt red and sore, and my chin stung above the itchy wool of my ratty old scarf. The wind was a knife. I walked quickly, head down.

"Nadia? Nadia!" A young voice gusting across the street. I turned and squinted.

"Josh?"

It was. He was with a group of boys and girls about his age, all of them muffled up in thick jackets and hats and jostling against each other, but he crossed the road to me. "I'll catch up with you," he shouted at them, waving them off. He seemed solider than I had remembered him, less pallid and weedy. He stopped a few feet from me and we smiled at each other a bit awkwardly.

"Joshua Hintlesham, I've been thinking about you," I said, aiming for the bright notes.

"How are you?"

"I'm alive."

"That's good," he said, almost as if there were some

doubt about the issue. He looked around edgily. "I should have got in touch," he said. "I felt bad. Coming around with Morris, all that. Everything."

It seemed more than five months ago since he had sat on my sofa, a pitiable heap of frail bones. I didn't know what to say to him, because too much lay between us: a great mountain of horror and loss and fear.

"Do you have time for coffee or something?" He took his woolly hat off as he spoke, and I saw he had dyed his hair a bright orange and put a stud in his ear.

"What about your friends?"

"That's all right."

We walked together without talking until we came to a small Italian café. Inside it was dim, hot, and smoky, and an espresso machine hissed and spluttered on the counter.

"Bliss." I sighed, and peeled off my coat and hat and scarf and gloves.

"I'm buying," he said, trying to be casual, looking pleased with himself and jingling the coins in his pocket.

"Okay, rich boy. I'll have a cappuccino."

"Anything to eat?" he asked hopefully.

I didn't want to disappoint him. "One of those almondy croissants."

I sat at a table in the corner and looked at him while he ordered. Jenny's eldest son, leaning over the counter with his orange hair, trying to be a man, trying on his cool and his confidence in front of me. He must have turned fifteen, I calculated. He almost was a man now. In a few years he'd be finished with school.

He set my coffee and croissant down in front of me. He had ordered hot chocolate for himself and he sipped it carefully, a small frothy mustache forming on his upper lip. We smiled at each other again.

"I should have got in touch," he repeated.

We took gulps of our drinks and looked at each other over the rims of the cups.

"I heard that you fixed Morris pretty good," he said.

"It was him or me."

"Was it really with an iron?"

"That's right."

"It must have hurt him."

"Oh yes."

"I guess I should be pleased about that," he said. "You know those Yakuza gangs in Japan? When they kill you, they do whatever they do until you're unconscious. Then they drag you outside and drive a car over and over you, breaking all your bones. There's a theory that you suffer pain on a very primitive level so you feel it even when you're in a coma and dying."

"Nice," I said, pulling a face.

"I felt for some time that I ought to do something to Morris. I thought of him hanging around with me and all the time him knowing what he'd done to Mum."

"I think that was part of the point."

"Then I thought, Fuck it. But maybe when he gets out."

"He won't get out until he's a doddery old man."

"A doddery old man with an arthritic knee," Josh said with a grin.

"I hope so. Fred will be out sooner. I was talking to Links about it. The trial won't be until next year, but for something minor like strangling your ex-girlfriend because she dumped you, he won't serve more than eight or ten years."

He put his cup down on the table and ran a thumb over his top lip, rubbing away the chocolate.

"I don't know what I want to ask you," he said in frustration. "I think a lot about asking you about it all, but now I don't know what I want to ask. I know what happened and everything; I know all of that—it isn't that." He frowned and stared hopelessly at me with those eyes of his that had always made me think of Jenny, and he looked suddenly much younger, like the Josh I remembered from our ruinous summer.

"You think there's something I should be able to tell you."

"Something like that," he mumbled, and drew a finger through a small heap of sugar on the table. I remembered saying almost the same to Grace, all those months ago on the heath. I took a breath.

"Your mother was murdered by Morris for fun. Then he picked on me, and if I hadn't been lucky you could have been sitting here with the next woman he chose, or the one after that. There's no reason. It could have been anyone, only it happened to be Jenny. And I'm really sorry," I added after a pause.

"'S'all right," he muttered, still making patterns in the sugar, not looking up.

"How's school?"

"I go to a different one now. It seemed a good idea to change."

"Yeah."

"It's better. I've got friends."

"Good."

"And I've been seeing someone."

"You mean a girlfriend?"

"No. Someone. To talk about things."

"Oh, well, that's good as well." I looked at him help-lessly.

"What about you?"

"Me?"

"What are you doing now?"

"This and that."

"You mean the same as before?"

"No, I don't," I said vigorously. I gestured to the small nylon hold-all tucked under my chair. "Do you know what's in that bag?"

"What?"

"Among other things, five juggling balls."

He looked at me as if he didn't understand.

"Five," I repeated. "What do you think of that?"

"That's amazing," he said, clearly impressed.

"My master plan is to get out of this work altogether, but in the meantime I haven't exactly been standing still."

"Show me," he said.

"Here?"

"Go on, show me."

"Do you really want me to?"

"I have to see it."

I looked around. The café was almost empty. I took the balls out of the bag, three in one hand, two in the other. I stood up.

"Are you paying attention?" I said.

"Yes."

"You have to concentrate."

"I'm concentrating."

I began. It went right for about one second and then they went everywhere. One hit Josh, one hit my empty coffee cup.

"That gives you the general idea," I said, and scrambled under the table for one that had bounced into the corner.

"Is that it?" he said, smiling.

"Well if it was easy, everybody would be doing it."

"No, it was great," he said, and he started laughing and laughing. Maybe this was my gift to Josh, and my good-bye: Nadia the jester, the one who didn't die, throwing colored balls around in a dark little café. A giggle, or maybe it was a sob, rose in my chest. I gathered the balls and put them back in the bag.

"I better get going," I said.

"Me too."

We kissed at the door of the café, once on each cheek, and then went out into the blasting cold. As we turned to walk off in our separate directions, he said:

"I still put flowers on her gravestone, you know."

"I'm glad," I said.

"I don't forget."

"Oh Josh," I said. "You're allowed to forget sometime. Everyone's allowed to forget."

But as I went down to the canal path and walked along it, toward my flat, I thought to myself: I can't forget. I won't forget them, the women who died. Zoe and Jenny. Sometimes I know that they are gone. They are not here, and never will be again, no matter how I wait for them, these women I never met. But I still catch myself believing that I will see them when I round the bend in the road, when I climb on board a crowded bus and make my way up the aisle looking for a seat, when I scan the faces in a moving crowd looking for a friend I was supposed to meet, when I open my eyes in the morning after a dream that seemed real, even when it was over.

I know their faces so well, better than the faces of anyone else, better than the face of my mother, my father; better than the face of a lover I once gazed at with passion and hope. I know their faces like my own face in the mirror. I have stared and stared at them, searching for clues, begging them to yield up their meanings, to help me. The tilt of a nose, the lift of a chin, the exact way she smiled, teeth gleaming; the exact way she frowned, with that little furrow between her eyes. Every wrinkle, groove, line, shadow, hollow, blemish, hurt.

I never met them, yet I miss them. I never knew them then, yet I know them now, when it's too late. I know them in a way no one else ever could. They would have known me too. We might not have liked each other, but we are sisters under the skin, for their fear was my fear, their shame was my shame, their rage was mine, and their panic, and their violation, and their sense that there was nothing they could do, and their knowledge that the horror was coming nearer and nearer. I know what they felt. I felt it too.

Others will gradually forget them, or at least they will let them go. That's how it should be when someone dies. The people who told them they loved them will say the same words to someone else. That's fine, that's right; that's the only way we can cope with life. We'd go mad if we remembered everything—and hung on to it. So they'll slide away. All their flaws and their irritating habits and their particular ways will fade, and they'll become vague, less vivid and less human. Too good to be true: blank, shiny surfaces where other people can stare at their own reflections. Their graves will be visited more and more infrequently; soon only on anniversaries and days of special importance. People will tell stories about how they once knew them, for proximity to tragedy makes us feel somehow important. They will use a reverent and hushed voice to talk of them: Oh yes, wasn't it terrible, what happened to Zoe, to Jenny? Wasn't it sad?

But I can't forget them like that. I have to carry them with me wherever I go now; through the life I have got back again, through the years they didn't have, all the love and loss and change they never knew. Every day I say to them again: Good-bye.

Please turn this page
for a
preview of Nicci French's
new hardcover novel

The Red Room

available from
The Mysterious Press
in August 2001.

Beware of beautiful days. Bad things happen on beautiful days. It may be that when you get happy, you get careless. Beware of having a plan. Your gaze is focused on the plan and that's the moment when things start happening just outside your range of vision.

I once helped out my professor with some research on accidents. A team of us talked to people who had been run over, pulled into machinery, dragged out from under cars. They had been in fires and tumbled down stairs and fallen off ladders. Ropes had frayed, cables had snapped, people had dropped through floors, walls had tipped, ceilings had collapsed on to their heads. There is no object in the world that can't turn against you. If it can't fall on your head, it can become slippery, or it can cut you, or you can swallow it, or try to grab hold of it. And when the objects get into the hands of human beings, well, that's a whole other thing.

Obviously there were certain problems with the research. There was a core of accident victims who were inaccessible to our inquiries because they were dead. Would they have had a different tale to tell? That moment when the basket slipped and the window-cleaners fell from twenty floors up, their sponges still in their hands, did they think anything apart from, Oh, fuck? As for the others, there were people who, at the time of their mishap, had been tired, happy, clinically depressed, drunk, stoned, incompetent, untrained, distracted or just the victims of faulty equipment or what we could only and reluctantly characterize as bad luck, but all of them had one thing in common. Their minds had been on something else at the time. But, then, that's the definition of an accident. It's something that breaks its way into what your mind is on, like a mugger on a quiet street.

When it came to summing up the findings, it was both easy and hard. Easy because most of the conclusions were obvious. Like it says on the bottle, don't operate heavy machinery when intoxicated. Don't remove the safety guard from the machine press, even if it seems to be getting in the way, and don't ask the fifteen-year-old with a week's work experience to use it. Look both ways before crossing the road.

But there were problems, even with that last one. We were trying to take things that had been on the edge of people's minds and move them to the front. The obvious problem with that is that no one can move everything to the front of their mind. If we turn to face a source of danger, something else has an opportunity to sneak up behind us. When you look left, something on your right has the chance to get you.

Maybe that's what the dead people would have told us. And maybe we don't want to lose all of those accidents. Whenever I've fallen in love, it's never been with the person I was meant to like, the nice guy with whom my friends set me up. It hasn't necessarily been the wrong man, but it's generally been the person who wasn't meant to be in my life. I spent a lovely summer once with someone I met because he was a friend of a friend who came along to help my best friend move into her new flat; the other friend who was meant to come and help had to play in a football match because someone else had broken his leg.

I know all that. But knowing it isn't any help. It only helps you understand it after it's happened. Sometimes not even then. But it's happened. There's no doubt about that. And I suppose it started with me looking the other way.

It was towards the end of a May afternoon and it was a beautiful day. There was a knock at the door of my room and before I could say anything it opened and Francis's smiling face appeared. 'Your session has been canceled,' he said.

"I know," I said.

"So you're free . . ."

"Well . . ." I began. At the Welbeck Clinic, it was dangerous ever to admit you were free. Things were found for you to do, which were generally things that people more senior than you didn't want to bother with.

"Can you do an assessment for me?" Francis asked quickly.

"Well . . ."

His smile widened. "Of course, what I'm actually saying is, "Do an assessment for me", but I'm putting it in a conventionally oblique way as a form of politeness."

One of the disadvantages of working in a therapeutic environment was having to answer to people like Francis Hersh who, first, couldn't say good morning without putting it in quotation marks and providing an instant analysis of it, and, second . . . don't get me started. With Francis, I could work my way through second, third, and all the way up to tenth, with plenty to spare.

"What is it?"

"Police thing. They found someone shouting in the street, or something like that. Were you about to go home?"

"Yes."

"Then that's fine. You can just pop into the Stretton Green station on your way home, give him the once-over and they can send him on his merry way."

"All right."

"Ask for DI Furth. He's expecting you."

"When?"

"About five minutes ago."

I rang Poppy, caught her just in time and told her I'd be a few minutes late meeting her for a drink. Just a work thing.

When someone is doing the sorts of things that are likely to cause a breach of the peace, it can be surprisingly difficult to assess whether they are bloody-minded, drunk, mentally ill, physically ill, confused, misunderstood, generally obnoxious but harmless, or, just occasionally, a real threat. Normally the police handle it in a fairly random fashion, only calling us in when there are extreme and obvious reasons. But a year earlier, a man who had been picked up and let go turned up a couple of hours later in the nearby high street with an axe. Ten people were injured and one of them, a woman in her eighties, died a couple of weeks later. There had been a public inquiry, which had delivered its report the previous month, so for the time being the police were calling us in on a regular basis.

I'd been in the station several times, with Francis or on my own. What was funny about it, in a very unfunny way, was that in providing our best guesses about these mostly sad, confused, smelly people sitting in a room in Stretton Green, we were mainly providing the police with an alibi. The next time something went wrong, they could blame us.

Detective Inspector Furth was a good-looking man, not much older than I was. As he greeted me, he had an amused, almost impudent, expression that made me glance nervously at my clothes to make sure nothing was out of place. After a few moments I saw that this was just his permanent expression, his visor against the world. His hair was blond, combed back over his head, and he had a jaw that looked as if it had been designed all in straight lines with a ruler. His skin was slightly pitted. He might have had acne as a child.

"Dr Quin," he said with a smile, holding out his hand. "Call me Guy. I'm new here."

"Pleased to meet you," I said, and winced in the vice of his handshake.

"I didn't know you'd be so . . . er . . . young."

"Sorry," I began, then stopped myself. "How old do I need to be?"

"Got me," he said, with the same smile. "And you're Katherine—Kit for short. Dr Hersh told me."

Kit used to be the special name my friends called me. I'd lost control of that years ago, but it still made me flinch a bit when a stranger used it, as if they'd come into the room while my clothes were off.

"So where is he?"

"This way. You want some tea or coffee?"

"Thanks, but I'm in a bit of a hurry."

He led me across the open-plan office, stopping at a desk to pick up a mug in the shape of a rugby ball, with the top lopped off like a breakfast egg.

"My lucky mug," he said, as I followed him

through a door on the far side. He stopped outside the interview room.

"So who am I meeting?" I asked.

"Creep called Michael Doll."

"And?"

"He was hanging around a primary school."

"He was approaching children?"

"Not directly."

"Then what's he doing here?"

"The local parents have started an action group. They give out leaflets. They spotted him and things got a bit nasty."

"To put it another way, what am *I* doing here?"

Furth looked evasive. "You know about these things, don't you? They said you work at Market Hill."

"Some of the time I do, yes." In fact, I divide my time between Market Hill, which is a hospital for the criminally insane, and the Welbeck Clinic, which provides assistance for the middle classes in distress.

"Well, he's weird. He's been talking funny, muttering to himself. We were wondering if he was a schizophrenic, something like that."

"What do you know about him?"

Furth gave a sniff, as if he could detect the man's stench on the other side of the door.

"Twenty-nine years old. Doesn't do much of anything. Bit of minicabbing."

"Has he got a record of sexual offenses?"

"Bit of this, bit of that. Bit of exposure."

I shook my head. "Do you ever think this is all a bit pointless?"

"What if he's really dangerous?"

"Do you mean, what if he's the sort of person who might do something violent in the future? That's the sort of thing I asked my supervisor when I started at the clinic. She answered that we probably won't spot it now and we'll all feel terrible afterwards."

Furth's expression furrowed. "I've met bastards like Doll, *after* they've done their crime. Then the defense can always find someone who'll come in and talk about their difficult childhood."

Michael Doll had a full head of shoulder-length hair, brown and curly, and his face was gaunt with prominent cheekbones. He had strangely delicate features. His lips in particular looked like a young woman's, with a pronounced Cupid's bow. But he had a walleye and it was difficult to tell if he was staring at me or just slightly past me. He had the tan of a man who spent much of his life outside. He looked as if the walls were pressing in on him.

His large callused hands were tightly clutched as if each was trying to prevent the other from trembling.

He wore jeans and a grey windbreaker that wouldn't have looked especially strange if it weren't for the bulky orange sweater underneath, which it failed to cover. I could see how, in an another life, another world, he might have been attractive, but weirdness hung about him like a bad odor.

As we came in he had been talking quickly and almost unintelligibly to a bored-looking female police officer. She moved aside with obvious relief as I sat down at the table opposite Michael Doll and introduced myself. I didn't get out a notebook. There probably wouldn't be any need.

"I'm going to ask you some simple questions," I said.

"They're after me," Doll muttered. "They're trying to get me to say things."

"I'm not here to talk about what you've done. I just want to find out how you are. Is that all right?"

He looked around suspiciously. "I don't know. You a policeman?"

"No. I'm a doctor."

His eyes widened. "You think I'm ill? Or mad?"

"What do *you* think?"

"I'm all right."

"Good," I said, hating the patronizing reassurance in my voice. "Are you on any medication?" He looked puzzled. "Pills? Medicines?"

"I take stuff for my indigestion. I get these pains. After I've eaten." He rapped his chest.

"Where do you live?"

"I've got a room. Over in Hackney."

"You live alone?"

"Yeah. Anything wrong with that?"

"Nothing. I live on my own."

Doll grinned a small grin. It didn't look nice. "You got a boyfriend?"

"What about you?"

"I'm not a poof, you know."

"I meant have you got a girlfriend."

"You first," he said sharply.

He was quick-witted enough. Manipulative, even. But not all that much more crazy than anybody else in the room.

"I'm here to find out about *you*," I said.

"You're just like them," he said, a tremble of rage in his voice. "You want to trap me into saying something."

"What could I trap you into saying?"

"I dunno, I . . . I . . ." He started to stammer and the words wouldn't come. He gripped the table hard. A vein on the side of his forehead was throbbing.

"I don't want to trap you, Michael," I said, standing up. I looked over at Furth. "I'm done."

"And?"

"He seems all right to me."

To my side I could hear Doll, like a radio that had been left on.

"Aren't you going to ask him what he was doing outside the school?"

"What for?"

"Because he's a pervert, that's why," said Furth, finally not smiling. "He's a danger to others, and he shouldn't be allowed to hang round kids." That was for me. Now he started talking past me at Doll. "Don't think this is doing you any good, Mickey. We know you."

I glanced round. Doll's mouth was frozen open, like a frog or a fish. I turned to go and from that point on I had only flashes of awareness. A smashing sound. A scream. A push from one side. A tearing sensation down the side of my face. I could almost hear it. Quickly followed by a warm splashing over my face and neck. The floor rising to meet me. Lino hitting me hard. A weight on me. Shouting. Other people around. Trying to push myself but slipping. My hand was wet. I looked at it. Blood. Blood everywhere. Everything was red. Unbelievable amounts everywhere. I was being dragged, lifted.

It was an accident. I was the accident.

To read more, look for *The Red Room*
by Nicci French.

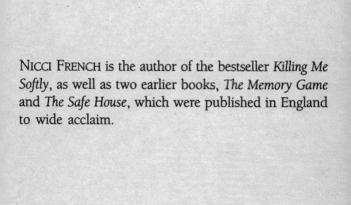

NICCI FRENCH is the author of the bestseller *Killing Me Softly*, as well as two earlier books, *The Memory Game* and *The Safe House*, which were published in England to wide acclaim.